ALEX MOVED STEADILY TOWARDS LAUREN.

Instinctively, she made a desperate lunge for the hack, but he reached it before her. His arm shot up beside her, effectively barring the door and blocking her from the curious gaze of any onlooker.

Trapped between the hack and his powerful frame, Lauren pressed into the carriage as he slowly leaned into her.

"God help me, but you intrigue me, Lauren," he murmured. "So full of surprises, aren't you?"

His nearness was a powerful drug on her senses. Her eyes fell to his mouth. The memory of that long ago kiss they shared came flooding back to her in the form of a queer tingle in the pit of her stomach. At the moment, she understood herself to be on dangerous ground. "I think you should leave me alone," she stammered.

"I think I should too, but I am afraid I cannot."

With that startling revelation, he leaned closer and gently laid his palm against her cheek.

He meant to kiss her.

And for one insane moment, she desperately hoped he would.

Praise for *The Devil's Love*
"A dazzling debut by a fine new talent."
—*Romantic Times*

Books by Julia London

THE DEVIL'S LOVE
WICKED ANGEL

Wicked Angel

Julia London

A Dell Book

Published by
Dell Publishing
a division of
Random House, Inc.
1540 Broadway
New York, New York 10036

ISBN: 0-440-22632-5

Printed in the United States of America

Published simultaneously in Canada

May 1999

2 4 6 8 10 9 7 5 3 1

OPM

Acknowledgments

Before I began writing, I had a perception of authors as solitary, somber figures who quietly observed life from the corner of some café with notebook and pencil in hand. I have discovered—in my case, anyway—that nothing could be further from the truth. I write surrounded by the support and help of many people.

I would like to thank my parents for instilling in me the belief and desire to be anything I wanted to be—well, perhaps with the single exception of my seventh-grade aspiration to be a merchant marine. Mother and Daddy gave me the foundation to be a writer, and they have not heard my appreciation enough.

I also would like to thank the rowdy bunch of Texans who are my entire extended family. They have taken on my writing as their own cause, demanding to know every detail, devouring my books, and gleefully promoting them to anyone who will listen—and many poor souls who would rather not, bless their hearts.

And last but not least, I would like to thank my editor and my friend, Christine Zika. Her insight and guidance are helping me to steadily improve my craft, and without her, I do not think anyone would be reading this today.

Chapter 1

Bavaria, 1828

Paul Hill felt the first stab of true panic—a young woman was wearing what he thought was one of his sister's gowns. And if he was not mistaken, she was also wearing a gold locket he had given Lauren on her sixteenth birthday. Standing in the dank foyer of a perfectly gothic castle, Paul feared he had arrived too late. As the woman searched for someone who could make some sense of his pathetic attempt at German, he wondered helplessly if once again he would find himself in a situation where he would be unable to help his sister. Swallowing past a lump of rising panic, he thought there could be a perfectly reasonable explanation as to why the woman was wearing Lauren's clothes and jewelry, though at the moment, that perfectly reasonable explanation escaped him.

He shifted, leaning against his cane to take the pressure from his crippled leg. If it were not for his infirmity, he might have been able to save her two years ago. He might have been able to provide for her and marry her well before

Uncle Ethan had come up with his detestable scheme. He might have—

"Entshuldigen Sie, Herr . . . ?"

Paul snapped from his ruminations and leveled a cold gaze on a man bent with age. "I have come for my sister," he announced grandly. The butler silently regarded him. Paul expelled a frustrated sigh; he did not have Lauren's knack for languages. *"Meine Schwester.* Lauren Hill."

The old man's face brightened noticeably. "Ah, Grafin Bergen! She will be quite pleased. We were not certain when you would arrive," he responded—in perfect English—and cracked a smile consisting of three teeth.

Startled, Paul straightened to his full height. "I demand at *once* to know her whereabouts!"

The old man's lips closed as he shuffled forward. "I should be perfectly happy to point you in her direction," he sniffed. "You need only ask. She is, at present, in the servant's quarters."

So they had forced her into servitude, the barbarians! "I should hardly think servant's quarters are befitting a countess," he snapped.

"Begging your pardon, sir, but the servant's quarters are just around the north side of the castle," the man responded indignantly as he pulled the massive oak-planked door open.

Paul pushed past him and moved as quickly as he could in the direction indicated. As he rounded a corner, laughter rose from a row of low-slung stone quarters built along the old curtain wall. Imagining the worst of indignities Lauren was being forced to suffer, he automatically groped at the small pistol he carried at his side.

Her most recent letter telling him of the death of her husband, Helmut Bergen, hinted that things were rather tense in the house. The new count, Helmut's nephew, Magnus, had taken exception to her unorthodox marriage to the old count. That was hardly surprising—their guardian uncle, Lord Ethan Hill, had arranged this preposterous marriage in exchange for the whole of the estate upon the old count's death, a feat he had accomplished without so much as a dowry. Bloody hell, if anything had happened to Lauren, he would strangle Ethan with his bare hands.

A chorus of German voices drifted up toward the slate sky as Paul attempted to quicken his pace, but it was nearly impossible on the wet stone path. Another burst of laughter sent his heart pounding against his ribs, and he lunged toward the first door he could reach. Flinging it open, he gripped the jamb to steady himself.

He might as well have flung open the gates to the cemetery just outside the castle walls and selected his spot. Surrounded by a group of people, Lauren stood in the center of the room dressed in a plain brown gown, her dark chestnut hair tied simply at her nape and draped carelessly over one shoulder. In the corner, a man towered over the group, wearing an expression of pure tedium. Judging by the expensive cut of his clothes, Paul assumed he was the new Count Bergen. And Lauren was smiling brilliantly at him.

Just as Paul had feared, whatever was happening in this stuffy room centered on his sister. Damn the girl, but she was clearly enjoying it. Unnoticed, Paul dragged himself through the door. He had half-expected to find her outside the cold stone walls, anxiously awaiting her rescue.

But no. Not Lauren.

She was cheerfully saying her good-byes, and as he glanced around the room, he noticed that several looked piteously enamored of her. He could surmise from her rather lengthy German monologue only that she was very thoroughly explaining, to each person individually, that she was leaving.

Paul loudly cleared his throat and succeeded in gaining the room's attention. Lauren paused in the delivery of her soliloquy and glanced over her shoulder. A bright smile instantly lit her face, and with a joyful cry, she pushed herself through the crowd, flinging herself into her brother's arms.

"Oh Paul! I am so thankful you have come! Oh, you cannot imagine how I have *longed* for you! I have missed you terribly!" she cried and kissed him fervently on each cheek. "Oh Lord, *look* at you! How *handsome* you are!" she exclaimed.

The warm sting of a blush started to creep up Paul's neck. He hastily grasped her arms and put her away from him as he warily eyed the crowd. "I have missed you, too. Are you quite finished here? The carriage is waiting," he said under his breath.

Lauren's laugh was musical. "Yes, just let me finish saying good-bye." She turned back to the crowd, grinning. They all grinned back at her. Everyone except Magnus Bergen, that was, and the frown on his rugged face made Paul shudder. Good God, but he was huge, and with features that appeared chiseled from stone, he did not present himself a happy man.

"Who is this?" Bergen asked, his English twinged with only a faint hint of an accent.

"My brother Paul," Lauren announced happily. For the benefit of the others, she added, *"Mein Bruder."* A round of "ahs" went up; the crowd beamed at him.

"Come, Lauren," Paul muttered. "A *hired* carriage is waiting." He gripped her elbow, intending to propel her from that overcrowded room as swiftly as possible.

"Wait!" Lauren exclaimed. "I forgot Herr Bauer!" She pulled away from him and moved back into the middle of the crowd, where a gardener of some sort was rummaging through a coarse hemp sack. He spoke in rapid German; the small crowd leaned forward, straining to hear. In a flurry of movement, he extracted a very large potato from the sack and very gently offered it to her, his voice having fallen to something of a whisper. Lauren leaned forward with a look of great concentration, then suddenly straightened and smiled warmly at the man. Bergen groaned impatiently and folded his massive arms across his chest.

"Oh, Herr Bauer, danke shoen!" she exclaimed, and affectionately patted his arm, causing the gardener to turn at least three shades of red.

So now Paul could add daft gardeners to the list of hopelessly besotted fools his sister attracted. Since blossoming into such a beauty, she attracted everyone. With thick, curly dark chestnut hair, unusual cobalt blue eyes that sparkled like sapphires, she had a smile that could easily disarm a man—yet she never seemed to notice the attention, and if she did, she was unaffected by it. Paul had never known her to primp, or to flutter her lashes, or to flirt in any way. Lauren was as exactly as one saw her, completely artless. So artless, she would accept a potato as a gift from a simpleton and think nothing of it. She was the most generous person he had ever known, completely accepting of everyone and everything.

God, how they needed her at Rosewood.

"Lauren!" Paul called impatiently. With a beguiling grin, and clutching the potato securely to her bosom, she obediently made her way to Paul's side, waving and calling a cheerful *auf wiedersehen* and *leben Sie wohl* to the lot of them. The moment she was within reach, he grabbed her elbow and dragged her forward.

Bergen emerged from the dank, overcrowded cottage close on their heels, muttering something in nonsensical German as Paul half-dragged his sister toward the carriage. "That is hardly accurate!" Lauren exclaimed to something the Bavarian said, and tossed a half-smile, half-frown over her shoulder.

Paul attempted to quicken the pace.

But Lauren, bless her cheerful heart, stopped once they reached the courtyard and turned to face the man who had once threatened to toss her out on her ear. "Farewell Count Bergen! You've been quite generous considering the circumstance, and I would have you know I am very appreciative of it!" She sank into a respectful curtsy.

Bracing his massive legs apart, Bergen folded his arms across his chest. "So you intend to leave?" he asked, frowning. "I thought we had an agreement."

Paul jerked a narrowed gaze to Lauren, fully prepared to do battle if he must. "An *agreement*?"

"Oh, *that*," Lauren said with an airy wave of her hand. "Count Bergen has some maggot in his head that I should perhaps stay and oversee the household. I *did* agree to help him, but only until you came for me. And now, here you are, so my part of the bargain is fulfilled." She smiled brightly at Magnus and nodded resolutely.

He snorted. "Bergenschloss suits you. Why would you return to that farm when you could oversee all of this as you see fit?" he doggedly continued, sweeping his arm across the old bailey and toward the main house.

Paul glared at Bergen. "You think to make my sister your *housekeeper?*"

"No, of course not!" the giant snapped. "Bergenschloss needs a mistress, and I am often away—"

"Magnus," Lauren said gently, "you know it is impossible for me to stay."

"Why?" Bergen started angrily. He quickly checked himself, running a hand through his flaxen hair as he contemplated the ground for a moment. "I admit I have said some things I regret," he added uneasily. "And I do not blame you for wanting to be away from here. But you have brought a measure of . . . *joy* to Bergenschloss, and I—*they*—want you to stay," he said, tossing a frown over his shoulder at the huddled group of servants standing several feet behind him.

Lauren beamed. "That is so very *sweet!* But I cannot stay."

Bergen fisted his hands on his waist. "You *can*."

Incredibly, Lauren walked to where the giant stood. The German looked at her strangely—so strangely, that Paul stepped forward, gripping his cane tightly in case it was needed. "My family needs me now, you know that," Lauren murmured, and then, much to Paul's amazement, she leaned up on her tiptoes and kissed him on the cheek. "But thank you for your kind words."

Bergen looked as startled as Paul felt, and for one long moment, he did not respond. Slowly, his face began to darken as he stood contemplating her; a muscle in his cheek jumped erratically. Paul realized he was holding his breath, waiting for the explosion he was sure would come. But Bergen surprised him by suddenly shaking his head. "Perhaps you will visit," he muttered, sighing heavily.

"I would like that very much," Lauren agreed.

"We shall miss you," he added irritably.

She peeked around his formidable frame and smiled at the servants. "I will miss everyone, too—even *you,* Count Bergen." With a little laugh and a playful wink for him, she turned and walked to the carriage. "Are you quite ready, Paul?"

Oh yes, *very* ready. He pushed Lauren into the waiting carriage and banged hard on the side before Bergen could speak again. As the carriage lurched forward, Lauren leaned out the little window, waving and calling good-bye, laughing as the servants stumbled over themselves to shout their farewells. The last thing Paul saw as the carriage rattled across the bridge was Bergen glaring after them, his arms folded tightly across his chest.

When at last they had cleared the castle walls, Lauren shut the window and settled onto the cracked leather seat. She smiled brightly. "Oh Paul, I am so *thankful* you have come! I have missed you dreadfully, and you would simply not believe how *erratic* Magnus Bergen has become!"

Oh, he could believe it. Rocking along the almost impassable Bavarian road, Lauren very cheerfully chatted away about the last few months at Bergenschloss, as if she had not been completely mad to sign over every last penny of her inheritance. As if it was perfectly reasonable for Bergen to go from threatening to hang her from the turrets to asking her to act as mistress of that monstrosity he called Bergenschloss.

"Count Bergen," he interjected irritably at some point in her string of chatter, "is an ass. How you manage to attract them all is beyond me."

"Count Bergen is *not* an ass. I think he is just rather lonely up here. He's accustomed to the city, you know. And I do *not,* by the by, attract . . . well . . . *asses,*" she added disapprovingly. "You know, I think you've grown an inch or two," she said, easily changing the subject.

Paul grinned sheepishly. "One and one quarter," he admitted proudly.

"Surely Mrs. Peterman has had to alter all your shirts to fit your shoulders! You look very well."

He blushed. "Well, I suppose I am a bit thicker than when you last saw me. I've taken to walking every day," he said, and launched into an eager discourse of the last two years, repeating the very things he had told her in his innumerable letters. Relating all that he had been eager to share with his beloved older sister since the day she had left Rosewood.

They could not reach Rosewood soon enough to suit Lauren. Having traveled for several days in stuffy mail coaches and a rickety old merchant ship, she was anxious to be home, to see the children again. "You are quite certain the children are all right?" she asked Paul for the second time as the post coach sped along a rutted highway snaking through the English countryside.

"Mrs. Peterman watches over those chicks like a mother hen. She would let nothing happen to them."

"And Ethan? Mrs. Peterman wrote his gout is worse."

"Gout!" Paul snorted disdainfully. "Ethan enjoys complaining, that is all."

Lauren frowned, studying her brother. Although he insisted things were fine, he had said enough for her to know that things were not so fine. He counted each coin in his purse every morning, and she did not have to be told his lack of appetite last evening was due to the lack of coin in his pocket.

She knew perfectly well that she had done the unthinkable when she had defied Ethan and had signed over her inheritance to Magnus. At the time it had seemed the noble thing to do, but she was beginning to think that perhaps her actions had been a bit impetuous. A wave of guilt began to creep through her, and she looked uncertainly at the tips of her worn boots. "I would imagine Ethan is rather angry—"

"What is done is done," Paul said. He paused, sliding a curious gaze to her. "But why did you do it? Give it all to Bergen, that is?"

Why? Because her two-year marriage had been a sham, because the senile old count had never so much as touched her, because her so-called inheritance rightfully belonged to his family. To Magnus, to be precise. "It did not belong to me. Uncle Ethan made a bargain, and I did not fulfill my part."

"Of course you did! You married him, did you not?"

Married him by proxy, yes. But the feeble old count had never understood who she was. "He was quite senile and never so much as touched me. He never really even knew me. My part of the bargain was to provide an heir, but I was never truly his wife. So, I did not fulfill my part."

Paul colored slightly and looked away from her, out the window. "Did Bergen take your things? I saw a woman wearing your gown—"

"Oh, no! That was Helga, the scullery maid, and well, she admired my gown, and as she did not have a proper thing to wear to her brother's wedding, I gave it to her. I really had no need for it." She laughed. "I am hardly called upon to entertain at Rosewood!"

Paul did not smile. "And the locket?"

"Now *that,*" she smiled, "was unfortunately but fairly lost in a card game." Her brother remained looking out the window, silent. Too silent. God, what had she done? The moment she had walked into Magnus's study with the paper relinquishing her claim to the Bergen estate and fortune, she could almost hear Ethan's bellows of protest from across the North Sea. Even Magnus had looked at her as if she were insane. Oh, *he* had understood the moment he had arrived from Switzerland what Ethan had done. The whole of Helmut's estate in exchange for an heir—how preposterous! A senile old man well past his eightieth year, the old goat had mindlessly signed an agreement that effectively gave her everything in exchange for nothing. Magnus had despised her because of the sham marriage, and the two of them existed uncomfortably for many months before Helmut's death.

When Helmut died, Magnus assumed the title and was finally free to say and do what he thought, and he heatedly accused Lauren of being a thief. Rightfully so, to her way of thinking. Ethan had taken horrid advantage of Helmut. She believed that so fiercely that she had made herself ignore Mrs. Peterman's letters, all of which hinted at the deplorable conditions at Rosewood. She *had* to ignore them, because she could not, in good conscience, keep the Bergen inheritance. Magnus, naturally, had been the first to agree with her. All right, he had softened somewhat over the last few weeks, if one could assume a man with a heart of stone could soften, but it had not changed anything.

Until this very moment, and she was mentally kicking herself for having turned over what might have been the only means to provide for Rosewood. "Good God, I am four and twenty," she blurted suddenly as the gravity of what she had done sank in. *"Four and twenty,"* she repeated, stabbing the air with her hands for emphasis. "How could I be so impetuous?"

"It is not your fault, love," Paul reassured her.

A surge of admiration washed over Lauren. God, how she loved her brother. To this day, she could not help feeling guilty about Paul's limp. It was the considerable opinion of Rosewood's stalwart housekeeper, Mrs. Peterman, that Lauren could not forgive herself for having emerged unscathed from the accident, for having been all of nine years old and arguing with a five-year-old Paul about who would be allowed to ride on the high seat with the driver, or for Paul's having been thrown clear of the wreckage that damaged his leg and killed their parents. Mrs. Peterman further reckoned that Lauren's guilt was what spurred her to work so hard for Rosewood. Lauren was less romantic about it— she worked hard because she loved her home.

In the first years after her parents' death, the estate had fared well enough, and Ethan had subscribed to the "out-of-sight, out-of-mind" theory of child rearing. Paul had continued his education at the parish school, and she had been placed under the stern tutelage of Ethan's wife, Lady Wilma Hill. Aunt Wilma proved determined to pound as much feminine grace and propriety into her charge as she possibly could. The old battle-ax had succeeded well enough before her death ten years ago, for all the good it did Lauren at Rosewood. After her aunt's death, she had refused to learn another blasted thing in the art of being a lady, and had thrown herself into the study of useful things, such as farming techniques, quotations and proverbs, and languages.

But the farm had slid farther toward the precipice of poverty over the years. While Ethan spent their dwindling inheritance as his legal status of reluctant guardian entitled him to do, Paul and Lauren had lived practically hand to mouth. What little land they owned that was not eaten up by the parish, was soon overused and unproductive.

It was Mrs. Peterman's idea to accept the first of their boarders ten years ago. His name was Rupert, a fifteen-year-old dullard and an apparent embarrassment to his affluent family. The parish vicar had arranged everything: in exchange for a place to put his son out of sight, Rupert's father provided a stipend that at least enabled them to keep food on the table. It turned out to be such a convenient arrangement, the vicar suggested to Mrs. Peterman that the parish would pay a small stipend to board orphans, and more had come over the years.

Their uncle had been happy to take the paltry stipends that came with the unfortunate children. Lauren had been quite content with the arrangement—until Ethan had convinced the feeble Helmut Bergen to accept an unheard of betrothal agreement, using little more than a small portrait of Lauren. She had balked, but in the end, under unbearable pressure from Ethan, she had done it for Rosewood and the children.

The children! How she longed to see them! There was Lydia, with fiery-red hair and big green eyes, and Horace, constantly dreaming of the day that he could be a *real* pirate. There was Theodore, who loved books as much as Lauren, and little Sally, the blond darling who worshipped Paul. And of course, Leonard, dear Leonard, the brightest and most tragic of them all. Born to a tavern whore, the poor child had been marred at birth with a purple birthmark that covered half his face.

Through the years, she had come to accept that in her parent's death was a blessing. Had it not been for that horrid spring day, she and Paul never would have known the boarders—they meant the world to her. And she had ruined the one opportunity they had to provide properly for them. What in heaven's name would they do now?

Lauren glanced at Paul, who had traveled thousands of miles to retrieve her, and impulsively grasped his hand. "Oh Paul! I gave it *all* away!"

Paul slipped a brotherly arm around her shoulders. "You

did the right thing, love, and we shall persevere,'' he assured her. ''We always have, we always will, and we shall do so without resorting to stealing from an infirm old man. You did the right thing.''

Chapter 2

Rosewood, southern England

Rupert, the first of the Rosewood boarders, was waiting at the post station in Pemberheath, perched in an old wagon pulled by two fat grays that looked as if they had not seen this side of a pasture fence in a decade. Thankfully, Rosewood was only three miles from Pemberheath, and Lauren's anticipation grew greater with each one. But when they turned onto the lane leading to Rosewood, her eagerness turned to shock. The once stately home was in such sad disrepair she hardly recognized it. The great green shutters, so grand in her youth, were faded with age, and one hung crooked from a single hinge. The paned glass windows her mother had been so proud of now boasted several cracks. The front lawn was overgrown with weeds, the fence was crumbling, and a thin, weak tail of smoke rose limply from one of four chimneys. Two kid goats chewed a section of weeds near the corner of the house.

"What *happened?*" she exclaimed with unconcealed mortification.

"We are somewhat short of funds," Paul mumbled wearily.

Short of funds? Judging by the look of the place, they had to be *destitute.* "But . . . we have *some* income, surely!" she cried.

"It's rather complicated," Paul responded gloomily. "I'll explain later," he muttered as the wagon rolled to a stop on the front drive. Rupert immediately jumped down from his perch, striding away for what he apparently considered the important task of corralling the kid goats.

The front door was suddenly flung open and a lad of almost twelve years scrambled outside shouting, "She's home! She's home!" A large, purple stain spread from the top of his forehead, across his left eye and cheekbone, and into his hairline. Lauren quickly alighted as the child rushed forward and threw his skinny arms around her legs. "Oh, Leonard! I am so very happy to see you!" She laughed gaily and hugged him tightly.

"Did you sail on a very large boat?" he asked anxiously.

"Yes, darling, we sailed on a *very* big boat," she responded, chuckling. "But we saw only one pirate."

"A *pirate!* But how did you *know* he was pirate?" he asked in awe.

Lauren laughed. "Why he wore a tricorn, a patch over one eye, and a sword at his hip, that is how I know!"

"Was he taller than Uncle Ethan?" another boy of around ten shouted from the door, hurrying toward Lauren. She quickly stepped into his path and caught him before he plowed her over. Hugging him tightly to her, she kissed his golden head.

"He was taller than Uncle Ethan and spoke a strange language," she confided, dropping to her knees.

"I *told* you Lydia! I told you there would be pirates!"

"I *know,* Theodore," a girl sniffed indignantly from the door. Lauren smiled and extended a hand toward the pretty twelve-year-old. Lydia started forward and was jostled as little Sally rushed outside, headed straight for Paul. Another boy, seven-year-old Horace, crowded in front of Lydia, his wooden sword stuffed in his belt. The children gathered around her like chicks to feed, and Lauren hugged them each, patiently answering the questions they shouted at her, and laughing gaily as she listened to their news.

"You better have a damn good explanation!" a surly voice boomed from the door. Lauren glanced up and swallowed a squeal of shock. At two o'clock in the afternoon, Uncle Ethan wore a threadbare dressing gown, a snifter of brandy dangling from two fingers at his side. But even more astounding was the fact that Ethan was . . . *enormous*. Good God, he had gained five stone, maybe six. His face was pallid, his jowls as fleshy as the obstinate old hog that lived on the premises. He had always been a large man, but this—*this* defied large. And for some inexplicable reason, it made her angry. Since Ethan had squandered their inheritance, he had come to live at the estate. Rosewood was destitute, but her uncle, well, he looked *remarkably* well fed. She stood slowly, dropped Theodore's hand, and folded her arms across her middle. "Good day, Uncle."

"What in the hell were you thinking?" he roared.

That did it. Lauren's eyes narrowed as she marched forward through the throng of children, her fists finding her hips. "What was *I* thinking? What were *you* thinking? You *promised* me, Uncle Ethan! You promised the children would be well tended!"

Startled, Ethan glanced sheepishly at the gaggle of children gathered around her. "I *did* care for them!" he blustered, his face turning red. "Do not attempt to turn the subject and don't talk to me of promises, girl! You broke yours!"

Marching to where her corpulent uncle stood, Lauren shouted, "I did nothing of the sort! We had a signed *agreement,* and it was not fulfilled! That money did not belong to me!'' Staring him straight in the eye, she silently dared him to disagree.

Ethan obviously was taken aback. He made a great show of straightening the lapels of his dressing gown as he muttered weakly, "Impertinent little wench."

But Lauren did not hear him. Mrs. Peterman had stepped out onto the drive, a slash of flour across her forehead and wisps of hair sticking out of her bun. With a squeal of delight, Lauren threw herself into the woman's arms. Hugging each other tightly, the two gleefully jumped up and down.

Ethan turned his hostility on Paul as he limped toward the riotous scene. "She signs it all away, and now she thinks she can do whatever she pleases! By God, she'll see differently, mark my words!'' he growled.

Paul lifted a dubious brow as he watched Mrs. Peterman and Lauren, arm in arm, turn and stroll inside. "Yes, she seems to be quaking in her boots." A smug smile lifted the corner of his mouth as he moved past his uncle, crowding with the children into the door behind his sister.

It had been just a little more than one month since her return to Rosewood, Lauren thought as she sat outside Dr. Stephens's drawing room. One month. Staring blankly at the wall, she marveled at what had happened in that time. First of all, Ethan had *mortified* her by announcing, almost the moment she had arrived at Rosewood, that he intended to marry her off again. That announcement had been followed by Mr. Thadeus Goldthwaite's attempted offer of marriage a scant four days later. It was enough to make her want to run screaming from the house.

Good *God!*

She was not even *remotely* interested in marrying again—not to some infirm old man as Ethan undoubtedly had in mind, and most certainly *not* to the round little apothecary, Fastidious Thadeus Goldthwaite.

A sound caught her attention, and looking up, Lauren

gasped in horror at the work Leonard and Horace had done to a bouquet of fresh cut flowers. Petals were strewn across the Oriental carpet and the small entry table, and only the stripped stems of the hothouse flowers remained in the hand-painted vase. Lauren scrambled to her feet and rushed forward to clean the mess before Dr. Stephens found it. Leonard moved to help her while Horace stood sullenly by.

"It's all right," Lauren hastily assured them, and searched for a place to discard the petals. There was no receptacle in sight except a canister reserved for canes and umbrellas. With a mischievous wink to the boys, she dumped the petals into the canister, then turned and held a finger to her lips before marching the children to the lone seat in the corridor.

She made them sit at her feet, her thoughts quickly returning to her dilemma. Though so very thankful to be home, she was absolutely sickened by the deplorable state of Rosewood. Paul had explained to her that because of escalating parish taxes, falling grain prices, and enclosures all around them that left the best lands to the wealthy, Rosewood was left with only a fraction of arable land, and that overused. "Representation is what we need!" he had blustered angrily. "There is no one in Parliament to look after *our* interests!"

She did not understand all that. But she understood that their land was so depressed it could not support a decent crop of grain, and even if it could, they could not afford the labor to harvest it, let alone the parish taxes. So she had racked her brain for a way to fix things.

She had been so intent on fixing things that she had not really paid Mrs. Peterman heed when she had tried to explain her solution for Rosewood. Lauren did not fully understand until the day Mr. Goldthwaite had come to Rosewood with herbs for the cough circulating among the children.

He then showed Lauren some of the herbs he had planted in the overgrown garden. The herb garden made Lauren think of the possibilities of trading the vine vegetables and fruits that seemed to grow rapidly and anywhere for supplies. Caught up in her ideas, Mr. Goldthwaite's botched attempt to kiss her surprised her so much that her heart had stopped for a moment. *"Mr. Goldthwaite!"* she had shrieked when the round man had unexpectedly clasped her in an ironclad embrace and pursed his lips. "Dear God, let *go* of me!"

The man turned as red as a fat ripe apple and quickly dropped his arms. Lauren had searched frantically for a club with which to brain him, but finding none, had brought her hands to her hips and glared at him. "Just what do you think you are doing?" she had demanded with all the authority of a countess.

The rotund shopkeeper had pulled himself up to his full height—roughly two inches shorter than her—and replied haughtily, "What do you *think* I am doing?"

Unfortunately, Lauren had startled them both by laughing, at which point Mr. Goldthwaite's color went from red to purple. "I am sorry, Mr. Goldthwaite, I do not mean to laugh. But you see—"

"I see very clearly, Countess Bergen," he said stiffly.

"Hill. Miss Hill," Lauren corrected. Much to Ethan's distress, she insisted on using her maiden name, believing she had no more claim to her title than she did the Bergen inheritance.

"I was given to understand from Mrs. Peterman that as you are now a widow—"

"Oh! Mr. Goldthwaite! Please, before you go any farther, you must understand my place is here at Rosewood. These children need me."

Fastidious Thadeus had puffed his barrel chest. "Indeed I *do* understand, madam, and I applaud your charitable disposition. I think such qualities are to be looked for in a wife, and you have those qualities in such abundance that I fully intend—"

"*Mr. Goldthwaite,* stop right there!" she had shrieked in horror, lifting her hand. "Please excuse me, sir. There is something I must do right away," she said unconvincingly, and had turned, intending to flee, but Mr. Goldthwaite had grabbed her hand and held it tightly. She had hastily jerked her hand from his grasp. "Mr. Goldthwaite, you must put all thoughts of me from your mind—"

"Miss Hill, you cannot begin to imagine how my heart—"

"I really *must* go inside!"

"But Miss Hill, there is something I wish to *say* to you!" he had shouted earnestly. Lauren responded by turning on her heel and fleeing the garden, her last sight of Mr. Goldthwaite tipping his hat after her.

When she flew into the kitchen, Mrs. Peterman greeted her with a strange, gleeful look. "*Well?* Did Mr. Goldthwaite have opportunity to speak with you?" the gray-haired housekeeper had asked, grinning unabashedly.

Lauren had collapsed onto a wooden bench. "God help me, but Thadeus Goldthwaite wants to *marry* me!"

"That's *wonderful*!" Mrs. Peterman squealed, clapping her dough-caked hands.

Lauren had gaped at her; she had obviously lost her mind. It was the most inconceivable, incredible, fantastic idea! "Mrs. Peterman, it is *impossible*!"

"Impossible?" the housekeeper had shouted. "It is *perfect*! You need to consider the practicalities of such a match, Lauren. He is a good man and a good provider. And he cares for these children—you cannot overlook that," she had blithely instructed her and had launched into such praise of Thadeus Goldthwaite that Lauren had begun to think the rotund apothecary must be kin to Hercules himself.

Sitting in Dr. Stephens's foyer, Lauren almost choked just thinking about how intent everyone seemed on her marital state. She would rather walk off a cliff than marry Mr. Goldthwaite or anyone else. *If* she ever married again, it would be for love. Yet it seemed the entire adult population of Rosewood wanted to see her married because of the *practicalities*. Oh, she understood their thinking. Obviously, the best hope for Rosewood was for her to marry someone of means, and as it was apparent that Ethan and Mrs. Peterman would struggle with one another to marry her off, she had desperately searched for another idea. If only she could make the farm profitable again, she reasoned, she could end this mad race to the altar.

Well, she had at last hit upon an idea, and it was that which brought her to the doctor's house today. The two children who accompanied her, despite their obvious energy to tumble on the carpet, were suffering from a cough that would not go away.

A door suddenly opened; Lauren shifted her gaze from the children to an elderly gentleman who was peering at her from above the tops of his wire-rimmed spectacles. "Who are you? Don't recall seeing you about," he said gruffly.

Lauren stood, and with a gentle command to the two children, politely extended her hand. "I am Lauren Hill."

"Hill? I knew a Miss Hill—Dear Lord, are you her? My, you have changed!"

"Yes sir," she said graciously, then glanced meaningfully at the children.

The doctor followed her gaze and peered at her charges. "Your children?"

"They reside at Rosewood."

"Ah, Rosewood, of course."

"They have a cough that will not go away," she informed him.

The doctor stepped around her, and with hands on hips, stared at the two children. Leonard, with the unsightly birthmark, looked him squarely in the eye. The younger boy fidgeted with his frayed belt. "Well, Miss Hill, bring them in and we shall see what can be done for a cough that will not go away," he said brusquely, then turned and marched back into the spacious drawing room.

Dr. Stephens walked to a shelf holding vials of various shapes. "Bring me a boy," he said absently as he studied one vial. He was not a man given to sentiment. He had gotten over that particular affliction several years ago. As a young doctor, it had occurred to him that he could not very well perform his duties if he was going to be emotionally affected by every unfortunate he saw. He knew Leonard, had known him since he was a baby and Leonard's mama had tried to drown the poor child. He had seen him sporadically throughout the last ten or twelve years and as would be expected, the boy was traumatized by the large port-stain that marred his appearance. As if being born to a whore and then orphaned were not enough strikes against him, he bore an ugly mark that made heads turn.

When he turned back to see what held the child, he could not keep his jaw from dropping. Miss Hill had apparently worked magic on the unfortunate little boy. Kneeling beside him, she was brushing his red hair from his eyes and whispering something to him with a smile that made even Dr. Stephens sit up and take notice. Leonard was standing tall, and, Dr. Stephens would later swear on his medical journals, the lad was smiling. He had never seen Leonard smile. Amazed, he watched as the lad marched toward him with a strong, proud countenance.

"Miss Hill says I might have a spoonful of delight," the lad announced.

"Beg your pardon?" Stephens managed to choke out as he looked down at Leonard. Miss Hill cleared her throat; Dr. Stephens glanced up in time to receive a pointed look from her.

"A spoonful of delight. To clear the cough," Leonard repeated.

"A spoonful of delight, is it? Well, let me hear you breathe, boy," he said, and pressed his ear against Leonard's chest. He checked the child for fever. "Yes, a spoonful of delight is just the thing," he said, astonished that he, notorious for his less than sympathetic bedside manner, should call the foul liquid he was about to pour into that child a *spoonful of delight*. He retrieved a bottle from the shelf and poured a large spoonful. "Well then, open wide," he said, and tossed the liquid down the boy's throat. Leonard swallowed, then turned to Miss Hill. She smiled charmingly and held out her hand. Immediately, he went and slipped his hand into hers, then pushed the other boy forward, who marched resolutely to Dr. Stephens's side.

"Miss Hill said I might get a *double* dose of delight," he said proudly. With a *humph,* Dr. Stephens bent to listen to the boy's breathing. She was right; Horace's rattle was worse than Leonard's.

"A double dose, then," he muttered, and poured the pungent medicine.

Horace swallowed the first mouthful without expression or comment, waited patiently for the second, then turned and walked back to Miss Hill. "How long will the delight last?" he asked her.

"I should think until tomorrow, would you not agree, Dr. Stephens?"

"I would," he said curtly.

"I think—and please correct me if I am wrong, sir—but shan't the boys begin to feel the delight tingling first in their toes in just a few moments? I thought so. Now boys, please have a seat near the door and do *not* touch anything. There is something I would discuss with Dr. Stephens," she said. Like perfect little gentlemen, the boys obediently took seats near the door.

By Dr. Stephens's account, everything he had just witnessed was a bloody miracle. Whatever she had done to bolster the confidence in the two young lads was worth every ounce of effort with which he could support her. Hell, he would just like to know how she had done it, if nothing else. "Miss Hill, I do not know what you have done—"

"You mean the flowers," she smiled with an airy wave of her hand. "I am dreadfully sorry about that; I am afraid I was a bit preoccupied," she said sweetly.

"Pardon?"

"The flowers. Unfortunately, I do not have any coin, or I would gladly replace them, but it's a condition I'm afraid I shall not see remedied for a time. Please don't say anything yet, because I come with a proposition. You see, the children of Rosewood are not receiving the medical attention they need." He must have looked puzzled as he adjusted his spectacles, because she explained quickly, "Oh, not bumps and bruises or *that* sort of thing. But the cough, illnesses of a more serious nature, are not called to the attention of a doctor until it is much too late, and the children spread those ailments so quickly that before you know it, the whole of *Rosewood* is infected, and I was thinking that perhaps we could agree to an arrangement whereby you might visit from time to time, not necessarily for coin, but something infinitely more agreeable, I should think."

Dr. Stephens had quit trying to understand the connection to flowers and had come to his senses, or so he thought. "Miss Hill, I cannot imagine what you've done, but you must know that I—"

"I am speaking of tomatoes, sir, tomatoes as big as *hams!* And beans, and pumpkins and cabbage! It seems that there is *some* talent to be had at Rosewood, and I daresay it is in the growing of fruits and vegetables. And we cannot possibly eat all the vegetables we grow, because they grow rather quickly, you see, and sadly, Mrs. Peterman has been throwing what we cannot eat to Lucy—I mean to say, to a rather enormous old hog. I am sure you are aware that hogs will do quite nicely on something less valuable than fruits and vegetables, so I am suggesting a trade of sorts—"

"Miss Hill!" Dr. Stephens fairly shouted. The young

woman blinked. He removed his glasses and pinched the bridge of his nose.

"Honestly, Dr. Stephens," rang another feminine voice," anyone with an ounce of sense knows it is a waste to give anything more than slop to a hog!"

Dr. Stephens groaned and opened one eye to see the Marchioness of Darfield standing in the doorway with her young daughter Alexa. The marchioness was a favorite of the doctor's, despite her very exasperating habit of ignoring his sound advice. With dark hair and violet eyes, she was as unusually pretty as the mysterious Miss Hill. He could not help noticing that standing side by side, the two women made quite a remarkable picture. "Lady Darfield, I was just about to say—"

"I think your idea is simply wonderful. My name is Abbey Ingram, and I should very much like to help."

Miss Hill smiled gratefully. "I am Lauren Hill. Are you familiar with Rosewood? It's a small estate, just a few miles from here, and I have been thinking how to make it a bit more self-sustaining. The children who live there—Well, I think they should learn as much responsibility as they can. But they cannot learn if no one trades with them, and unfortunately, no one comes to Rosewood. That is, with the exception of the *apothecary*, but *he* can hardly be counted on to take so many vegetables in trade, and—"

"Miss Hill! If you please, I was *trying* to say what you have done for those two boys is quite remarkable, and I would be more than happy to help you in any way that I can, including taking *tomatoes* as big as *hams* in trade!" Dr. Stephens bellowed.

The two women looked at him as if he were mad. Lady Darfield lifted a censorious brow and muttered in a soft aside, "I was quite certain he would agree."

"Really? I was not at all certain, but I had rather hoped he would. Unfortunately, we are rather short of funds," Miss Hill responded.

"Oh, you mustn't worry about that!" Lady Darfield said cheerfully. "Dr. Stephens should hardly be concerned about payment; he does quite nicely for himself. He will gladly look after your wards!"

Miss Hill beamed at him. "I rather suspected he was not as crabby as he would have me believe. So you think he could be counted on to help?"

"Absolutely!" Lady Darfield nodded enthusiastically.

Incredulous, Dr. Stephens looked from one woman to the next, both wearing alluring smiles that would have sent a lesser man to his knees. Without a word, he turned abruptly and marched back to his desk.

By the time Lauren Hill finally left—with *two* bottles of delight in exchange for a crate of tomatoes to be delivered the next morning—the women had agreed to meet at Rosewood the following day to discuss further what could be done. As with everything, Abbey Ingram had jumped in with both feet. She beamed happily at Dr. Stephens as he examined a cut on Alexa's knee, insisting that she, too, knew all along that he was not nearly as "crabby" as he would have her believe.

Over the next few weeks, Lauren established a trade of produce for medicine, flour, and twice weekly help with the sewing. Barren wheat fields were given over to pumpkins and gourds, and tomatoes and berries flourished along every fence. Each morning after completing their lessons, Lauren and the children would weed and water their little vegetable fields.

The children delighted in their work. They measured the growth of the melons each day, searched for cucumbers hidden among the leafy vines, and arranged the pumpkins to their satisfaction. Their little kitchen garden was soon large enough to support a few more kitchens, and with the help of Abbey, who made a point of engaging in the trade herself, the townsfolk of Pemberheath slowly began to soften toward the children and their "trade."

As late summer turned to fall, Rosewood began to show signs of resembling the modest country home it had once been. Lauren managed this despite having to care for her slovenly uncle while intermittently arguing with him about her future. Paul was very silent about what *he* thought she should do, but at his request, she had bargained for two books on investments. He was very mysterious about his plans, but every once in a while he would look up from his books, run a hand through his dark brown hair, and smile. His light blue eyes twinkling with excitement, he would assure her that all at Rosewood would soon be well.

Lauren desperately hoped he was right. There was more need at Rosewood than a fledgling vegetable trade could support. With Abbey's help, she began to plan for a future that included dairy products and wool to be traded for more substantial assistance.

She cherished her friendship with the marchioness. For once in her life, Lauren understood the quotation, *"of all the heavenly gifts that mortal men commend, what trusty treasure in the world can countervail a friend?"* And contrary to what she might have expected, Abbey did not seem remotely concerned that she was penniless. Even when Mrs. Peterman blithely informed the marchioness that Lauren was, in reality, the widowed Countess of Bergen, Abbey did not seem to mind that Lauren had been less than forthright about her identity.

The two women grew even closer, oddly enough, because of Fastidious Thadeus. In constant pursuit of Lauren, he had finally worn her to the limits of her patience and she had confided her dilemma to Abbey. When Abbey was through laughing—she insisted that Lauren was no more suited for Mr. Goldthwaite than she was for the now infamous old hog,

Lucy—she helped Lauren steer clear or her ardent admirer. But poor Mr. Goldthwaite could not be convinced; he never missed an opportunity to stare at Lauren with all the longing of a dog trapped on the wrong side of a door.

Chapter 3

Sutherland Hall, England

Alexander Daniel Christian alighted from the sleek traveling chaise the moment it rolled to a halt in front of his massive Georgian mansion in Southampton. With a curt nod to a footman, he swept through the double oak doors and into the marble foyer where two more footmen waited with his butler, Finch.

"Welcome home, your grace," Finch said with a bow.

Alex tossed his hat to a footman. "Finch," he responded blandly, and handed the butler his leather traveling gloves. Another footman in the silver and blue livery of the Duke of Sutherland stepped forward to divest him of his cloak. "You may inform my mother I have returned. Where shall I find the correspondence?" he asked as he straightened the French cuffs of his silk shirt.

"The study, your grace."

Alex nodded and strode swiftly down the marble corridor, his polished Wellingtons clicking softly beneath his determined stride. He did not glance at the new damask wall coverings, nor the dozens of roses displayed on the consoles along the hall. As he crossed the threshold of his study, he shrugged out of his coat, tossed it carelessly to an over-stuffed chair of dark green velvet, then strolled to the intricately carved Louis XIV desk in the middle of the large room. "Whiskey," he said to a footman and picked up the correspondence. Settling gracefully into a chair of burgundy Corinthian leather, he sifted through the stack of letters that had accumulated during his two weeks in London. In addition to standard business correspondence, there were a few invitations to social events. Those he tossed aside. His eyes fell upon a missive sealed with the signet of his solicitors in Amsterdam. Ignoring the whiskey the footman placed at his elbow, he tore it open. Scanning the letter quickly, he cursed softly.

Christ, he had more trouble with that blasted trading company! He abruptly crumpled the report of yet another loss and tossed it across the room in the general direction of the fire. As if the rash of recent losses wasn't enough, Britain's tariffs were strangling him. If he actually *had* cargo, the import taxes were so damn high as to make it almost economically unfeasible.

Restlessly he stood and picked up his whiskey, dismissing the footman with a terse nod as he crossed to the bank of floor-to-ceiling windows. He stared at the massive green lawn and gazebo at the edge of a lake marking his brother's grave. Alexander Christian, Viscount Bellingham, was not supposed to be the Duke of Sutherland with all the attendant responsibilities of the family fortune. *Anthony* was supposed to be the duke—*he* was supposed to be the second son with lesser titles and the luxury of time to indulge in the pursuit of worldly adventure.

Some might argue that he had seen enough adventure to last a lifetime, but he could not agree. When Anthony was very much alive and performing quite nicely as the duke, Alex had been plagued with stifling ennui. When an old family friend had reported the treasures he had found in

Africa, Alex had eagerly accepted an invitation to accompany him on a return trip. That experience in the Serengeti Plain had whetted his appetite for raw adventure. Since then, he had traipsed the Himalayas, had sailed to the Orient, and had discovered the wilds of North America.

It was a lifestyle that suited him well and one for which he still yearned, but a tragic accident on horseback unexpectedly claimed Anthony's life five years ago. He bitterly recalled being abruptly summoned home to find his beloved brother truly dead and himself an instant duke. The change in his responsibility was almost as instantaneous as the change in attitude of those around him—old and new acquaintances alike were suddenly scraping their knuckles in front of him. And in addition to coping with his loss he suddenly found himself at the head of a powerful dukedom and a vast fortune. He no longer had the luxury of several months to leisurely explore the world.

For five years now, he thought wearily, he had been a duke. Five years it had taken to grow accustomed to being *the* center of attention. Five years to learn the intricacies of the family holdings and accept the enormous responsibilities of being a duke, not the least of which included the production of heirs. At least Anthony had made that part of his responsibility easy enough, and he had, finally, set a wedding date with Lady Marlaine Reese, just as everyone expected him to do.

Anthony had been promised to Marlaine almost from the moment of her birth. The Christian-Reese family alliance was almost legend. His father Augustus had befriended the young Earl of Whitcomb before either had married, and the two had formed a monopoly of sorts through their partnership in iron manufacture. The Christian-Reese factories had successfully underpriced other factories for the production of cannons, guns, and ironworks during the Peninsular War, making both families obscene profits. The two men were of like minds, and the powerful voting bloc they formed in the

House of Lords had further solidified their long-standing friendship. Everyone knew that a Christian-Reese vote on a bill was as good as passing it.

It was perfectly natural that their children should continue the alliance, and Anthony was quite content to marry Marlaine, even though he was fifteen when she was born. Alex remembered she was always a pretty, affable girl, but she was still in the schoolroom when Anthony died. When she made her debut three years ago, Alex had determined she was as good a solution to his ducal responsibility to produce heirs as he was likely to find. His title required a good business arrangement in a marriage, and Marlaine was definitely that. Moreover, she was trained to be a duke's wife, was pleasant enough, and was a comfortable, quiet companion. As those things went, she would make a good wife, and he had finally offered for her—as everyone expected he would do—two years ago when she had turned twenty-one.

The sound of the pocket doors sliding open interrupted his thoughts, and Alex turned.

"Welcome home, darling." His mother, Hannah, glided into the room, followed by Marlaine on the arm of his younger brother, Arthur.

Alex crossed the room to greet her. "Thank you, Mother. I hope I find you well?"

"Of course! A small ache in my back is all I have to complain of," Hannah said with a smile. "And it is not worth mentioning. You should be quite pleased to know that Lord and Lady Whitcomb are visiting Lady Whitcomb's sister in Brighton. As it is such a short drive, I invited Marlaine to visit this weekend."

"I am quite pleased," Alex said, and kissed Marlaine on the cheek.

She blushed slightly, shifting her smiling gaze to the carpet. "You look fatigued. Have you been sleeping?" she murmured.

"I am fine, Marlaine."

"Are you quite certain? You look as if you have something on your mind," she insisted.

"It's business." Extending his hand to Arthur in greeting, he added, "East India."

"What, again? By God, Alex, we should withdraw!"

Alex chuckled as he sat on a leather couch. Arthur dropped beside him while Hannah took a seat near the hearth. Marlaine picked up Alex's discarded coat and folded it carefully over one arm before joining her there. Alex reported the contents of his correspondence to Arthur, absently playing with his empty whiskey glass. Unnoticed, Marlaine rose from her seat and crossed to Alex's side. "A drink, darling?" she asked softly. He glanced briefly at her as he handed her the glass, and returned his attention to Arthur, who was quite adamantly reviewing the pros and cons of investing in the East India Company. Marlaine returned with a fresh whiskey and handed it to him with a quiet smile.

From the corner of his eye, Alex watched her as she returned to her seat. He had the brief, blasphemous thought that on occasion, she behaved like a well-trained dog. Sitting prettily with his coat folded across her lap, she smiled softly at the others without breathing a word. In contrast, Hannah sat on the edge of her chair, leaning forward and listening intently to her sons as they spoke of high tariffs and the need for economic reform. Every so often, she would interject her own opinion.

They talked until Finch appeared and, moving immediately to divest Marlaine of Alex's coat, announced a bath had been drawn for his grace. Alex tossed the last of the whiskey down his throat and stood. "If you will excuse me, Mother. Marlaine," he nodded, and began to stride across the thick carpet. "I assume supper at the usual time?" he asked over his shoulder.

"Eight o'clock, dear. Lord and Lady Whitcomb will be joining us."

Alex nodded, and walked out the door, Finch trailing behind.

Hannah Christian, the dowager Duchess of Sutherland, peered over the rim of her wineglass at Alex and sighed softly. His handsome face and warm green eyes betrayed no emotion whatsoever. It was silly, she knew, but she had worried about him since the day he had assumed the title. In contrast to Arthur, who enjoyed each day as if it was a new beginning, Alex seemed to take each day too seriously, as if the success of each one was his own private responsibility.

It was perfectly ridiculous, in her humble opinion. He was a strong and capable leader, with a sharp mind for business details that had enabled him to expand the family's holdings beyond her wildest imaginations. He could manage the family fortune standing on his head and, as his leadership was also highly regarded in the House of Lords, he could be the toast of all London if he so desired. Certainly the *ton* had tried to make him so. He was one of the most sought-after personages in all of Britain. A young duke, excessively wealthy and exceedingly handsome, his influence was unparalleled among the peerage. Yet he seemed forever bored—at times, even anxious. Her gaze shifted to Marlaine sitting on Alex's right, her quiet smile reserved for him alone. Alex hardly seemed to notice her.

That's what Hannah hated about the whole betrothal. He hardly *noticed* Marlaine.

She casually sipped her wine as she contemplated the pretty blond. She had nothing against Marlaine; she was a pleasant, well-bred young woman, the daughter of the affable Earl of Whitcomb, and a very suitable match for a duke. But not her son. Hannah wanted Alex to know the sheer joy of love she and her beloved Augustus had known, that complete adoration one feels for a true soul mate. She wanted her son to marry for love, not for some arcane sense of responsibility. She had hoped that in some dark corner of his soul, Alex might *want* to love the woman he would marry. That maybe, just maybe, he would realize Marlaine did not strike the chord in him that made him want to move mountains just to please her.

Alex's gaze met hers across the table, and he very subtly lifted a brow, as if inquiring what she was thinking. Hannah shrugged helplessly. He smiled faintly and shifted his gaze to Arthur, who was relating some outrageous event that had occurred at a rout of the infamous Harrison Green, much to Edwin Reese's considerable amusement. Hannah had noticed that other members of the youthful set hung upon every detail of a Harrison Green affair, but Alex, as usual, looked bored.

His mother was mistaken—Alex was not bored. He was quietly plotting to entice his future father-in-law into supporting a set of reforms sure to make their way out of the House of Commons next Season. Reforms that would lower the sky-high tariffs he was paying on his shipping line.

When supper was concluded and the women retired to the green salon, Alex, Arthur, and Lord Whitcomb stayed in the dining room for the customary cigar and port. Alex absently watched the hands of the porcelain mantel clock as Arthur and Whitcomb discussed a pair of hunting dogs. Convinced the expensive timepiece was winding down, Alex checked it against his pocket watch.

"Are we boring you, Sutherland?" Whitcomb grinned. Startled, Alex hastily shoved his pocket watch out of sight.

"He's smarting over another reported loss from East India," Arthur said, chuckling.

"That so? Never thought dallying in shipping was the way to go," the elderly earl remarked.

"It would be quite profitable if the tariffs weren't so damned high," Alex said.

Whitcomb shrugged. "Those tariffs also keep foreign

grain from coming to our shores and competing with what you grow out here, son.''

''Yes, and when the domestic markets are flooded, it keeps the smaller farmer from exporting his grain to the continent.''

Whitcomb chuckled and puffed on his cigar. ''Don't know why you'd worry about that. From what I hear, most of them can't afford the labor tax necessary to harvest the grain to begin with. It's not as if they are competing with your exports.''

''My point exactly, Edwin. Competition is healthy. This country is long overdue for economic reform. Taxes are strangling the shipping and agricultural industries—the system is antiquated and lacks equity. Just think of the profits you would realize in your factories if the labor tax was equalized across all industries,'' Alex said calmly, and took a long sip of his port, eyeing his future father-in-law above the rim.

''Perhaps,'' Whitcomb said thoughtfully. ''Can't deny the countryside suffers worse than the manufacturers. But I don't like the reform package the Radicals are pushing— they want to do away with the whole parliamentary system, I fear, and the first step would be allowing the Catholics a seat. Can't have that, you know.''

Alex did not immediately respond. Catholic emancipation was a point of great contention among his peers, but he honestly could not care less if Catholics held a seat in Parliament. ''All I know is that we need relief and a new, *fair* system of taxation. Perhaps next Season we could work together toward a more palatable set of reforms.''

Whitcomb smiled as he drained his port glass. ''I might be amenable to that. Always enjoyed a good fight in the Lords. Well, gentlemen, shall we see what the ladies are about?'' He did not wait for an answer, but shoved away from the table. Alex and Arthur dutifully followed him to the green salon, where they sat quietly listening to the ladies talk of engagement parties for two hours more.

Later, as Alex stood in the foyer with his mother, he heard Marlaine mention that she and Lady Whitcomb would return the next day to discuss the winter engagement party. He managed not to snort impatiently.

Two days later, having escaped the tedium of Sutherland Hall, Alex stopped at a rushing stream so his stallion, Jupiter, could drink. He had been chasing the same buck all morning, but the animal was wily and knew how to evade him. He guessed he was at least five miles from his hunting lodge, Dunwoody. Only a day's ride from Sutherland Hall, he often came to Dunwoody for a few days of respite from his title. Or his wedding.

Rubbing his eyes, he dropped the reins as Jupiter drank and considered calling it a day. His thoughts drifted to Marlaine. She, of course, had not wanted him to go hunting. She had fretted about it, anxious that something might happen to him and she would not be there to care for him. He had rather salaciously suggested she come along and take care of all his needs, but Marlaine had grown wide-eyed with mortification at the mere suggestion. He had never bedded Marlaine, respecting her ironclad determination to hold on to her virtue until the very last possible moment.

So he had come alone, unable to endure one more day of idle chatter about their wedding. Marlaine and her mother were insisting on an event during the Season—meaning he had several long months to wait until he could bed her. And several long months to listen to talk of trousseaus, wedding breakfasts, engagement fetes, and bridal trips. Dear *God*.

She had whimpered when he left. He had responded to that maidenly display by telling her she best get accustomed to his absences. He had left her standing at the great entrance to Sutherland Hall, cautioning him with all sincerity to have a care for his person. Have a care, indeed. He had scaled mountains and forded roaring rivers without a nurse-maid and supposed he could manage to hunt alone for a few days.

A sound in the brush startled him, but he never saw the animal. Jupiter suddenly reared, neighing loudly. Caught off guard, Alex grabbed the reins and fought to contain the massive horse, almost falling from the saddle for his efforts. Horse and rider rushed headlong across the stream and into the brush, blinded by dense foliage and shackled by the thick undergrowth. When Jupiter burst through the thicket into a small clearing a few moments later, Alex pulled up hard, finally gaining control. The incident left them both panting; they stood in the clearing, each fighting to regain their breath. He became aware of a stinging in his leg and looked down. His buckskin breeches were torn and his shin was bleeding where he had obviously slammed up against a thornbush.

"What then, have you never seen a hare, old boy?" He soothingly patted the steed's neck, and attempted to turn back. Jupiter moved awkwardly, neighing softly when his right foreleg came into contact with the ground.

"Christ." Alex sighed wearily and dismounted. He felt for broken bones, thankfully finding none. Nevertheless, Jupiter was in no mood to use the sprained appendage.

"Bloody, bloody hell," Alex muttered, and glanced around him. Dunwoody lands were vast but oddly shaped, and he could not be completely certain he was still on his property. He impatiently removed his hat and ran a hand through his thick hair as he debated what to do. He hated the thought of leaving Jupiter, but without knowing the full extent of his injuries, he could not chance walking him very far without risking serious damage. Walking to Dunwoody was out of the question; he had ridden too far. If he was not mistaken, the village of Pemberheath was due north, perhaps a mile or two more. At least he hoped so.

He reluctantly tied Jupiter's rein to a low limb of a tree

and covered his heavy rifle in a pile of leaves. "Mind you keep an eye on it," he said lamely, stroked the stallion's nose, and walked out of the clearing, headed north to Pemberheath.

Chapter 4

Traipsing through the wheat stubble, Lauren could not see the hog, Lucy, anywhere. It was unusually warm for the time of year, and she paused to loosen the collar of her work gown. She absently examined a wheat stalk Lucy had stomped in her escape and wondered how long hogs lived. Lucy had to be positively ancient by now, and the older she got, the more obstinate she became. For reasons beyond Lauren's ability to understand, the children loved her. The last time Lucy had gotten it into her head to take a stroll in search of new fodder, it had taken the considerable efforts of both her and Rupert to lure her home, and she had not gone so far that time. As Rupert had taken Ethan and Paul to Pemberheath, she would have to corral Lucy by herself. She had no earthly idea what she would do once she found the walking ham, but if she did not return with her, the children would be frantic.

She came to the edge of the field, but still no Lucy. Beyond the barren wheat field was an orchard of new apple trees, donated by Abbey's friends, Lord and Lady Haversham. Beyond that, a few spindly stalks of harvested corn. And farther still, a field of pumpkins, which Lauren had already bartered for enough tallow to last the next two months.

Dear Lord, but it was terribly warm. The heavy mane of her hair was making her neck sticky, and she attempted to knot it, but her efforts did little more than keep a few errant strands from her face. She wiped a hand across her brow and continued plodding through the field, shaking her head at the damage the enormous pig had caused as she had rumbled through the cornstalks.

She found Lucy in the middle of several destroyed pumpkins, happily munching away. "Oh *no!*" Lauren groaned. As she approached, the headstrong hog moved in front of the pumpkin she was devouring and glared at Lauren.

"Lucy, come away from there!" she insisted, fully cognizant that Lucy had never heeded a single command in her long life. Lucy responded with a loud, warning snort. Lauren slowly circled her, thinking that if she could grab the last pumpkin in the row, the ham might follow her. But the moment Lauren reached for the pumpkin, Lucy charged. With a shriek, Lauren jumped out of the way. Lucy had *never* charged her. Standing between Lauren and the half-eaten pumpkin, Lucy began to paw the earth like a bull. Lauren cautiously backed away, but it did not convince the swine of her good intentions, and she continued to paw the earth, snorting wildly. Besides food, Lauren knew of only one thing that would calm Lucy.

She sang, a little frantically, a song from a Shakespeare play. If there was one thing Helmut had liked in his declining health, it was a good play. English, German, or French, it made no difference. A variety of plays had been staged at Bergenschloss at great expense, and if Helmut liked one in particular, it was played several times.

"Who is Silvia, what is she? That all our Swains commend her?" Lauren sang softly, then paused. She quickly

resumed when Lucy angrily pawed the ground again. *"Holy, faire, and wise is she, The heaven such grace did lend her, that she might admired be. . . ."* Lucy stopped pawing and regarded Lauren suspiciously. *"Is she kinde as she is faire? For beauty lives with kindness: Love doth to her eyes repaire, to helpe him of his blindness: And being help'd, inhabits there. . . ."*

Putting aside, for the moment, that it was utterly *ridiculous* to be standing in the middle of a pumpkin field singing to a hog, Lauren had no idea what to do. If she stopped, Lucy was prepared to charge. But she could hardly stand here singing all day like a simpleton. Trapped between the wood fence and Lucy, Lauren tried to think while she sang.

Alex paused and removed his coat, then lifted his foot. Just bloody grand. A stone had pierced a hole in the sole of his very, *very* expensive boots. What he paid for the custom-made leather Hessians should have guaranteed him a walk all the way to Scotland and back. He slung his coat over his shoulder and continued, wincing every so often when he managed to step on a pebble and spear the bottom of his foot. God, he had never been so completely miserable. First that stubborn buck, then Jupiter, and now his boot. And to top it all off, he was positively melting under the bright sun. Alex angrily yanked at his neckcloth, muttering an oath or two against his tailor as he did, when an unusual sound caught his attention.

He had to be hearing things.

He paused, straining to listen. A gentle, lilting voice lifted on the breeze from nowhere. *"Holy, faire, and wise is she, The heaven such grace did lend her . . ."* Yes, he was definitely imagining things. That was a song from *The Two Gentleman of Verona*. He almost laughed at the notion of some crofter singing a song from a Shakespearean play. With a derisive chuckle, he shook his head and started forward again, but quickly drew up short. *"Then to Silvia, let*

*us sing, that Silvia is excelling; She excels each mortall
thing upon the dull earth dwelling. To her let us Garlands
bring . . .''* He most definitely was not hearing things.
Alex turned slowly toward the sound and quietly sucked in
his breath.

God Almighty, it was no crofter.

Standing nearby in a field was a vision of a woman.
Woman? She was an *angel*—with dark chestnut hair loosely
knotted in the middle of her back, tiny curls of it swirling
softly about her face. God, but she was *beautiful*. Classic,
patrician lines, a small, straight nose, full lips the color of
roses, the voice of a wren. Alex shook his head and squinted
at her again. Had he been walking in the sun too long? Was
this some kind of dream? He moved slowly toward the
fence, captivated by her voice and extraordinary beauty. A
movement to his right disrupted his attention, and he reluctantly shifted his gaze from the vision.

This was no dream.

It would not include such an enormous, mean-faced hog.
Alex quickly shifted his gaze to the angel and frowned. Nor
would an angel be wearing a plain brown dress and a pair of
thick-soled, clumsy boots. The angel was just a young
woman who was . . . hell, he didn't know *what* she was
doing. Except standing in a field. And singing to a hog.

He was suddenly embarrassed to be staring at her as if
she were some priceless piece of art. At the very least, he
ought to ask if she knew how far it was to Pemberheath. He
braced one leg against the rough-hewn fence and called,
''Good day!''

Both the hog and the woman started, jerking wide-eyed
looks of surprise to him. A moment passed; the woman
warily slid her gaze to the hog, and the hog to her.

Then the hog suddenly charged.

With a cry, the angel whirled and headed for the fence,
her long hair flying out behind her like some surreal banner.
She ran for her life, and so did that huge swine. Alex

dropped his coat and held out his arms, intending to help her. But the hog, which had to outweigh her by a factor of at least four, was moving with alarming speed and gaining on her. She must have sensed it because she glanced over her shoulder and shrieked. Reaching the fence just barely ahead of the swine, she ignored his outstretched arms and hurled herself across the structure in a cloud of brown wool and silken hair, landing squarely on top of him. His hands somehow found her waist, but the impact caused him to lose his footing, and the two tumbled to the earth, rolling down a short embankment.

Unexpectedly flat on his back, Alex blinked up at the clear blue sky, momentarily uncertain as to what had just happened. Another clouded moment passed before he realized his hand was trapped beneath her firm derriere. Before he could do anything about it, his view of the blue sky was abruptly obscured by the angel's lovely face, a pair of vivid cobalt eyes narrowed menacingly, and the banner of hair spilling over her shoulder and pooling onto his chest.

"Are you *mad*?" she fairly shrieked, and jumped to her feet.

A little stunned, Alex slowly pushed himself up onto his elbows, eyeing her warily as she brushed the dirt and grass from her gown. "Am *I*?" he asked incredulously. "Madam, I was not the one singing to a hog!"

"You *startled* her! She was doing quite nicely until then, did you not see that?" the vision shouted at him.

Rather astonished, Alex struggled to his haunches, retrieved his hat, and stood. The lass was yelling at him. No one ever yelled at him. No one ever so much as lifted their voice. Most never really *spoke* to him. "I may have startled her, but what about you?" he shot back. "That hog was intent on swallowing you whole, and there you stood, singing like some actor on a stage!"

"A *stage*? I was *calming* her, how could you not *see*

that?'' she cried, and punched her fists to her slender hips to better glare at him.

''*Calming* her? That's absurd! You silly little chit, she could have killed you!'' he shouted.

''And just who are you calling a *silly little chit*?'' she fairly shrieked, then as quickly as a cloud scuds across the sky, the anger slipped from her face.

And she laughed.

Not the polite titter to which he was accustomed from women, but a deep, heartfelt laugh. Her hands splayed across her middle as if to keep the laughter contained, and she bent backward with glee. Her hair reflected the sun's rays in the rich dark gold streaks as it drifted toward the earth. Her rose lips stretched over a row of even, white teeth, and she laughed so hard that tears seeped from the corners of her brilliant blue eyes. Quite unaccustomed to such an artless display of gaiety, Alex nervously shifted his weight to one leg.

''D-Do you s-see?'' she gasped as she lifted a hand and delicately wiped a tear from the corner of her sparkling eye. ''We are *arguing* about an obstinate old *hog*!'' she cried gleefully, and followed it with another peal of melodious laughter.

He supposed he should be thankful she was not hysterical after the scare, but merely amused. *Greatly* amused—her dulcet laughter was infectious. ''Are you hurt?'' he asked, a grin slowly spreading his lips.

She shook her head, making the tiny wisps of curls dance around her flawless face. ''No,'' she said, giggling, ''are you?''

''No.''

She peeked up at him through thick, curly lashes. ''I am quite mortified, you know! I landed right on top of you! I thought you would . . . you know . . . *move*.''

Alex chuckled as he bent to retrieve his coat. ''My intention was to help you step over the fence.''

She laughed roundly. "And did you think with that beast
on my heels I would tiptoe across?"

"I rather suppose I did," he admitted sheepishly. God,
but her smile was as brilliant as the damned sun beating
down on them.

"I am Lauren Hill," she offered, and extended her hand.

A faint, indescribable tingle waved through the pit of his
stomach as he took the long, graceful fingers into his and
closed around them. "Alex Christian," he muttered, his
eyes riveted on her hand. Belatedly remembering himself, he
glanced up. A bit of color infused her cheeks as she slowly
withdrew her hand. Her gaze dipped to the tips of her
chunky boots as she clasped her hands demurely behind her
back.

"It would appear the hog has decided that as a meal, you
are not worth the effort," he remarked.

Her head snapped up, and gasping softly, she leaned to
one side to see around him. "*Now* where has that silly hog
gone?" she muttered under her breath. "Honestly, the way
Lucy keeps running off, you would think we never feed
her!"

"Lucy?"

"We named her Lucy eight years ago when it became
apparent she was much to old to be a very good Christmas
dinner."

"I see. And do you often sing to Lucy?" he asked, another, uncommon grin curling the corners of his mouth.

"No," she said softly, her eyes riveting on his lips, "only
when she is irritated."

He wished to high heaven she would not stare at his
mouth like that. Uncharacteristically flustered, he turned
abruptly toward the field. "Lucy apparently likes pumpkin."

"Yes, exceedingly well." Frowning, Miss Hill walked to
the fence. Alex's legs moved of their own accord, but his
gaze followed the soft sway of her slender hips and the dark
chestnut curls bouncing lightly just above them. He recalled

the feel of that round little bottom, and amazingly, he had an unmistakable urge to touch those curls, just above those hips. She turned suddenly, startling him. "Are you lost?"

"Lost?" he stammered.

"Lost. I hope I am not too forward, Mr. Christian, but is there a reason you are, you know, *here*?"

Alex was so captivated by her dark blue eyes and so startled by the uncommon address that he was momentarily unable to think of an answer. "Ah, well. I suppose one could say I have lost my bearings." *If not my mind,* he added silently. "My horse drew up lame, you see, and I was walking for help. I thought the village of Pemberheath was nearby—"

"Three miles more," she offered helpfully. "Where is your horse?"

"A small clearing a few miles south of here. Perhaps you would be so kind as to point me in the proper direction?" he asked, feeling uncomfortably absurd to be looking at her with all the admiration of a schoolboy. But hell, he was only mortal, and she possessed the most remarkable eyes he had ever had the good fortune to see.

"You shall come to Rosewood! I can send Rupert for help when he returns from the village," she offered, then smiled so charmingly he had to swallow. Rosewood, he had heard of it. Rupert? Was she married, then?

"Is your husband presently at home?"

"Husband?" she asked, confused, then abruptly laughed. "I am not married, Mr. Christian. Rupert lives at Rosewood—I mean, with my uncle, my brother, and me. Oh, and Mrs. Peterman," she added hastily.

It astounded him that he should be so pleased she was not married. "I would be most obliged if Rupert could find help." Still smiling, she gracefully flicked a thick strand of curls over one shoulder. Alex's eyes followed the movement, and he swallowed again. Hard.

She motioned toward a barely discernible path. "I am afraid it's a bit of a walk," she said apologetically.

"My only regret is that I cannot offer you the comfort of a carriage."

She giggled as if that was the most perfectly ridiculous thing he could have said, which, of course, it was. "Oh, it is much too nice a day for carriages, Mr. Christian. It should be many months before we enjoy such fine weather again."

Fine weather? He was positively stifling. Limping slightly, he fell in beside the enchanting creature. Her eyes landed upon the slash of dark red seeping through his expensive buckskins, and he said, "A bramble bush, I think."

"I beg your pardon?"

He motioned to his leg. "Jupiter slammed into a bramble bush, I think," he clarified.

"Yes, bramble," she murmured, and turned her attention to the path in front of them. But not before he noticed the heightened color in her cheeks. They walked for several minutes before either spoke.

"Where did you learn the song you were singing?" he asked.

"It's a ditty from a Shakespearean play," she said with a graceful but dismissive flick of her wrist.

"The Two Gentleman of Verona," he said.

Surprised, Miss Hill snapped a wide-eyed gaze to him. "Why, *yes*! How did you know?" She beamed, clearly delighted.

How did he know? He was a generous patron of the arts, had boxes in the finest theaters and concert halls across Europe. But all of that seemed a bit too pretentious under the circumstances. "I am quite a fan of Shakespeare," he said simply.

"Ah, the *'Sweet Swan of Avon,'* " she said with a sigh.

Alex arched a brow. Singing Shakespeare and now quoting Ben Jonson? "You have read Mr. Jonson?"

The angel laughed lightly. "We may be a bit off the

beaten path, sir, but we are not so remote we do not have a book of English literature.''

He nodded, silently regarding her as they continued along. Dressed in that plain brown frock and those awful boots, she looked like a simple country lass. But her speech was that of a gently bred woman, and she was obviously well read. It was an unusual dichotomy, one he could not quite understand. One he did not need to understand, not when she was looking up at him with those vivid blue eyes. She brought a hand to her brow and raked a loose curl from her forehead. For the second time, Alex was seized with a desire to touch the riotous curl of her hair.

''Do you read poetry?'' she asked. He nodded, mentioning a couple of his favorites. He was astounded—she knew them all, and rattled off little stanzas of her favorite poems. He was completely mesmerized, stunned that he had found this unusual creature in the middle of a pumpkin field.

After a quarter of an hour more, a barn came into view. Three dairy cows mowed the grass in a large circle, tended by a young boy. She noticed him looking at the barn, and admitted proudly, ''We just birthed a calf. Horace is quite convinced one of the bigger cows will smush the little fellow, so he has appointed himself its guardian.''

Amazed by the extraordinary leap of his stomach at the mention of her children, Alex glanced toward the mill. ''How many children do you have?''

''Five at the moment. Sometimes one or two more.''

He should hardly have been surprised; the small kernel of disappointment he felt was ludicrous. He had the impression that country people bred continuously, and why should he care how many children she had now or had lost? Country children were, unfortunately, susceptible to disease and death. ''You have five children?'' he asked again, angry with himself.

She shifted her dark blue gaze to him, saw the obvious look of wonder on his face, and burst out laughing. ''Oh no, sir, not *mine*! The children at Rosewood are our wards. Or-phans," she clarified, "except for Rupert." Another child suddenly appeared on the crest of a hill, behind which Alex noticed the four chimneys of a small manor house. Miss Hill lifted her hand and waved. Absurdly relieved that they were not her children, Alex followed her to the barn. The young boy tending the cattle, who looked to be no older than seven or eight years, rushed forward to greet them.

"Horace, have a care where you step!" she called, then laughingly wrinkled her nose. "Our cattle, few though they are, are quite prolific in their production of fertilizer."

He was about to remark that he was quite sure it was a trait common to all cattle, but the shouting caught him off guard. He thought the other boy had been hurt, and jerked around. With inhuman effort, he managed to keep from gap-ing at the boy's hideous birthmark. "Really, Leonard, he is *not* a pirate," Miss Hill said, laughing. "He is a country gentleman who has lost his way." *And my mind,* Alex si-lently reminded her, *especially my mind.* The unfortunate young lad was smiling brightly at Miss Hill. She touched his temple, smiling at him as genuinely as if the child were Adonis himself.

Dear God, she *was* an angel.

For the second time that day, Alex felt he was watching a dream. The boys looked adoringly at Miss Hill, and the an-gel with the voice of gold laughingly regaled them with Lucy's adventure, lovingly touching them as she spoke. Cer-tain he was rudely gaping, Alex clenched his jaw tightly shut and tried to remain as expressionless as he knew how.

"Mr. Christian, may I introduce Leonard?" she smiled, gesturing toward the birthmarked child, "and Horace."

"Good afternoon," Alex heard himself say.

"Good afternoon, sir," they chirped in unison.

"We have four more boarders at Rosewood," Miss Hill said. "Sally, Theodore, and Lydia are inside. Rupert and my brother, Paul, are with my uncle in Pemberheath."

"It's Theodore's turn to watch Sally," Leonard informed him. As Alex imagined that Sally had some horrible malady, Miss Hill instructed the boys to run ahead and inform Mrs. Peterman they had a guest.

"I will race you to the top of the hill!" Horace shouted, and the lads immediately scampered ahead, toward the house.

"It is the dinner hour. I rather imagine you must be famished," Miss Hill said. Alex dragged his gaze from the boys and smiled. "I would not think of imposing."

"It is no imposition, sir. You are very welcome."

"If you are quite certain, I admit I am indeed rather hungry." He would probably never know what compelled him to agree. Part of him wanted to look at the child's birthmark again, to see if the others were similarly afflicted. But another part of him wanted to look at the angel as long as he could. All of this—Rosewood, Lucy, and the angel beside him, intrigued him on a level he could hardly fathom. She had already started toward the crest, and he quickened his step.

Lauren did not realize how fast she was walking. God, was she *addled*? The invitation to dinner had no sooner tumbled out of her mouth when it occurred to her that Ethan might have returned. Blanching at the very thought, Lauren quickened her step, wanting to reach the house before he did, mortified that such a dignified, educated, *handsome* man might meet *Ethan*. Good *God*!

She was practically running by the time she reached the house, and would have run straight inside and up to her room had Mr. Christian not stopped her with a gentle hand on her arm. She gasped and immediately looked down to see if her arm was on fire. It certainly felt like it was; a strange, tingling sensation spread quickly to her chest. Catching her breath in her throat, she looked up at him. Lord, but Alex Christian, whoever he was, had to be the most handsome man she had ever clapped eyes on. He was tall, well over six feet. His brown hair was threaded with a sprinkling of gold, and he had warm green eyes that could melt ice. They were certainly doing a fine job of melting her where she stood.

"I beg your pardon, Miss Hill. I did not mean to imply I was *that* hungry!" He grinned at her. Lauren's cheeks burned; how foolish she must look, running to the dinner table like Lucy to her slop. He looked as if he expected her to say something, but Lord Almighty, she could not help staring at him. His face was rugged and square and deeply tanned, his shoulders broad and muscular, his legs powerful. She silently commanded herself to stop being ridiculous and laughed nervously at his jest. She felt the heat in her cheeks, and was never so glad to see Mrs. Peterman in all her life as when the housekeeper stepped onto the back steps, her arms wrapped around a huge ceramic bowl. She glared at Mr. Christian as she furiously stirred the contents of her bowl.

"Mrs. Peterman, may I introduce Mr. Christian?"

"How do you do, Mrs. Peterman," he said politely.

She growled and shifted a narrowed gaze to Lauren. "That blasted hog is back in her pen. I sent Leonard after you, thinking she might have killed you at last!"

Lauren laughed tightly, cringing inwardly at how strange she sounded. "She certainly tried, but Mr. Christian was kind enough to help me."

"Miss Hill is too generous. It would be more accurate to say she survived in spite of my help."

"Are you in the habit of roaming the open fields, Mr. Christian?" Mrs. Peterman snapped. Lauren winced. Mrs. Peterman was still smarting over her rejection of Fastidious Thadeus, and since then had treated every eligible man in a ten-mile radius of Pemberheath as a blackguard.

"His horse drew up lame, Mrs. Peterman. I brought him here so that Rupert might help him," she muttered, and cast an imploring look at the housekeeper.

"Rupert is not here," Mrs. Peterman said, and pivoting on her heel, marched into the kitchen.

Why didn't the earth just open and swallow her where she stood? She tried to smile. "Mrs. Peterman is rather protective."

"I can certainly understand why," he smiled.

Those simple words caused another rush of heat to her face. Bewildered, she proceeded into the kitchen, not daring to see if he followed. Incredibly, he did. She asked Lydia to show him where he might wash and had to nudge the young girl to move, as she was gaping in awe at the handsome stranger. The moment Mr. Christian left the room, Lauren whirled to Mrs. Peterman. "Please, *please* tell me Ethan is not here!" she moaned, sinking onto a stool.

Mrs. Peterman did not deign to look up from the stove. "He is not here, and you should thank the stars he is not! What are you thinking, dragging a perfect stranger home from the fields?" she snapped.

"His horse was injured! Should I have left him wandering about?"

Mrs. Peterman gave her a stern look as she thrust a large bowl of stew at her. Lauren ignored it; she could not explain to herself, much less to Mrs. Peterman, that she might very well have escorted him to hell and back for one of his warm smiles. Or that her heart pounded at the sight of those powerful legs moving in those *very* tight buckskins. She marched to the dining area set up for the children and placed the bowl rather loudly on the old scarred table. It startled Theodore, whose nose was buried in a book. Just ten years old, he devoured every book brought into the house. Next to him was Sally, Theodore's charge for the day. Sally was only four, so her supervision was a responsibility shared by the older children.

"Leonard said you brought a pirate to dinner," Theodore remarked hopefully.

Lauren smiled and handed several wooden bowls to him, motioning for him to set the table. "Leonard is mistaken, darling. Mr. Christian is a gentleman with a lame horse. I rather doubt he has ever been on a boat.''

Theodore pondered that as he carefully placed the bowls around the table, then brightened. ''Sometimes pirates *act* as if they are gentlemen. Perhaps he just *said* that so as not to frighten you.''

''I assure you, he is not a pirate, but a man in search of a good horse doctor.''

''Yes, but maybe he was riding for his ship when his horse was hurt!''

''We are many, many miles from the sea, darling,'' Lauren said, running her hand over the boy's blond locks.

''But he *had* to go that way, Miss Lauren!'' Horace shouted from the door, then ran to take a seat at the table. ''Leonard said the constable would find him if he took the main road!''

''The constable?'' She laughed. ''And what do you suppose the constable would do if he found Mr. Christian? Without the booty of a raid, he should have no grounds to detain him. I am afraid Leonard is filling your head with tales from his own imagination.''

''I hardly think your story is much improvement,'' Mrs. Peterman huffed from the kitchen door. She placed two freshly baked loaves of bread on the table, which Lauren promptly began to slice.

''It is not a *story,* Mrs. Peterman,'' she said with cheerful patience. ''It is fact!''

''Oh, he is a pirate,'' Leonard said with great authority as he came into the small dining area. ''He is wearing pirate boots. Very *fine* pirate boots.''

''These boots,'' Mr. Christian drawled, ''would not suit the lowest of pirates, I assure you.'' Lauren looked up; her country gentleman filled the narrow doorway with his athletic physique, and smiling at the children as he was, started the giddiness in her all over again. She looked down and noticed she had cut a chunk of bread the size of brick. She hastily made three slices of it, then smiled broadly at Mr. Christian, helplessly aware that she was on the verge of making a complete cake of herself.

She motioned to a chair. "Please be seated, Mr. Christian. And I pray you, do not fault these boys overmuch. Since Paul began reading fantastic stories of pirates to them each night, they believe every grown man is potentially a marauder of the high seas." Lydia was still standing in the door, still staring at Mr. Christian. "Lydia," Lauren said softly, and the young girl slowly walked to the table, no more able to tear her eyes from him than Lauren could. Usually, Lydia could talk of little else than Ramsey Baines, with whom she was desperately in love, but she sat across from Mr. Christian, gawking at him with such awe that Lauren wanted to laugh. She knew *exactly* how she felt.

"I am *not* a pirate," he informed the children, "nor have I been a pirate in at least five years. I was forced to stop that practice several years ago. Constable Richards . . ." he paused and glanced slyly at the children. With the exception of Sally, who was molding a slice of bread into a doll shape, the children's faces were filled with expectant terror. He shrugged carelessly. "Forgive me. I would not bore you with the details," he said, and helped himself to a generous portion of stew.

Lauren stifled a delighted giggle as she nudged Lydia to take a piece of bread. "Constable Richards? How very ironic," she said as she pushed a bowl in front of Sally. "They say he pursued a ruthless pirate for many years." She paused and glanced thoughtfully at the window. "He never caught him—they say it haunts him to this day. But surely he is not the *same* Constable Richards."

She glanced at Mr. Christian, who returned her gaze with a mischievous smile. Incredulous, the children all paused, their attention riveted on Mr. Christian's anticipated answer. "Surely not," he agreed slowly, and the children's shoulders sagged almost as one with disappointment. "Unless, of course, you refer to *Robert* Richards?'' The children suddenly sat forward, their spoons freezing between bowl and mouth as they jerked their gazes to Lauren.

''Why, *yes,* I do indeed! Do you know him?'' Of course he did, and Mr. Christian began to weave a fantastic tale of adventure on the seas, sprinkled with exciting and very close encounters with the imaginary Constable Richards. The children were spellbound, hardly tasting their stew. Lauren was hardly immune to his charm, either. She wanted to hug him for treating the children with respect and dignity. She wanted to cry that he did not seem to notice Leonard's horrid birthmark. Her admiration of Mr. Christian, already dangerously high, grew with alarming leaps and bounds during the course of that meal.

Unfortunately for them all, with the notable exception of Mrs. Peterman, dinner was over far too soon. Lauren reluctantly sent the children to their chores, kissing the tops of their heads as she firmly sent them off. They all wanted to stay with Mr. Christian—so did she.

And she might have contrived a way to do it had Mr. Goldthwaite not picked that very inopportune time to call. The banging on the front door came just as she poured tea. A moment later, the apothecary marched into the small dining room carrying a large bunch of wilting daisies, his apple cheeks flushed. If there was anything worse than Ethan, it was Fastidious Thadeus. Why did he have to call *today?* ''Good afternoon, Mr. Goldthwaite,'' she said wearily.

''Afternoon Miss Hill.'' He sniffed. ''I have taken the liberty of bringing you some daisies. They are quite the rage just now, and I thought they should brighten your dressing table nicely,'' he said, his small brown eyes sliding to Mr. Christian.

''Thank you, Mr. Goldthwaite,'' she said evenly, ''but I do not have a dressing table.'' She stood politely to receive the blasted flowers and brought them quickly to her face to hide her mortification. Oh God, she could not bear to imag-

ine what Mr. Christian must be thinking! "Mr. Goldthwaite,
may I present Mr. Christian?" she said coolly, and hearing
Mrs. Peterman behind her, turned and thrust the daisies into
her hands, for which she received another disapproving
frown.

"How do you do, Mr. Goldthwaite."

"I do very well, sir. I have not seen you here before. Are
you a benefactor?"

Lauren groaned.

Mr. Christian politely ignored the indecorum of such a
question. "Miss Hill very kindly brought me here after my
horse went lame. I am off to Pemberheath now in search of
help," he said, coming to his feet.

Lauren felt a moment of panic, and rushed too eagerly,
she damn well knew it, to his side. "Rupert has not yet
returned, Mr. Christian, but I am certain he shall be along
shortly—"

"Nonsense! I should be happy to take Mr. Christian to
Pemberheath! But I pray you, sir, we must leave at once. I
should not have stopped as it is, but as I had the daisies, it
would not do to let them wilt," Mr. Goldthwaite said, and
started immediately for the door.

"I should be most obliged, sir." Mr. Christian turned
and smiled warmly at Lauren. "Miss Hill, I cannot thank
you enough for your hospitality. Good day, Mrs. Peterman,"
he nodded to the unsmiling housekeeper, and followed Mr.
Goldthwaite as he waddled quickly from the room. Unbalanced by a surge of unfamiliar emotion, Lauren looked helplessly to Mrs. Peterman, receiving a hapless shrug in
response. Knowing she should do *nothing* but bid the gentleman a good day, Lauren grabbed his forgotten hat from a
wall peg and rushed after him.

"Mr. Christian!" she called as she stepped out onto the
drive. He turned, his green eyes sparkling with his smile.
She thrust the hat at him. He grasped it with one hand and
pulled lightly, but she did not let go. "Ah . . . thank you,

sir, for helping me out of a rather peculiar predicament,"
she said nervously. What in heaven's name was she *doing*?

He chuckled softly. "I was hardly any help, Miss Hill."

"Mr. Christian, if you please!" Thadeus shouted from
his curricle. Lauren scowled mightily at him then turned a
winsome smile to her gentleman.

"If you should ever have reason to be in the area, it
would please the children enormously if you would call,"
she said, and instantly ashamed at her brazenness, nervously
averted her gaze. "I, ah . . . they so enjoyed your tale."

"Miss Hill—"

"*Mr. Christian!* I really must be going!" Mr. Goldthwaite bellowed from the carriage. Good *God,* she would
have liked to have knocked that stout little peacock from his
perch and stuff him full of daisies!

"Thank you again, Miss Hill," Mr. Christian said. Yet he
remained standing in front of her, his eyes crinkling in the
corners with his smile.

"You are very welcome, Mr. Christian," she sighed, gazing up at him.

His smile turned into a charming grin. "Miss Hill . . .
the hat?" Lauren looked down; she was still clutching the
hat. Horrified, she let go of it so quickly that he took a step
backward. Chuckling, he turned toward the carriage.

Oh, how very *grand!* She had succeeded in making a
complete blockhead of herself! Mr. Christian looked at her
again when he had settled onto the narrow little seat next to
Mr. Goldthwaite. With a jaunty wave she hoped looked very
carefree, Lauren pretended to be examining a tattered vine
that had attached itself to the stone exterior of the house.
When she heard the carriage pull away, she wished for a
thousand deaths. For herself *and* Fastidious Thadeus.

Alex managed one last look behind him as the carriage
raced away from the shabby manor house. His initial assessment was correct—she was an angel, and a very provocative
one at that. As Mr. Goldthwaite sent the carriage careening

around a bend in the road, Alex grabbed his hat and the seat at the same time. "In something of a hurry, are you?" he asked dryly as the carriage righted itself.

"I have *many* pressing matters," the little man fairly spat out. "I should never have called today!"

"Have you known Miss Hill long?" Alex asked, knowing full well that she was the cause of Mr. Goldthwaite's angst. He could hardly blame the poor man. She was as captivatingly beautiful as she was kind, the sort of woman that could bring a man to a state of blind devotion.

"I have been very well acquainted with Miss Hill for most of her life."

"I am sure she is a good friend," Alex remarked for wont of anything better to say.

Mr. Goldthwaite snorted loudly. "*Friend?* We are practically *betrothed,* sir!" he snapped angrily.

Alex had no idea what the understanding was between the two of them, but in his humble estimation, Mr. Goldthwaite had a better chance of marrying Lucy than Lauren Hill.

Chapter 5

With his feet propped upon a footstool, Ethan was sitting directly in front of the fire when Lauren marched into the drawing room carrying a tray of medicinal soup. The unusually warm weather had turned unusually cold, and Ethan had not stopped complaining since the first gray clouds had appeared. Kicking the door shut, Lauren marched to where her uncle sat and placed the tray down with such force as to spill the soup.

"Don't be slamming that door, lass. I have a headache," he grumbled. Lauren said nothing as she poured him a cup of tea. "What, are you still sulking over Rupert?" he sighed, and reached for his brandy, ignoring the tea.

"You promised me, Uncle Ethan," she reminded him sharply.

Ethan moaned his exasperation. "He is a grown *man,* Lauren. If he wants an ale, who am I to deny him?"

"Putting aside, for the moment, that the two of you could have been *killed* driving that old wagon in such a state, you know Rupert cannot absorb spirits like other men! It has taken him two full days to recover!''

"Do not bother me with that now," Ethan groaned. "My gout is flaring up again."

Lauren sighed loudly. There was no reasoning with Ethan. She supposed she should be grateful that as he so rarely left the drawing room, he was no real threat to Rupert's safety. Bless Rupert, but he thought Ethan had practically hung the moon. How his simple mind had concluded *that* was the biggest mystery of all. "Please eat your soup, Uncle. Mr. Goldthwaite gave me some herbs that should help ease your pain," she said, and bent to retrieve a discarded weekly paper.

"Goldthwaite! I do not like him sniffing around your skirts, do you hear me? The pillows, child . . ."

"Mr. Goldthwaite understands I do not return his affections," she lied, adjusting the pillows behind Ethan's back. Apparently, there was *nothing* she could say to convince Fastidious Thadeus *or* Mrs. Peterman of that. "But he is so terribly generous to us, I cannot ask him to stay away."

"Then *I* shall do it! I cannot make a match for you with that little hummingbird constantly underfoot," Ethan grumbled, and slurped from his bowl of soup. Lauren shook her head and began to walk toward the door. "Good God, what are you wearing?" he suddenly barked.

She paused and glanced down at the pair of trousers and heavy linen shirt Paul had outgrown many years ago. "Trousers." She continued to the door.

"Mind me, lass! There will be no man wanting to marry you in that!" he called after her. Mind him, indeed, she thought, and shut the door loudly. His constant talk of marrying her off—and it was *constant*—was beginning to wear on her. She marched to the foyer and removed a woolen coat from a peg. Everything was beginning to wear on her, she realized, as she plunged her arms into the coat.

"Where are you off to this morning?"

Lauren glanced over her shoulder at Paul as she pulled a woolen cap over her head. He limped into the foyer and leaned against the wall, his arms folded across his chest. "I should salvage what is left of the pumpkins," she muttered.

"Have Rupert do that. There is no need for you to toil."

"Thanks to Uncle Ethan's superior choice of a drinking partner, Rupert is behind in his chores. And I am in great need of a solitary task," she said sharply, reaching for gloves.

"Is anything wrong?" Paul asked.

Immediately regretting the unleashing of her foul disposition, Lauren smiled weakly. "Nothing that a little time alone will not cure, I assure you." She walked out the door before he could question her further.

She had no hope time alone would cure her. It wasn't that Ethan had allowed Rupert to get so incredibly intoxicated, although she was still quite angry about that. It was just—*everything.* Everything had turned upside down since Mr. Christian had come to Rosewood two days ago.

Damn it, she could not stop *thinking* about Mr. Christian.

She dreamed about him at night, thought about him all day, and yesterday, at a distance, had even mistaken the vicar for him. That was laughable, since the vicar was nearly seventy years old. Never had anyone had such an impact on her. She had never been so much as smitten that she could recall—unless she counted Donovan Williams, who had sparked her great admiration by pulling her hair when she was eight.

But even Donovan Williams could not possibly hold a candle to Mr. Christian. She had never met such a handsome, masculine, *kind* man. He liked poetry, he liked the children, and he did not even seem to object overmuch to Lucy. And beyond those admirable traits, he made her skin tingle in a strange sort of way, made her giggle for no apparent reason, and when he looked at her, dear *God,* her knees turned to water. Lauren sighed miserably as she tromped the path to the pumpkin field, pulling a battered wooden cart behind her.

All right, so she was smitten. What exactly was she to do about it? Mope about like some lovesick schoolgirl? Mr. Christian was not coming back. He was probably at home right now, probably with a *wife* for Chrissakes, and probably had already forgotten the whole thing.

If only *she* could forget.

"Miss Lauren!"

Lauren closed her eyes and moaned softly before turning to face Leonard as he came bounding down the path. "Paul said I should help you."

It took every ounce of energy Lauren had to muster a smile. Damn Paul! Now that he was twenty, he had decided it was his duty to look after her. Sometimes he treated her as if she might break with the slightest breeze! She loved Leonard with all her heart, and at any other time, would have welcomed his company. But not today.

"All right. You may watch for pirates while I pick what is left of the pumpkins." She took his hand in hers, and pulling the cart with the other, continued her march to the pumpkin field.

Leonard did a fine job of guarding her after finding a stick that made a suitable sword. For nearly an hour, he climbed again and again onto the fence and leapt to the ground, shouting *en garde* before he tackled a swarm of imaginary pirates. Despite her miserable mood, Lauren could not help smiling at his exuberance. Tossing the last pumpkin in the cart, she quickly counted. There were fourteen in all, which would pay for only one month's supply of tallow. It was not enough; she needed at least two months supply, if not three, to last the winter.

As she stood in the middle of the field pondering that little problem, Leonard ran up behind and punched her in the back with his stick. Startled, Lauren shrieked and whirled around.

"Arm yourself!" he cried.

Lauren's hands found her hips; her brows snapped into a foreboding vee. "All right, you brigand," she said, squatting to retrieve a stick. *"En garde!"* Much to Leonard's delight, she lifted her stick, assumed a fencing position, and stabbed at the air. She pushed Leonard backward, then allowed him to advance on her. Back and forth they went, laughing gaily at their play.

"Miss Hill?"

Her head snapped around at the sound of that voice. She had just a glimpse of his handsome face before Leonard drove his stick into her unguarded belly. Startled, she toppled onto her rump with a bounce, knocking the breath from her lungs.

"Dear God, are you quite all right?" Mr. Christian asked, suddenly on his knee beside her. He put a steadying arm around her shoulders as she gasped for air.

"Mr. Christian," she rasped, "I have concluded you are quite determined to see me slain in a pumpkin field."

He laughed. "And I believe you are quite determined to give me every opportunity!" His arm slid around her and she was suddenly lifted to her feet. Her breath still would not come, but it had nothing to do with her tumble. Mr. Christian bent over her, peering into her face, a slight frown creasing his forehead. God, but his hand covered the whole of her ribcage. She smiled sheepishly as his strong arm slid away from her. His green eyes flicked to a point past her shoulder, and she suddenly remembered Leonard and turned.

The boy was gaping at her, clearly mortified by having toppled her. "I am sorry!" he cried. "I thought you were looking!"

She laughed, tousling his hair. "You will be the finest pirate yet, Leonard. My goodness, but you are *very* quick. That is very important in sword play, wouldn't you agree, Mr. Christian?"

"I would consider it more important than footwork or strength," he agreed solemnly.

"There, you see?" She smiled, cupped his face in her hands, and kissed him lightly on the forehead. "Do you think you could pull the cart to the barn?" she asked sweetly.

"Are you truly all right?" he asked, his eyes revealing his worry.

Lauren laughed. "I am perfectly fine, darling. It will take much more than a tumble to harm me."

Leonard looked skeptical, but accepted it. He turned to Mr. Christian and mumbled, "Good day, sir," and ran off to wrestle with the old cart. Lauren and Mr. Christian stood side by side, watching Leonard pull the cart up the path. Well, Mr. Christian was watching. She was trying very hard to hide the fact that his physical presence was making her shiver. That, coupled with her sheer mortification at having been found playing pirates in a pair of boy's trousers, caused her to unconsciously wrap her arms around her middle.

"You are chilled," he remarked suddenly, and shrugged out of his coat, draping it across her shoulders before she could answer. The smell of spicy cologne, so faint as to almost be imagined, wafted across her senses.

"You . . . you must be wondering . . ." Lauren stammered as they watched Leonard disappear into the next field.

"Only if Lucy is as hungry as all that," he quipped.

A giggle escaped her. "No doubt she is, but she is forbidden to eat the pumpkins. I have already promised the crop in trade for tallow."

"Pardon?"

Lauren grinned at him. "For candles. I had enough pumpkins to trade for two months worth of tallow, but as best I can figure, Lucy has left me with enough for one month. And if she eats *that,* I am half-tempted to render her hide in exchange."

Mr. Christian said nothing for a long moment; his gaze

slipped to her mouth. Lauren's pulse began to race. "I should be happy to provide you with enough tallow, Miss Hill. You need not trade your pumpkins."

She thought her giggle was absurdly shrill. "Thank you, Mr. Christian, but that is why I grew them in the first place."

"For tallow?" he asked, incredulity evident in his voice.

"For trading. I did not think of tallow at the time, but Mrs. Pennypeck said she could use them in her bakery, and as her husband had more tallow than he needed, it seemed a very good trade. Leonard thought of it."

"So"—he grinned, his gaze dipping to her shirt and trousers—"you trade pumpkins."

"And . . . and apples and tomatoes when they are in season," she muttered, conscious of a heat creeping up her spine. "And then, of course, if there is extra milk . . . not that there is any surplus of that, really, but one day we'll fill buckets."

He lifted his eyes and smiled. A perfectly gorgeous smile, full of what seemed hundreds of white teeth. Her knees were turning to water. Dear God in heaven, she was going to swoon. She took an unconscious step backward. "I . . . I did not know you lived near here."

"I am temporarily at a hunting lodge."

He *hunted*. Oh, but he *looked* like a hunter, all tall and lean and muscular, and . . . God, he was looking at her mouth again. "Is he all right, then?" she asked weakly.

Mr. Christian's brows sank in confusion. "Who would 'he' be?"

"Your horse."

He tossed his head back with a shout of laughter. "Yes, Jupiter is quite all right. Seems he was not as lame as he would have had me believe. Would you like to have a look at him?" he asked, and gestured to where Jupiter was tethered.

Yes, she would like to have a look. She would like to look

at anything but him, lest she topple onto her rump again. "Very much," she said, smiling.

Jupiter was an enormous black stallion, and had the effect of making Rosewood's two old grays look like fat ponies in comparison. Mr. Christian gave her some carrots from his saddlebag, and Lauren stood on a large stone so she was eye-level with the beast, laughing delightedly as she fed him. She asked him what he hunted, and he talked of stalking a buck that had eluded him for three days running. She gathered from his conversation that he was at the lodge alone, and imagined him sitting at night, quietly reading from a book of poetry. She stroked the stallion's nose, a faint smile on her lips.

"Would you like to ride him?" Mr. Christian asked when the carrots were gone and the horse grew restless.

Lauren blinked. Ride that enormous thing? She had never ridden a horse any more daunting than one of the old grays. "I do not know . . ." she hedged, staring into one of the horse's big round eyes.

Mr. Christian chuckled. "Allow me to return the favor of your rescue and escort you to Rosewood. The air is decidedly cooler; I shouldn't be surprised if it rains soon." Lauren looked askance at him. He quirked a brow. "Are you afraid?" he asked, his amusement apparent.

Lord, *yes*! Nevertheless, she flashed him a lopsided grin. "Unfortunately, sir, *'I fear dishonor more than death.'* "

He laughed at the Homeric quip. "Come then," he said, smiling broadly, "I cannot allow you to be dishonored." He stepped aside and bowed gallantly. "Madam, your carriage awaits." Lauren stepped off the stone and walked slowly to the horse's side. "Put your foot in the stirrup," he said from behind her. She could hardly reach it, but the moment her foot made contact, he caught her by the waist and vaulted her onto Jupiter's back. She landed astride the huge horse and quickly grabbed the pommel to keep from sliding right off the other side. In one fluid movement, he swept up behind her, and reached around her to gather the reins. "Well then, are you on?" He chuckled, his breath fanning her cheek.

She was *on* all right, practically *painted* onto his lap, pressed against his brick wall of a chest. His muscular arms surrounded her. His powerful thighs enveloped her own, and she was struck by how tiny her legs looked next to his. She was having difficulty breathing; her pulse was racing at a clip. "I . . . I think so," she breathed.

"Do not be afraid," he said gently. "With that death grip you have on the pommel, there is little chance you will fall."

He nudged Jupiter into a trot, and the force of movement propelled her, impossibly, even further into his body. She nervously yanked the musty wool cap from her head when it came into contact with him; he lifted a hand to smooth her curls from his face. She was acutely conscious of every muscle in his body, every movement of his limbs in guiding the horse. His essence seemed to penetrate her, filling her senses, burning her skin everyplace they touched.

She thought she had died and gone to heaven.

When they reached the barn, she asked him to stop, coming up with the lame excuse of needing to check on the calf. Her uncle would strangle her if he saw her riding astride in front of a stranger, in *trousers,* no less! Mr. Christian obliged, alighting with the grace of a bird before reaching up for her. He lifted her effortlessly, allowing her body to brush the full length of his until her feet touched the ground. Her legs would not hold her; she stumbled to one side before righting herself. He flashed a lopsided, lazy grin that suggested he knew what she was feeling.

It embarrassed her to no end to be so terribly transparent, and she nervously swung his coat from her shoulders and thrust it toward him. "Thank you, Mr. Christian. That was most kind," she said as confidently as she could.

"It was my pleasure, Miss Hill." He smiled, donning his

coat. He shoved his hands in his pockets, regarding her with a faint smile. Lauren stood self-consciously, not knowing what to say or do next. Nervous, she twisted the wool cap in her hands.

"You seem to grow a lot of vegetables," he said, nodding toward a fence where the vines of a squash plant were fastened.

"We, ah, we seem to have a knack for it," she said softly, entranced by his pale green eyes. "Would you like some?"

The green eyes landed on her again, lingering there. "Remarkable," he murmured.

"Oh!" She blushed. "It's not really so remarkable. We don't grow much wheat anymore . . ." Unexpectedly, he lifted his hand to her temple, brushing a single curl from her face. The gentle touch of his fingertips sent a flame racing through her. "The, ah, the taxes, you know, are quite high," she muttered inanely.

"I was referring to you. Truly remarkable," he said quietly, then grasped her hand and brought it to his lips. Oh God, oh *God,* his lips were so *soft*! With a smile, he dropped her hand and stepped away, swinging up onto the back of his horse. "Good afternoon, Miss Hill." He touched the brim of his hat in something of a salute, and sent Jupiter galloping back the way they had come.

Lauren stood rooted to her spot for a long moment, lightly touching her temple where his fingers had been. When he had at last disappeared from sight, she pivoted and flew to the manor house, bursting through the back door with an absurd giddiness. When Paul asked her what had come over her, she laughed and replied enigmatically, "Nothing that a little time alone did not cure." With a beatific grin for her brother, she floated up the stairs to her own room.

It was very odd, Alex thought, that he should be so absorbed in a young woman of such a different class. But he had to admit that he was enchanted. Lauren Hill was as full of surprises as she was smiles. And she was beautiful. Bloody hell, she was *gorgeous*. Seeing her dressed in boys' trousers had almost been his undoing. She was one feminine curve after another, with a full bosom, a slender waist, and gently rounded hips atop what he imagined were two very shapely legs. After their little ride on Jupiter's back, the torturous feel of her body against his own had lingered for two days.

In Pemberheath yesterday, she had caught him off guard again. He had happened upon her at the dry goods store, dressed in a light blue wool gown, her mass of curls neatly coifed and hidden beneath a bonnet, arguing with the proprietor over the price for milled flour. An angel in blue, he thought, whose blue eyes danced excitedly when she paused in her very elegant dressing down of the proprietor to cheerfully thank him for the tallow he had sent to Rosewood.

It had just begun to snow when he escorted her outside, having sweetly and successfully demanded a fair price for the flour, confusing the poor shopkeeper with more than one obscure quotation befitting the situation. He would never forget her glee when she caught a fat flake on the tip of her tongue. She had laughingly remarked that he seemed to bring a change in weather whenever she saw him, but he thought it nothing compared to the storm brewing inside him.

Alex turned the curricle, a sled trailing behind, onto a road leading to Deadman's Run. He had so dubbed the hill only yesterday, when this maggot of an idea had taken hold. Strangely enough, he had found himself rather frantically thinking of ways to see her again as she had tossed the bag of flour into the wagon and climbed up next to Rupert. He had impetuously blurted an invitation to sled. To *sled?* He had not sledded since he was a boy. And just where in the hell did one get a sled? Fortunately, he discovered that the blacksmith sold them—for a king's ransom. Old sleds apparently belonging to some ancient ancestor. He had worked until the early hours of the morning getting the thing in working order.

As the curricle and horse lumbered through the snow, he absently wondered why he did not tell her who he was. He had thought to, but it just seemed so inappropriate. And it hardly seemed to matter. He would be gone in a few days, likely would never see her again. And besides, there was something very peaceful about being a man without a title.

As promised, Miss Hill was at the top of the hill with the children, looking quite fetching in a red cloak and her chunky boots. The boys were a mass of fidgety arms and legs, absolutely beside themselves with anticipation. Lydia seemed a little preoccupied, and every time Alex turned around, she gaped at him as if he had three eyes. Little Sally, the darling with a mass of blond curls, still had the tears of disappointment on her chubby cheeks because, she tearfully informed him, Paul had not come.

"Good day, Mr. Christian," Miss Hill greeted him cheerfully, a luscious smile on her lips. She turned that smile to the children. "Mr. Christian has claimed he possesses great skill when it comes to sledding. He practically demanded he be allowed to show you."

He had said no such thing. His eyes narrowed playfully. "And Miss Hill insisted that she could outsled me, and demanded the opportunity to demonstrate."

She shot him a devilish look. "Why, Mr. Christian, that sounded positively like a challenge."

"Indeed it was, Miss Hill." He glanced meaningfully to the top of the hill. "Well, Leonard, shall we show them how it is done?" Theodore and Horace instantly clamored around Leonard, instructing him. Leonard nodded to all their advice, assured them he knew what he was doing, and taking the sled from Alex, proceeded eagerly up the hill.

As Alex waited for Leonard to position the sled just so, he watched Miss Hill laughing with the orphans, his heart filled with a peculiar admiration. Gathered around her skirts, their upturned faces filled with adoration, he knew how important it must be to receive the gift of her winsome smile. It never occurred to him to so much as look at a child on the rare occasions he was in their company. He would not be doing so now, except that was where he could find her. And oddly enough, these children delighted him. He swallowed past an uncharacteristic swell of emotion as Leonard dusted the snow from his mittens.

"I think I should ride in front," he whispered loudly, "but I will help you steer. Miss Hill said you might be a bit rusty." Alex arched a brow as Leonard eagerly clambered onto the front of the sled. He got on behind him, feeling very awkward with his long legs bent up as they were. "Miss Hill, if you would turn your attention to the slope," he called. Smiling, she dropped to her knees in the snow, one arm around Sally.

"Don't worry," Leonard said solemnly. Grinning, Alex pushed off. The sled began to careen down the hill; he expertly guided it around a large protruding rock, through two trees that served as an obstacle course, and then onto the flats at the bottom of the hill, where they coasted to a stop. Laughing wildly, Leonard immediately leapt up and raced for the top of the hill.

Theodore and Horace went next, flying fearlessly to the bottom. Lydia was equally fearless, riding with Leonard, and even little Sally took a turn, crying the length of the run with Theodore. Satisfied the children would not kill themselves, Alex walked to where Miss Hill stood. "So," he drawled, "have you determined it safe enough to have a go of it?"

"Lydia has convinced me it is quite breathtaking," she said, smiling coyly. "But I confess, I rather think it is safer to go with Theodore than you, sir."

Alex smiled mischievously and impulsively took her gloved hand in his. "If you are assured that I can at least drive the thing, I should very much like to take you down, Miss Hill.''

"Would you call me Lauren?'' Her question startled him; she asked it as if it were some tremendous personal favor.

"On one condition,'' he muttered. "You go down that hill with me.''

She laughed charmingly. "I am quite prepared, sir. You will not find a braver woman in all of England.''

He believed that was true. With his arms and legs wrapped firmly around her, they sped to the bottom of the hill, Lauren laughing gaily, fearing nothing. In the flats, Alex pulled the sled to a stop and clambered to his feet. Exhilarated, he yanked her to hers. She found that amusing, and laughing with one another as if they were old friends, the two trudged to the top of the hill, turning the sled over to the children once again.

They stood to one side as the children took turns sledding, chatting about Rosewood. She explained the demise of the family home, and how she and the vicar had schooled the children. With a proud gleam in her eye, she spoke of her vision for Rosewood, where orphans could come and learn the skills they needed to be happy, contributing adults. In her vision, Rosewood was not the run-down, overused and overtaxed farm it was presently. It flourished with life. He could not help but think of the call for reforms by people just like the Hills, with the same hopes and dreams, who were desperately trying to survive. "Paul says we must have fair representation in Parliament to fix things,'' she had said. Paul was right, and for the first time since assuming the title, Alex could see how very important that notion was.

Alex in turn told her about his quest for the buck, omitting the small detail that he had not looked for the ornery beast since the day he had found her fencing with Leonard.

And he asked her to call him Alex.

When a bank of gray clouds began to creep into the sunny day, Alex suggested to Lauren that it was time she took the children home. Theodore protested, grabbing Lauren's hand and imploring her to go with him for one last run. "Would you mind terribly much?" she asked Alex with a charming smile.

As if he could deny that smile a blasted thing. "I will wait with the children at the bottom of the hill," he told her, and with a wink for Theodore, herded the gaggle to the bottom.

She and Theodore were having quite a discussion at the top of the hill. When Theodore climbed in front, Alex clenched his jaw. Lauren intended to steer. Theodore looked a little pale as the sled started down the hill, but Lauren was grinning as they picked up speed. Alex sucked in his breath as she shakily steered the sled toward the two trees. He took a step forward as the sled skimmed the edge of the rock and headed straight for one tree, his pulse pounding in his neck when he realized how quickly they were sledding. Alex heard a sharp intake of breath, and was not sure if it was he or Leonard who shouted to mind the tree.

She managed to veer around the tree at the last possible second, but the sled came perilously close to the trunk and spun out of control. Thick fingers of fear closed sharply around Alex's heart as he helplessly watched the tumble of her red cloak fly across the snow. The shouts and screams of the children startled him from his shock; he and Leonard raced for the fallen riders.

She was lying face down, her cloak a stark, ruby red puddle in the snow. Alex scrambled up the hill, slipping and sliding in his haste to get to her. When he reached her, Theodore had come to his feet and stood above her, a look of sheer panic on his face. The lad nodded that he was unhurt to Leonard's frantic question. Alex fell to his knees and placed his hands gingerly on her back. Thank God, at least she was breathing. She made a sound, and he quickly rolled her to her back.

Lauren flung her arms wide, her blue eyes sparkling vividly as she burst into melodious laughter. Stunned, Alex sat back on his heels and stared at her. Her cheeks stained deep pink with the excitement, she *laughed*.

"I think my cloak caught the rudder!" she happily attempted to explain, and struggled to sit up. His heart pounded mercilessly in his chest, and Alex sat heavily in the snow. Still laughing, Lauren struggled to her feet, smiling cheerfully at the two young boys. "I am sorry if I frightened you, but I am really quite all right."

"Aye," Leonard mumbled, obviously still frightened. Theodore could only gape at her.

Alex stumbled awkwardly to his feet. "You gave me quite a start, madam."

Lauren chuckled and brushed the snow from her cloak before lifting her beaming face to his. "It is quite exhilarating, is it not?"

"Quite," he said evenly, and glanced at the children. "She is fine," he said gruffly, and with a firm grasp on her wrist, turned on his heel and marched down the hill, annoyed that his heart continued to slam against his ribs. As far as he was concerned, the little chit was banned from sledding for life. Lauren ran to keep up with him, and when they reached the children, she laughed at her exploit, until none of the faces around her showed any sign of fear.

It was not until Alex was at Dunwoody with a port under his belt that he could finally relax from the scare that fearless little chit had given him. It was not until he had three ports under his belt that he could stop analyzing why that was.

Chapter 6

Lauren paused from her chore of mending a protective wire cage the cattle had destroyed around a sapling and examined her progress. She frowned; she simply had to stop day-dreaming if she was *ever* going to complete this chore.

Honestly, she had not put in a full day's work since Alex Christian had tried to help her over that fence. For two full weeks, she had thought of little else than the country gentleman who had appeared from nowhere to capture her imagination and her heart. He had so fully occupied her thoughts that she could hardly concentrate long enough to see a task through, and kept forgetting things that had to be done. Even now, on her knees amidst a tangle of wire, she was imagining an intimate, candle-lit supper with Alex. Dressed in formal black attire resembling what she had seen Magnus wear on occasion, he was gazing at her with eyes of warm green. And of course, *she* looked fabulous, wearing a magnificent gown of blue satin, trimmed in seed pearls that matched the wreath of pearls on her head. Naturally, he complimented her profusely.

With a laugh, she shook her head and wrapped the wire around a fat stick protruding from the ground. The intimate supper was just one of her many little dreams. There was the daydream in which he worked beside her in the fields, sweat glistening on his muscular forearms as he proclaimed her the wisest of all women for having established her trade. And the one in which he played with the children on a luscious green and impeccably trimmed front lawn. There was the daydream in which she rode behind him on Jupiter, her arms clasped tightly around his rock hard middle as they galloped across lush meadows.

She sat back on her heels and smiled up at the sky. And there was her favorite, the one in which he took her in his arms, his green eyes piercing through to her very soul, a seductive smile on his lips. The one in which his head descended, excruciatingly slow, his lips parting slightly—

"Lauren?"

She gasped, turning sharply toward the sound of Alex's voice. Leaning against a tree, his hands shoved deep in his pockets, he had obviously walked up from the pumpkin field. Heat immediately flooded her cheeks—God, he had not actually *seen* her thinking about the kiss, had he? "You startled me." She laughed nervously, and brushed the back of her hand against her cheek in a vain attempt to erase the stain of embarrassment.

"Jupiter is just below in the pumpkin field, I hope you don't mind."

"Not at all!" Jupiter could graze in the drawing room for all she cared. Smiling, she pushed herself to her feet, shaking the dirt from her cloak. "I am glad you have come! The children have talked *so* much about you, my brother Paul insists on meeting this sledding pirate," she said. "He is beginning to think you are a figment of our imagination."

"Perhaps another time," he said simply.

His response struck her as oddly distant. Surely he was not surprised she would want to introduce him to her family.

She had little choice; Paul knew she had seen Mr. Christian on a handful of occasions now, and had demanded he be brought round to meet him. Lauren had hedged at first, telling him that Alex was a visiting gentleman whom she happened to encounter from time to time. But after the sledding, Paul had quizzed her suspiciously. What sort of man, he asked, invited the children sledding without meeting her family? She had made light of it. But then she had met Alex, quite accidentally, one afternoon in front of Mrs. Pennypeck's bakery, and they had strolled about Pemberheath. Paul had heard about it from Mr. Goldthwaite, who had turned so red when he had seen them together that she feared his heart would rupture. Paul had *demanded* to meet the mysterious country gentleman then.

"He will not bite, you know," she laughed nervously.

He smiled thinly, his expression far too serious as he pushed away from the tree. "There is something I must say to you."

Her heart skipped a beat at the absurd thought that flitted through her mind. Good God, she was hopeless! He had not given her *any* sign that he would be interested in anything more than the casual friendship they enjoyed. Nonetheless, she blushed profusely. "Judging by the look on your face, it must be a very serious topic, sir. Something very grave, indeed. Did you forget the name of the local poet I told you about?" His smile deepened a bit, but Lauren was struck by the peculiar, almost remorseful look in his eyes.

"No, I have not forgotten," he said quietly. He took another reluctant step toward her and glanced at the sapling.

She did not like the look on his face, not at all, and swept the wide-brimmed straw hat from her head to give her trembling hands something to hold. "The cattle, they rub against it, but the tree is so small they have almost killed it," she explained, and looked at the sad tree, her mind racing, her words filling the awkward silence. "I cannot seem to fasten the wire," she added softly.

"I am leaving on the morrow."

Leaving? Lauren caught her breath; she felt as if he had just punched her in the gut. He could not be leaving, he simply could not! A tidal wave of confused emotions swept over her, and she fought to maintain some modicum of decorum. "I . . . I don't know what to say. I thought . . . I suppose I thought . . ." she stammered uncertainly, her eyes riveted on the wire.

"I came only temporarily, to hunt, but I have stayed longer than I should have. I have responsibilities—"

"Responsibilities?" she blurted. Oh God, he was married, and for the last two weeks she had been dreaming about him like some silly, smitten schoolgirl, practically *drooling* each time she saw him. He must think her the biggest fool!

"I have a home and family," he was saying. Her mind quickly rifled through all the possible scenarios she could have imagined, but this had to be the worst. He was *married*. "My brother has corresponded recently that there are matters requiring my immediate attention."

Lauren wanted to die right where she stood. Her face flaming, she could not bring herself to look him in the eye, certain that her every thought, her every little fantasy, was plainly evident on her face. "Well, there you have it," she blustered unthinkingly. "I am sorry . . . I mean, the *children* will be very sorry, but if you have responsibilities, I would be the last person to think you should not attend to them right away. Responsibilities are very important—I try to instill in the children the importance of responsibilities all the time, and I certainly would not want them to think that Mr. Christian does not take his responsibilities seriously, and of course they *would* think so if you continued to stay at your hunting lodge without thought to—"

"Lauren," he said softly. Only then did she realize he had moved to stand only inches from her. She hoped to high heaven he could not see she was fighting for breath, that she

was silently dying in front of his very eyes. When his hand
lifted to her cheek, she gasped at the roiling wave of sweet
hysteria his touch shot through her. "I wish I did not have to
go, either. But I must."

"Oh," she said, and shrugged lightly, still unable to meet
his gaze. "It's quite all right, Mr. Christian, truly it is." He
took a step closer, his fingers trailing along the line of her
jaw. Her heart began to slam against her chest in terrifying
rhythm. "The, ah, the children . . . they will miss you,
but—"

"Will you?"

She bit her tongue to keep a shout of mad laughter from
bubbling forth. Was he mad? Could he not *see* just how
badly she would miss him? She slowly lifted her gaze to his,
having no earthly idea what one said on such a monumental
occasion as this. His hand slid to the nape of her neck, his
green eyes piercing hers, just like her daydream. "Will
you?" he repeated softly.

Everything in her screamed to be aloof, to not let him
know just how much she would miss him. "Maybe," she
choked out.

A faint smile appeared on his lips, and he bent his head,
his lips descending to hers. Holy Mother of God, he was
going to *kiss* her! After days of fearing it, her knees finally
buckled, and she stumbled backward against the wire cage.
He smiled lazily at her complete discomfiture, and slowly,
deliberately, leaned down until his lips touched hers.

The sensation of it rocked her.

Her body strained for air. His hand caressed the nape of
her neck while the other slipped around her waist and pulled
her into him. Her breasts pressed against his chest, and she
wondered, insanely, if he could feel her heart slamming fit-
fully against him, threatening to break violently free. His
lips moved lightly across hers, softly shaping them, tasting
them as if they were some delicacy. His tongue flicked
across the seam of her lips, and she heard herself moan

softly. The pressure of his lips quickly intensified; she must have sighed, because his tongue was suddenly in her mouth, sweeping her teeth, her tongue, and the valleys of her cheeks. His hand cupped her face, his thumb gently stroking her cheek.

An exquisite pressure began to build in her chest, filling the space her pounding heart did not. She feared she would very well explode from the feel of his sweet breath mingled with hers and almost hoped she would. He pressed tightly against her, seeking to meld his body to hers, and she realized her body answered, curving into him, melting against him. It was the single most incredible experience she had ever had, and she felt herself slipping away on a wave of unprecedented sensual desire.

Then suddenly, it was over.

He lifted his head. His eyes swept her face as he ran the pad of his thumb over her bottom lip. With a lingering, tender kiss to her forehead, he stepped away. Stunned, Lauren could only gape at him. "It has been my very great pleasure knowing you, Lauren Hill," he said quietly, and reached up to carefully brush a curl from her temple. She thought he would speak again, but he abruptly turned, walking toward the fence with his head down and his hands shoved deep in his pockets.

She stood rigid, her chest heaving with each frantic breath, watching his long, determined stride until he disappeared into the pumpkin field. Only then did she notice she had destroyed her hat.

In the formal dining room of Sutherland Hall, Alex pretended to listen to his mother's recital of news contained in Aunt Paddy's latest missive from London. He stared at the massive silver candelabra in the center of the dining table, privately contemplating the last two weeks. Home now for two days, he could not stop thinking of Lauren Hill.

He had no idea what had possessed him to kiss her like

that. Perhaps it was the look of genuine despair in her blue eyes when he had announced his departure, something he had done with no finesse at all. Perhaps it was just plain desire—he understood, of course, that he desired her. Who would not? She was beautiful, artless . . . And nothing more than a pleasing dalliance for the space of a fortnight. He had had no right to kiss her so familiarly.

Familiar, hell. He had been completely unprepared for the impact of that kiss. That unusual, enchanting young woman had responded so achingly that she had almost knocked him from his boots.

"Alex?" Marlaine said softly. Hesitantly, he shifted his gaze to her. "I received a letter from my cousin, Daphne Broadmoore. She is coming home to Brighton next week, to Aunt Melinda's. Before I end my visit there, I thought to bring her round."

"Of course," he mumbled.

Marlaine blinked her wide brown eyes. "I hope you don't mind terribly. But now that we are engaged, it's really the thing to do," she explained.

The thing to do. Alex wondered, absurdly, if Marlaine would ever think wearing trousers and fencing a small boy was the thing to do. "I do not mind at all," he said, and motioned for the footman. "Thompson, bring round the whiskey, will you?" He smiled at Marlaine and gently squeezed her dainty hand.

God, he needed a drink.

It was the thing to do.

Chapter 7

Rosewood, four months later

Paul moved slowly down the narrow hall to the drawing room, dreading the meeting with Ethan. A summons from his uncle was never good news, and he was sure this had to do with Lauren. It had to be; their funds were almost depleted, and the profits from this year's corn crop had been worse than expected. If he knew Ethan—and he did—there could be only one reason for this sudden little family meeting.

He entered the drawing room where Ethan was seated, as usual, in front of the fire. Lauren was quietly picking up the mess around him. "At last, he joins us," Ethan grumbled.

"What is it, Uncle?" Paul sighed, limping to the hearth.

"I have news," Ethan mumbled irritably, and poured a brandy. "There is a trust, reverting to Paul on his twenty-first birthday," he abruptly announced.

Trust? There was no trust! Paul's sense of foreboding began to heighten. "I beg your pardon?" he said slowly. "*What* trust?"

"Now don't get overwrought. It is not a *big* trust, just a

little something your grandfather put aside, the stingy old—''

"Why have I not been made aware of this before now?" Paul demanded, the foreboding turning swiftly to anger.

"Well, as you could not *have* it before you reach your twenty-first year, I did not see the point."

Paul was about to tell him *exactly* the point, but Lauren startled him with a gleeful laugh. "This is *wonderful* news! Oh, Paul, you shall have money to invest, just as you have wanted!" Beaming, she whirled toward Ethan. "How much, Uncle?"

"Five thousand pounds," he muttered.

Lauren clasped her hands to her chest. "Five *thousand* pounds?"

"But I borrowed it," Ethan said bluntly.

Stunned silence filled the room as Ethan casually sipped his brandy. At length, Paul found his voice. "You *borrowed* it?"

"For Chrissakes! I had to have *something* to set her up in London, didn't I?" Ethan blustered. "You think a Season is bought with a bloody song?"

It took Paul a moment to realize what Ethan was saying. He glanced at Lauren; she looked completely stricken. "*Ethan!*" he roared, the cry reverberating throughout the house. "What have you *done*?"

"What any man would do in my situation," Ethan said simply, and turned away. Anger exploded in Paul's chest; he lunged across the small room for Ethan, his hands grasping for his fleshy throat. Lauren flew between them, unbalancing him and causing him to stumble backward.

"Am I to expect everyone in this godforsaken house is mad?" Ethan bellowed, and straightening his lapel, lifted the snifter, intending to sip. But Paul lunged again, slapping it from his hand and knocking the glass and it's precious contents to the worn carpet.

"By God, you will find yourself *dead* if you touch me

again!'' Ethan roared, and attempted to push himself from his chair.

"Stop it, *stop it!*" Lauren cried, and pushed Ethan into his chair. "Paul! Whatever he has done does not warrant violence! And *Ethan!*" she snapped, leveling a heated gaze on their corpulent uncle. "You had best have a good explanation for stealing Paul's inheritance!"

"I did not *steal* it! I am your legal guardian! I had every right and every reason!" Ethan shouted, and looked helplessly to the carpet where his snifter lay on its side. "Is it not obvious to the two of you that we are in need of funds? This little spot of hell can't produce a bloody stalk of *wheat*,'' he grumbled, and gestured meaningfully toward the window and the Rosewood estate beyond.

"You have *stolen* from me!" Paul responded contemptuously, his rage barely contained.

"*I* am executor of this estate, not *you!*" Ethan shouted defensively. "I will determine what is to be done! You cannot know the pressures I feel, having a bunch of outcasts—''

"*Ethan!*" Lauren gasped. He groaned irritably and heaved himself over the arm of the chair to retrieve his snifter.

"What have you done with the funds?" Paul breathed, working very hard to keep his voice even.

"I told you," Ethan shrugged, and reached for his decanter of brandy. Lauren snatched the glass container and moved quickly out of his reach, holding it tightly to her chest. Ethan motioned furiously for her to return the decanter. "I will not tolerate your impudence, Lauren."

"What have you done with it?" Paul bellowed.

Ethan slid a heated glare to Paul. "I engaged a modiste for your foolish sister, I sent a sum to retain a London house from my good friend Dowling for the Season, and that, as they say, is that!"

"A *modiste*?" Lauren gasped.

"You heard me," Ethan mumbled, and motioned for the

brandy, but Lauren held the decanter hostage. "Oh, *fine*! You probably thought I would marry you to that idiot Goldthwaite! That little pumpkin would not bring as much as a bloody shilling to this place!"

"What are you saying? Have you *betrothed* her?" Paul asked.

"No, I have not *betrothed* her," Ethan scoffed. "Not yet! But *I* am giving her a London Season and *I* will make a good match for her! What, did you think we could go on this way forever? With the likes of *Goldthwaite* sniffing at her skirts, for Chrissakes? I had to take matters into my own hands! I am sending her to London, and *this* time, she will not give it all away!" he bellowed.

Paul stumbled toward a chair, sank into it, and stared helplessly at Ethan. He had expected this, but not with *his* money—money he did not know he even had! Of course he knew Lauren must marry. As hard is it was to maintain Rosewood, there was little choice. But *he* had wanted to be the one to make a good match for her. Lauren wanted to marry for love—she had told him that more than once. And he wanted to be the one to settle on her behalf with a man she could love. Ethan, he would give her to the highest bidder.

"Oh, Uncle, you cannot mean what you say! You cannot send me away! What about the children?" Lauren cried.

Ethan turned his fleshy face to his niece. "What about them? Mrs. Peterman will tend them as she always has," he said roughly. "Oh come now, what use are you here, lass? The longer you work in those fields, the sooner your looks will fade, and then what use will you be? Even that mindless little apothecary won't want you then!" he blustered, and shifted a wary glance at Paul. "For Chrissakes, stop looking at me like that! Bloody hell, it's not like you will *lose* your precious trust. I merely borrowed against it!"

"Oh, that's rich, Uncle," Paul scoffed. "Exactly how do you think to repay it?"

"With a betrothal agreement, what else? In exchange for her hand, I will extract an annuity and the paltry sum of your trust!"

"Without a dowry? You have no dowry!" Paul angrily reminded him.

Ethan shrugged indifferently. "Don't need a dowry with a face like hers, you know. A man would just as soon have a beauty in his bed as another estate to tend. And there is always Rosewood. Not much of a place, but good enough for some, I'd wager, and I reckon you won't deny your sister a share in it if it comes to that."

Lauren gasped softly; silence filled the room as brother and sister gaped at Ethan. At last, Lauren spoke. "Have you no *conscience*? Was your barter with the count not enough? Am I to have no say at all?"

Ethan rolled his eyes. "Bloody hell, you make it sound as if I am the first man to give a lass away for an annuity. It is the way of things, girl."

Lauren shoved away from the wall with that remark, her blue eyes sparkling with fury. She slowly shook her head. "I will not go to London. I will *not*! When and *if* I marry again, it will be to a man of *my* choosing, not *yours*!"

Ethan snorted his opinion of that and drained the trickle of brandy left in his glass.

She was going. Staring blindly at London through the dingy window of a hired hack, Lauren pressed her lips firmly together. She had steadfastly refused Ethan's ridiculous plan at first, had even laughed at him in her indignation. That had enraged him; he had threatened to marry her to Thadeus Goldthwaite if she did not comply. Granted, *that* prospect had her walking on pins and needles for a few days, but she knew he had little to gain from a marriage to Fastidious Thadeus, and had brazenly ignored him.

So he had done the one thing that could force her into anything.

She was on the front lawn one afternoon when the vicar came for Lydia. He explained, much to Lauren's horror, that as Lydia had resided at Rosewood for the last three years without benefit of stipend, Ethan had written they could no longer afford her keep. The vicar had dutifully found a convent willing to take the young girl.

Lauren glanced at her uncle filling the narrow seat across from her and winced as she recalled the terrible row that had caused. As unfeeling as a rock, he had casually informed her that they could not afford to keep the children at Rosewood, and further, the only way they could *possibly* afford it was for her to marry well. Bless him, but Dr. Stephens, having heard about the ruckus from Abbey, had quietly paid Ethan three months of Lydia's keep. And Lauren had realized on that horrid afternoon that she would go to London.

Paul, having confirmed the existence of his trust with the family solicitor, was the one who finally convinced her she had to go. She *should* be married, he said; she was, after all, fast approaching the grand age of five and twenty. He had wrested a promise from Ethan that she at least would have a say in any offer for her hand, a great concession on Ethan's part. He reminded her that there was no other hope for Rosewood, and despite her optimism about her trade, there was still the problem of barren land and high taxes. And furthermore, he had argued, it was not outside the realm of possibility that she might actually fall in love with a man in London.

Paul was right. At least this way, she would have some control over her fate. Not like before, when Ethan had found the oldest and most senile match alive for her. It was, she very well knew, the only way she could save Lydia and the children at the moment. Deep down, she knew it was really the only way she could save Rosewood.

So she had reluctantly agreed. Yet she privately doubted a decent man was to be found among London's aristocracy. Lauren knew how the *ton* lived. Marriages were made for

gain, adulterous affairs abounded, and she could not imagine
that a single one of them could look at her charges without
lifting their noses.

More important, she was quite certain not one of them
could compare with Mr. Christian, the man she had not been
able to purge from her heart.

When she had finally conceded, Paul insisted on accom-
panying her and Ethan to London. Lauren had pleaded with
him to stay at Rosewood for the sake of the children, but he
would have none of it. He had railed about his duty to her
and Rosewood. He was a *man* now, he insisted, and would
not allow her to go to London without proper escort. Furthermore, he harbored some fantastic notion that he would
carn back all that Ethan had borrowed and more by investing
the money he was sure he would win at the gaming hells. He
had taught himself to gamble, he explained, and according
to Dr. Stephens, he was quite good.

So the three of them had trooped off to London after
tearful good-byes to Mrs. Peterman and the children, and
repeated assurances from Dr. Stephens that he would look
after things.

And so here she was, she thought sadly, trying to appear
as if the whole sordid event were tolerable. They rode in
silence—with the exception of an occasional grumble from
Ethan—to the Russell Square town house he had rented
from his old traveling companion, Lord Dowling.

When the hack finally stopped in front of the small
house, the front door flung open, and a middle-aged man
with a shock of white hair appeared on the front steps as
they climbed out of the conveyance. "Lord Hill," he said,
as if announcing their arrival to the street.

"Bring round a brandy, man," Ethan groused as he waddled up the steps to the door, and unceremoniously pushed
past the butler as Lauren and Paul trailed behind. In a blatant
disregard for protocol, the butler looked at Paul, and then
Lauren, and shrugging, moved to pass them. He muttered

the name of Davis in doing so, and Lauren supposed that he
meant to convey his identity.

"I am Paul Hill, and this is my sister, Countess Bergen,"
Paul responded. At that gentle reminder, Lauren flushed terribly, hoping that the butler—at least she *thought* he was the
butler—would not see how that irritated her. Paul knew how
angry she was at Ethan for making sure the entire population of London knew she was a countess. They both knew
very well how she felt—it was hardly her title to bear, seeing
as how she had been little more than a glorified nursemaid
to Helmut. Nonetheless, Ethan had written long letters to his
friends bragging about the "the countess." The title, he had
boasted to her, would bring him a few pounds more.

The butler shrugged again and disappeared inside. Exchanging dubious looks, Paul and Lauren hesitantly followed.

The interior of the town house was a shock to Lauren's
senses. The small entry was papered in red and light blue,
and in the corner stood a full suit of armor, taking up so
much space that one had to step around it. Walking into the
front parlor, Lauren stifled a gasp. Lined with dark paneling,
it boasted various armaments of war from every century in
every conceivable space. She would have thought it a man's
study had it not been for the pianoforte at one end and a
scattering of plush, floral print chairs and a couch about the
room. Various works of arguable-quality art lined the walls,
interspersed occasionally with a delicate china sculpture. It
was the oddest mix of styles and furnishings she had ever
seen, and she could not help thinking it was all very hideous. And very fitting.

Davis reappeared as she removed her bonnet, carrying a
tray with one brandy and a stack of letters. He attempted to
hand the letters to Ethan, but he waved them away as he
helped himself to the snifter. Davis abruptly thrust the letters
at Paul. "Correspondence," he muttered. Paul took the

small stack; Davis shuffled across the room and disappeared through the door.

"My God, these are invitations for Countess Bergen," Paul exclaimed.

Lauren jerked around, her eyes landing on the small stack he held in his hand. "Invitations?"

"Marvelous, marvelous!" Ethan gleefully exclaimed, and slurped his brandy. "Read them, go on!"

Paul opened the first one and frowned. "This is from Lady Pontleroy of Mayfair, inviting Countess Bergen and escort to a supper party, Wednesday next. And this one is from Lord and Lady Harris . . ."

"But . . . but how do they know me?" Lauren exclaimed.

"Ah, my good friend Dowling has done it! The coot owed me a personal favor, but I did not think he would have sufficient time before he was off to the Americas. Lord and Lady Harris? Now there's a feather in your cap. Aye, appearances are everything to this set! They would much prefer to have a title at their table than their own flesh and blood." He laughed and tossed the rest of the brandy down his throat. "You will do well to remember that, lass"

Lauren hardly knew what to say to that. Ethan was worried about appearances? Good God, so was she. From all of London's appearances thus far, this was going to be the longest few weeks of her life.

Chapter 8

Alex sighed impatiently and glanced at his pocket watch. He had been escorting his great aunt, Lady Paddington, for a turn about the blasted park for a good half hour now, yet she showed no signs of tiring. Aunt Paddy, as the family affectionately called her, clasped her plump hands tightly in front of her and contentedly surveyed a group of young women strolling together. "Mrs. Clark said that Arthur most decidedly has his eye on the pretty Miss O'Meara, did you know? Unfortunately, she comes from a rather large family," she said with a nod toward the young lady in question.

Alex could not, for the life of him, imagine what the size of her family had to do with anything. "Really?" he remarked with bored indifference. "I rather thought Arthur was interested in Miss Delia Harris."

"Oh! Arthur is uncommonly stubborn! He pays particular attention to a different girl at every event!" she groused. "There is Miss Charlotte Pritchit. Nice girl—it's her *mother*," Paddy whispered, and looped her arm possessively through Alex's. "Good day, Lady Pritchit, Miss Pritchit!"

she called cheerfully. Alex slid his gaze to Lady Pritchit, who, in her near gallop to reach them, was dragging her meek daughter behind her.

"Lady Paddington, how do you do?" the mother asked breathlessly, her eyes slanting conspicuously toward Alex. He graciously inclined his head, noting that the plain young woman kept her eyes on her shoes as she curtsied. "And good day to you, your grace. I had not heard you were in town," Lady Pritchit said as she coyly smoothed her elaborate lace collar.

"Really? So *The Times* has not yet posted my every move?" he asked with not a little sarcasm.

Lady Pritchit's lips curled away from her teeth in a laugh that sounded something like a horse. "Indeed, it has not! Will you be in town for the Season, then?" she asked bluntly.

"I have not as yet firmed my plans, Lady Pritchit."

"But surely you will attend the Harris ball? It is to be the event of the Season! My Charlotte was just introduced at court, and is quite looking forward to the affair," she said eagerly, and none too subtly elbowed her daughter in the ribs. Miss Pritchit grimaced slightly, but did not look up.

"His grace has *many* engagements, Lady Pritchit," Paddy answered haughtily before Alex could open his mouth. "I am *quite* sure he has not determined which he will attend as yet!"

Lady Pritchit's lips formed a silent *O*. An awkward moment passed before she realized she had nothing else to say. "Well. Perhaps we shall have the pleasure of seeing you at the Harris ball, your grace. Good day, Lady Paddington." She reluctantly curtsied and grabbed her daughter's arm, who had yet to look up from study of the tips of her slippers, and beat a hasty retreat.

Aunt Paddy snorted with disdain at the woman's retreating back. "I cannot believe the cheek of that woman!" she bristled indignantly. "That young girl may have debuted at court, but she has nothing to recommend her. Mrs. Clark believes Lady Pritchit has some distant connections, but none so great that she should set her sights on anything higher than a baron, for heaven's sake!''

Alex nudged his aunt forward before she became apoplectic, and they continued walking, Paddy chattering in a string of inanities that Alex barely heard until she suddenly gasped and pointed to a black landau. "Oh my, it's *her*!''

Alex glanced across the park but noticed nothing other than a woman's foot disappearing inside the carriage. Lord van der Mill, an old coot with more money than he knew what to do with, was escorting her. "Who is 'her'?'' he asked with polite insouciance.

"The *countess*, Alex! Ah, such a lovely woman, and so tragic! It must be terribly difficult to be widowed at such a tender age,'' she sighed sadly.

Alex looked again at the landau as it pulled away from the curb. "Which countess would that be? I do not recall hearing of any death among the peerage.''

"Not in *England*. In *Bavaria*!'' Paddy exclaimed as if he were dense. "Count Bergdorf, Bergstrom, something like that. Oooo, it's the most romantic story, really. She met the count on the continent, and he was positively swept away by her charitable disposition and agreeable looks, and mind you, *she* fell quite in love with him—he was terribly dashing, and *very* wealthy, according to Mrs. Clark, who heard it all from Lord Dowling. So strong was their attachment that they married quickly and repaired to his native Bavaria. Ah, but he was tragically taken from her in a fatal hunting accident,'' Aunt Paddy recounted. As the landau disappeared into the crowded street, she sighed with all the longing of a schoolgirl.

Above her gray head, Alex rolled his eyes and made a mental note to tell Arthur to stop bringing Aunt Paddy those ridiculous novels.

* * *

As Lord van der Mill's landau rocked away from Hyde Park toward Russell Square, Lauren sat with her arms folded across her middle, her eyes on her lap. She wore one of her mother's old gowns she had altered to resemble the latest fashions. It was no prize, but it was not so bad as to warrant Lady Pritchit's indelicate comments. She had hoped upon seeing the saber-tongued woman that Lord van der Mill would proceed past. But no, he had stopped to chat. At the end of the conversation, Lady Pritchit had eyed Lauren's gown from the high neckline to the flounced hem, and had remarked, much to her daughter's obvious horror, that Lauren's gown resembled one she had seen at a wake many years ago. On the *deceased.*

Lauren smiled absently at Lord van der Mill as he expounded on the reforms the Commons was debating. She was discovering, much to her dismay, that the further she penetrated the *ton,* the more her feminine vanity was making itself known to her. Ethan's promise of a modiste had not materialized, naturally, and she was beginning to feel very conspicuous as she moved among Britain's most finely dressed. Paul tried to help; he had taken to the gaming tables almost the moment they had arrived in London, eager to test the skills he had practiced for years at Rosewood. Although he had been moderately successful, and had managed to pay for a new gown here and there, they were not nearly enough to suit the *ton*'s standards. Angered by her vanity, Lauren glanced out the window and frowned. She had never cared a whit about dresses and frills and hats and gloves before now.

God, her unprecedented self-consciousness was almost enough to send her to a convent. But Ethan's constant parade of old, blue-veined men was humiliating. She had taken to disappearing when Davis would knock on her door and announce, "Caller!" Her penchant for doing that, however, had been the subject of many heated arguments with Ethan.

She sighed wearily, oblivious to Lord van der Mill's increasingly agitated discourse. The only bright spot so far was Miss Charlotte Pritchit, whom she had met at one of those awful affairs, and the two had become instant friends. Charlotte's singular misfortune was having the world's most disagreeable mother. If a man so much as looked in Lauren's general direction, Lady Pritchit took it as a personal affront to Charlotte.

Lauren had not understood how deeply the woman disliked her until she heard her remark loudly at a supper party that the senior lords of the *ton* would not appreciate their sons courting a *foreign* woman with unknown connections in Britain. It took Lauren several minutes to realize she was referring to *her*. A few of the women gathered around Lady Pritchit that evening had nodded knowingly, although Lauren was unclear as to why. The men she had met were not heirs to the throne! Lady Pritchit obviously considered Charlotte a strong contender for *any* hand.

When Lauren had received an invitation to Mrs. Clark's home, Lady Pritchit had become, apparently, enraged. It seemed that Mrs. Clark's constant companion, Lady Paddington, was the great aunt of a duke or some such muckety-muck. Charlotte had apologetically informed her that Lady Pritchit was concerned she might meet this duke first, and therefore lure all the eligible hangers-on to her cause. Lauren had taken that to mean the old battle-ax had thrown another one of her infamous fits. Lauren had insisted to Charlotte that she was not the least bit interested in some stuffy old duke *or* his friends. Charlotte believed her, for all the good that did her.

She glanced at Lord van der Mill, who had become quite red in the face. Really, she thought as she observed the least odious of Ethan's suitors, she had met many eligible young men, but none suited her. They were too finicky, too snobbish, too effeminate, too old, or too young. None of them seemed as strong or as kind or as *masculine* as Mr. Christian. Against her will, she ended up comparing all men to him, then berating herself for making the entire situation so bloody impossible. Impossible because she found herself looking for Mr. Christian in every ballroom and salon—not a suitable match, as she was supposed to do.

Dear Lord, she tried; she really *did* try to look for the admirable qualities in the men she had met. But if she had to be married, she wanted to marry a man as virile as Mr. Christian. And as handsome. And *definitely* someone who would kiss her as he did. A little shiver ran up her spine at the memory and she smiled.

She was still smiling as the landau rolled to a halt in front of the Russell Square town house. Lauren automatically extended her hand to Lord van der Mill. "Thank you, my lord, for a very pleasant afternoon," she said sweetly.

Shaken from his diatribe, Lord van der Mill glanced uneasily out the window. "Well, so we've come to Russell Square, have we?"

"Indeed we have, my lord."

A coachman opened the door at the exact moment van der Mill grasped her hand. "Countess Bergen, if I may. Your uncle has been good enough to allow me to call three times now, and I think it obvious there is a certain, how shall I say, a certain and *mutual* esteem between us. It is as opportune a time as any to come to some understanding, don't you think?"

Oh *God,* an understanding? The only understanding she could *possibly* have with Lord van der Mill was that there would *never* be an understanding between them. He looked at her expectantly, his tongue flicking nervously across his antique lips. She blinked. "Have you the time, my lord?"

Startled, he asked, "The *time*?"

"Yes, please, the time?"

His pale face pinched. He reluctantly dropped her hand and withdrew a timepiece, at which he impatiently glanced. "It is four o'clock, madam."

"I should really be more attentive! I promised my brother

to help him with a—this afternoon! Thank you again, my lord,'' she said, and grabbing her reticule, launched herself with all haste from the landau. ''Good day!'' she called, waved cheerfully, and walked as quickly as she could. Davis appeared at the door as she sprinted up the walk, and Lauren gratefully bounded up the steps and rushed through the opening before Lord van der Mill could call her back.

In the tiny foyer, she sagged against the wall as Davis peered at the landau, praying that Lord van der Mill would not mention this little episode to Ethan. She was imagining all the possible outbursts that would bring when she became aware of someone staring at her. Slowly, she turned her head; a man stepped in front of her, and Lauren shrieked.

''Magnus!''

He merely nodded, his hands clasped behind his back as he carefully regarded her.

''Count Bergen! What are you doing here?''

Magnus dropped his hand from his back and presented her with a large bouquet of roses. ''For you,'' he said simply.

Stunned, Lauren took the flowers without even glancing at them. ''But what are you doing here?''

''I have come to London on business.''

''Wh-*what* business?''

Magnus frowned at Davis, standing at the door. ''Is there someplace we might talk?'' he asked, and with his head, motioned toward the parlor. Still gaping, Lauren watched him walk to the parlor door and pause, peeking rather timidly inside before disappearing inside. She glanced at the roses in her hand and slowly shook her head. The whole world had gone mad, utterly mad. She deposited the roses in a giant Grecian urn Davis occasionally used as a doorstop and followed Magnus into the parlor.

''Count Bergen,'' she said as she crossed the threshold and folded her arms across her middle, ''I demand to know what you are doing in London. Not just in London, but *here,* at Russell Square.''

With his finger and thumb, Magnus picked up a bear claw that had been preserved for time immemorial, the bridge of his nose wrinkling with disgust. ''I am obviously here to see you,'' he said as he gingerly replaced the trophy. ''The *Kartoffelmann* thinks of you. He has made a . . . shrine.''

In spite of her shock, Lauren burst out laughing. ''The Potato Man built a *shrine*?'' Magnus glanced up from his study of a candlestick made of an old sword hilt and nodded solemnly before moving on to a rather strange painting of two fairies and a dog. ''But . . . but how did you know I was here?''

''I had the direction to Rosewood. Frau Peterman directed me here. Helga sends her regards,'' he said, and produced a small, folded parchment. Lauren crossed the room to take the letter.

''Frederic has moped about since you left. He is not inclined to perform his duties,'' he continued.

Lauren smiled at the memory of Magnus's nervous valet. ''Frederic is too finicky for you. You should send him to Paris, where he can do some meticulous fop justice.''

Magnus suddenly turned, his light blue eyes riveting on her face. ''He would happily perform his duties if you were at Bergenschloss. The *Kartoffelmann* would perhaps allow one of his precious potatoes to be eaten. And Helga would stop moping about.''

Lauren covered her mouth with a gloved hand, stifling a burst of surprised laughter. Magnus arched a pale brow. Good God, he was serious! Yes, the whole world had gone *quite* mad. ''I cannot come to Bergenschloss! I have responsibilities here!''

''Marry me and you will not want for responsibilities.''

''*Marry* . . . ? Have you forgotten that you once wished to hang me from the castle walls?'' she asked, trying desperately to contain her mirth at the absurdity of his offer.

"I have not forgotten."

"Pardon, but I should think even *you* might see the irony in that!" She laughed.

Magnus frowned and contemplated the tips of his fingers for a moment. He looked at her again. "I have thought about you often. You could be very happy at Bergenschloss."

She could barely contain the hysterical laughter bubbling in her throat. "Magnus! I *cannot* marry you!" she squeaked. He lifted one impatient brow high above the other, and her hysteria began to give way to shock.

"What is it that you think you cannot have in Bavaria? Orphans? You may tend them there if you like," he offered.

"Orphans?" she cried, and fought to check her rising panic. "I appreciate your offer, indeed I do. But my place is in England. I have Rosewood to think of—"

"I will provide for Rosewood."

"But the children! They need—"

"Bring them."

Stunned, Lauren gaped at him. At length, she slowly shook her head. *"No,* Magnus. I cannot marry you."

With a face of stone, he asked, "How shall I convince you?"

"How much will you offer?" Ethan asked from the door.

Startled by the intrusion, Lauren whirled around to face her uncle. "Ethan, I said *no!*"

Ethan ignored her, his gaze locked on Magnus. "How much?" he asked again.

"Who are you?" Magnus inquired.

"Lord Ethan Hill, sir, her uncle. What is your offer?"

Magnus's eyes flicked the length of Ethan's massive body before casually inquiring, "How much do you want?"

Lauren jerked around to the German, her hysteria now giving way to anger. "I said no! *No!*"

As if she had not even spoken, Magnus flicked a stoic, blue-eyed gaze from her to Ethan. "What are your terms?"

With a shriek of exasperation, Lauren flung her hands in

the air and marched for the door. "You may talk all day if you like, the both of you! Go ahead, but I will *not* marry you!" Ethan and Magnus both regarded her impassively, as if she had just announced she preferred fish for supper.

"Ethan, you and I had an agreement!" she cried. He shrugged. She whirled toward Magnus. "I told you in Bavaria I could not live there!" When Magnus did not respond, she pivoted and marched angrily from the room, blinded by the fear that Ethan would actually strike some bargain with him.

The two men watched her march away before turning to look at one another. Ethan picked up a decanter of brandy and two glasses. "Shall we talk?" He grinned, and motioned his guest into an overstuffed red velvet chair.

Chapter 9

Two days later, at an afternoon reception held in honor of a war hero-turned-brilliant-parliamentarian, Lauren sighed and leaned against a colonnade. Lord and Lady Granbury's ballroom was positively filled to capacity, but she found the reception desperately boring. She would not have come at all had Ethan not demanded she allow Magnus to escort her to the event. Knowing the whole *ton* would be in attendance, he had determined that if his ridiculous attempts to settle a betrothal agreement with Magnus did not come to fruition, he would not waste the opportunity to parade her about.

Paul had come along, too, he said, "to keep an eye on things." Lauren suspected the real reason was the chance to meet Sir Robert Peel, the Home Secretary. Her brother was quite glowing in his admiration of Peel and his progressive reforms; in fact, he had disappeared into the crowd the moment they arrived, using his cane to forge a path.

She glanced at Magnus standing beside her; he winked subtly. She attempted a weak smile, but she did not feel like smiling. She did not feel like doing anything except crawling into her hideous bed with the purple and green velvet curtains and pulling the pink counterpane over her head. This was miserable; she would have cheerfully granted Rosewood to the first person to rescue her from the watchful eyes of her latest suitor.

Her *suitor.* For two whole days since appearing at Russell Square, he had suffocated her with his presence. He paid no heed to her declaration that she did not *feel* for him as she ought if she were to honestly consider marrying him. He seemed to think that the requisite feelings would come of their own accord. Lauren was not even remotely convinced of that and craved a respite from his suit, if only for a few moments. Now seemed as good a time as any, and with a devilishly charming grin, she turned and faced him. "Magnus?" she asked sweetly, "Will you excuse me? I am in need of the retiring room."

Magnus did not even blink. "Of course," he said. "I shall wait here for you." Surprised by the relative ease of that, Lauren hurried in the general direction of the retiring rooms. In her haste to escape, she collided with Lady Paddington.

"Good heavens! Countess Bergen! What a delight! Look here, Mrs. Clark! Look who I have had the good fortune to bump into!"

"Countess Bergen!" Mrs. Clark exclaimed in the exact same chirp as Lady Paddington. "Lady Pritchit said you had gone back to Bavaria!"

"No, dear, she said she *hoped* Countess Bergen had gone back to Bavaria," Lady Paddington corrected her.

"Really?" Mrs. Clark asked, surprised. "I am quite sure she said the countess had left! And I thought that it simply could not be, as I had the good fortune to encounter your uncle, Lord Hill—we were childhood friends, you knew that, did you not, my dear? And I was quite certain that he would have mentioned something as noteworthy as your departure—"

"Countess Bergen, we simply *must* contrive a gathering," Lady Paddington interrupted. "There is so much more of Bavaria I should like to know about. I know your last outing was a bit harried, what with Lady Thistlecourt and all, but we are not usually so—"

"Incorrigible!" Mrs. Clark loudly interjected.

"Incorrigible," Lady Paddington echoed as if she had thought of it.

Mrs. Clark bent her head toward Lauren and whispered loudly, "Hortense Thistlecourt could learn a thing or two of grace from *you,* Countess Bergen. You lost what, eight or nine rounds at the loo table? Goodness, I know it was several, because I remember thinking I had never seen *anyone* lose so many hands in one outing! Was it your first experience with cards, dear? Oh, it doesn't matter. The point is that you were terribly sporting about the whole thing!"

"I have so wanted to invite you for supper, Countess. I don't mind telling you that I am simply mad to hear all about your tragic love," Lady Paddington blithely interjected. "My nephew is all agog about the prospect of meeting you but declares he hasn't had the fortune! I cannot imagine why, I said to him—Mrs. Clark says that you have attended some of the most fashionable of routs, and lord knows *he* is always in attendance. Would you?"

"Would I?" Lauren asked, completely befuddled by the two women.

"Would you be disposed to a small gathering?"

"I am most obliged, Lady Paddington, and would look forward to the privilege of knowing your nephew."

"Wonderful! I am hosting a little gathering Thursday next, at precisely eight o'clock. Now dear, you understand I do not mean the duke. I am, of course, referring to my nephew Lord David Westfall. I am afraid the duke is bit of a recluse when it comes to such gatherings. Swears he does not care for them."

"Oh my no, the duke does not care for them!" Mrs. Clark unnecessarily confirmed.

"Yes, but does that suit?" Lady Paddington breathlessly finished.

"I beg your pardon?" Lauren asked carefully.

"The day, dear, does it suit?"

At that point, she would have agreed to anything. And in truth, a supper party with the delightfully batty widows would prove a nice diversion from the constant attention of Magnus. "It suits perfectly, madam. If you ladies will excuse me, I am in dire need of the retiring room," she said, and attempted to take her leave. But Lady Paddington had not quite finished her thoughts on the subject of the now infamous incident at the loo table.

Alex halted dead in his tracks at the first glimpse of the crowded reception room. He had come for Marlaine and her mother, but the last thing he wanted was to suffer through an inquisition, alone, unguarded, in a ballroom full of matrons and their debutante daughters while their bored husbands stood idly by. The place was positively jammed to the rafters with those he called the prowlers—elderly women in Aunt Paddy's set who roamed from drawing room to park to ballroom and back again, intent on the latest piece of gossip. And if there was no gossip, they were just as intent on inventing it.

He was pondering how on earth he might retrieve Marlaine when he noticed the woman in the lavender gown. The young woman was truly stunning; he would even say breathtaking. She had a classic profile, a luscious red mouth, and flawless, creamy skin that stretched tautly across high cheekbones. He watched as she drummed long, tapered fingers against one arm while she listened to his aunt's chatter. From his vantage point, he could admire all her feminine traits, of which, he could not help noticing, she had many. Enjoying his leisurely perusal of her, he suddenly realized he had met her before. He was struggling to put a name to the face when the young woman smiled.

Alex almost choked. He knew that smile; he would know *that* smile anywhere. Bloody hell, it was his angel! It flabbergasted him; she was the *last* person he would have expected to see here! He could not believe it—the beauty with eyes of cobalt blue was in town for the Season! But what was she doing *here*? Dear God, she was not in search of a husband, was she? What else could explain it? And just how in God's name did she expect to accomplish *that*? He would hardly expect her to have the requisite connections, and even if she did, she could *hardly* be recommended to a family of Quality. She lived in a run-down manor with a group of unwanted children, for Chrissakes! She chased hogs in the fields and traded pumpkins for tallow! What member of the *ton* did she hope to snare with those astonishing credentials?

He realized what he was thinking and frowned. It should not matter to him in the least how she hoped to accomplish what all women sought to accomplish. She was none of his concern—but God, he had thought of her often in the last months. In his mind, he had held her up as a paragon of virtue, an angel among mortals, a goddess among the damned.

His angel suddenly moved away from Paddy and Mrs. Clark, toward the far end of the ballroom. A fragment of treasured memory jolted Alex from his languid stance; his eyes riveted on that lovely derriere. He was suddenly and overwhelmingly compelled to speak with her. With his head down, he began moving quickly around the perimeter of the crowd.

She disappeared into the crush. He looked frantically about the room, thought he had lost her until she suddenly emerged again, walking briskly through doors opened onto the gardens. He started after her, but was quickly intercepted by Sir Robert Peel. "What a pleasure, your grace! We were just speaking of you! Is it true? You intend to champion reform in the Lords?'' the diminutive man asked.

''I have considered it, Sir Robert,'' he said, conscious of the crush around them straining to hear every word.

''A worthy cause, indeed, your grace. But the economic reforms the Radicals would see include more than just a change in the tax laws, as I am certain you are aware,'' Peel said carefully.

Alex knew he referred to changes in parliamentary representation—allowing Catholics a seat, to be precise. And he also knew the Home Secretary, while progressive in his ideas, was not in favor of change as radical as that. ''Indeed? I shall have to examine their platform carefully,'' he said evasively. ''If you will excuse me, sir,'' he said, and walked away before he could be questioned further, out into the gardens.

Damn it, he had lost her. His eyes scanned the overabundance of rosebushes of which Lady Granbury was inordinately fond. Had she returned to the crowded ballroom? Had he just imagined it was she?

Surely he had only imagined it.

As he turned, a flash of lavender at the far end of the gardens caught his eye. Perhaps he had imagined it, but he would not rest until he knew. He walked purposefully in the direction of that splash of lavender with absolutely no idea what he would do or say. Only one thing was certain—if it was she, he had to look into her eyes again.

Bloody hell, it *was* her. She saw him as she reached the gate of a small arbor, fenced off from the rest of the garden. Her remarkable dark blue eyes rounded in surprise, followed by a devastating smile that conveyed her delight and made his heart leap to his throat. He clamped his jaw firmly shut. What in the hell was he *doing*?

Lauren was wondering the same thing as she fumbled helplessly at the wrought iron gate. How had he found her? Had he come for *her*? Her heart began to beat with an anxiousness that took her breath away. In a moment of great anticipation, she brought both hands to the gate and yanked hard until the stubborn thing flew open. Conscious that she was grinning like an idiot, she passed through the gate, swallowing deep gulps of air to smother her excitement. Did she dare to hope? Dear God, did she dare to *believe* he had come for her? Her heart thumping wildly, she smiled brilliantly, frantically thinking what to say.

He shoved his hands into his pockets and stared at her for a long moment before speaking. "Miss Hill. It is a pleasure to see you again," he said stiffly.

Lauren laughed with absurd glee. "Mr. Christian, it is an enormous pleasure to see *you* again!"

He blinked. Shoving his hands deeper into his pockets, he said, "You look remarkably . . . well."

"Oh!" She smiled, blushing. "Thank you! So do you!" Her hands found the little fence at her back, and curled around the rails in something of a death grip. Good God, her heart was beating so strongly she was certain she would be airborne at any moment. And her cheeks were beginning to ache from the broad smile she could not keep from her lips.

His green eyes flicked to a rosebush at her side, then riveted on her face again. "Might I inquire as to what you are doing here?"

With that one question, he swiftly killed all of her fabulous hopes. He had not come for her. Come to think of it, he did not seem particularly glad to *see* her. No, he actually looked uncomfortable! His expression hurt her. Why did he not just kick her in the shin? She responded sharply, "Perhaps I should inquire the same of you!"

He looked startled. "I beg your pardon. I meant only that I am very surprised to see you in London. I did not think . . . ah, that you . . . would necessarily . . . *enjoy* . . . the Season."

Lauren faltered. It was not what he had said, but how he had said it. He thought she did not belong here! Maybe she did not, but who was he? The bloody king of England? The last time she checked he was a country gentleman, with no more right to be here than she had! "I *necessarily* enjoy it very much," she lied.

He nodded absently as his gaze floated to her mouth, swept the full length of her gown, and then traveled slowly to her eyes again. A heat crept up her neck and quickly flooded her cheeks at his frank perusal. Dear *God,* she had not remembered him being so terribly handsome.

"I hope it is a success for you, then," he said flippantly.

A *success*? Lauren's eyes narrowed. "I beg your pardon, Mr. Christian, but whatever would you mean by that?"

He quirked a dark brow. "Just that most unmarried women partake of a London Season for one particular reason, is that not so?"

The truth infuriated her. "And what concern is it of yours?" she snapped.

He smiled then; her stomach sank at the unexpected dazzle of it. "Please forgive me. I suppose I am a bit astounded to find you here." Astounded. Astounded that a woman like her would attend a fancy reception. She frowned; his green eyes seemed to pierce her, which enraged her almost as much as the lazy smile on his lips. "You are right; it is none of my concern, and naturally, I wish you all the best in your endeavors for a good match," he said.

A heartfelt panic in Lauren's throat threatened to choke her, and she looked nervously to the gravel path at her feet. Humiliated, she desperately wanted to disabuse him of the notion that *she* was looking for a match—*Ethan* was! "Mr. Christian . . ." She glanced up at him, only to be unbalanced by the depth of his green eyes. Really, she did not remember the arrogant swine being quite so handsome. For some reason, her brain chose that moment to remember he likely was married. She frowned; she might be in town for a particular reason, but he was a glib horse's ass. "Please excuse me. I should rejoin my party in the ballroom,'' she said icily.

He shifted uncomfortably and glanced up the gravel path. "Pardon, madam. Please allow me to explain myself. I merely wondered what would bring you to London, as I thought your heart belonged to Rosewood, and then, of course, it dawned on me, and I am—''

She unconsciously released a quiet shriek of frustration. "If you please, Mr. Christian, unless you have been charged with the royal authority for this interrogation, I hardly see what difference it could possibly make to you *what* I am doing in London!'' She lifted her chin, pleased with herself for thinking of a rejoinder with a brain completely numbed by the sight of him.

She was not the only one who was numb. Startled by his own discomfiture and her apparent indignation, Alex's gaze swept the eyes framed with long, dark lashes, the slender neck, and the inviting swell of her bosom. Lauren's eyes sparkled with great irritation, and he thought them the most enchanting eyes he had ever seen. He clasped his hands behind his back, absently wondering why her entry into the marriage market should annoy him so. And why was she so angry with him for stating the obvious?

"Miss Hill, it is certainly no concern of mine what you are doing or *not* doing in London. I simply remarked that it surprised me. I should think you would not find that so terribly odd given that I have seen you sing to a hog, fence a young orphan, and sled into a tree,'' he attempted to jest. "By all means, if it is matrimony you want, I am quite certain you will be very successful.'' He thought he was handing her a compliment, but her sparkling eyes narrowed dangerously.

"Is that so?'' she said in a very low, very soft voice. "You cannot imagine how it warms my heart to know you approve, Mr. Christian. Thank God, I should be able to sleep tonight now that I have your implicit approval! If you will excuse me, sir, I should go inside where *gentlemen* do not remark on a lady's motives for attending a silly afternoon reception! Good day, sir!'' she snapped, and with a curt toss of her head, marched past him.

Bloody hell, what had he said? Stunned, Alex watched the gentle sway of the angel's hips and the grace of her movement in spite of her near sprint. He thought about her dark blue eyes as she skipped daintily across the path of a couple. She disappeared through the doors and, shrugging in bafflement, he followed her inside.

Much to his considerable annoyance, he found himself looking for her. The angel was not hard to find; she quite naturally stood out among everyone. She was in the company of a young man leaning on a cane. He assumed it was her brother Paul, as the children of Rosewood had said enough for him to know about his infirmity. That he was relieved it was her brother irritated him.

But it was nothing compared with the swell of irritation when a very large and very handsome golden-haired man joined her. Lauren smiled up at the stranger, and he very instantly and possessively put his hand on the small of her back to lead her through the crush toward the door. Angry that he was even remotely curious, he was positively mystified by the unusual twinge of jealousy in his chest.

''Alex?''

He turned sharply toward the sound of his fiancée's voice with a sheepish grin. She smiled sweetly. Gazing at her lovely smile, he was glad that *she* was his betrothed, and not some petulant woman who sang to hogs. He could not help himself; he slipped an arm around her waist and pressed a tender kiss to her forehead that made her skin heat beneath his lips.

She pulled away from him with a nervous laugh and glanced shyly around them. ''Oh my, what has come over you? I am sorry you had to wait.'' He grinned unabashedly and kissed her forehead again. Marlaine's cheeks fused pink and she cast a demure gaze to the floor, the nervous little smile still on her lips. "Darling, *please*. What will people think?" she whispered sweetly.

"I don't give a damn," he answered, and laughed when Marlaine's eyes grew wide.

Chapter 10

The Season commenced with a vengeance in the three days that followed the Granbury reception, and Lauren attended more routs and teas than she had in all her life. Every day was spent madly dashing here and there in order to be seen in all the right places, and the constant social whirl was beginning to take a toll on her measly wardrobe.

Standing in the ladies retiring room at the Harris ball, Lauren tugged at the gown of sapphire blue brocade, the skirt draped with a thin layer of chiffon. She was squeezed so tightly into the thing, she very much feared her bosom would spring free with the slightest misstep. Her discomfort was made even worse by the fact that she found it impossible to dress her own hair without Mrs. Peterman to help her. She had resorted to a simple twist—hardly the height of fashion.

She tugged at the gown one last time before leaving the retiring room and emerged onto a crowded landing. Slowly, she made her way to the dining salon, where a large buffet had been arranged with an elaborate display of food. Swiping a bite of cheese, she pushed onto the ballroom, where large crystal chandeliers ablaze with dozens of candles hung from elaborate ceiling friezes. At the far end, five sets of French doors opened onto a wide balcony and the gardens beyond, allowing air into the packed house.

Lauren gratefully accepted a glass of punch from a footman and stood to one side, surveying her opulent surroundings—until she saw Magnus standing at the bottom of the great curving staircase. His eyes slowly traveled the crowd; he saw her at almost the exact same moment she saw him.

Lauren frowned.

Magnus actually grinned.

And he began to move steadily in her direction. Lauren sighed, downed her punch, and with a stealth a jewel thief might have admired, moved swiftly and silently along the wall, her eyes trained on the crowd for any sign that the Bavarian was gaining on her. In so doing, she stumbled upon Charlotte Pritchit.

"Goodness, Charlotte, what are you doing back here?" Lauren gasped once she realized she had collided with her friend behind the wide leaves of a tall green plant. In her bright pink satin gown and newly cropped hair, Charlotte reminded Lauren of a miserable china doll. "You look faint! Are you quite all right?"

"You would look faint, too, if your mother was arranging your dance card for you," Charlotte muttered.

"But don't you *want* to dance?" Lauren asked.

"Of course I do, but she won't allow me to dance with just anyone! They must be titled, and not just any title but only an earl and above," she muttered helplessly. "She harbors some fantastic notion that I shall dance with the Duke of Sutherland, of all people! She honestly believes a single quadrille with him will create an *interest*," she said disgustedly.

"Is he here?"

"I don't *think* so! He rarely comes to these events, and

even if he did, he would not be remotely interested in dancing with me, I can assure you!'' Charlotte groaned miserably.

"Oh, Charlotte," Lauren laughed, "why on earth not? I cannot imagine what man would *not* want to dance with you!"

Charlotte smiled meekly. "That is exceedingly kind of you, but you do not understand. The Duke of Sutherland is one of the most popular men in all of England. Every woman in this *room* will want to dance with him. If he determines to dance—and he never does—he should not deign to look at me! And dear God, if he *should,* my mother will make an absolute *cake* of herself!"

Lauren shrugged. Obviously another aristocrat with an overinflated view of himself. A man like that would not suit Charlotte at all. "He is a cabbagehead," she said with great authority, missing Charlotte's look of horror. "I have an idea! Come with me to the far side of the room—your mother cannot possibly see us there! You can say you lost your dance card and stand up with whomever you please!"

Charlotte gaped at Lauren as if she had just spoken heresy, but slowly, a tremulous smile spread across her lips. "I don't know," she said hesitantly. "My mother can be quite ill-tempered."

Lauren suppressed the urge to snort her agreement with that. "Come! She cannot possibly think of dragging you from the dance floor without causing a scene. Besides, I know a man who has a proper enough title to suit her, and he shall be happy to stand up with you," she said with supreme assurance. She grabbed Charlotte's hand, determined that Magnus should be the first to escort her onto the dance floor.

The Duke of Sutherland and Michael Ingram, the Marquis of Darfield, having come from the gentleman's smoking room, stood uncomfortably at the entrance to the

ballroom. Surveying the crowd, Michael sighed unconsciously, bringing a grin to Alex's face. If there was a person who despised the Season's events, it was his old friend,
Michael. Once known as the Devil of Darfield, Michael had
shunned society with a vengeance until his delightful wife,
Abbey, had come along and changed everything. He attended the events now, but reluctantly. Earlier, the two had
escaped to the smoking room, where they had stayed just
long enough for Michael to divest Alex of two hundred
pounds in a card game.

Alex shared Michael's lack of enthusiasm, and this ball
was no different than countless others. The house was filled
to overflowing, the rooms were stifling, the champagne
tepid, and the dance floor a moving obstacle course. But
Marlaine enjoyed it, and he had to admit, she looked particularly lovely tonight. He had been very proud to dance with
her.

"Ah, there is the happy marchioness now," Michael said
dryly, nodding in her direction. In the center of a group of
admirers, Abbey was laughing gaily. "If you will excuse
me, old chum, I think I shall go to my wife before White-
hurst carries her off," he said, and walked into the crowd.
Grinning, Alex turned his attention to the crowd, looking for
Marlaine. He peered closely into the crush, until a flash of
light upon a gem or crystal caught his eye.

His eyes riveted on the object, all thoughts of Marlaine
suddenly vanquished from his mind. Just a few feet from
him, Miss Hill glided across the edge of the dance floor with
a firm grip on Miss Pritchit's hand. His pulse quickened at
the mere sight of her; it was little wonder; the angel was
absolutely stunning.

She and Miss Pritchit stopped and put their heads together, giggling at something or someone on the dance
floor. Her smile was infectious; like a bright star, it illumi-
nated those around her. And those sparkling dark blue

eyes—God, they were enchanting. It was hard to imagine
they had flashed with anger three days ago. . . .

Just what had he said, anyway?

The more he thought of it, the more irritated he became.
What exactly *had* he said to cause such ire in her? Jesus, he
had merely wished her well! She acted as if it were some
grand secret that women came to London in hopes of a good
match.

He was so intent on the angel that Lady Harris was able
to easily intercept him. "Your grace! I am so glad to have
found you in this mob! I should very much like to introduce
you to someone," she purred, and linked her arm through
his.

"At your service, Lady Harris," he replied automatically, but he did not take his eyes from Miss Hill, who was
now talking with the same blond man he had seen with her
at the reception.

Lady Harris playfully tapped his arm with her fan. "I
should very much like to introduce you to the Countess
Bergen. She is from the continent after all, and I thought
perhaps you had met her before."

Alex realized they were moving in the direction of Miss
Hill. He watched as she turned to Miss Pritchit and introduced her to the stranger. "I am quite certain I have not,"
he responded politely.

"Well, you should very much enjoy meeting her now.
She is truly a delight! Such joie de vivre! I wish you could
have seen her just last week. That girl lost at *least* twelve
rounds of loo to Lady Thistlecourt, who lorded it over us
all with the decorum of a *skunk*! Honestly, Hortense
Thistlecourt thinks she positively *owns* the loo tables! And
do you know the dear girl simply laughed, declared to Lady
Thistlecourt she was honor bound to seek a rematch, and
then blithely offered to fetch her a drink? Can you imagine?" Lady Harris babbled.

Alex only vaguely heard his hostess. The golden stranger

was escorting Miss Pritchit onto the dance floor, and the angel was smiling as if she had just eaten a fat cow. She further startled him by calling after the stranger in German, telling him to please try and smile. "Excuse me, Lady Harris, but where is the Countess?" he asked impatiently, wanting to be done with it so he could speak with the angel.

"Why, she is just there," she responded happily, and nodded toward Miss Hill.

Alex looked at Lady Harris, then at Miss Hill. "I beg your pardon?" he choked out.

"One can hardly miss her!" Lady Harris laughed. "The dark-haired woman in the sapphire gown. She is quite lovely, is she not?"

God in heaven, for the first time in his life, Alex was utterly speechless. Where in the hell had Lady Harris come up with the idea that Lauren Hill was a countess—the *Bavarian* countess of whom everyone spoke? It was impossible! The little chit had never made mention of a *title*! "I think there must be some mistake," he uttered.

"Oh, there is no mistake, I assure you! *That* is Countess Bergen!" Lady Harris cheerfully confirmed.

Lauren chuckled to herself as Charlotte and Magnus disappeared into the crowd of dancers. Magnus had not liked it one bit, but Charlotte had almost swooned. Well, he *was* a handsome man; she had to give him that. When he smiled. Which was rarely. Nonetheless, he was *trying* to be charming.

"Lauren!"

She whirled toward the sound of Abbey's voice. With a small squeal of delight, she rushed into the open arms of her friend.

"Where on earth have you been? Not a word from you since you left Rosewood! I should be mortally offended, you know!" Abbey gushed, then held her at arm's length to examine her.

"Oh, Abbey, you cannot imagine how sorely I have missed you!" Lauren cried.

"When are you coming again to Pemberheath? The new barn at Rosewood is finally finished, but it is positively too grand to be a barn! The children are quite proud of it."

"I miss the children *dreadfully,*" she moaned genuinely. "Uncle Ethan has promised we may visit in a fortnight."

"Oh my, your gown is *beautiful,*" Abbey proclaimed honestly.

"Do you really think so? I have had the worst luck finding a seamstress."

"Really?" Abbey beamed. "I know of one who is quite affordable. I commission *all* my gowns from her—"

"I beg your pardon, darling, but shall you not introduce us?" Glancing to her right, Lauren saw a tall man with finely chiseled features and soft gray eyes. Lord, but he was handsome—almost as handsome as that arrogant Mr. Christian. She quickly covered that forbidden thought with a bright smile.

"Michael, darling, I am so very pleased to finally introduce to you Countess Bergen," Abbey happily replied.

Lord Darfield took her hand and gallantly bowed very low over it. "A true pleasure," he said charmingly. "My wife speaks very fondly of you and your enormous tomatoes."

Lauren graciously curtsied. "I am quite fond of your wife, too, my lord," she said, laughing lightly, "but it is her patronage of my tomatoes that makes me adore her!"

"You are being kind, Countess Bergen, for I rather think we both know it is an obsession. We have eaten so many tomatoes at Blessing Park that I rather fear they may sprout from my ears!" the marquis exclaimed as he took two glasses of champagne from a passing footman and handed them to the women.

Lauren laughed as she brought the flute to her lips.

"Countess Bergen!"

Lauren smiled helplessly at Abbey. The way Lady Harris kept introducing men to her, she would have sworn the woman had been retained by Ethan to find her a match.

"Countess Bergen! Please allow me to introduce you to his grace, the Duke of Sutherland."

She reluctantly looked over her shoulder—and instantly choked on her champagne, spraying the marquis's coat sleeve. A *duke?* Her country gentleman was *the* Duke of Sutherland? The marquis grabbed the flute from her hand before she dropped it and Abbey slapped her soundly on the back. The so-called duke did not make the slightest attempt to keep the insolent smile from his lips. With exaggerated flourish, he pulled a white handkerchief from his breast pocket and offered it to her. "My apologies for having startled you, madam," he said with polished grace.

"Oh dear, I am *dreadfully* sorry!" Lady Harris said in horror. Shocked senseless, Lauren nervously grabbed the handkerchief from him and indelicately wiped her mouth and hand. She could not take her eyes from him, let alone speak. Abbey broke her trance by stealthily kicking her with her foot, and Lauren obediently stumbled into an awkward curtsy. The *duke*, blast him, grinned broadly. "Your grace," she heard herself rasp, "what a pleasure to make your acquaintance."

With a smile of great amusement, he took her hand and brushed his lips across her knuckles, his gaze on her face. "The pleasure is all mine . . . *countess.*"

"I had hoped you had met before," Lady Harris said, looking pointedly at Lauren's hand, which was still in the duke's.

Abbey gaped at her as Alex grinned cheerfully and slowly released her hand. "I am quite certain I would recall the enormous pleasure of encountering such a celebrated . . . and lovely . . . countess," he said smoothly.

Lauren blanched and covered her mouth with a half-cough, half-choke. She glanced uncomfortably at a beaming

Lady Harris. "His grace has traveled often to the continent, Countess," her hostess chirped. "Perhaps he has met that wonderful cousin of yours, Count Bergen? Shall we call him over?"

"Cousin?" Alex interrupted politely, his all-too-knowing smile deepening.

"No, no, not exactly," Lauren stammered. Alex quirked a brow. Lady Harris, Abbey, and Lord Darfield all leaned forward as if afraid they might miss her explanation. "I mean, that he . . . He would be the nephew of my husband. Was the nephew. Is," she stupidly attempted to clarify. Completely disconcerted, she clumsily thrust the handkerchief at Alex. "Thank you," she mumbled.

"No, my lady, I would that you keep it. You may need it again," he said, and had the audacity to wink very subtly. At Lord Darfield's choked laughter, Lauren's pulse surged with mortification, and even worse, some indefinable emotion that made a rash of heat flood her face. She thought of a million retorts she should have made, but the scoundrel had turned her tongue to mush. She could only stand helplessly as he greeted Abbey with sophisticated charm. "Lady Darfield, as always, an immense pleasure."

"Alex, really, you stand on such formality," Abbey laughed, and gave him a familiar hug.

"Sutherland, you surprise me. I've never seen you advance so deeply into a ballroom," Lord Darfield grinned insolently, and turned to his wife. "Speaking of ballrooms, darling, they are playing a waltz."

"Yes, but I should very much like to—"

"I am quite certain the countess will be here a while longer?" he said to Lauren. "Excellent," he said to her dumbstruck nod, and practically pushed his wife toward the dance floor.

"Perhaps the countess would do me the honor?" Alex asked cheerfully.

Dance with him? Oh no, not on her *life* would she dance

with him. "Ah, no thank you . . . you see, my friend Charlotte—"

"Posh!" declared Lady Harris, and tapped Lauren's arm with her fan. "Charlotte Pritchit can fend for herself!" The duke smiled smugly at that. "I shall wait here and explain to Miss Pritchit if you like," she insisted, and gave Lauren a little push.

Bloody hell, but there was no graceful way out of it. The scoundrel smiled as if he had never been more amused. She considered giving him the cut direct for having lied to her if nothing else, but she could hardly do so without bringing undue scrutiny on herself, and well the rogue knew it. "Certainly," she said with a cool glower, and deliberately placed her hand on his arm as if she were touching a leper. He grinned, covered her hand with his, and escorted her to the floor.

As he led her through the crowd, Charlotte's words suddenly popped into her head: *He is one of the most popular men in all of England.* Dear God, all this time she had been dreaming about the Duke of Sutherland! *Not* a country gentleman, a *duke*! A rumble of panic began to build in the pit of her stomach.

Still grinning when they reached the dance floor, he bowed and swept her into a waltz, whirling her toward the middle of the floor before she could even lift her skirts to give him a perfunctory curtsey. The stab of panic only sharpened when she noticed how easily she fit within his arms. How on earth could she have been so naïve as to mistake him for a country gentleman? Dear God, there was a marquis, a duke, and an earl or two residing near Pemberheath. Why had she not seen it? And Holy Mother, he danced with such *grace*. He was probably trained on the continent, because one simply did not possess such skill of movement. He danced like he kissed . . . blast it all, she *would* have to think of that *now*! Bloody marvelous! She had been quite thoroughly kissed by a *duke*! Shaken by the ex-

traordinary turn of events, she could do little more than stare
at his snowy white neckcloth.

It was tied so perfectly that it naturally led her to glance
surreptitiously at his formal attire. He wore black tails in
which his square shoulders filled every inch, and a white
satin waistcoat that fit his lean waist with no room to spare,
just as he appeared in her daydreams. She dared to look up,
to where a brown curl had fallen across his bronzed forehead. He smiled languidly, just oozing dukelike charm.
"Well, well, Miss Hill. You seem to be faring much better
than I thought."

Lauren snapped awake at that. "Countess Bergen," she
corrected stiffly.

To her great irritation, he feigned surprise. "*Countess?*
My apologies, madam. I could have sworn you first introduced yourself as simply Miss Hill."

"Then perhaps we both misunderstood, for I could have
sworn *you* first introduced yourself as a gentleman," she
shot back. He flashed an irrepressible grin before pulling her
close to avoid colliding with another couple. When they
were safely past, he did not release her, but kept her close.
Too close—his cologne tickled her nose.

"Forgive me, but I am rather mystified. You failed to
mention your lofty connections when first we met," he remarked with a cheerful smile.

Yes, but he had not exactly told her who *he* was! Oh, he
was the *epitome* of pomposity! "Could it be, sir, that you
have duped a whole *range* of acquaintances into thinking
you are a gentleman? And by the by, you certainly failed to
mention *your* connections!"

His deep, rich laugh sent a peculiar shiver down her
spine. "*Touché,* madam. At the time, it did not seem appropriate. I did not think it wise to startle you with my identity
after your brush with near disaster, nor did I think Mrs.
Peterman would be terribly amused. But as to your name, is

it Lauren Hill—or is that yet another false identity?'' he asked, twirling her about again.

"As I said, it is *Countess* Bergen,'' she countered angrily.

His bold green eyes danced with merriment. "Ah, yes. Of course it is.'' The look in his eye made her uncomfortably warm, and she tried to put some distance between them. But he stubbornly tightened his hold on her. "Perhaps I should ask it another way. Imagine my surprise to see you first as an impoverished miss chasing a hog, and now, a celebrated countess from Bavaria. Surely you can understand how one might wonder?''

Her anger soared with indignation, and it was only intensified by his devilish smile. Did he think that he was the only one worthy of a title? Well, *that* was hardly surprising! All the aristocrats *she* had ever known thought themselves absolutely infallible! All right, that consisted of her uncle and Magnus Bergen, but nonetheless, they also possessed the tendency toward intolerable arrogance. But theirs *paled* in comparison to *this*. "I am surprised, my lord duke, that you are obviously unaware it is terribly impolite to ask such probing questions of a lady.''

"And a countess, you forgot that,'' he agreed amicably.

"You seem to delight in interrogating me!'' she blustered angrily. "Do you think I am not a little miffed that you did not reveal yourself to *me*?''

"It is hardly the same thing. Now I should very much like to know why you concealed your identity from me.''

Oh, so now she had *concealed* it. Her brows snapped together as she pressed her lips tightly together.

"Oh, that will not do,'' he said of her frown. "You should smile and nod as if my conversation is terribly fascinating, which it is. Anything less than that will have every occupant of this ballroom, including myself, wondering why the Countess Bergen should be so angry with the Duke of Sutherland. Why don't you instead entertain us both by telling me just how, exactly, you came by this mysterious new title?"

She opened her mouth to speak. But glancing furtively around them, she thought twice about shouting that she had not just come by her title any more than *he* apparently had, and that his supposed indignation was no more valid than her own. She clamped her mouth shut. There was certainly more than one pair of eyes on them, including those of Charlotte Pritchit, and naturally, Magnus. Only Paul's surveillance was missing, but he was in the gaming room. She caught sight of Charlotte again, wistfully watching her. In the space of that moment, Lauren concluded she could not escape the arrogant duke without a scene, that she would have to tell him something to appease him in a very few minutes, and that she should at least get some small concession for being forced to his will. A good punch in the nose was more to her liking, but she would settle for a small token of kindness.

"All right, she whispered angrily, and forced a smile to her lips. "I shall tell you how I came by my title." He inclined his head in a show of victory. "On one condition," she added coolly. "You must agree to dance with Miss Pritchit."

A shout of laughter escaped him. "Charlotte Pritchit? I shall need more than your little story to entice me to that!"

"You heard me," she breathed, then catching herself, graced him with a smile she hoped he would think sincere.

He did not think it terribly sincere, but it had to be the most alluring smile he had ever seen. "Well?" she demanded. "Will you agree to dance with Miss Pritchit?"

Alex chuckled. Beautiful, bold, and practical to the end. "May I ask *why*?"

"Because." She smiled sweetly, glancing across the ballroom. "It would be a nice thing to do."

That reasoning hit him like a left jab from nowhere. A *nice thing to do*? "Is that all? Or do you have any other odious trades in mind?'' he asked, bowing chivalrously as the music came to an end.

Her exceptional eyes danced like fire. ''What a *perfectly* arrogant thing to say! Dancing with Miss Pritchit is *hardly* odious! Honestly, you aristocrats are all alike!''

''I beg your pardon, madam, but we *aristocrats* are cut from the same cloth as *countesses,*'' he said, his fingers closing tightly around her elbow as he led her from the dance floor.

''Do we have a bargain?'' she demanded.

It *was* a very small price to pay. ''All right. I shall ask the little mouse to dance!''

With a firm nod of agreement, Lauren jerked her arm free and marched off the dance floor as if leading a charge. He deftly caught her elbow again. ''You will incite the crowd into believing there is a fire if you walk out of here like that.''

''I would get this over and done!'' she murmured furiously, but paused long enough to snatch a flute of champagne from a passing footman. She took a sip—a good, *long* sip—and slammed the half-empty flute onto a table. Shooting him a look of total exasperation, she marched out into the cool night air with him close on her heels, leading him to a semisecluded spot on the popular balcony.

He settled one hip against the railing and folded his hands in his lap. ''Well?''

She glanced out over the moonlit gardens and exhaled a long, agonized breath. Her eyes were amazing; they were the most bewitching things he had ever seen. His gaze wandered the sweep of her slender neck, the graceful swell of her bosom, and the long, lean line of her body in that provocative gown.

''All right,'' she said, turning slowly toward him. He reluctantly dragged his gaze to her face. ''I was married to a very old, very senile man,'' she said slowly. ''My uncle betrothed me to Count Helmut Bergen of Bergenschloss—

that's in Bavaria, you know. The ceremony was performed by proxy, so I did not know how . . . how *infirm* he was until I arrived there.'' She paused; he kept his expression intentionally bland. She suddenly looked down and brushed an imaginary piece of lint from her gown. ''The terms of my betrothal were an heir in exchange for a generous annuity, and then, naturally, the estate upon his death.'' Lauren glanced up at him through the veil of her dark lashes; he made sure she could read nothing from his expression. She took another deep, steadying breath. ''Helmut died several months ago.''

''A hunting accident?'' he asked.

She surprised him greatly with a snort and roll of her eyes. ''Apparently you have heard my uncle's more romantic version. I am afraid he died of natural causes brought on by a positively ancient age. And since he never—I mean, since I had not provided the heir, I thought the inheritance forfeit. So I gave it to the new count, and he happened to agree rather strongly with my assessment. He thought I should return to England without delay.'' She demurely clasped her hands together, rocking unconsciously onto the balls of her feet and back again. ''I did not tell you my true title at Rosewood, because it seemed . . . well, *empty*. I was married scarcely two years, and really, Helmut was never quite certain who I was. And I would have preferred to stay at Rosewood,'' she said, her brows dipping into a momentary frown, ''but as we are struggling, my uncle is quite determined I shall marry again. It was *he* who spread the word of my title, not I!'' She glanced shyly at him. ''Really, one hardly has need of a title at Rosewood, so it did not seem to matter.''

It only mattered in that it served to increase her allure. This woman was fascinating. Certainly she had to be the only woman in all of Britain who did not think a title mattered, or who would give her inheritance away. ''Your uncle is right. A title will greatly improve your chances of a suitable match,'' he absently remarked.

He was caught off guard by the narrowing of her lovely eyes and the fists she clenched at her sides. ''You *are* an arrogant *swine*,'' she breathed.

''*Now* what have I said?'' he asked, surprised.

''Is everyone in this town as obsessed as you with what makes a good *match*?''

Alex laughed. ''I see we are bound to have this discussion again. All right then, is it not why you are here?''

She gasped, whether from surprise or indignation, he was not sure. It suddenly occurred to him that she was incensed because she had already made a match. ''Forgive me, perhaps you have received an offer? Who is the golden-haired man I have seen you with?'' he asked casually.

Her lovely face reddened, and he thought for a moment she might positively explode. Or punch him in the nose. ''Your grace, I owe you no further explanation, nor, I should think, do you *require* any,'' she said icily. ''As we have now established, hopefully to your great satisfaction, that I have a *right* to be here, I will thank you to leave me alone!'' With that, she turned abruptly on her heel and marched to the ballroom, her hips swinging pertly. Bloody hell, what had he said this time?

She did not see him for a long time after that. She made a point of not looking but finally gave into the overwhelming temptation. There he was, leaning against a column, smiling in that self-satisfied way of his as she danced a quadrille with Lord Wesley. She quickly looked away, but after a moment, she could not resist another peek. He was still watching her . . . and he watched her until the conclusion of the dance. As Lord Wesley escorted her from the floor, he inclined his head toward Charlotte, standing in the oppressive company of her mother. Lauren's heart skipped a beat. To dance with the duke would mean so *much* to Charlotte.

Almost fearing what he would do, she watched nervously as he made a great show of walking over and asking Charlotte to dance. She could see Charlotte's bright smile and her mother's near faint. She could not help smiling as he escorted Charlotte onto the dance floor. He nodded, ever so slightly, in acknowledgment of her unspoken gratitude. Lauren did not care for the impact that small, intimate exchange had on her senses, and turned away.

But she was smiling.

When Magnus insisted on a second dance, she realized she was searching for the duke over and over. Each time he seemed to catch her looking at him, and each time he gave her a smug grin, as if he knew what a wreck he was making of her emotions. She yanked her gaze away and nodded at something Magnus said, vowing to herself she would not look again.

And she did not, not really.

Standing next to her fiancé, Marlaine followed the direction of his gaze onto the dance floor. A small wave of disappointment swept through her when she found the object of his attention. The countess was now dancing with Lord Hollingsworth. With a twinge of queasiness, she glanced furtively at her betrothed again. Surely it was only her imagination that he kept staring at the countess. But when he excused himself, his eyes still on the countess, she turned away from the dance floor, her face devoid of any color.

She was *not* imagining things; she had not imagined a single thing all night. All right, Alex was often in the company of other women. But it never meant anything, and he always came back to her, *always*. This time would be no different. She walked away from the dance floor, confused and unthinking.

"Are you going to allow that?"

Marlaine gasped. She had stumbled upon her mother and

father, standing together near an open window. She swallowed. "Allow what?"

Lady Whitcomb frowned disapprovingly. "Are you going to allow your fiancé to pant like a dog over the countess?" she whispered loudly.

"Now Martha," her father said soothingly, "Sutherland is a popular fellow."

"Not nearly as popular as the countess, it would seem," she grumbled. "He has hardly taken his eyes from her."

Marlaine looked across the dance floor. Alex was where he had been most of the evening—near the countess. Catching a sigh in her throat, she reminded herself that he hated balls, and the countess was only a distraction. He was just amusing himself. She had nothing to fear. Nothing. "He shall be along soon, Mother, I know he shall," she said, desperately wanting to believe it.

Her mother made a sound of disagreement, but her father quickly spoke before she could voice her opinion. "What say we get a bite to eat? All this dancing makes a man hungry," he said kindly, and ushered the two women from the ballroom.

None of the Reese family noticed the man with the cane standing to one side, staring at his sister and the Duke of Sutherland.

Headed home in a hired hack, Paul was still reeling from the remarkable notion that Sutherland had eyes for his sister. The man was not only a duke, he was *famous*. Some called him a Radical for leading the reform movement in the House of Lords. He was bold, his ideas refreshingly original. He was, in Paul's estimation, exactly what the country needed in Parliament. Engaged to a beautiful woman, he was planning a marriage that would create a family alliance *The Times* predicted would be of enormous consequence in the next decade. And he was blatantly flirting with his very own sister. Paul looked at Lauren. Settled against the squabs, she gazed dreamily out the dingy window, a contented smile on her lips. "Enjoy yourself?"

"Hmmm," she nodded.

"Meet anyone of particular interest? Or did Count Bergen keep them all at bay?" A small smile curved her lips, but Lauren slowly shook her head. "I was beginning to think you might have developed some attachment for the Duke of Sutherland," he said quietly.

Lauren's eyes shot open and she laughed. "*Him*? Hardly!" She laughed again, but it was a feigned laugh, he knew. That rake had impressed her.

"He is engaged, you know," he said carefully," to Lady Marlaine Reese. Earl Whitcomb's daughter."

Clearly startled, Lauren jerked her gaze to him, her eyes roaming his face. "Engaged?" she echoed, her voice small.

"You did not know?"

She blinked, then looked down at her lap, shrugging. "No, but why should I? I hardly know the man, and you know how aristocrats can be. Very particular about who is introduced to whom," she said, then added so softly he could barely hear, "besides, he does not particularly care for me, I think."

Paul remained silent on that point. But she could not be more wrong.

Chapter 11

"Thank you, Finch, I'll show myself in."

From his desk, Alex glanced up as his younger brother sauntered across the thick carpet and dropped onto a leather couch. Grinning broadly, he stretched his long legs in front of him and shoved a hand into the waistband of his trousers.

"What," Alex asked dryly, "puts such a smile on your face this afternoon? Are you pleased with yourself? Or some trifle?"

Arthur chuckled gleefully. "A trifle. Seems the entire *ton* is talking about the Duke of Sutherland this morning."

"Indeed?" Alex drawled.

"Indeed, your most exalted grace. I take it you have not heard the gossip?" Arthur asked, his hazel eyes sparkling with gaiety. Alex shook his head. "Then you may very well be the only person in London not to have heard how the aloof Duke of Sutherland paid uncharacteristic attention to a widowed countess. A beautiful, Bavarian countess."

Alex rolled his eyes. "Thank you, Arthur, for that titillating piece of gossip. Should you not be on your way to your exclusive interview with the editor of *The Times*?''

Arthur's delighted laughter filled the large room. ''Then you deny it?''

Alex shrugged; he was quite accustomed to the daily rumors and innuendoes surrounding him. During the Season he was often the subject of much drawing room speculation after an event like the Harris ball. ''I do not deny dancing with Countess Bergen. If one terms that 'uncharacteristic attention,' then I suppose I am guilty.''

''And I suppose the fact that your secretary dispatched two dozen roses from the Park Lane hothouse this morning is just a coincidence,'' Arthur said nonchalantly.

A slow smile worked at the corner of Alex's mouth. He leaned back, propping a booted foot against the expensive, hand-carved mahogany desk. Clasping his hands behind his head, he grinned fondly at Arthur. ''*That* is the very reason I leave the business details to you. You rarely miss the little things that may appear insignificant to others.'' Arthur inclined his head in acknowledgment of the compliment. ''But you should have confirmed the destination of those roses. They were sent to Marlaine Reese.''

''Yes, the roses were sent to Marlaine,'' Arthur grinned, ''but the gardenias were sent to Russell Square.''

Alex laughed heartily. ''All right, if you must know, it would seem I insulted the countess. She does not like to be reminded that I first saw her staring down an enormous hog.''

''I beg your pardon?''

Alex grinned and nodded. ''Met her near Dunwoody last fall as she was about to become a hog's next meal. Tried to help her and almost broke my neck for it.'' Bemusement creased Arthur's forehead at the irreconcilable image. Alex laughed. ''A rather old, cantankerous hog at that. They both hail from a small estate by the name of Rosewood.''

A light of understanding dawned on Arthur's face. ''I

see—I don't suppose that was the reason you stayed a week longer than you had intended?''

"Of course not," Alex scoffed, unconsciously averting his gaze to the stack of papers in front of him.

"I was given to understand the countess had only just arrived in England. According to Paddy, she was recently widowed by a hunting accident.''

"Aunt Paddy," Alex said dryly, "believes what she wants to believe in addition to every single thing Mrs. Clark *tells* her to believe.''

"Nonetheless, she does seem to have appeared from nowhere. I have not had the pleasure of meeting the countess, but I have met her brother. They say he has amassed a small fortune in the gaming hells of Southwark," Arthur remarked. "Seems to be unusually clever with cards.''

"You don't say? I would not have guessed him a gambling man. By the look of things, they have not a shilling to spare. But then again, I would not have guessed her a countess.''

"Apparently you have *some* interest in the woman," Arthur remarked jovially. "But far be it from me to make light of your little diversion.''

"It is not a diversion, dear brother. Have you forgotten I will be married at the end of the Season?" Alex asked, smiling.

"I have not—have you?" Arthur laughingly shot back, and stood to leave. "I shall take my leave of you before you impale me with that letter opener. Incidentally, Mother has closed the Berkley Street house in favor of my home on Mount Street. Swears she cannot abide being alone.''

Alex snorted. "She has not abided being alone in twelve years. I think it time we convinced her to sell it.''

"We can certainly try, but you know as well as I that she is of the opinion one never sells property unless one is destitute or dead. By the by, do not forget that we have been properly shamed into attending Paddy's little supper party tomorrow evening. Shall I tell her to expect her favorite nephew?''

"Please do. And tell her I will attend as well," Alex said with a grin.

Across town, Paul counted again the fifty pounds he had collected at the Harris's gaming tables last evening. Coupled with his winnings from a recent foray into Southwark, he now had sufficient funds to provide a proper wardrobe for Lauren. If God granted him a little luck, in six weeks he would have enough to pay the interest on what Ethan had borrowed against his trust. Fortunately, he was winning with regularity and was beginning to build a tidy sum large enough to invest in the private securities with a decent return. He had studied his investment books in earnest, and was convinced he could achieve his ultimate goal of providing for Rosewood.

He folded the bank notes and stuffed them into his breast coat pocket as Davis entered the room. "Count Bergen," he announced, then with some flourish pivoted and made his exit. Paul grimaced to himself; he did not particularly care for the German, much less the prospect of Lauren living in Bavaria. Magnus entered carrying a massive bouquet of lilies.

"Good morning, Count Bergen," Paul sighed. "Are those for me?"

Magnus did not so much as smile. "Is Lauren about? I would like a word with her."

"Unfortunately, she is asleep. We arrived home quite late last evening."

"Yes, I know," Magnus said absently.

Paul regarded Lauren's suitor impatiently. "Has it occurred to you that perhaps she does not care to be so closely watched?"

"Yes," he said simply, and glanced about the room. His

gaze landed on a table near the front windows, where a cluster of gardenias rested next to an arrangement of roses.

Paul followed his gaze and smirked. "As you can see, you are not the only man who vies for her attentions."

"Perhaps not, but your uncle is agreeable to my terms," he responded gruffly.

"Yes, but is Lauren?"

The German's eyes narrowed menacingly. He abruptly moved toward the table, dropped his bouquet on top of the gardenias, and turned on his heel, walking out of the room without a word. Paul glanced at the window, smiling quietly as he watched Magnus emerge from the house and bound down the steps, walking briskly in the direction of Covent Garden. "Apparently, she is not," he answered himself, and still smiling, returned to his books.

She had absolutely *nothing* to wear, and moreover, Lauren was in no mood to attend the supper party at Lady Paddington's. It was *his* fault—since the Harris ball she had not been able to get Alex off her mind. Unwilling to admit that he attracted her like no other man, and absolutely frantic that he did, she anxiously tore through her measly wardrobe. Why on earth should she feel any attraction for him? He was *betrothed* for Chrissakes! She angrily yanked a gown from her wardrobe and examined it with a critical eye before tossing it on the bed with the others.

She was being ridiculous! She had absolutely no business even *thinking* of him. She was in London for one purpose, and that purpose did not include making moon eyes at a duke. He probably thought of her as little more than another conquest, anyway—if he thought of her at all, that was, and she was quite certain he did not. This was absurd; she could not possibly care less *what* he thought of her!

Sighing with frustration, she planted her hands on her waist and surveyed the gowns strewn about her small room, settling without enthusiasm on a demure gown of midnight blue obtained from a so-called affordable seamstress. She told herself it hardly mattered what she wore. There would be no one in attendance who would spark even the slightest interest for her. There never was. The only man who came even remotely close to interesting her was—

"*Stop* it!" she angrily chided herself. She picked up a glass pendant and donned it, then strolled to a full-length mirror and gazed pensively at her reflection. As much as she despised her reason for being in London, she actually enjoyed the parties, the glittering lights, and the fabulous costumes. But it was all an illusion. Her place was at Rosewood with the children, and it was to Rosewood she would soon return. With or without a suitable match.

Yes, and what, exactly, constituted a suitable match? She hoped she might at least meet a man whom she could learn to *like*. Having been exposed to the best London had to offer it seemed less and less likely that love would enter into it. Actually, she had given up that ridiculous ideal the moment Ethan had seriously considered Lord van der Mill's offer. Now, she only hoped she could *respect* her future husband.

Her gaze traveled to the vanity and the bouquets of wilting flowers. The roses were from Lord van der Mill, whom Ethan kept on the end of taut string, ready to yank at the first sign the old man might see his way to outbid Magnus for her hand. Magnus had sent the others, as he did every day. He was trying very hard, and for some reason, had sent her *two* bouquets after the ball.

One corner of Lauren's mouth tipped upward. For some extraordinary reason, Count Bergen had changed his mind about her and was now rather determined in his pursuit of her. He had taken a town house on fashionable Bedford Square, he said, to be nearby if she should change her mind. And when she had told him she resented his constant surveillance, he had responded very matter-of-factly that it was necessary, because she would not allow him to see her any other way.

One had to respect such dedication to a cause. And she did respect him, but she could never *love* Magnus. Oh, she was fond of him in a friendly sort of way, had always been, even when he had suspected her of cheating his uncle and had wanted to haul her off to the Bavarian authorities. But she simply could not summon more than a feeling of friendship for him.

With a soft sigh, she walked to the window and parted the pale green drapes. Looking out onto Russell Square, she contemplated that perhaps she was not quite ready to give up on love. Unfortunately, she did not have the luxury of time to wait for it—she had to marry if she wanted to save Rosewood. She had to settle soon, and no handsome, arrogant duke was going to stop her.

No matter how badly she wanted him to.

Lady Paddington, with an ostrich feather bobbing precariously from her coif, appeared in the foyer to greet Lauren upon her arrival. "Oh, *Countess!* I am so pleased you could attend my little gathering!" she crowed with genuine delight. "Ah, but you look so lovely this evening! I daresay you and Lady Marlaine are the loveliest of women," she rushed on before Lauren could get a word in. "You shall become instant friends tonight, I am certain of it."

Oh, wasn't life *grand!* She could spend the entire evening listening to Lady Marlaine gush about her blasted fiancé!

"Come and let me introduce you to her and her mother, Lady Whitcomb. Lord and Lady Pritchit and their daughter Charlotte are also here. I rather think my nephew Lord Westfall might be interested in dear Charlotte," she whispered conspiratorially. Lauren swallowed her bitter surprise as Lady Paddington chatted on. Lady Pritchit grew increasingly hostile to her, particularly after she had made the unforgivable sin of dancing with Sutherland. As if she had been given a choice. ". . . and of course, Mrs. Clark," Lady Paddington finished.

Lauren missed the names of the other guests, but she had heard enough to know that this would be a tedious evening. She forced a gracious smile and followed Lady Paddington into the gold salon, her attention immediately drawn to a woman on her right. She had seen her at the Harris ball with Alex. Close up, she was even prettier than she had realized, with a head of silver blond ringlets that complimented her gown of pale blue. Pastels were obviously all the rage, and she did not have, in her vast wardrobe of eight evening gowns, a single pastel.

"Countess Bergen, may I introduce Lady Whitcomb, and her daughter, Lady Marlaine?" Lady Paddington asked with great formality.

Lady Marlaine curtsied politely, and reflexively, so did Lauren. She felt completely inadequate in her dark gown as she gazed at the perfectly put together Lady Marlaine. "A pleasure to make your acquaintance, Lady Whitcomb," she murmured, aware that her face flushed, "and yours, Lady Marlaine."

"The pleasure is undoubtedly mine, Countess Bergen," the younger woman responded smoothly. "We have heard so much about you."

Lauren smiled as Lady Paddington tugged on her sleeve. "And here, of course, are Lord and Lady Pritchit!" Lauren offered a polite greeting for the sake of propriety, noting that the countenance of Lord Pritchit was a stark contrast to his wife's ever-reproachful look. Next to them stood a very uncomfortable Charlotte, who spoke so timidly that Lauren could barely hear her. ". . . and my nephew, Lord David Westfall."

Lauren smiled at the handsome young man. "It is my distinct honor to make your acquaintance, Countess Bergen," he said with an appreciative smile, and with a grand flourish, bowed over her hand.

"Of course, you know Mrs. Clark," Lady Paddington continued, and Lauren turned away from the charming Lord

Westfall to greet the widow of a Royal Navy captain who never seemed to be very far from Lady Paddington's side. "And last but certainly not least, my nephews, his grace, the Duke of Sutherland, and Lord Christian."

Lauren's stomach twisted. It was *inconceivable!* He could not *possibly* be the same duke or nephew associated with Lady Paddington! Gritting her teeth, she glanced to her left.

It was not, apparently, so wholly inconceivable.

Smiling quietly, the duke was clearly enjoying her discomfiture for the third time. His brother, who bore a great resemblance to him, was grinning unabashedly. Lauren glanced demurely at the floor for a brief moment, striving to regain her composure before anyone noticed she had lost it. Naturally, *he* already had. "Madam, it is truly a delight to meet you again," the cretin intoned.

Reluctantly, she offered her hand. His laughing eyes caught her gaze as he brought her hand to his lips—she felt herself color and silently cursed him for it. "Your grace, I was hardly expecting to see you again," she muttered.

He grinned and leaned dangerously close, quietly startling her. "No, I daresay you were not," he murmured, and then, "allow me to introduce my brother Arthur. The Countess Bergen of Bavaria."

"It is a great honor, Countess Bergen," Lord Christian said smoothly. "I have heard many compliments about you and see they were genuinely spoken."

She deliberately gave him as enchanting a smile as she could muster. He looked a little stunned; no doubt he thought she was as bold as a tavern wench, but she did not care. As long as the Duke of Swineland saw that she would gladly smile at anyone but him, she had accomplished her little goal. She flicked a smug gaze to the duke. Not only was he not in the least perturbed; his green eyes were dancing gaily.

Lady Paddington wasted no time in ushering her into a

seat directly across from Lady Marlaine and her mother while she loudly commanded Dillon to bring her a sherry. Lauren smiled brightly at Lady Marlaine, her pulse racing madly as Dillon handed her a small crystal glass.

"Lady Paddington is quite beside herself. She so rarely entertains," Lady Marlaine said apologetically as the rotund woman bustled off.

"Oh?" Lauren asked innocently.

"Years ago, she delighted in entertaining. But then again, the boys were always in residence—they preferred this side of the park to Audley Street."

"The boys?" Lauren asked politely, and glanced up momentarily from her study of the brown liquid in her glass.

"The Christian brothers," Lady Whitcomb stiffly informed her. Lady Marlaine added wistfully, "and Anthony, of course."

Lauren nodded politely and looked at her sherry again. Anthony. Had she met an Anthony? "I am afraid you have me at a disadvantage, madam. I do not believe I have met an Anthony."

Lady Whitcomb's brown eyes widened with surprise, but her daughter kept a polite expression. "Anthony was the former duke, Alex's brother. He was taken from us five years ago."

Alex, she called him Alex. And his brother had died, had been taken from *us*. She took a fortifying sip of the vile sherry.

"May we join you, ladies?"

She wasn't sure if it was the sherry or the deep timbre of his voice that caused the strange little shiver to run up her spine. The rogue did not want an answer; he had already settled onto the settee next to Lady Marlaine. And he was staring at her. Good God, he was *maddening*. Lauren dropped her gaze to the carpet as Lady Marlaine made polite conversation with Lord Christian about a new mare Alex had obviously given her as a gift. The Duke of Swineland interjected from time to time, but Lauren was acutely aware that he watched her—she could feel it. She, on the other hand, watched one of his polished shoes swing comfortably next to the other, and kept staring at that foot until Lord Westfall joined them. Grateful for the distraction, Lauren smiled charmingly.

Alex thought he was going to have to throw some cold water on his cousin. But then again, that blasted little angel had a way of smiling at a man that left him prepared to grovel at her feet. Damn it all, in that modest gown of midnight blue, she was the epitome of elegance; even Marlaine's renowned beauty seemed to pale in comparison. Lauren Hill or Countess Bergen, whoever she was tonight—was enchanting.

Dangerously so.

"The countess was telling me last evening that she enjoys the country," he remarked casually to David, and received a quelling frown for it from the angel. He raised his brows in feigned innocence as David quipped, "Which one?"

She turned an alluring smile to David and laughed softly. "I am from Rosewood—perhaps you have heard of it? It is near Pemberheath."

"*Rose*wood?" Lady Whitcomb coolly interjected, pronouncing the word as if it left a terrible taste in her mouth. "I have not heard of it. It is your home, then?"

"Yes," Lauren beamed. "You may think me biased, but I do believe it is the most beautiful place in the world." She proceeded to rattle off the attributes of that run-down estate as a hint of rose crept into her porcelain cheeks. No wonder he had mistaken her for an angel.

Alex realized she was telling a story about Rupert, and noticed that while Arthur and David enjoyed it immensely, Marlaine wore an oddly stoic expression. Lady Whitcomb looked horrified. "Oh no!" Lauren laughed at David's question. "Rupert is *quite* big. Nevertheless, there he was, bouncing around atop that bleating calf like an Indian rubber ball, his eyes as big as balloons! Leonard and I chased him nearly to the village and back,'' she said with a giggle.

"Who is Leonard?" Marlaine asked politely.

"Oh, he is my ward. I have five altogether." She said it with an unaffected smile, her pride evident. Marlaine exchanged a look with her mother that left Alex with the distinct impression she was embarrassed for Lauren.

David, of course, was more than happy to oblige the pretty countess. "Near Pemberheath, you say? I must contrive a reason to visit," he said. Like a puppy, he eagerly responded to her attention, and began to tell a story of his own encounter with a herd of cattle, drawing laughter from the group. For reasons he could not and did not want to understand, it irritated Alex.

When supper was announced, Alex was seated at the head of the table as was due his rank, Marlaine on his right. Arthur had quite smoothly managed to seat himself next to Lauren, as had David. Throughout the first course of turtle soup, Alex furtively watched Lauren as he tried to respond to Marlaine's chatter. God, but she had an engaging smile, especially when she laughed. And she certainly laughed freely with Arthur, he thought irritably.

He became aware of Marlaine saying his name, and dragged his eyes from Lauren to his fiancée. "My, but you seem preoccupied this evening," she whispered, smiling. When he did not respond, she blushed self-consciously. "Mother and I are attending the opera tomorrow night, and I thought that you might like to accompany us."

"The opera? I thought your mother was returning to Tarriton for the weekend," he said blandly.

Marlaine's smile faded a bit and she glanced shyly to her right. "Don't you recall? Grandmama is doing much better now, so Mother decided to stay and assist the duchess with the wedding preparations."

"I seem to have forgotten. But I should be pleased to

accompany you," he said simply, trying to listen to Lauren's conversation.

Marlaine suddenly leaned forward. "Alex? Do you think we might take a turn about the park tomorrow afternoon?"

He had no idea what prompted that, but she knew very well that he could hardly endure such trivialities. "I am engaged tomorrow afternoon," he said flatly. Her face paled at his curt response, and she straightened slowly as a chorus of laughter rose from the other end of the table. Expressionless, Alex turned to the other guests. "Did I hear reference to a potato?" he asked, glancing at Lauren.

"Countess Bergen was just telling us that in Bavaria, the potato is so essential to the average diet, they have raised it to the level of deity!" Mrs. Clark cheerfully informed him. "What did you say, Countess Bergen?"

Lauren shrugged sheepishly. "Just that there is an old saying: *'It is better that it make you sick than you do not eat it at all.'* " Polite laughter was heard around the table.

"And tell them about the Potato Man," Mrs. Clark prompted. Lauren blushed but politely summarized the story she had just shared by admitting there was a daft gentleman who fancied he saw people's faces in various potatoes. Lord Pritchit demanded to know exactly how that could be, and Lauren hesitantly explained more fully about the Potato Man. As she spoke, she received increasingly disapproving looks from Lady Pritchit and Lady Whitcomb. It was so typical, Alex mused. The *ton* did not countenance differences in background or culture.

But Arthur laughed appreciatively at her story. "Did you have opportunity to travel beyond Bavaria, Countess?" he asked.

"Not often, but I had the good fortune to travel to Paris. I think it one of my favorite places. What is your favorite place, Mrs. Clark?" she asked, artfully turning the conversation from herself.

Interrupted from her diligent work on a turbot filet, Mrs.

Clark looked up from her plate and blustered, "Oh my! I suppose it is London! Paddy and I went to Paris once, but we did not care for it. Too foreign or something."

"Plus je vis d'etrangers, plus j'aimai ma patrie," Arthur quipped. Lauren laughed gaily.

"What? What did he say?" Mrs. Clark demanded.

"It's from a French play, Mrs. Clark. Let me think, loosely translated . . . *'the more foreigners I saw, the more I loved my homeland,'* " Lauren offered.

She spoke French *and* German? The woman's surprises were never-ending. Alex hid his amazement behind a mouthful of fish as Mrs. Clark frowned at Arthur. "Well, I suppose that's *exactly* what I thought!" she exclaimed to polite laughter.

"Normandy is particularly lovely in the fall," Marlaine interjected. "We plan to travel there after the wedding." An awkward silence fell over the room, save Aunt Paddy's slurp of her wine.

"Do you travel, Lord Christian?" Lauren asked after a moment.

"I've taken the grand tour, of course, but unlike my roving brother, I have spent most of my life in England. I, for one, prefer British soil to all other," he said, to which Lord Whitcomb offered a hearty "here, here."

Impulsively, Lauren recited: " *'I traveled among unknown men, In lands beyond the sea. Nor England! Did I know till then what love I bore to thee!'* " She grinned. But the other guests, momentarily taken aback by her recitation, grew quiet.

"Wordsworth," Alex said quietly from the end of the table.

Lady Pritchit sniffed disdainfully and stabbed her fish. "They *do* teach poetry in the girls' schools, your grace! My Charlotte also knows poetry. Recite something, Charlotte," she hastily bid her daughter. Charlotte's face mottled with terror.

"Oh, that is hardly necessary," Lady Paddington said, attempting to intervene.

"But she is quite poetic! Go on, dear, recite something!" Lady Pritchit said a little more forcefully. Clearly mortified, poor Charlotte clumsily attempted to recite a passage from *The Canterbury Tales* with the magnanimous help of everyone at the table, who called out what pieces they could recall. Alex stole a glimpse at Lauren as the others butchered the work. She glanced shyly at him with what he would have sworn was a faint smile of gratitude. Inexplicably, his chest tightened, and he hastily turned his attention to Charlotte.

After dinner, the women retired to the drawing room, leaving the men behind to enjoy their cigars. Lady Paddington began to tell a rather convoluted story about the hiring of a housemaid, during which Mrs. Clark frequently clarified what she thought were the salient points. Lauren was simply too confused to listen to their prattle. In all her twenty-four years, she had never been so affected by the mere *presence* of a person, but Alex Christian was able to turn her inside out. She could *feel* him in a room, aware that his eyes were constantly on her, whether she was looking at him or not. Worse yet, she was keenly aware of his lovely fiancée, and she had heard enough tonight to know that theirs would be the wedding of the decade. The very thought made her queasy.

Dear God, this was slowly becoming the longest supper party she had ever attended, longer even than the one where Herr Mietersohn, sitting next to her husband, Helmut, tried to grope her under the table while a Frenchman delivered an excruciatingly boring monologue about the revolution. In broken German mixed with French, no less.

But this was *far* worse. All Alex had to do was smile, the corners of his eyes crinkle, and her stomach would flutter madly. She was a giddy little fool—no, *imbecile* was a better description. Alex Christian was as far removed from her as a person could be, yet here she sat, practically pining for him. While she was sitting with his fiancée, for Chrissakes!

She wearily glanced around her. The women were listening to Lady Paddington—except for Lady Marlaine, who smiled nervously when Lauren caught her staring at herself and Charlotte.

When the men finally rejoined the ladies, her tension soared. Lord Westfall came immediately to the circle of women and sat next to Charlotte, causing the poor girl to turn two shades of red. The duke sauntered over and chose a seat next to Lady Marlaine—directly across from her, of course. As if he sensed what that did to her, he flashed an indolent smile.

She retaliated against the raw impact he had on her by immediately engaging Lord Westfall in conversation, hardly noticing when Charlotte seemed to sink in her seat. For the rest of the insufferable evening, Lauren managed to avoid any conversation with the duke at all. Trying gamely to include Charlotte, she chatted with Lord Westfall about the horse races at Ascot. Although a bit of a dandy, she discovered that Lord Westfall was charmingly witty and personable. When she confessed she had been to Hyde Park only twice, she was actually rather pleased when he asked if he might drive her around the next day.

As Lord Westfall mapped out a plan for their excursion, she was conscious of the duke watching her. Having endured his unnerving scrutiny long enough, she was vastly relieved when Lady Whitcomb stood to leave along with Lady Marlaine. Alex also came to his feet, prepared to escort them home. Lauren kept her eyes on her lap as the trio bid all a good night. When at last the departing guests made their way to the door of the drawing room, she could not help stealing a final glimpse of him. Though he was speaking with Arthur, he was looking straight at her. He smiled very faintly at her blush before following the ladies out.

Lauren sagged when he left, the tension finally leaving her.

"Come sit and talk with me, Countess," Lady Paddington called from her armchair. Oh God, no more conversation, she thought, but reluctantly did as she was bid. The moment she seated herself on the footstool, Lady Paddington eagerly leaned forward. "I think they make a handsome couple, don't you?" Beaming, she nodded toward Lord Westfall and Charlotte, still seated on the settee.

"Indeed, madam."

"You should invite Miss Pritchit to join you for your little turn about the park tomorrow. My dear David would like that very much. Now stay a bit, will you? I rather think my nephew is enjoying Miss Pritchit's company, but she will be uncomfortable if you go," she whispered. She could hardly refuse, and the longest supper party in the history of mankind fast became eternal damnation as she sat and listened, stupefied, to Lady Paddington and Mrs. Clark turn a discussion of a new wool cloak into an argument about the proper care and feeding of sheep.

When at last Lord Westfall stood to go, she smiled and assured him she would remember their engagement on the morrow. She very carefully did not look at Lady Pritchit, but she could feel the daggers the woman was staring at her. When Lord Westfall finally made his exit, Lauren stood, determined to take her leave.

"Might I offer you a ride?" Arthur asked after she had wished Lady Paddington and her guests good evening.

"Oh no, but thank you kindly," she said, and with an airy wave, slipped into the foyer before he could press the issue. "Where might I find a hack?" she asked the butler breathlessly as she quickly slipped into her cloak.

"I shall call one for you, milady."

"No! I mean . . . do not trouble yourself. I shall walk to the park—surely I might engage a hack there?"

"Forgive me, ma'am, but I could not recommend it. Wallace! A conveyance for the lady!'' he snapped, and pulled the front door open. Lauren hurried after the dispatched footman, who looked as if he were on an afternoon stroll as he moved down the street toward the park. She debated calling out and urging him to hurry. Never in her life had she wanted to be gone from a place so badly. She just wanted to go home so that she might forget this horrid evening. God, she was such a *fool* for letting Alex unnerve her so badly.

She turned eagerly toward the sound of a coach turning onto the street, her face falling when she saw the ducal crest. It couldn't be. It simply *couldn't* be. Dear God, was she in *hell*? She turned so that her back was to the coach, listening as it drew to a stop. The coach door flung open; she heard the fall of expensive heels on the cobblestone, and mouthed an unladylike curse when the footfall stopped just behind her.

"My, my, if it isn't the countess. I rather thought David would have escorted you home by now so that he might speak to your uncle about his intentions," he said mockingly.

One thing was certain—his extreme arrogance had not lessened since the ball. "I beg your pardon, your grace, but should you not be with your fiancée?" she snapped.

His chuckle was soft and low. "Perhaps. But I promised Arthur a nightcap at White's."

She could feel him standing very close to her; it was just a strange coincidence that her stomach seemed to climb to her throat. She took a nervous step forward. "Well then, just run along and fetch him why don't you? A driver will be along for me any moment." A long moment passed as she waited for some response, but he said nothing. What was he doing? Why did he just stand there? She waited, the curiosity killing her, the need to look almost overwhelming. When she could not endure it another moment, she abruptly peeked over her shoulder.

The insufferable man was grinning.

"Oh! By all that is holy, you are the most *unbearable* man!" she cried impulsively.

His grin deepened. "That is a rather heavy mantle, but I shall very graciously consider the source."

"I beg your pardon? Whatever do you mean by *that*?" she gasped, truly affronted.

"I mean, Countess Bergen," he said, sobering, "that since our reacquaintance at the Granbury reception, you seem quite put out with me."

Put out with him? Really, just because he seemed to think *she* was a fortune-seeker while *he* was to be married to a very pretty woman, she was not *put out* with him. Not in the *least*. The hired hack turned onto the street.

"I had honestly hoped the gardenias would take the edge off your disdain."

That startled her. "The gardenias? But they were from—" Oh God, she had thought they were from Magnus, but she had not actually looked at the card! Her heart started to beat erratically. He had sent her *flowers*! And gardenias, her very favorite!

"Ah, I see," he said quietly. "Too many suitors."

"I . . . I did not know," she murmured as her thoughts tumbled wildly over one another. Why had he sent her flowers? What had the card said? What had the bloody card *said*? She glanced at him over her shoulder and smiled graciously. "They . . . they were lovely. Thank you."

A strange emotion flickered in his eyes. "Not nearly as lovely as the recipient," he said quietly.

That unexpected and tender compliment washed over her. Unsteadily, she took a step toward the curb as the hack rolled to a halt. The footman jumped down from the rear running board, and moved toward the little door.

"Hold!" Alex suddenly barked. Startled, Lauren jerked around to face him. He began to move steadily toward her. Instinctively, she made a desperate lunge for the hack, but somehow, he reached it before her.

"Hold, driver!" he called as his arm shot up beside her, effectively barring the door and blocking her from the curious gaze of any onlooker. "Thank you, that will be all," he said to the footman. The man glanced uneasily at Lauren, but not one to argue with a duke, he quickly pivoted on his heel and disappeared through the gate.

Trapped between the hack and his powerful frame, Lauren pressed into the carriage as he slowly leaned into her, bracing his weight against the hack. His eyes flicked across her bosom, lingered on her pursed lips, then traveled slowly to her eyes. "God help me, but you intrigue me, Lauren," he murmured. His sweet breath fanned her cheek, sending a convulsive shiver down her spine. "So full of surprises, aren't you? I can't help but wonder if that giant is worthy of your affections."

His nearness was a powerful drug on her senses—her knees shook and she frantically clutched her reticule to her stomach. "Who . . . Magnus?" she mumbled thoughtlessly.

A lazy smile stretched his lips, contradicting the dark, pointed look in his green eyes. "Yes, him."

Unconsciously, her eyes fell to his mouth. The memory of that long ago kiss came flooding back to her in the form of a queer tingle in the pit of her stomach. Intuitively, she understood herself to be on dangerous ground. "I—I think you sh-should leave me alone," she stammered.

"I think I should too, but I am afraid I cannot." With that startling revelation, he leaned closer and gently laid his palm against her cheek. Lauren drew a sharp breath at his gentle touch, astounded by the heat that quickly spread down her neck.

He meant to kiss her.

For one insane moment, she desperately hoped he would, but when she felt his breath against her lips, fear, propriety, and the image of Lady Marlaine caused her to bring her hand up and push against his chest. *"Don't do it,"* she whispered frantically.

The husky timbre of her voice sent blood pumping furiously through Alex's veins. He covered her hand with his and pressed it tightly against his racing heart. She gasped; her gaze locked on his hand. God, but he was powerless to resist her, and slowly he leaned down until his mouth brushed lightly against her full lips. Jolted by the warmth of her breath, he groaned softly and leaned into her, delicately painting her lips with his. The tension left her jaw, and he swept his tongue inside the forbidden sweetness, savoring the faint taste of wine, the smooth veneer of her teeth.

He could feel the tremble in her slender body and he deepened the kiss, wanting to fill his senses with her. Her head tilted backward as his kiss grew more insistent; her fingers slowly fanned across his rapidly beating heart. Dangerous desire spiraled through him, unfurling rapidly in his groin.

The sound of voices shook him; Lady Pritchit's sharp voice calling good night shattered the moment. Stunned, he jerked his head up and pivoted about, dropping Lauren's hand from his chest. The Pritchits were at the threshold of his aunt's house, preparing to leave. He stumbled backward as Lauren clumsily pushed past him and climbed into the hack unaided.

She had dropped her reticule. He was, uncharacteristically and overwhelmingly, embarrassed. He hastily picked up the little beaded bag and handed it to her. Lauren refused to meet his gaze, staring straight ahead, clearly mortified. He shot a look at the driver and commanded hoarsely, "Russell Square."

A rush of shameful anxiety escaped his lungs as the carriage turned toward the park. The guilt and shock at what he had just done warred with the heat of her, the *taste* of her that still coursed through his veins. He ran a hand through his hair, realized he was trembling slightly, and shoved both hands in his pockets. That was, he thought madly, a *very* close call—in more ways than one.

He turned and walked shakily out of the shadows and toward the house, calling a greeting to his aunt.

Chapter 12

Lauren's sleep was unsettled after that reckless kiss. In the morning she awoke with feelings that were new to her, and conflicting thoughts of Alex. The only thing that saved her from going completely mad was the arrival of two letters from Rosewood. Davis thrust them at her the moment she finished breakfast; with a delighted cry, Lauren closeted herself in the small dining room to read them.

Mrs. Peterman, in her weekly letter, proudly reported a bumper crop of tomatoes, which Fastidious Thadeus was doing his best to trade at his apothecary shop. The second letter filled her with joy. In her sprawling girlish handwriting, Lydia used many exclamation points to relay the news that Ramsey Baines had smiled at her after church services. After a long, rambling discussion of that monumental event, she wrote that Leonard and Rupert were repairing another fence, and that Theodore requested a book of poetry if there were funds for such an extravagance. Horace had fashioned a pirate's hat from one of Lauren's old bonnets and could not be persuaded to remove it, even when Mrs. Peterman had threatened to cut his head off at the neck. Sally, bless her heart, missed Paul so badly that she made him the guest of honor at all her imaginary tea parties, which she hosted at least twice daily.

A haze of unshed tears filled her eyes. She missed the children desperately, but Ethan's promise of a trip to Rosewood had been put off for another fortnight. He had railed at her when she protested, claiming that it was her own fault, and when she decided on one of the two good offers he had for her hand, she could return to Rosewood.

If that was to be the prerequisite, she might never see Rosewood again. She was suddenly reminded of Magnus repeating his offer just two nights past, and his avowal that he was prepared to wait for her answer as long as it took. It was touching in a way; his rugged face looked almost hopeful, as if he somehow believed that she could come to love him. In another place and time, she might have considered his offer. *Might* have. But at that moment and more so now, the only thing she could think of was Alex, and her heart unexpectedly twisted in her chest.

With a heavy sigh, she glanced at the clock. There was still enough time to respond to Lydia's letter before Lord Westfall called. Better she occupy her thoughts with something before despair swallowed her whole.

Alex galloped to a lake in the middle of Hyde Park and reined the mare to a sharp halt. Pushing his hat back from his forehead, he frowned at the water as the horse drank her fill. Marlaine's demeanor this morning still perplexed him. He had offered to take her to the park as she had requested last evening, but she had looked at him strangely and had asked in that soft way of hers if he did not have a previous engagement. After explaining his appointment had been canceled, Marlaine considered him curiously for a long moment, then politely declined, citing a headache.

She did not have a headache. No, she was rather extraordinarily perturbed by his invitation, that had been clear. She had obviously mistaken his gesture of conciliation as something altogether odious. It had irritated him to the extent that he had come to the park alone—an event, he mused, that was as unprecedented as it was boring. It was not as if he did not have a mountain of work waiting for him and a speech to prepare for the Lords. He would take the mare around again, he decided, then return home.

He did not allow himself to think why, exactly, he had come in the first place. Nor did he dare to think about that kiss last night. What must he have been thinking? *Bloody, bloody fool.*

He tugged the horse around and started forward, his thoughts still on Marlaine's reticence. Surely whatever ailed her would be forgotten with a new bracelet. Mulling it over, he turned onto the main path just as David's phaeton rounded a bend ahead of him. His cousin didn't see him. He was too engrossed in his conversation with Lauren.

Alex felt an immediate constriction in his chest at the sight of her with David. How ridiculous! He had heard them make plans for the drive today—bloody hell, it was the reason he had come, whether he wanted to admit it or not. He slowed his horse to a walk, greatly irritated with himself. This was *absurd.* He was engaged to be married, had his pick of the prettiest mistresses in London, and had absolutely no business chasing about the park on the slim hope of seeing a young woman. It mattered little that her kiss had ignited him—he should go home and stop this *pointless* pursuit.

Inexplicably, he did not move as the phaeton headed straight for him. "David!" he called. His cousin's head jerked up, and seeing Alex, he hastily pulled the carriage to a halt. Lauren, shading her eyes with her hand, looked up, her blue eyes slicing across him. For a brief moment, she looked almost sick. It did not set well with him at all, and he shifted uncomfortably in his saddle.

"Sutherland! What a surprise!" David grinned.

"Good day, David. Countess, it is a pleasure," he said coolly.

"Thank you," she answered tightly, and glanced at her lap.

"Nice piece of horseflesh you've got there. Must be the mare you gave Lady Marlaine?"

Alex flinched inwardly at the mention of Marlaine. "It is. She is not comfortable riding her just yet."

"Ah, not a better day to practice, either," David said wistfully. "I thought to take Countess Bergen around to Kensington Gardens. Why don't you tie her to the back of the carriage and ride along?"

Lauren's mouth dropped open, clearly appalled by the suggestion. *That* made him angry, angry enough that he impetuously decided that she would just have to put up with him. No country countess was going to keep him from enjoying a very fine afternoon. "Grand idea, Westfall," he said, and swung a leg over the saddle, dropping quickly to the ground. He secured the mare's reins to the back of the phaeton, reminding himself that she was just another woman, even if she did happen to be the only one in all of London who could not abide him. He marched around to the side of the phaeton and hauled himself onto the seat. David had climbed down to adjust the harness, and Lauren, damn it, was staring at him as if he had sprouted horns.

He had not sprouted horns, in Lauren's humble estimation. He had become, impossibly, even more ruggedly handsome in his brown coat and skintight buff breeches. She recalled that she once thought he looked like a man who scaled mountains. Scaled them? He probably *rearranged* them!

"Countess Bergen?" Lord Westfall said, motioning at the carriage seat. She moved a fraction of an inch and busied herself with rearranging her skirts. When Lord Westfall vaulted upward, practically landing in her lap, she did not so much as breathe. She scooted another fraction of inch toward the duke. Lord Westfall wriggled uncomfortably and cast a meaningful look at her. She reluctantly scooted another inch, then another, until her escort was satisfied and her thigh was pressed tightly against the duke's iron one.

The chestnut lurched forward with a slap of the reins, and the sudden movement of the carriage caused her to pitch against Alex. Lauren frantically righted herself, perching precariously on the edge of the seat with a spine as straight and stiff as Lady Pritchit's attitude.

"Where did you find the mare?" Lord Westfall asked.

"Rouen."

France? Dear God, the expense of bringing that horse across the channel must have been greater than the price of the horse itself!

"A trotter then?" Lord Westfall continued.

"Yes."

Lord Westfall chuckled. "Lady Marlaine must get on her back if she's to learn to ride her."

"She will," Alex responded curtly.

Her escort laughed cheerfully. "Yes, I rather suspect she will," he grinned, then lapsed into a monologue about horse-breeding in Rouen, a subject, apparently, with which he was well acquainted. Lauren barely heard Alex's clipped responses, she could scarcely even breathe with his thigh searing an imprint into her own. She concentrated on her lap, stealing furtive glimpses of those powerful thighs. His strong hands, encased in supple leather gloves, rode lightly on his knees. She remembered the feel of his palm on her cheek, and a furious blush crept into her face. Mortified by her body's sudden revolt, she did not notice they had come to the gardens until Lord Westfall pointed out a particularly colorful patch of columbine.

"Lovely," she muttered.

"Why, they are the best in all of England," Lord Westfall exclaimed as he brought the carriage to a halt.

"Perhaps Countess Bergen is indifferent to flowers," Alex remarked coolly.

Indifferent? If only he knew! She risked a look at him then. His jaw clamped firmly shut, he returned her gaze with a look of cool displeasure.

The mare began to neigh, jerking at her tether. "She's a bit unsettled, Alex. You might have to ride it out of her," Lord Westfall said, peering over his shoulder.

Apathetically, Alex asked, "Want to give it a go?"

Lord Westfall jerked forward to peer around her, grinning eagerly. Oh *no,* he was going to leave her with him! She tried to catch his eye, but Lord Westfall was far too enamored of the mare, and did not hesitate to toss the reins to Alex as he clambered out of the carriage with boyish enthusiasm. "Perhaps a quick turn about the park. What say I meet you at the entrance? You don't mind, do you, Countess?" he asked, but had already untied the mare.

She honestly had no idea if she minded or not, because she could not even *think.* Speechless, she watched Lord Westfall swing up onto the mare's back and rein in tightly to keep her from bucking. With a jaunty wave, he galloped off, his coat billowing behind him. She was still watching him in disbelief when the carriage started forward.

"You shall see him again, do not fret," Alex muttered. "I promise I shall not assault you, so you may ease that look of horror."

A gasp of surprise lodged in her throat. Oh, she was horrified, all right, of what his mere presence did to every fiber of her body.

"What is the matter, Countess? Cat got your tongue?" he demanded, glancing irritably at her from the corner of his eye.

"No," she said hastily. "I just . . ."

"Just what?" he demanded.

She swallowed nervously. "I just . . . I suppose I am not *accustomed—*"

"I am sorry," he interjected, his jaw clenching tightly. "I am hardly accustomed to accosting women on the street, either. I must have drank too much port," he muttered.

Too much port. God, how very deflating—a drunken moment to him, a snatch of heaven to her. She glanced at her hands clasped tightly in her lap, fighting another surge of strange emotion bubbling to the surface. She was a damned fool, but she had her pride, and she would rather die than let him see how that admission hurt her. She suddenly giggled. "Oh, *that*. You must think nothing of it! Of *course* it was the port! No, no, no, I was referring to Lord Westfall. I am unaccustomed to being left for a horse!" Her laughter sounded shrill to her ears.

His jaw flinched. "Please accept my apology," he muttered, and focused his gaze on the road ahead.

"Well, of course I shall!" she said with irrational gaiety. "We won't speak of it again."

He muttered something under his breath, but the hard edges of his face seemed to soften. "And I apologize for David, too, but my cousin lives for horses. He would have suggested it himself before the end of our drive, I assure you."

Lauren risked another glance at him, recalling how that stern mouth had so tenderly touched her own. She realized she was trembling, and nervously cleared her throat, afraid to utter one single word for fear that it would come tumbling out in some incoherent, gushing way. She could not think of him like that. She had no *right* to think of him like that. "It's . . . it's a pity Lady Marlaine could not join you for a ride—I think she would have liked it very much. You will give her my regards, won't you?" she chirped, wincing inwardly at her foolish, *foolish* remark.

"Naturally," he muttered. A muscle in his jaw jumped erratically. She forced herself to turn away and concentrate on the scenery. They rode in silence for what seemed an eternity, until they came to a lake. Alex unexpectedly brought the carriage to a halt. "It has been many years since I have gone so deeply into the park; one tends to forget the beauty of it."

"It's wonderful," Lauren agreed wistfully.

He paused, looking out at the lake, seemingly a bit more relaxed. "Would you like to walk about?" he suddenly asked, and leapt to the ground before she could answer. Through no will of her own, she nodded, and the next thing she knew, his broad hands had grasped her waist to lift her down. As her feet touched the ground, his hands stilled on her waist. He looked closely at her. Too closely. Lauren felt herself color, and quickly stepped away before he could see how he stirred her.

She thought she heard a faint sigh as he gestured toward a path leading into a copse of willows. She obediently moved, and they walked, side by side, neither speaking. The sounds of human voices, horses neighing, and the creaks and moans of a dozen carriages began to fade as they wandered deeper into the grove. Under normal circumstances, it would have been a beautiful, peaceful walk, but Lauren could not dismiss the nagging thought that she should not be alone with him. She should definitely not be alone with him.

But she did not ask him to turn back.

"When I was a boy, my brothers and I spent many hours exploring this park. If I am not mistaken, we should find a small clearing just ahead."

He was right. The grass was tall and damp in the seldom-used clearing, and as she fidgeted with her skirts so as not to ruin the hem, Alex strolled to the edge of a small pond and went down on his haunches to drink. The thigh that had touched hers was suddenly bulging against the fabric of his breeches. God, but it was exceedingly warm, she thought suddenly, and impulsively removed her bonnet as he splashed water on his face. The muscles in his back strained against the fabric of his coat; she tried to imagine what his bare back looked like. It was a mistake; she felt a queer sensation in her belly as she gazed at him. She abruptly pivoted on her heel and strolled across the clearing before her thoughts went any further.

Alex, too, was trying to keep his thoughts simple, but it impossible. God help him, he had once noticed only her eyes, but now, he took in everything—her trim figure, the way her gown hugged every feminine curve, the taper of her elegant fingers from which her bonnet dangled carelessly. He noticed little things, like the way she worried her bottom lip when flustered, or how she demurely dipped her gaze to the ground when in repose. And now, the way she strolled across the clearing, seemingly without pretense or guile.

Her hair was knotted at her nape, and he remembered it as it was in the pumpkin field when he had first seen her— thick, wavy and unbound. He stood slowly with the fleeting image of her lying naked in his bed, her luxuriant hair framing her. Bloody hell, he had no business being here. He tried to think of Marlaine, tried to remember her eyes. Marlaine's eyes were large, brown, and pretty.

But they did not sparkle; not like Lauren's.

She stopped to inhale the fragrance of a lilac bush. The thought of her married to that German suddenly invaded his thoughts, pricking at him like a thorn. It was none of his concern, none at all, but that angel was too enchanting, too pretty . . . too *good* for the Bavarian. She was too good for any man, any man but—

He stopped himself right there.

Lauren turned away from the lilac bush, absently swinging her discarded bonnet, and smiled nervously at him.

"I am curious," he said at length, "how did you manage to escape Madgoose? He never seems to be far from your side."

A slight frown creased her brow. *"Magnus,"* she corrected him, "is my friend. There are times he accompanies me, and times he does not. He is only visiting London."

Alex arched a dubious brow. "Really? I have not seen him *visit* with anyone but you."

"That's because," she said with a pert toss of her head, "he does not know many people in London. And he does not care for small talk."

"Does he care for orphans?" he snapped. His own remark surprised him. It was terribly rude, but he smiled with satisfaction when her brows snapped to a dark V.

"As a matter of fact, he came to London by way of Rosewood. He has met the children and finds them delightful."

"I suppose he must if he is to win your hand."

She folded her arms tightly across her middle. Her bonnet bounced at her side, telling him that a foot tapped anxiously beneath her skirts. "He is not going to *win* my hand," she said with great authority. "Count Bergen is a . . ." She glanced at the ground. The bonnet grew still. "And when is your wedding planned?" she suddenly asked.

God, right to the gut. It wasn't enough that he felt a complete heel for what he had done to her last night, or that she seemed to think it was little more than a moment's indiscretion. It wasn't enough that his desire to see her again confused him on a level too deep to fathom. But she had to mention Marlaine, the *one* person in all of bloody England he did not want to think about at the moment. "August," he ground out.

"Lady Marlaine shall make a lovely bride." She attempted to smile, but it seemed to be painted on her face. Her eyes said something altogether different.

"Not as lovely a bride as you will make," he said softly.

Lauren gaped at him. "I beg your pardon, your grace, but I find your compliments . . . rather perplexing," she said, frowning.

Perplexing and damned annoying, he would grant her that. But not nearly as annoying as a streak of unwarranted, unfounded jealousy. Alex swept the hat from his head and shoved a hand through his hair. She cocked her head to one side, frowning prettily at him. In the dappled light beneath the branches of a willow, her face reminded him of a fine painting in which one discovered something new every time one looked. His pulse began to beat at a clip. "Do you enjoy paintings?" he asked idly.

Surprise scudded across her face. "Pardon?"

"Do you enjoy paintings? Portraits, that sort of thing?"

She looked at him as if he had just asked her to shoot his expensive mare. "I—I—why do you ask?" she asked warily as he strolled toward her.

"You remind me of a portrait."

"A portrait?"

A priceless portrait at that, he thought, and at the moment, the view was his alone. "Does that disturb you?"

"Well . . . *what* portrait?" she asked suspiciously.

He casually circled her, covertly admiring her from all angles while he pretended to take in their surroundings. He came to a deliberate halt behind her, taking in the flush of her neck, the soft curve of her shoulder. *" 'Mine eye hath played the painter and hath stelled thy beauty's form in table of my heart. My body is the frame wherein 'tis held, and perspective it is best painter's art.' That portrait,"* he murmured. Clearly taken aback, an alluring pink hue arose in her cheeks as he slowly circled to stand in front of her. She shyly dropped her gaze to the buttons of his waistcoat. "Shakespeare," he murmured, "wrote about you."

Her lashes slowly lifted. "False flattery, your grace."

"I assure you, it is not. I part company with the dictates of etiquette when it will not allow a beautiful thing to be honestly and openly admired." Her blush deepened, and for the first time since the Granbury reception, she smiled fully, knocking the breath from him. Instantly consumed with the desire to taste those full, rose-colored lips, he impulsively brushed his knuckles across her cheek. She drew a soft breath at his unexpected touch, and in one blinding moment,

Alex saw his angel. The sparkling cobalt eyes, the dark lashes, the slightly parted lips. "You are," he murmured unthinkingly, "an incomparable beauty. And that, madam, comes from the depths of my being."

She hastily took a step backward. "I don't understand why you keep *saying* those things, your grace," she said nervously. "It's not right—"

"There was a time you would call me by my given name. Say my name, Lauren." He closed the distance between them, his fingers reaching for the bend where her neck curved into her shoulder, her skin like satin to the touch. Her blue eyes widened. "Say my name," he said again as one hand gently cupped her elbow and pulled her toward him.

"A-Alex," she stammered. A shudder coursed his spine. *"Alex,"* she repeated softly.

When his lips brushed across hers, she shivered convulsively and sent another alarming bolt of desire through him. God, she tasted sweet. His hand tenderly caressed her neck as his lips slowly and artfully softened hers. A strong tide of pleasure began to flow through him—he anchored her to his stark arousal, his chest almost burning from the sensation of her body pressed against him. He felt her hands slide around his waist, gripping him tightly as she timidly parted her lips.

Lord in heaven, he was on fire. He slipped his tongue into her mouth, swirling it about her soft depths. When her tongue cautiously brushed between his lips, he imploded with unprecedented need.

Whatever she had done must have startled him, Lauren marveled, because his grip suddenly tightened. His tongue thrust against hers with an urgency so fierce that it battered at her defenses and lured her into responding with equal intensity. Somehow, the simple knot at her nape came loose; her hair tumbled around her shoulders and he grasped a fistful. Impossibly, he deepened his kiss, the stroke of his tongue urging her to want him. Oh, she wanted him, as badly as she had ever wanted anything. She pressed herself against him, amazed by the shocking sensuality of his hardness against her belly. When his hand slid down her neck to cup her breast, she gasped against his mouth and reflexively met his burning ardor with her own. Yet she had no idea how to give him everything she was feeling, to match his hunger.

The experience jarred her. It also sent an alarm rattling in her brain, and she suddenly broke away, surprising even herself. Alex slowly lifted his head and touched his fingers to her temple. *"Angel,"* he murmured.

The remnant of his kiss and his seductive words stirred deeply within her. His eyes, their liquid depths unfathomable, floated across her face. Her gaze fell to his lips, and suddenly, she realized what she had done. She had allowed herself to be thoroughly kissed by a man betrothed to another woman, had allowed him to stoke an unimaginable desire within her. How *easily* she had allowed it! It was so wrong, so very *wrong.* "Oh *God*!" she choked. She closed her eyes against his handsome visage, but it did no good. He immediately attempted to encircle her in his arms, but distrustful of her own body, Lauren pushed against his chest.

"Don't," he hastily whispered. "Don't think. Don't do anything, Lauren, just let me hold you," he said, reaching for her.

Terror engulfed her; she desired him as she had never desired anything in her life, and the depth of it scared her to death. "No, no—this is *madness*! We cannot do this!"

"Lauren—"

"No!" she shrieked.

He immediately dropped his hands. He stared at her, his eyes searching her face. Unsteady, she watched his chest rise and fall with each ragged breath. In a desperate attempt to clear the longing from her mind, she counted them—one, two, three, four—Fear melted away to humiliation. Like a tart, she had willingly accepted his advances. Her pride completely shattered, she whirled away from him. "You must think me terribly wanton—"

"Lauren!" he said sharply, and grabbing her shoulders, forced her around to face him. "Don't *ever* say that!" he said angrily. "If there is any blame to be had, it is *mine*." He stooped down so that they were on eye level and peered intently into her eyes. "But there is something very strong between us, Lauren, you cannot deny it!"

He spoke so earnestly, she believed he felt the turmoil, too. Slowly, she shook her head. "I don't deny it."

His eyes seemed to glow like fire. "When I see you, when I am near you, I lose myself. I—" He caught himself. He straightened, looking blindly over her shoulder. "I just lose myself," he repeated beneath his breath, and pulled her into his embrace.

God, she had been lost since he first appeared at Rosewood. Even then, she had wanted this man with all her heart. Confusion, extraordinary longing, and a sense of terrible distress rifled through her. She buried her face in his shoulder. "I am lost, too," she muttered, unconsciously voicing her thoughts aloud. "But it is so wrong! Nothing can come of it."

She felt the tension in his body, then his hands slid from her, falling leaden to his sides. "I know, angel. It can never be," he mumbled wearily. "It can *never* be."

He sounded so ravaged that her heart sank with despair. He had just ignited a flame in her that would not be doused, not for the rest of her life, she was quite certain. It was so grossly unfair. She turned away from him, blinking back a rush of tears as she fumbled madly with her hair. "I . . . I want to go home," she gasped.

"Of course." He gestured solemnly toward the path, his eyes downcast. Desperate, she preceded him, walking swiftly to the phaeton, afraid to look back. When she reached the carriage, she tossed her bonnet onto the seat and hauled herself up, afraid that he would touch her and start the inferno blazing in her again. He climbed up beside her and wordlessly signaled the chestnut forward.

The drive around the park was painfully silent, and she was relieved to see Lord Westfall waiting for them near the entrance. He was grinning, and as they rolled to a stop he reached down to pat the mare's neck.

"Fine mare, Alex . . ." He paused, glancing at Lauren. A strange look came over his face that she immediately read as disgust. Mother of God, she could have died of shame. Lord Westfall flicked a cool gaze to Alex. "I should see Countess Bergen home," he said curtly, and slid off the horse.

Alex did not hesitate to trade places with him. He mounted the mare swiftly, then glanced at her, his blank expression seemingly carved from stone. "Good day," he said, and turned the horse in the direction of Pall Mall. Her chest tightened painfully as he galloped away.

The carriage abruptly swayed, bringing her back to her senses. She glanced shyly at Lord Westfall. He was obviously trying very hard to pretend as if nothing was amiss, but was failing miserably in his efforts. She had never felt more ashamed in her life.

Nor had she ever felt more terribly confused.

Chapter 13

Still highly agitated by the experience in the clearing, Lauren stomped into the town house and flung her bonnet onto an entry table, not noticing Davis until he picked it up. "Parlor," he announced, and extended a hand for her reticule. Marvelous, she thought. Ethan would probably demand to know if she had gleaned Lord Westfall's annual income during their drive.

But it was only Paul and he was alone in the parlor. She suppressed the urge to groan as his eyes swept her disheveled appearance, from the top of her head where wisps of hair had come loose from her attempt at a coif, to the grass stains on the hem of her gown. He raised a brow high above the other. "Dear Lord, were you caught in a storm?"

With a harried shrug, Lauren looked down at her gown. "The wind is bit brisk today."

"It looks as if your carriage rolled over," he said, eyeing her suspiciously.

"The grass was wet."

Paul frowned. "I understood you to say that Lord Westfall was driving you."

She did not like the tone of his voice at all. On top of everything else, it was enough to drive her to drink. She marched to a cart in the corner of the room and picked up a decanter of sherry. "He *did* drive me. But we met his cousin, and Lord Westfall wanted to ride his horse. It's from Rouen, and he is quite fond of horses, so while we were waiting, we had a short turn about," she muttered evasively.

"We?" Paul asked.

Good heavens, was this an inquisition? "His cousin," she said, frowning.

"His cousin? Who is his cousin?" Paul demanded.

"The Duke of Sutherland," Lauren muttered.

"The *Duke* of *Sutherland*?" her brother loudly exclaimed.

Lauren impatiently discarded the sherry. "Yes! The Duke of Sutherland!"

"He is engaged!"

"I am aware of that!" she snapped, and picked up a bottle of whiskey.

Paul moaned irritably. "This won't do, not at all. You are inviting scandal!"

That did it. She set the whiskey aside and turned to face her brother. "I went for a *drive,* Paul, a simple drive! Why on earth should that invite scandal? And just what do you think I have to *protect* from scandal?"

Clearly taken aback, Paul peered closely—a little too closely to suit her. She suddenly feared he could see Alex's kiss on her lips, and turned abruptly, picking up a decanter of port. "You have your good name to protect, and you know it," he said softly. "You cannot hope to make a decent match if there are salacious whispers about you and Sutherland. And rumors certainly won't help his work."

"*His* work?" she asked, flabbergasted.

Paul suddenly sat forward, his expression earnest.

"Don't you know who he is, Lauren? He is, at the moment, the *only* champion of reforms in the House of Lords!" Lauren made a sound of impatience in response to that; Paul's face darkened. "Let me say it another way. If, by some bloody miracle, the reform bill should pass the Commons, it must then pass the Lords! Sutherland is the only one who can see it through, and I daresay even *he* can't do it without Whitcomb's support! Rumor has it that Whitcomb is lukewarm to reform for several reasons, and would probably welcome a good excuse not to support his future son-in-law!" he exclaimed. At Lauren's look of bafflement, Paul fell backward in his chair, exasperated. "Don't you *see*? Sutherland's progressive leadership could be squelched with just a *hint* of scandal, and *particularly* one affecting his fiancée!" he declared roughly.

Confused at his reasoning, Lauren frowned. "I don't understand what that has to do with—"

"It has everything to do with Rosewood!" Paul loudly interjected. "The taxes are killing us, you know that! The laws are designed to protect the wealthy, not people like us—"

"The land is overused at Rosewood, Paul! *That* is what is killing us!" she countered angrily.

"It would not matter if Rosewood were the most fertile land in the country! Unless something is done about high taxes, we cannot afford the labor necessary to *work* the land! And the only person powerful enough or influential enough or *willing* to change all that is *Sutherland*!"

Stung, Lauren shrugged indifferently. Paul fairly exploded. "Don't pursue him!" he shouted.

Outraged by that accusation, Lauren gasped. "I am not *pursuing* him!"

"Sutherland is above your reach. He is one of the most influential peers of the realm, and he is to be married at the end of the Season. If *he* is paying *you* any particular attention, it is because he would trifle with you!"

She gaped in disbelief at her brother, who was now, apparently, an expert on the Duke of Sutherland. What could he possibly know? *He* had never met Mr. Christian or been kissed by a duke. He had no idea the myriad feelings that man could evoke, feelings that were *still* rifling through her and turning her inside out. She placed the port on the drink cart. "I have had a rather long day. Please excuse me." Turning on her heels, she walked swiftly to the door.

"Do not see him again, Lauren," Paul warned.

She whipped around, her eyes narrowed with anger. "I understand the duke resides on Audley Street, Paul. Perhaps you should dispatch a messenger to inform him that as I am so wholly unsuitable as a *friend,* he should cease to present himself every blasted place I go!" she exclaimed, and sailed through the door before he could utter another word.

Several miserable days followed in which she could think of little else than Alex. As if it made any difference, she mourned the fact that he was so far above her in social situation. *Miles* above her—so high that she could no longer even pretend. Mr. Christian, the stuff of her dreams, was gone, and in his place was the very handsome Duke of Sutherland. She rebuked herself for desiring him so completely and hopelessly, *particularly* since he was engaged. Particularly since he was so bloody *prominent.*

She read every paper she could get her hands on, devouring the news of what was happening at Parliament with a mixture of awe and resignation. Some said the Duke of Sutherland was a Radical, a dangerous man with a dangerous agenda. Others said his progressive thinking was just what the country needed, that his foresight was inspirational. The middle class cheered his efforts; the Quality sniffed disdainfully that his quest for economic and social reform would lead to Catholic seats in Parliament. Some editorials hinted that his motives were not altogether pure—the duke's shipping empire stood to gain from the very reforms he touted.

Nonetheless, *The Times* called one of his many speeches to the august membership of the Lords brilliant. He argued that unfair representation and oppressive taxation, the very reasons England had lost America, were now the very reasons England could lose its own people. Reform, he insisted, was not an academic debate, but imperative to the health and well-being of the Crown.

As political pundits argued in print whether Sutherland was helping or hurting the reform movement, on one thing they all agreed: Reform could not pass the Lords without the influence of the Duke of Sutherland, and Sutherland could not garner enough influence without the Earl of Whitcomb. No one could dispute the importance of the Christian-Reese family alliance.

But the dailies gave every indication that the Earl of Whitcomb was less than enthusiastic about reform—apparently, the popular earl did not want to include Catholic emancipation in the reform movement. He was purported to have said that while some change was vital to the nation, too much change was dangerous.

As Lauren pounded her fist into her pillow for the hundredth time one night, she realized Paul was right. Alex was fighting an uphill battle, a battle for reforms that Rosewood desperately needed. Any hint of impropriety would taint what good he had done or could hope to do, particularly, she gathered, among the old guard, who did not tolerate public indiscretions. And as nothing could *ever* come of her consuming desire for him, her only hope was to put him out of her mind, to avoid him at all costs.

If only it were that easy.

God help her, if she closed her eyes, she could still feel his hands and lips on her. She could still smell his cologne, see his handsome face and green eyes. His kiss had ignited a fire in her that was left smoldering, and nothing, apparently,

would extinguish it. God knew she had tried, but she was
incapable of suppressing her thoughts of Alex or the overwhelming desire to be held by him again. He had awakened
in her the powerful desire for a man's touch. The fiery kisses
they had shared had only scratched the surface of what she
instinctively knew could be between a man and a woman,
and she ached to know it all, to feel him inside her, his
hands and mouth on her skin, his breath on her neck. And
damn it, it seemed *nothing* would ease such extraordinary
yearning—as the poet Keats had once put it, *"yearning like
a God in pain."*

But it could never be.

Nothing short of a miracle could change anything. There
was nothing she could do but put him out of her mind, once
and for all, and concentrate on the task of finding a suitable
match. She had to think of Rosewood, and above all, she had
to stay away from him. It was bloody impossible to be near
him and not want him, and utterly devastating to desire him
so fiercely.

Lauren tried to cope by focusing on a weekend trip to
Rosewood. Ethan had finally relented, and they planned to
leave in two days' time. The anticipation helped to buoy her
spirits, and she busied herself as best she could. She took to
visiting the Haddington Road Infirmary to fill the time. She
had gone once with Paul to visit an old school chum of his
who had fallen into ill health. As they had walked down the
corridor, several patients looked up, hopeful that they had
come to visit them. Realizing how lonely some of them
were—particularly the elderly—Lauren had been drawn
back. It meant so much to the patients, and it filled a void in
her.

She donned a new soft-green gown one glorious morning
after a solid week of putting Alex from her mind. It was a
perfect day for the Darfield garden party, and she had promised Abbey she would come. Actually, she was looking *forward* to the garden party, anxious to pass the time until the

following morning when they would leave for Rosewood. That, she mused, was a sign she was finally able to put some distance between her feelings for Alex Christian and the reality of who he was—the Duke of Sutherland.

Alex Christian, however, was a man obsessed.

Taunted by her memory, he had tried to erase Lauren's image with copious amounts of port, but it had not helped—nor had what little sleep he had gotten. He was not even deterred from his thoughts after meeting Lauren's rather odious uncle in the company of Mrs. Clark and Aunt Paddy one day, or the rather frightful discovery that the ignominious man was a childhood chum of Mrs. Clark. There was nothing on God's earth that could turn his thoughts from the angel—not Marlaine, not his impending nuptials, not even Lauren's very cool behavior toward him.

Two nights past, he had bumped into her at the Fordham mansion. Although she had managed to avoid eye contact with him, he had been unable to keep his eyes from her. In a sumptuous gown of ice-blue silk that left little to his imagination, she had smiled thinly, mumbling her rather terse responses to his small talk, all the while studying the tips of her slippers. And then Madgoose had intervened. That damned German was beginning to irritate him greatly—so greatly that he had walked away without even excusing himself.

Yet he had unwillingly glanced back and had caught Lauren looking at him. The unreadable expression in her vivid blue eyes was almost as disturbing as seeing her dancing with Madgoose later, laughing at something he said, and smiling that devastating smile of hers.

It had almost undone him.

It had also left him feeling intolerably restless.

The restlessness had continued well into the days that followed. At the Vauxhall Gardens fireworks display, he had chafed with unease for the better part of two hours as he sat with Marlaine in a box reserved for dignitaries. No matter how hard he tried to keep his thoughts on his fiancée, he could not keep his mind from wandering to Lauren. When Marlaine requested a walk about, he was grateful for the distraction, and had led her on an aimless stroll through the crowds.

He did not see Lauren until he was almost upon her.

Standing near Madgoose in the dim evening light, she did not notice him, either. Staring up at the dark sky, she smiled brilliantly as a charge exploded in the night air. Spellbound, Alex watched as she tilted her head back and stretched her arms out, as if his angel sought heaven's light. As the glittering light had faded from the sky, she had uttered, " *'The Sun*'s *rim dips; the stars rush out; at one stride comes the dark.'* " The stanza was from *The Rime of the Ancient Mariner,* one of his favorite poems. It had stirred him so deeply he had hardly heard Marlaine speak his name, or notice the cold glare Madgoose had bestowed on him. They had walked on, just as Lauren turned. He was certain he had seen a flicker in her eyes, a brief surge of . . . *something.* But her eyes had quickly shuttered and she had turned away again, pretending not to have noticed him.

He was a man obsessed.

One bright, sun-drenched day, Alex smiled thinly at Marlaine's enthusiasm for the Darfield garden party. For her sake, he was prepared to endure the chatter of the prowlers for hours if he must, but when he walked out onto the terrace with Marlaine on his arm, he heard Lauren's gentle laugh. It shook him—for some reason, he had not thought that she would be there.

Bothered by the strange churning of his gut, he stiffly greeted Michael and Abbey then kissed his mother, who had arrived earlier with Aunt Paddy. He then took a seat—prudently, he thought—as far away from Lauren as he could get. Only then did he allow himself to look at her.

"Your grace, you have come just in time!" Paddy insisted with great exuberance. "Honestly, there can be no consensus gained among us! You shall help us, shan't you?"

"I shall certainly try, Aunt. What seems to be the issue?" he asked, stealing a glance at Lauren. Smiling serenely, her eyes fixed on a point in the middle of the group. He had the distinct impression she was determined not to look at him.

"As you are to be married in St. Paul's Cathedral at precisely eleven o'clock in the morning—"

"On a Friday," clarified Mrs. Clark.

"On a Friday, and as it is a summer wedding, I thought that pews would be most handsomely set off with lilies of the valley, but your dear mother has suggested white roses."

Alex exchanged a weary look with Michael. "I shall be quite happy with whatever Marlaine decides." He smiled at his bride-to-be; her fair cheeks pinkened as she shyly returned his smile.

"Oh, that is not very helpful a'tall! Very well, then, we shall inquire of Countess Bergen *her* opinion," the elderly woman decreed, and turned her head so sharply that the ringlets about her face bounced like fat little sausages.

Lauren's head jerked up, her serene smile gone. "*My* opinion? I, ah, think either one would be very lovely," she murmured uncertainly to Paddy's nod.

Paddy frowned. "Come now, surely you have an *opinion*?"

"She is not required to have an opinion," Lady Thistlecourt imperiously informed her. Paddy shifted an impatient look to the terror of the loo tables.

"Paddy," Hannah interrupted lightly, staving off an imminent argument, "what if we mixed them? Lilies and roses?"

"Lilies and roses? How very odd," Mrs. Clark mused. Paddy snorted at what she obviously considered a preposterous suggestion and looked expectantly at Lauren.

She paled, glancing nervously at the flagstones. "I, uh, cannot say," she murmured.

"Oh come now, dear. What *flower* do you prefer?"

"I adore gardenias," Mrs. Clark suddenly interjected, "don't you, Countess Bergen?"

She responded to the question by choking on a swallow of punch and turning wide blue eyes to Mrs. Clark.

"My goodness, what on earth is wrong, Countess Bergen?" Hannah exclaimed, coming swiftly to her feet.

Lauren's laugh was nervously high pitched. "Why, nothing!" she insisted, and attempted to wave the duchess away, but Hannah was quickly at her side. Lauren looked panicked; she stumbled to her feet, her gaze scudding across Alex before settling on Mrs. Clark. "W-Would you believe," she said nervously, "that I cannot tolerate sugar? I did not know the drink was sugared, and I took a very large drink of it, and well, I simply cannot take sugar!" She smiled brightly. Too brightly, Alex thought. The reference to gardenias had truly disturbed her. *Good.* He hoped she was suffering at least a little. He certainly was.

"But that is your second glass," Mrs. Clark observed.

"Is it?" Lauren asked weakly. She laughed again, and carefully placed her punch on a table. "I rather think a bit of air is all I need." A bit of air, indeed, Alex thought dryly.

"What a marvelous idea. Would you mind terribly if I joined you for a turn about the gardens?" Marlaine asked.

Astonished, Alex gaped at his fiancée. It was so unlike her, so *very* unlike her. He peered at her closely, wondering madly what was going through her head, but she carefully avoided his gaze.

"Why, that . . . that would be lovely," Lauren calmly responded, but her stunned expression belied her words. Suddenly very uncomfortable, Alex looked from Marlaine to Lauren and back again. As the two women started down the garden path, Alex glanced at his mother. Hannah regarded him curiously enough, but worse yet, Lady Whitcomb, who was seated next to Hannah, was staring daggers at him.

"Hmmm . . . that could be trouble," Michael uttered as his gaze followed the two women. Horrified, Alex jerked a startled gaze to him. Michael chuckled. "They will probably return with the notion of lilies, roses, *and* gardenias on every pew!" He shrugged when Alex closed his eyes and slowly shook his head.

Marlaine nervously clutched at the seams of her pink gown as they walked, wondering what on earth she did now. If only Alex had not looked at Countess Bergen the way he did! She was quite determined *not* to be upset by it, but Lord, she could hardly help herself. It was such a *different* look, unlike any he had ever directed at her. And when the countess had surged to her feet, obviously discomfited about something, her feminine instincts had warned her that she must do *something* to stop what was happening between Alex and this woman. But she was not the impetuous sort, and now, having found her way into this walk, she felt completely inept to take such delicate matters into her hands.

"Lady Darfield has quite a green thumb," the countess remarked. "I understand she grows many of the roses herself."

"I . . . I should like to grow roses at Sutherland Hall when I am married," Marlaine blurted uneasily. The countess said nothing, but looked away, toward the roses. Well there was no going back now, Marlaine told herself, and apprehensively plunged ahead. "I shall be so very happy when we are married, you know. Alex is so wonderfully kind to me, even though I am not nearly as . . . as exciting as other women he might have chosen."

"Oh," muttered the countess, almost inaudibly. "I am sure the duke thinks you are perfect."

Marlaine laughed tightly. "I am not sure what he thinks, but I—I mean, *he*—" Words escaped her. Honestly, she had no idea how to convey her frustration and fear. From the corner of her eye, she glanced at Countess Bergen. She was staring intently at the path in front of them, her bottom lip between her teeth. She looked pained—so pained, that Marlaine found a glimmer of confidence, and hastily continued. "In truth, I have no idea the depth of his feelings, but I am quite certain he is rather fond of me—he has said I shall make him a comfortable wife. And he agrees entirely that our betrothal is very right . . . and . . . and . . . *important.*" Marlaine winced, pausing as she searched for the right words.

"Yes, I can see that it is a very important match," the countess muttered weakly.

Surprised by the apparent affect she was having on her, Marlaine took a fortifying breath. "Yes, well, naturally, as he is a duke, his marriage is quite important for a number of reasons. I am sure you can appreciate that our betrothal is the concern of many. My father and Alex are quite influential in the Lords, you know, and of course, they share interest in some factories in the south. Everyone watches them to see what they will do. It's a very high compliment, and God forbid, if something were to *happen,* it would be horrible—not just for *me,* you understand, but for many others."

"Yes."

The countess's response was even weaker than before; she looked as if she might be ill. They rounded the far end of the garden and started back toward the terrace and lawn, where a game of lawn bowling was starting. Lady Paddington called out to them, gesturing for them to join the game. Marlaine smiled and waved, but stopped in the middle of the garden path, forcing her companion to stop, too. Emboldened by the countess's obvious distress, she turned and faced her fully. "In truth, madam, ours is a very important match. Not only am *I* very much in favor of it, but so is Alex, and certainly so are our families. You understand, if . . . if something should *happen,* it would very well ruin my reputation. And I . . . and I would be quite devastated to lose him." There, she had said it. She felt an enormous sense of relief.

The blood seemed to drain from the countess's face. Her blue eyes turned glassy, and she quickly looked at the ground between them. "Lady Marlaine, I think you worry for naught. As you said, his grace is quite fond of you. I cannot imagine what would happen to change a thing," she said, and slowly, cautiously, looked up.

She had won. Dear God, she had won! "I was hoping you would say that," Marlaine murmured. Suddenly, she wanted to be gone from those vivid cobalt eyes. "I see they have started a game of lawn bowling. I should very much like to play. Will you please excuse me?" She did not wait for the countess to answer, but quickly walked away, her heart hammering loudly in her chest. She fairly flew to the lawn, a bright smile on her face as she joined the others. Marlaine had never felt more triumphant in her life.

Humiliated, Lauren slowly followed, trying to ignore Lady Paddington's insistent wave. Intense guilt threatened to suffocate her as she reflected on Lady Marlaine's thinly veiled plea. Woodenly, she walked toward the lawn, feeling very much like a doxy. As she reached the edge of the lawn, Mrs. Clark's blue ball went sailing wide and long, skipping into an arbor bordering the rose garden.

"Oh my! Fetch that, will you dear?" Mrs. Clark called to her. Lauren waved and walked quickly to the arbor. Once inside, she collapsed onto a wrought iron bench, taking several deep breaths in an effort to maintain her composure. She heard a sound behind her and jerked around, half-expecting to find Lady Marlaine staring at her with soft brown eyes.

But it was Alex who stood at the entrance to the arbor, his hands behind his back, his green eyes intent on her face. "Are you . . . are you all right?" he asked hesitantly.

Lauren jumped to her feet. "I . . . I can't find the ball," she lied.

"It's just here," he said simply, and pointed to her right, where the ball lay in plain view.

A flame of embarrassment flooded her face. "Oh! Well, there you have it!" She attempted to laugh as she swiftly retrieved it. She turned, clutching the thing to her chest, but Alex blocked her exit. "Now it is found, so I shall return it right away—"

"Lauren, are you all right?" he asked softly.

She could not look at him. She could not hear that voice. Something inside her began to crumble, pitching her toward a torrent of tears. "Yes! Of course I am!" she insisted, and attempted to walk past.

Alex put his hand on her arm. "Did . . . did Marlaine upset you?"

Lauren blushed furiously. *Stay away. Don't let him see. Don't let him see.* "I should really return this ball—"

"Lauren, look at me," he quietly insisted.

She desperately wanted to look at him, but was only a fraction away from sobbing as it was. She swallowed convulsively past the hideous mixture of guilt and yearning burgeoning in her chest.

"*Look* at me."

She steadfastly refused to meet his gaze. "I thought we agreed," she murmured desperately.

"Agreed? To what? That we would never speak again?" he asked sharply. "That you would never look me in the eye again? I don't recall agreeing to anything, least of all *that*!"

Lauren closed her eyes, gathering every ounce of strength she could muster. She would not succumb, she would *not.* "Please, I really must return . . ."

"Look at me!" he demanded, his fingers curling tightly around her elbow.

Panic rose swiftly, and she jerked away from him, wrenching her elbow free of his grasp as she turned toward him. "I *can't* look at you! I can't bear it!" she cried. "We *agreed*!"

His eyes rounded with astonishment. "You are right," he said softly. "We did agree. We agreed there is something undeniable and very strong between us." He took a cautious step toward her. His soft green eyes flicked to the others through the boughs of the arbor, then to her, penetrating her anger. "I do not mean to torture you, angel, but I cannot get you out of my mind."

Dear God, neither could she, and for that she almost hated him. "Please don't say that. Don't *say* that," she whispered, and clutching the blue ball fiercely, walked out of the arbor.

Chapter 14

Alone in his study, Alex stared at a mountain of paperwork. Work had proven impossible; the restlessness in him of late was seemingly eternal, making normal activity intolerable. The turmoil of his thoughts and the memory of Lauren's anguish in the Darfield's arbor yesterday burned him.

What in the hell was the matter with him? Why this woman captivated him so was baffling—he was not a man who brooded about women, but he had done nothing but that since discovering her at the Granbury reception.

Disgusted, Alex abruptly stood from his desk, walked to a walnut sideboard, and poured a sherry. Finishing it in one gulp, he was reaching for more when the door opened and Finch stepped across the threshold. "Her grace the duchess and Lady Marlaine," he announced. Alex nodded curtly and lowered the glass, hardly prepared to make chitchat with Marlaine.

The worried look on his mother's face as she rushed through the door surprised him. Marlaine, her face pale, followed a few feet behind. "Mother? What is it?"

"Oh darling, I was with Marlaine and Lady Whitcomb this morning going over the details of the wedding breakfast when they received some terrible news," Hannah exclaimed.

A stab of panic hit him squarely in the gut, and Alex jerked toward Marlaine. She dropped her eyes to the carpet. Quickly, he went to her, taking her delicate hands in his. "What news, Marlaine?"

"It's *Grandmama*," she burst forth on a sob. "Oh Alex, she has taken a turn for the worse! Mama and Papa are preparing to leave for Tarriton right away!" A large tear slipped from the corner of her eye.

He swept it away with the pad of his thumb. "Then you must go to your Grandmama right away. Finch, have the barouche brought round."

"Yes, your grace."

Marlaine sniffed, fighting valiantly to hold back her tears. Alex draped an arm around her shoulder and cupped her head against his shoulder. "Ah, darling, I am so very sorry," he murmured.

She suddenly gripped the lapels of his coat. "You will come with me, won't you Alex? I cannot bear the thought of that journey alone, truly I cannot!"

He unconsciously stiffened as a fleeting thought of Lauren skipped across his mind. "Marlaine, you are very strong when you must be."

She choked on another deep sob. "No, Alex, I am *not* strong, not at all! I cannot face it! I had so wanted Grandmama to see us married—I *promised* her she would see it! Oh please, you must come with me!"

He hesitated—excuses tumbled in his brain, and he marveled at how easily they had come to him. Over the top of her head, he glanced at his mother, but quickly averted his gaze. It hardly mattered—he could feel her eyes burning a hole through him, her disapproval emanating across the room and swallowing him whole. How could he blame her?

Marlaine would be his wife in a matter of weeks, and he was hesitating, actually thinking of ways to avoid the trip to her grandmother's deathbed. God, what in the bloody hell was the matter with him?

"I . . . I understand you are needed here. I know how important your work is," Marlaine mumbled, obviously trying to convince herself. "But . . . but Tarriton is only a two-hour drive from London." She looked up at him with large, glimmering brown eyes that made him feel instantly and terribly contrite.

"Of course I will go with you," he said soothingly, and pressed a kiss to her forehead, despising himself and his faithless thoughts.

Tarriton, an enormously grand estate just north of London, had been awash in steady drizzle for the three days since their arrival. Alex could not recall a time he had visited Tarriton when it had *not* rained. It was a dreary place, made even more so by the fact that a woman lay upstairs, hovering between life and death. For three days there had been no change in the status of Lady Whitcomb's mother. She did not improve, she did not worsen. At times, she was awake and lucid, but for the most part, she simply slept.

On the first day of the family's deathwatch, Alex had occupied himself with the work he had brought along, completing it and dispatching it to London before the evening shadows had begun to lengthen. He had begun the second day by wandering aimlessly from room to room, which had only increased the insufferable restlessness he felt. So he had attempted to read, but found he could not concentrate long enough to comprehend it. In the afternoon, he had briefly debated the necessity of parliamentary reform with Lord Whitcomb, but it was obvious the earl had little interest in politics with illness oppressing his house. Alex had tried to cheer a sullen Marlaine, but she was inconsolable.

The family's evening meal was a morose affair. They ate

mostly in silence, attempting half-hearted conversation about the wedding, until Marlaine had begged to be excused, saying she could not discuss the wedding while her grandmama lay suffering in a room just above her. The entire meal was greatly disconcerting to Alex—for some reason, he felt as depressed about the wedding talk as he did the deathwatch.

On this, the fourth morning, Alex had gone out for an early morning ride to clear his head of the discontent threatening to drown him. The whole of Tarriton was beginning to feel like a banishment, entrapping him in a world where conversations drifted from the dying, to overdone weddings, and back again. Extremely agitated and short-tempered, he had ridden for over an hour, getting drenched to the bone, but quite unable to rid himself of the agitation at his core. Moreover, he was quite unable to rid his thoughts of Lauren.

Tremendously disturbing thoughts.

Having done everything he knew to cure himself of the restlessness, and having failed miserably, Alex sat alone in the earl's study, staring blindly at the large expanse of windows. The only sound in the room was the steady *tap tap tap* of the quill he absently drummed against the desktop.

A familiar wave of guilt swept through him. This was how he repaid Marlaine's loyalty—by dreaming of Lauren, by thinking of her constantly. He had tried to see Marlaine differently, to desire her, but thoughts of the angel with eyes of blue had rooted, unwelcome, in his mind and heart. He was a bloody fool—he had a duty to Marlaine. Yes, and that *duty* was eating away at him, a little every day.

Why he was so interested in a country lass with an obscure title confounded him. Bloody hell, his "interest" had turned his ordered world upside down. What in the hell was it about Lauren that made him so insane with longing? She was beautiful, true. But he had known many beautiful women and had never felt such a peculiar sense of urgency about seeing them, not even when his physical need of them was at its greatest. It was not actually lust that bewitched him, although he certainly seemed to have plenty of *that* in store. Perhaps it was her wit, or her unusual gift for languages, or her amusing penchant for tossing in little quotations from English literature when the conversation warranted. She was a clever woman.

But he did not normally *dream* about clever women.

It could be her genuine kindness. She had a certain quality he admired and envied. He recalled her charming tale of the Potato Man, her insistence he dance with the mousy Charlotte Pritchit because it was a "nice thing to do," her acceptance of Paddy's leaden conversation. And God knew Abbey Ingram thought she was a saint incarnate because of her attention to those unfortunate children at Rosewood.

Yes, he thought as the quill's tempo increased, he had all the symptoms of being hopelessly besotted. Frustrated, he tossed the quill onto the desk and stood, moving to the window. Jesus, the need to look deep into those dark blue eyes was slowly devouring him. He wanted to feel her body beneath his, hear her melodic laughter. He wanted to listen to her sing, recite some little poem, and experience the impact of that devastating smile on all of his senses.

Bloody hell, his desires were intolerable, insupportable, and infuriating! He was a *duke,* for Chrissakes! He had responsibilities to his title and to Marlaine, not the least of which were marrying and producing an heir. He should be paying attention to the details of managing his vast estates, *not* daydreaming about a woman constantly shadowed by a giant Bavarian! He should be helping Marlaine plan their wedding trip, *not* wondering when he might see Rosewood again.

But the truth was that while he was a duke, he was also a man. And this man wanted Lauren Hill, the rest of the world be damned. He had tried to find conviction of purpose in the deepest recesses of his soul, but to no avail. He just could not conjure the will to fight his increasing desire.

He heard the door open and steeled himself—as he did every time a door opened in this house—for the news that Grandmama had died. He turned slightly, glancing over his shoulder.

Marlaine was smiling. "It's wonderful news! The doctor says she is somewhat better."

"Truly?" he asked, surprised.

She hurried toward him, her hands clasped tightly at her waist. "She is not out of the woods, but he believes there may be reason to hope!" she said brightly.

"That's marvelous news, Marlaine."

She beamed at him. "Yes, isn't it?"

He extended his hand to her; she came willingly when he pulled her into his arms. "It is my fervent prayer that she survives to see you happily married," he said softly, and kissed the top of her head.

"I am very optimistic," she said, nodding hopefully, and with a timid glance at the door, pulled away from him, out of his arms. Alex shoved his hands in his pockets and resumed his position in front of the window. "Mama's spirits are much brighter. She said we might have a game of loo after supper," she added.

"I shall look forward to it," Alex muttered, already dreading it.

The next morning Marlaine was glad to see a few feeble rays of sun had broken through the clouds as she descended the stairs. They all needed a little sunshine to chase away the gloom. Although Grandmama had not improved through the night, she had not worsened, and the doctor had said that was the most important thing.

She made her way to the dining room, hungry for the first time in days. She was pleased to find Alex there, reading a paper, the remains of his half-eaten breakfast pushed aside. "Good morning," she said, smiling.

He glanced up and gave her a weak smile. "Good morning."

"Grandmama is the same," she said, her smile fading a bit. "But the doctor said we should be much encouraged if she did not worsen in the night."

"Ah, that's excellent news." He turned his attention to the paper.

The invisible wall was coming between them again, she thought, and walked to the sideboard and slowly helped herself to some eggs and toast. Alex had been distant with her for some time now, but then again, the strain had been hard on everyone. Preparations for such a large wedding were so very stressful anyway, and coupled with a family crisis—well, it was hard on everyone. "Shall I fetch you something?" she asked.

"No, thank you," he mumbled from behind his paper. Shrugging, she took a seat to Alex's right. He continued to read. "Have you seen Papa this morning?"

He did not look up. "He has gone to the stables, I think. Said a mare is about to foal," he muttered absently.

She pushed her eggs to one side of the plate and picked up a slice of toast, disturbed that she felt so . . . inconsequential. Determined to prove herself wrong, she tried again. "What are you reading?"

He glanced briefly at her from the corner of his eye—impatiently, she thought. "The commerce news."

"Oh," she murmured, and took a bite of toast as she examined his profile. He looked strange—bored, perhaps. Rather uneasy. Honestly, it was the same restless look he had worn for days now, as if he was waiting for something. She shook her head, annoyed at her thoughts. Of course he was restless. *Everyone* was restless, waiting for Grandmama to improve or take a turn for the worse. It was little wonder Alex would be on edge—after all, he hardly knew Grandmama. He had come to Tarriton to be with *her,* she reminded herself, and she had hardly tended to him.

He needed a distraction. "Mama informs me that Lord and Lady Harris will be in Paris when we wed. Lord Harris has some business there that cannot be postponed," she said nervously, scattering her eggs about her plate.

"Ah, well. I am quite certain they have attended enough weddings to last a lifetime," he said indifferently, and turned a page.

"Lady Harris gave us a set of beautiful port glasses as a wedding gift. They are heavy crystal, and Mama says one can find that sort of crystal only in Belgium." Her eggs were now scattered across the entire plate, toast notwithstanding.

"Hmm. That was very thoughtful."

A vague sense of fear began to rise in Marlaine, and it was not the first time she had experienced it. Oh, she was keenly aware of how little they had in common. He liked horses, she did not. He was concerned with politics, but she liked balls and gardening. Sitting there, desperate for conversation, she could not think of a solitary thing that would particularly interest him. But it wasn't because of their differences. Her eyes narrowed. He was *bored*.

Unnoticed, she leaned back in her chair, staring at him. He was bored, all right, and he had been bored since Countess Bergen had attended the Harris ball! As many times as she had tried to convince herself there was nothing to fear, he had acted distracted, as if he would rather be *anywhere* than with her. He was *bored*, damn it!

She abruptly dropped her fork in her plate.

The loud clatter startled Alex; he jumped, turning quickly to her. "Is something wrong?"

"I should very much like for you to walk in the gardens with me, Alex. The sun has come out, and it looks to be a fine day," she said, resolutely folding her arms across her middle.

Slowly, he lowered the paper, studying her warily. "If that is what you would like."

She pushed away from the table and stood. "What I would *like,*" she snapped irritably, "is some companionship!" She did not wait for his response, but moved swiftly for the door, half-tempted to bolt for her rooms.

Alex had the good grace to put the paper aside and follow her. Halfway down the corridor, he caught her elbow. "Slow down," he said softly. He opened the door leading onto the terrace, and gestured for her to precede him. Once outside, he slipped her hand through the crook of his arm and led her toward the gravel path wending through the shrubs. They walked slowly, neither speaking. Marlaine's initial twinge of fear began to give way to anger. Mama had told her about men; she knew of their needs, their roving eyes. Alex was no different, nor did she expect him to be. *Honestly* she did not, but she thought he should have the decency to be properly interested in their wedding, to give her at least *some* measure of interest! Unconsciously, she sighed heavily.

"I hate to see you fret," he said quietly. She jerked a startled look to him. He smiled down at her, a warm, caring smile. "Your Grandmama is feeling better. Perhaps she will pull through." His words were so tender that they brought her to the verge of tears. Hastily, she looked away, her insides churning. There was so much she wanted to say, so much she wanted him to understand. She had found the courage to speak her mind once before, but this somehow seemed harder.

She nervously cleared her throat. "Alex, I know about Countess Bergen," she said, her voice barely above a whisper.

"I beg your pardon?" he asked coolly.

"I mean, I have noticed how you . . . how you *look* at the countess."

He stopped abruptly and turned to face her. "What nonsense is this?"

"I am not imagining things," she said weakly. His green

eyes narrowed uncertainly. "I . . . I understand, of course. She is very beautiful."

"Sweetheart, you are quite mistaken—"

"Please do not deny it!" she quickly interjected. "I am not a little girl. I *see* how you look at her." Alex looked astounded, and it angered her. Did he think she was blind? "It's all right. I know how men are, Alex. But . . . but . . ." She paused, inwardly grasping for courage. Alex reached for her hand, but she shook her head and brought her hand up, stopping him, before raggedly continuing. "I know how men are, but I do not think you have given me a proper chance, Alex. I shall make you a good wife; I swear it on my life. But you must give me the opportunity to show you!"

Stunned, Alex stared at her. Her bottom lip quivered slightly, her brown eyes glimmering with unshed tears. Good God, what was he doing to her? He felt a surge of remorse as he looked down at the young woman he had determined would make him a good wife two years ago. Serene and quiet, Marlaine had never asked him for anything, yet she was compelled to ask him for the chance to be a good wife.

A deep shame rumbled through him, and he anxiously shoved a hand through his hair. She had never asked him for a bloody thing, had never done anything but be the perfect lady, and he had forced her to ask for his respect. He hated himself for that. He hated the turbulence, the restlessness Lauren had brought him. He was suffering through each day, tormented by thoughts of a dark-haired angel, when all the while a sweet young woman stood by, eager to be his wife. All at once her serene nature seemed so much more desirable, so much *easier* than the turmoil Lauren created in him. What demon had *possessed* him?

"I know I am not as . . . *lively,* or pretty, but I—"

He grabbed her hand and yanked her into his chest. "Marlaine, you are a beautiful woman, and I should be very proud to have you as my wife. I am sorry, sweetheart, I am so sorry I have caused you any pain.'' Marlaine's lips parted slightly with surprise; for the first time in at least a month, Alex wanted to taste those lips. ''I shall make you a good husband, too, if you will give me the chance,'' he said, and impulsively kissed her fully on the lips. Marlaine stiffened in his embrace; her arms dropped to her sides as his hands swept down her spine. Alex gentled his kiss, his tongue sweeping lightly over the seam of her lips. She stood as rigid as a marble statue, her eyes squeezed shut, her lips glued together. He stroked the nape of her neck and caressed her spine, trying to relax her. She did not relax. Rather, she tolerated him. With a kiss to her cheek, he let her go. The poor girl was beet red, quite embarrassed.

''Alex, I . . . Mama and Papa are just inside!'' she whispered.

''It's all right, Marlaine. It's quite all right,'' he lied.

The tension seemed to leave her body, and she sagged against his chest. ''I shall be a good wife,'' she muttered. Alex understood. She would be a good wife, all right, dutifully submitting to him like a sheep. In the meantime, she would keep her maidenly virtue intact until she was required by law to submit to him. He sighed and folded her in his arms. There was nothing to be done for it.

Grandmama slowly improved over the next two days, but the doctor warned the family that she was not yet out of danger. He stressed that she could take a turn for the worse at any moment. So they continued to wait. Alex tried very hard to be a dutiful fiancé, seeing to Marlaine's welfare. The restlessness had not yet disappeared, but he was hopeful that it would eventually go away. She was, he kept telling himself, a perfectly good match. Someday, he would be grateful she had shown him such patience.

He was in the library searching for something to read

when the Reese family butler found him. "Beggin' your pardon, your grace, but a messenger has come."

"A messenger?"

"From London, your grace."

He nodded. "Send him in."

The man who appeared in the door of the study had obviously ridden hard. Alex strolled across the room to meet him. "What message?" he asked.

"From Lord Christian, your grace," he announced, and thrust a grimy, folded parchment at him. "He bid me tell you that you are needed in London." Alex nodded, fished in his pocket for some coins, and directed the man to the kitchens. He unfolded the parchment and scanned it quickly. Arthur wrote that the issue of Catholic emancipation was expected to pass the Commons on the morrow. But the Lords was a house divided, the members turning on one another over this divisive issue. Alex's presence was urgently needed if the reform measure had any hope of successfully passing the upper house.

Alex carefully folded the note, trying desperately to ignore the feeling of immense relief, the sense that he had been released from custody. He would not allow himself to think of anything but reform, of what he would say to the Lords. He pivoted on his heel and strode from the salon, in search of Lord Whitcomb.

He would be in London by late afternoon.

Chapter 15

Alex could not believe what he was doing. Sitting in a phaeton at Russell Square, an armful of gardenias in his lap, he could not believe he was actually *calling* on her. Good God, he could not even remember the last time he had called on a woman. But he really had no choice—after two increasingly restless days and nights in London, he had determined that he needed to see her and somehow resolve his internal struggle. Or go mad. Assuming, of course, he was not already *completely* mad.

He had been sitting in front of the town house for at least fifteen minutes. When he had first turned onto the square, he had seen the Bavarian coming out of the house with a crate of what looked to be tomatoes perched on his shoulder. Alex despised the handsome giant for being in London, for following her every move. For carrying the bloody crate of tomatoes.

An elderly couple passed and peered curiously at him. With a sigh, he forced himself to climb out of the phaeton. Gathering the gardenias, he walked to the front door and knocked. A slight man opened almost immediately and eyed him with great suspicion. "Good day, sir. Might I inquire if Countess Bergen is in?"

"Card," the man stated.

Alex dutifully fished a card from his coat pocket and placed it on the tray the old man thrust at him. The butler glanced at the card, then startled Alex by shutting the door in his face. He shifted uneasily onto one leg, feeling perfectly ridiculous waiting on a stoop like an eager young dandy. Fortunately, the white-haired man soon opened the door again. "Parlor," he said, and with his head, motioned in the general direction. Alex nodded his thanks and stepped inside. Remarkably, he managed to contain his great surprise as he took in the unusual decor. The only outward deference he gave it was to peer closely at a full suit of armor as he walked to the door the butler had indicated.

He stepped across the parlor threshold and glanced about. Much to his disappointment, Paul Hill was sitting alone in the room. "You must be Mr. Hill. I am Alex Christian, the Duke of Sutherland."

"I know who you are," Hill said, and slowly pushed himself from his seat, straightening to attain his full height of about six feet, and limped around to the front of the desk.

Alex self-consciously shifted the gardenia bush he carried. "Might I find Countess Bergen in?" he inquired, chafing at the need to inquire at all.

"No. She has gone out with Lord Westfall," Hill said icily, and folded his arms across his chest, more for balance, it seemed, than affectation.

Annoyed to learn she was in David's company again, Alex sighed. "I see."

"Do you?"

The bitter tone of his voice surprised Alex. "I beg your pardon?"

"My sister is not a sophisticated socialite. She is a simple young woman, and I cannot, for the life of me, understand why you pursue her.''

That was what Alex would call getting to the point. The damned gardenia bush was really beginning to irritate him, and he impatiently shifted it to his other arm. ''Excuse me, Mr. Hill,'' he answered coolly, ''but I am not *pursuing* your sister. I am paying a social call.''

''I will not stand idly by while you toy with her!'' Hill announced, his young chest swelling. ''There is no earthly reason you should call on her—she is beneath you in social standing, and as you are to be married to Lady Marlaine, I can only conclude you are trifling with her!''

Astonished by the accusation, and moreover, the kernel of truth in it, Alex's eyes narrowed menacingly. ''Mr. Hill, I will forgive your unwarranted attack on my character this one occasion. If you think my acquaintance with Countess Bergen requires some social stamp of approval, you are mistaken,'' he huffed, and angrily swallowed past the swell of hypocrisy that surged to his throat. ''Perhaps I should call at a more convenient time.'' Without waiting for a reply, he strode out of the parlor, the damned gardenias still in his arms.

He walked swiftly past the butler busily oiling the hinges of the armor, and suddenly paused. Jerking around, Alex thrust the bush at the diminutive man. He took it without so much as a blink and promptly placed it between the feet of the armor. With an impatient roll of his eyes, Alex marched to his carriage and vaulted onto the seat. He urged the roan to a fast trot, uncertain of where he was going. He caught a bitter laugh in his throat—lately, it seemed, he was uncertain about every goddam thing under the sun.

At precisely two o'clock the next afternoon, Alex arrived at Russell Square on horseback, dismounted without a moment's hesitation, and gave a tuppence to a young lad to stable his horse. He walked purposefully up the narrow little path to the front door and rapped sharply. "Good afternoon," Alex said when the door was pulled open. "Kindly inform Mr. Hill I have come to call on his sister. *Again.*"

The strange little butler did not bat an eye, but shut the door in his face as he had done yesterday. Alex leaned casually against the door frame until the door opened a few moments later. "Parlor?" Alex drawled. The butler's stoic expression did not change; he simply nodded and stepped aside. Depositing his hat and gloves on a small table, Alex strode through the foyer, his mind vaguely registering the fact that the armor had changed locations since yesterday.

The parlor was empty, and he noticed for the first time the bizarre mix of furnishings and hunting memorabilia. He was quickly distracted when he heard the clip of a cane on the planked floor of the hallway. "Looking for me?" Hill smirked as he limped through the door. His expression impatient, he moved for an armchair.

"I would prefer your sister, but I have no doubt I will not find her at home," Alex said as Hill lowered himself into the chair.

He eyed Alex's neckcloth and tight-fitting waistcoat. "You are correct," he said.

"Let me guess. Driving with Lord Westfall?"

Smirking, Hill shook his head. "Count Bergen."

Alex glanced impatiently at the plain ceiling. "I could not have imagined anyone would enjoy driving about the park as much as your sister."

"What she enjoys is no concern of yours. My sister does not desire you to call."

"I suppose she told you that?" Alex asked with a sardonic laugh.

"I believe her precise word was *'cabbagehead.'* If I were in your shoes, I should forget this insanity."

"You are not in my shoes, Mr. Hill," Alex said evenly. "And believe me, you would not want to be. As I am, it appears to me the only thing to do is to wait." He sat himself on a red settee.

That caught Hill's attention. "I beg your pardon?" he asked incredulously. "You cannot simply *wait*."

"And exactly who," Alex asked quietly, "will stop me?"

Hill froze, his face turning red. "You offend my uncle's hospitality!"

Alex smiled. "Your uncle is at Wallace House for the day. I should know—my Aunt Paddy complained for a good half hour about that unfortunate turn of events." Hill's face grew even darker. Alex shook his head. "I desire to speak with your sister, sir, and short of having to duel that German for the honor, my only other recourse is to wait here for her return."

"You cannot insinuate yourself into her life when she would not have you there!" Hill insisted.

Oh, but he could. Alex looked at the young man across from him, his uncertainty and discomfort apparent. He was certain Hill had no idea what it was like to have his gut burn with longing, to fight sleep so the dream of a woman's touch would not come to taunt him. "Is it she who does not want me in her life? Or you?" he asked quietly. Hill's eyes widened; Alex took a deep breath. "You are a fine man to protect your sister so ardently; she is quite fortunate."

Hill looked at him warily, unsure how to respond. "It is a responsibility I do not take lightly."

"Of course not. But the fact of the matter is, there are times when a man must weigh his responsibility against circumstances beyond his control."

Hill scowled. "And what is that supposed to mean?"

"Only that at times, regardless of a man's situation, he encounters someone so extraordinary that he must follow his instinct. I do not trifle with your sister, sir. I *could* not—I respect her far too much. I would not seek to harm her in any way—but her friendship is very important to me. So important, I would defy convention in order to speak with her. I *must* speak with her.''

Hill said nothing, clearly confused. Alex smiled thinly. ''Might you at least offer a man a drink after such an admission?''

Hill hesitated; slowly, he pushed himself out of the chair and limped to the sideboard. ''Port? Or do you prefer whiskey?'' he asked stiffly.

''Whiskey.''

Hill poured him the drink, then helped himself to a port. He resumed his seat, looking out the window as he sipped. Alex was prepared to wait, to argue, to duel if he must. He could hardly blame Hill for being angry; this was the epitome of gall, he knew, but desperate times called for desperate measures. They sat in silence for what seemed hours, until Hill gulped the last of his port and glanced at him sidelong. ''How long do you intend to wait? They could be hours yet.''

''As long as is necessary.''

With a snort, Hill hoisted himself up again. He went to the sideboard and grabbed the decanter of port and brought it back to his chair. Seating himself, he pulled the stopper from the decanter and tossed it aside. He poured another glass, then set the decanter roughly on a table, causing Dowling's stuffed bear claw to lurch eerily. ''Lauren is right, you know. You *are* an arrogant fool. I suppose Lady Marlaine knows of your gentlemanly call?'' he asked.

Alex frowned at him over the rim of his glass. ''Rest assured that my betrothal does not preclude an honest friendship among the fairer sex.''

''Do not patronize me, Sutherland. I am not stupid.''

The lad had backbone; he would give him that. ''No, I would never say you were stupid.'' Alex came to his feet and went to the sideboard. ''Far from it.'' Following his reluctant host's lead, he picked up the container of whiskey and returned to the settee with it. ''Your forays into Southwark alone have proven as much. It is a very clever man who wins so consistently.''

The glass of port stilled halfway to Hill's mouth. ''How would you know of that?''

''Word travels, my friend,'' Alex grinned. ''I understand your winnings are not insignificant—the German must require a sizable dowry.''

Hill eyed his port. ''It is no doubt inconceivable to you that Bergen does not require a dowry. Imagine, a marriage without the requisite business exchange. My winnings are for Rosewood. Ah, but that's a subject you know nothing about, as it is not something which would amuse you,'' he said arrogantly.

''On the contrary, I am quite familiar with Rosewood,'' Alex admitted. Hill's head shot up, his eyes narrowed with unspoken accusation. Chuckling, Alex lifted a hand in supplication. ''Do not assume the worst. I stumbled across it when my horse drew lame one day. Quite by accident, I assure you.''

Clearly stunned, Hill's blue eyes widened as they searched Alex's face. ''*That* was you? Mr. Christian?''

''Of course it was me! Surely you knew that?'' Alex laughed.

''*Christian.* Bloody hell, I should have known!'' he groaned, closing his eyes.

''I do not suppose that endears me to you?'' Alex asked with an irreverent chuckle.

Hill shot him a disapproving frown. ''Does it make you any less a duke? Does it change your imminent marriage? Does it improve my sister's situation in any way?''

Hell, there was no good response to that, Alex thought, and wisely chose not to answer. He tossed back his whiskey and poured another. Just what *did* he intend to do with Lauren when he saw her, other than be near her and breathe her in?

Nor did Paul trust what the duke really wanted, and it

unnerved him. Friendship? He had trouble believing that
was all. He poured another port, eyeing Sutherland with
suspicion. Good God, how had he missed such an obvious
connection? Alex Christian, Duke of Sutherland, Mr. Christian. Why had he not put two and two together? Why hadn't
Lauren told him? Because, he angrily reminded himself, *she*
knew he was Mr. Christian, the country gentleman with
whom she had fallen madly in love. And every time the
subject of Sutherland had come up, Paul had done his
damnedest to warn her of the scoundrel's intent. Dear Jesus,
they had argued bitterly about it at Rosewood last weekend.
He had suspected her feelings. She, of course, had heatedly
denied it, but now everything was crystal clear to him.
Lauren loved this wretch. This wretch who was capable of
changing nations with a simple speech.

There was every indication that Catholic emancipation
would pass the Lords, and that was due in no small measure
to Sutherland's steady persuasion over the last two days.
Paul should know—he had followed every word of the de-
bates. The prospect excited him. If Catholics were given a
seat in parliament, other reforms leading toward equal representation could not be far behind. And with fair representation, or rather, a representative protecting the interests of
small estates such as Rosewood, there was every possibility
the family home could flourish once again. Only yesterday,
he had joined in holding the Duke of Sutherland up as the
people's hero. The image of that powerful change agent was
hard to reconcile with the man sitting in his parlor just now.

"The weather is quite nice for the time of year, wouldn't
you agree?" the duke asked idly. Paul thought that a perfectly ridiculous remark from such a visionary, seeing as
how it rained four out of every seven days since he had been
in London, and said so. Sutherland took exception to Paul's
characterization of London being a dark pool of all sorts of
deviant behavior, which led to a debate over the merits of
London in general. Slugging back drinks with abandon, the

two turned the discussion into a heated debate ranging from Parliament to foreign trade, in which Sutherland obviously was heavily invested, to the government and private securities, with which Paul was extremely well acquainted. And then, miraculously, the two men began to agree on the types of reforms that were needed to foster a healthy economy. Paul even went so far—after his fifth glass of port—to commend the duke's most recent speech on that very topic.

After three hours, Paul and Alex had argued about every conceivable social topic under the sun, had drunk enough liquor that both men were blurry eyed, and still had not resolved the unspoken question of Lauren hanging between them. Paul was unyielding on that front. With every glass of port, his duty to his sister became more entrenched. Alex was prepared to camp on the settee if he must, but as that was no solution, he came up with the drunken notion of a bet.

"All right, Hill," he said, grinning, the contents of his glass sloshing dangerously close to the rim as he struggled to perch on the edge of the settee, "you think you have such a way with cards, why not put your mouth where your money is?"

"Put it wherever you like, Sutherland, but I will put my money in my mouth," Paul tried to correct him.

Alex frowned and waved a hand at him. "No, no. A wager. Here it is." He paused to stifle a drunken belch, wiping the palm of his hand across his dangling neckcloth. "All right. Here it is," he repeated.

"What is the wager?" Paul asked, as if he had missed it.

"I am *thinking*," Alex castigated him, and closed his eyes tightly shut, trying to recall the perfectly brilliant idea he had just had. It suddenly came to him, and he opened his eyes, grimaced at the wave of dizziness, and gave himself a moment to focus. "Here it is. I want to attend the opera. Shall we cut cards?"

"For what?" Paul asked, clearly confused.

"For the *opera.*"

"I do not want to attend the opera with you!" Paul said disdainfully, and took another long drink of his port.

"Good *God, not you. Lauren,*" Alex exclaimed with horror.

"You are awfully familiar with my sister, sir," Paul snapped.

"Obviously not as familiar as *Madgoose!* Bloody hell, how many times can one carriage circle that damned park?" Alex shouted.

Paul chuckled. Alex glared at his young adversary, steadying himself against the arm of the settee until the room stopped spinning. When he could at last focus, he glared at Paul. "Cut cards?" he repeated.

"Let me get this straight," Paul slurred, and attempted to lean forward, only to fall backward again. "If you win, I should take Lauren to the opera."

"No!" Alex roared, and mumbled an impatient curse under his breath. "If *I* win, *I* shall take Lauren to the opera," he said, thumping himself on the chest. "The highest card wins. It's all very, very *simple,* Hill."

"But what if *I* win?" Paul demanded.

That gave Alex pause. Busily trying to fit a bottle stopper in the whiskey container, he wavered, frowning at the bottle. "You should get something," he agreed.

"Yes! I should!" Paul exclaimed, bobbing his head in furious agreement.

"Well . . . do you like my horse?" Alex asked.

Paul dismissed the offer with a wave of his hand. "No use for it."

"I have some fine hunting dogs at Sutherland Park," he offered. "Do you like to hunt?" Paul sighed, looked pointedly at the cane propped against his chair, then at Alex. "Oh," Alex muttered sheepishly, "that wouldn't do, would it? Let me think . . . I have money."

Paul's face lit up. "Yes! Money! Two thousand pounds!" he exclaimed gleefully.

Alex frowned. "Two thousand pounds? My God, man, it is only the opera!" he scoffed.

"But it is my sister!"

"Good point," Alex agreed cheerfully, and fit the stopper in the neck of the whiskey bottle. His triumphant smile faded rapidly when he noticed his glass was empty.

"Then we are agreed," Paul said firmly. He stood up—a little more smoothly than would be expected—grabbed his cane, and staggered to a writing desk. "Best two out of three?" he called over his shoulder as he searched for the playing cards, which were stacked neatly on top of the desk.

"Two out of three," Alex agreed. Paul found the cards after a moment, made some remark about the housekeeping, and pitched to the settee, sitting heavily next to Alex.

"You had best hope you not lose, Sutherland. Two thousand pounds is very, very . . . much . . . money," Paul mumbled.

"Not to me," Alex blithely admitted, and reached for the cards. He made a great show of cutting them, going very deep into the deck, and lifted a two of diamonds. He groaned and fell against the back of the settee, draping one arm over his eyes with exaggerated flourish.

"Ha!" exclaimed Paul an instant later, laughing gleefully. Alex peeked out from beneath his arm; grinning like an idiot, Paul danced a six of spades in Alex's face. Bloody hell, he needed a miracle.

Paul went next, drawing an eight of clubs. This time, Alex abandoned any pretense at flourish and closed his eyes to cut the deck. He drew a ten of diamonds. Hill's expression did not change but for the single quirk of a brow. "I assume you will accept a bank draft," Alex said dryly.

"Naturally," Paul agreed amicably.

As Paul clumsily shuffled the deck, Alex suppressed the urge to laugh. He would lose, he knew it in his gut, but to come this close to winning was, at the moment, terribly amusing. He grinned at Paul. "Nine o'clock tomorrow evening," he said easily, tossed back the last of his whiskey, and cut the deck, drawing the queen of hearts. Paul's eyes flicked to the card. With a moan, he stared at the cards for a long moment before reaching to cut what was left of the deck. He slowly turned the card over in his hand. He and Alex gasped simultaneously and lifted startled gazes to one another.

The three of spades.

Alex had gotten his bloody miracle.

"You cannot take her without chaperone!" Paul shouted angrily.

"No, no, of course not. Paddy, she goes, too," Alex muttered, stunned by his luck.

The room grew silent as both men stared at the three of spades in Paul's hand. At length, Paul spoke, his voice ragged. "Give me your word."

Even in his state of inebriation, Alex did not have to ask what he meant. "You have it," he responded quietly. Paul tossed the losing card onto the floor and pushed himself to his feet. Once he had steadied himself on his cane, he looked down at Alex without emotion. "I have your word," he reiterated.

Alex nodded mutely and watched as Paul made his way from the parlor. Only then did he fall back against the settee in complete elation, reminding himself not to forget his horse on the way out.

Chapter 16

Wrapped in a hooded cloak, Lauren stared out through the door of the barouche at the brightly lit windows of the opera house. She expected Ethan to pawn her away like some worthless trinket, but *never* Paul. He had tried to justify his actions by blaming it on the port, and when that had not worked, by insisting it was not good to provoke the duke, who had, after all, won this night fairly. Lauren had vehemently objected to being bartered, for which Paul had again apologized. But then he had insisted she attend, adamant that whether she liked it or not, the Hills honored their debts. Ethan, damn him, had chortled his agreement, excited at even the remote possibility of a duke as a suitor. So here she was, stuffed into a coach with *him* and a chatty Lady Paddington, forced to honor Paul's foolish, *foolish* bet!

Faint strains of music drifted to her ear as Alex helped her and Lady Paddington from the coach. She could not deny that in spite of being *completely* humiliated by the drunken wager, she had desperately longed to see him. At the moment, however, all she wanted was to give him a good piece of her mind, maybe even wipe that lazy smile from his face. She bounced up the stairs behind him and Lady Paddington and stalked inside, pausing to push away the hood of her cloak.

Lady Paddington, adjusting her fat little ringlets, exclaimed loudly when she saw Mrs. Clark. "Wait here," Alex said low, his voice carrying a hint of warning. With a pointed look, he swiftly proceeded to escort Lady Paddington to a corner where Mrs. Clark and another elderly woman stood. By *God,* he was a scoundrel! She lifted her chin and angrily jerked at the frog of her cloak. She yanked it from her shoulders and shoved it at an approaching footman, pausing to apologize for almost punching him in the chest before leveling a heated gaze on the wretch as she smoothed the skirt of her blue-green satin gown.

Oblivious to the crush of people hurrying to their seats, she glared at him as he conversed with Lady Paddington's friends. She suddenly realized that Lady Paddington was walking away with Mrs. Clark. Where in the hell was her chaperone going? Did he honestly think she would sit alone with him? The man was too arrogant by half! She impatiently shifted her weight onto one hip, waiting for him to come and explain himself. He turned toward her as Lady Paddington disappeared into the corridor, and smiling, gestured mildly for her to join him. The lout was going to make her walk across the grand foyer to *him*! He was not only arrogant, but also crass, and *dammit,* so bloody handsome!

Furious, Lauren marched across the expanse of the grand foyer. Alex extended his hand as she reached him. She glanced at his hand, then settled a scathing glare on him, punching her fists on her hips. "You, sir, are a . . . a *reprobate*!"

He lowered his hand and bowed. "And you, madam, are a vision." Lifting his other hand, he offered her an elegant gardenia corsage.

Where had *that* come from? Shrugging, Lauren folded

her arms across her middle and glanced away, swallowing hard against the feeling that simple gardenia gave her. It was difficult to make eye contact with him; his gaze was so penetrating, she felt completely raw. Even now she could *feel* his eyes on every inch of her. She wondered if he was comparing her to Lady Marlaine. Self-conscious, her gaze slipped to the marble floor and the tips of her blue green slippers. His silent perusal seemed to go on for an eternity until she thought she would scream. Finally unable to bear it another moment, she jerked her head up. "Well? Do I pass your inspection?" she snapped. Naturally, his lopsided grin made her knees weak.

"More than you know," he replied, and motioned toward the gardenia he held.

She rolled her eyes. "See here," she blurted impatiently as she took the blasted flower. "That little *wager* between you and Paul should be disqualified on the grounds that the *object* of the wager was not a willing participant!" She succeeded in piercing her flesh with the corsage's pin. Grimacing, she added, "There should be a *law* against such stupid, stupid bets!"

Obviously enjoying her efforts to pin the corsage, he merely lifted a brow. She managed to secure it, and angrily folded her arms across her middle. "Happy? Honestly, I don't care if you are!" she rushed on before he could answer. "If you even *remotely* resembled a gentleman, you would not force me to come here tonight like . . . like some *booty*. Please, concede that my brother's debt to you is satisfied and allow me to return home!"

"I am afraid that is not possible," he said pleasantly, his green eyes sparkling with unconcealed mirth.

"And why not?" she demanded, tossing an uneasy glance behind her.

"Because you are hardly in a congenial mood to hear anything I might say. No, I rather think we shall wait until you are quite disposed to converse with me like a lady."

Lauren stilled at the insult. *"Swine!"* she gasped.

"Oh, now that's terribly original." He grinned at her.

Speechless, she dropped her fists to her sides. "I have never, *never in my life,* met a more arrogant, outrageous, *rude* man!" she choked out.

He cheerfully inclined his head in concession of that assessment. "And I have never met a more intractable woman in all of mine. Shall we?" He offered his arm as if were the most natural thing to do.

"And just where is Lady Paddington?" she demanded, refusing to take his proffered arm.

"She would like to sit with Mrs. Clark for a bit. She'll join us later." Lauren glared hatefully at his arm, unmoving. With a devilish grin, he shook his head. "Lauren. You know very well to leave now is not practical. Your brother wagered your presence tonight and lost. It was a legitimate wager, and a gentleman always honors his debts. If you persist in this temper tantrum, you will cause quite a lot of unwelcome attention—not only tonight, but also when I demand satisfaction for Hill's debt. So let me ask you again. Shall we?"

Oh, dear *God,* she wanted to claw that self-satisfied smirk from his face. *"Fool!"* she muttered.

"I beg your pardon, was that a yes?" he asked, clearly amused. With a glower that would have sent most men running, she slapped her hand down—hard—on his forearm. Grinning in that omniscient way of his, he escorted her up the great staircase, chuckling at her efforts to keep as much distance as possible between them by stretching her arm out as far as she could without toppling over.

At the end of a long, carpeted corridor, a footman stepped ahead of them and opened a carved door onto a richly appointed box. There were four velvet chairs, a small occasional table with two crystal flutes and some chocolates, and a bottle of champagne chilling in a stand. His hand landed on the small of her back. He guided her into a chair at the polished brass railing, taking her hand in his to seat her. She hated him for touching her and sending an unwanted jolt up her spine. He seemed to know it; with a graceful flip of his coattails, he seated himself next to her and grinned unabashedly.

"Where is Lady Paddington?" she asked, feeling suddenly self-conscious.

"Just there," he said, nodding to his left. "Don't fret so. She can see you at all times, so you are quite safe." Lauren glanced uneasily across the crowded house. Lady Paddington and Mrs. Clark waved their fans; Lauren smiled and lifted a gloved hand in return. *Foolish, foolish wager!* She glanced at the ornately decorated ceiling, at the orchestra, even her corsage—*anywhere* but him. They were in one of the largest boxes in the house, directly across from a gentleman she recognized as the Duke of Wellington. To her great surprise, he inclined his head in her direction, and she smiled brightly before she realized he was nodding to the brute who accompanied her. Embarrassed, she surreptitiously glanced around. Other patrons were watching them closely, too. Despite her deep flush, she tried to maintain an expressionless facade.

When Alex touched her hand, she almost jumped out of her skin. She glanced at him from the corner of her eye as he leaned toward her with quiet smile. "I think," he said charmingly, "they are admiring your beautiful gown."

An inadvertent chuckle escaped her. He was a clever man, she would give him that, but in some respects, he was as thick as the fog outside. She wore a very plain, unadorned gown. "They are most decidedly not admiring my gown."

"Why not? I think it is beautiful."

She turned slightly to see if he trifled with her, but he looked genuinely sincere, and against her will, it pleased her enormously. She unconsciously opened the fan she had borrowed from Abbey and waved it in her face. "It is functional," she muttered.

He chuckled. "Functional, is it? Well, I do believe it is

the loveliest gown I have ever had the opportunity to admire on a woman.''

Good God, was he mad? A bit in his cups? He had to be one or the other, because each time Lauren had seen Lady Marlaine, that beautiful creature had been dressed in the finest *haute couture,* which included a variety of pastels and frills. Lady Marlaine most decidedly did *not* dress in dark colors with little adornment. ''You should not leave your quizzing glass at home, your grace, if you cannot see better than that.''

Alex smiled quietly as the curtain was drawn. ''I wish you would call me Alex,'' he murmured. But the first strains of music had been played, and Lauren did not respond, losing interest in him and everything else.

He barely heard the music at all, and had to keep reminding himself to breathe. The woman simply took his breath away. Dressed in a shimmering gown the color of peacock feathers, her skin glowed radiantly. Her bosom swelled enticingly above the low-cut bodice, and a single strand of dark chestnut hair that had escaped her simply elegant coif draped sensuously across her eye. And those eyes, dear God, those eyes that had haunted him the past week sparkled brilliantly.

She was completely enraptured with the performance. With her hands clasped tightly in her lap, she leaned forward, hanging on every note. He could not take his eyes from her classic profile, or the loose strand of hair that fell again each time she delicately brushed it from her face. He drank her in, practically paralyzed by the overwhelming desire to touch her, to caress her skin, to taste her lips.

The power of his emotion completely bewildered him.

It was the power of the music that helped to relax Lauren. As the curtain was pulled for intermission, she sighed contentedly and fell back against the velvet chair, her hand resting lightly on her throat.

''You seem to enjoy the music.''

She smiled in unspoken agreement, and risked looking at him. In the soft glow of the candlelight, he looked extremely virile. As he handed her a glass of champagne, the rich brown waves of his thick hair brushed his collar. His green eyes were soft and liquid, and his lips, pursed just slightly, reminded her of the explosive kiss they had shared. A shiver unexpectedly raced through her.

"My God, you are more beautiful than I imagined you would be." His eyes casually flicked the length of her.

The compliment startled her; the flute wavered in her hand. "You should not say such things."

He smiled. "Why not? I told you once before I believe beauty should be openly and honestly admired. Did you think I jested with you?"

"I did not believe you," she admitted truthfully.

His green eyes danced dangerously. "Angel, if you believe nothing else, believe this. You are the most enchanting woman I have ever known."

Oh God, she desperately wanted to believe it. Lauren realized she was trembling. She put down the champagne flute and clasped her hands tightly together in her lap. Alex did not say anything, but regarded her so tenderly that her pulse began to race. Slowly, he reached across the gap that separated them and carefully laid his hand upon hers. She swallowed a gasp at the gentle gesture and stared at his hand, his strong, broad hand, lying simply, easily, across her own. It was so *comforting,* so safe. She saw each dark hair, the way his long fingers tapered, the way the ruby cuff links looked like drops of blood against the stark white of his shirt.

"I wanted you to come tonight, but not for the reasons you think," he said softly. "I apologize for my methods, but I had to see you again."

A flood of emotion began to course through her; she could not drag her eyes from his hand. "I thought we agreed." It was her voice, but she would have sworn some-one else spoke.

He was silent for a long moment. "I am very sorry," he finally uttered, "but I cannot honor whatever it is you think we agreed to."

Lauren drew a steadying breath. "But you must. We agreed, nothing can come of it! Lady Marlaine—"

"No." He cut her off. "Just tonight, let us not speak of anything else. Let us have just one night, Lauren, one night, only you and me . . . no one else."

She was mad to even consider such a request, to let her guard down, even for a moment. Yet her heart was of a different opinion, and she lifted her gaze from his hand and looked at him. The earnestness in his expression amazed her; it was with a yearning she understood too well. He suddenly lifted her hand and kissed her gloved knuckles. "One night. You want it, too, I think, as badly as I do."

Unable to answer him, she dragged her gaze to his hand again. She should deny it. She should demand he fetch Lady Paddington. Mother of God, could she allow herself this pleasure, this single moment in time? It seemed so *easy*— they were in a crowded opera house. Nothing could possibly happen! It was meaningless! It was *possible*. For only one night. He mistook her hesitation and slowly released her hand. Lauren impetuously grasped it and held it in her lap. "Just one night," she whispered.

Alex moaned with relief and leaned closer, his forehead almost touching hers. "One *blessed* night, angel," he whispered, his breath fanning her cheek. He brushed the strand of hair from her temple, leaving a trail of sparks to flow through her.

She gripped his hand tighter. "But . . . but we cannot sit here . . . we must converse. We must *talk*," she said hesitantly. "Do you, ah, play an instrument?" she asked nervously.

He chuckled at her nervousness and fondly squeezed her

hand. "There were some singing lessons, but the instructor eventually convinced my mother she was throwing good money after bad. Three boys, and none of us had the temperament for the arts. We preferred hunting to singing, mud to paints."

"You had an older brother," she stated.

"Yes, Anthony. Died in a fall from his horse and broke his fool neck," he said, a hint of bitterness in his voice.

"It must have been terribly difficult to lose a brother and inherit such an important title all at once."

Startled, Alex blinked. How on earth could she know that? "He was the duke," he heard himself say. "I was the second son. It was an arrangement that suited us perfectly. There are times I find I have yet to adjust completely."

He was still marveling at that unprecedented revelation when she asked, "What did you do?" He must have looked puzzled, because she quickly clarified, "When you were the second son, I mean."

"Chased things," he said with an enigmatic grin, caressing the inside of her slender wrist.

"Chased things?" she echoed.

"Pursuits of a cerebral nature," he said, smiling, "the search for adventure."

"Ah, so *'thy chase had a beast in view.'*" She laughed lightly at the Dryden poem, an appealing blush rising in her cheeks. "I should not tell you so, but the first time we met, I thought you looked like a man who had climbed mountains."

Whether it was the treasure of a glimpse into her thoughts of him, or the fact that he had indeed scaled mountains, he did not know, but he was inwardly startled. "I have climbed a few," he said simply.

She grinned with delight. "You *have*?"

The impact of that gorgeous smile hit him squarely in the chest—how he had longed to see it! He chuckled warmly.

"I beg your pardon, Countess, but do you think a duke is incapable of climbing mountains?"

She flashed a charming smile and leaned forward, unwittingly affording him a tantalizing view of her cleavage. "I rather suppose I thought a *duke* might send a footman ahead to do his climbing."

"Not all dukes rely on their footman for such things," he said in a lightly admonishing tone. "Some of us relish the experience of all things physical in nature." Blushing prettily, she tossed him an impertinent grin. "And what did you do before you married your count?" he asked as his fingers stroked her palm.

"I don't know." With an unaffected shrug of her shoulders, she smiled. "I suppose I tended things. Paul, the children, the animals. My uncle, when he found time to visit Rosewood."

"Your guardian uncle? I had opportunity to meet him recently. Did he not live at Rosewood with you?"

"He preferred the continent." She smiled again. "I must check the rules of foolish wagers, your grace. I should think a discourse on my uncle was not included with one night at the opera."

He briefly wondered what it would take to learn every last thing about her, but nodded congenially. "Perhaps not. But I do think the wager entitles you to call me by my given name."

Lauren smiled shyly. "For just one night, Alex," she murmured, and turned eagerly toward the stage as the orchestra picked up again.

Across the house, Mrs. Clark snapped open her fan with a practiced flick of her wrist and leaned toward Aunt Paddy. "I told you so," she muttered behind the fan's cover.

Aunt Paddy surreptitiously slid her gaze to the ornate ducal box as she pretended to study a cuticle. Countess Bergen looked particularly lovely this evening; but then again, she always looked as if she had arisen from spring's gardens. "You have an overactive imagination," she sighed wearily.

"Admit it, Clara. Just look at the way he speaks with her! I daresay that smile on his lips has not wavered since he set foot in the box! Nor has he stopped looking at her. I am telling you, Sutherland has a particular attachment for the countess."

"He has nothing of the sort! He is quite in love with Lady Marlaine, and is merely biding his time until the poor creature returns from Tarriton!"

"You simply cannot abide it when I am right," Mrs. Clark sniffed. "Look there, he is holding her hand!" she whispered frantically. Both women gasped audibly when the duke lifted the countess's hand to his lips. "Now *that* is not friendly interest, if you ask me," Mrs. Clark murmured.

"I did not ask you that I recall! Really, why must you read so much into an innocent situation?" Paddy asked, a little desperately.

Mrs. Clark rolled her eyes and waved her fan for some air. "I know you are inordinately fond of the duke, Clara, but he and Countess Bergen have more than a passing interest in one another. Your nephew Westfall certainly believes so—you recall what he said about the park? And why do you suppose the duke sat you here this evening? He hasn't come for you as he said he would, and it is not out of regard for *my* feelings, I can assure you! If you don't believe me, just look at Count Bergen! I would wager *he* does not think it a friendly interest, either!"

Both women slyly shifted their gaze to the box next to them, where Count Bergen sat stiffly in the company of Lord and Lady Harris. He stared at Countess Bergen, had stared at her since he had seated himself during the first act. "That poor, poor man. He simply adores her," Mrs. Clark said sadly.

"And she adores him, Mrs. Clark. Everyone knows she

will soon accept his offer and return to her beloved Bavaria," Paddy proclaimed.

"My dear"—Mrs. Clark sighed, as if speaking to an ignorant child—"even *Count Bergen* knows she does not *adore* him. She is tolerant of him, to be sure, and I would even go so far as to say she is somewhat fond of him, but she *adores* your nephew."

Aunt Paddy frowned mightily at her companion. "As I live and breathe, Elizabeth, you know *nothing*. Goodness, he is to be married in three weeks! The dear boy is not a fool— he knows a good circumstance when he sees one, and he would do nothing to jeopardize that! He is very kindly escorting Countess Bergen to an opera, nothing more!"

"Honestly, Clara, you of all people should know that men do not confine themselves to good circumstance! Lord Paddington hardly confined himself to your tidy little fortune, now did he? The duke is a man, my dear, a man who is quite simply captivated by a beauty!" Simultaneously, the women slid their gaze back to the duke's box. "Dear *Lord,*" Mrs. Clark exclaimed, "they are terribly admiring of one another, aren't they?"

Lauren was smiling into the duke's eyes, and he—well, even Paddy could not ignore the fact that he could not take his eyes from her. "I tell you, he adores Lady Marlaine!" she insisted weakly, and huffed with exasperation when her good friend lifted an imperious brow.

Chapter 17

When the curtain finally fell to thunderous applause, Alex smiled as Lauren leapt out of her seat in enthusiastic praise of the performance. When the last bows were made and patrons began to file out of the house, she turned to him, her face flushed with excitement. "It was *marvelous*," she said, beaming.

Extraordinary as it was, he would do just about anything to put such joy in her face. "I am glad you enjoyed it." He suggested they have another glass of champagne as they waited for the crush to clear the house. While he poured, she laughingly compared this performance to the plays she had seen at Bergenschloss.

"Frau Batenhorst had the good fortune to see a play in Munich as a young girl, and she was thereafter convinced that every actress worth her stage bows should wear ostrich feathers. It did not matter what role she was assigned, she wore her feathers. I do not believe I shall ever forget the sight of her playing a poor farmer's wife with that plume of ostrich feathers sticking out every which way!"

Alex laughed, infected by her enchanting laughter. It was, he recognized, one of the most charmed evenings he had ever spent.

"Grafin Bergen!"

Until now.

Annoyed, Alex glanced over his shoulder at the German Giant and frowned mightily at the intrusion. But his blood began to boil when Lauren smiled broadly at the foreigner. "Magnus!" she gasped. "What a surprise!"

It rankled Alex that she would so easily call that monstrosity by *his* given name.

"Pardon the intrusion, but I saw you from over there," he said, motioning vaguely across the hall.

"Oh," Lauren murmured, her face coloring curiously. Bergen shifted cold blue eyes to Alex and studied him openly before remarking to Lauren, in German, that he did not know she was a particular friend of the duke. Lauren hesitated, then laughed politely. She responded in German that she was a particular friend of his aunt, Lady Paddington, who was visiting another box. A knowing smirk creased the count's face as he countered that Lady Paddington apparently was not aware of their friendship, as she had remained in a separate box throughout the entire performance, and had just left with her companions.

Alex would have liked to stuff the count's smirk into the back of his throat. "Count Bergen apparently does not understand that in England, a widow does not require a constant chaperone. But then again, Germans are hardly noted for their keen mental insight," he said coolly, taking great satisfaction in the surprise that flitted across the beast's face upon realizing he had understood their exchange. Lauren frowned at Alex, which did not make him feel contrite at all.

It made him angry.

The count's eyes narrowed dangerously. "Perhaps not. But Germans are known for—*Rittertum*—" He paused, looking hesitantly to Lauren for the right word.

"Chivalry," she muttered, her face growing pale.

"Chivalry. We do not allow our women to be placed in questionable circumstances," Bergen finished.

"Indeed? I suppose you prefer to keep them in your sight at all times, to the point of stalking their every move?" Alex quipped coldly.

Beside him, Lauren's frown deepened. "You exaggerate, your grace! Bavarians are kindly reverent of their womenfolk," she said, the lightness of her voice belying the murderous look in her eyes.

An irrational anger boiled in Alex's veins. It was impossible to accept that she might harbor some affection for *this* man while he practically had to beg her to smile. "I beg your pardon, Countess. I did not realize that in Bavaria it was considered *kind* or *reverent* to take an inheritance from a young widow and send her away. Perhaps in Bavaria, that sort of behavior is the *height* of chivalry," he countered nastily.

Lauren fairly vaulted from her seat, and sensing an impending explosion, Alex came just as quickly out of his. He recklessly grabbed her hand, slipping it into the crook of his arm and clamping tightly so she could not escape him if she so desired.

"Don't be a fool, Sutherland," the count said, his hands fisted at his side. "I will not tolerate your insults."

"Magnus!" Lauren exclaimed softly. "Don't take offense. Please, I promised Paul to come safely home. He would be angry to hear of a public dispute."

Bergen did not seem to hear her, but glared hatefully at Alex. "Magnus, *please,*" she said again.

The muscles of his jaw worked frenetically as he considered her. With some effort, he finally spoke. "I will speak with you another time," he said simply, and with a withering look for Alex, turned and walked out of the box.

"Good evening!" she called after him, then turned such a burning look to Alex that he actually winced. She impatiently yanked her hand free of his arm. "You are *despicable*!"

"Pray tell, what is my crime? That I take exception to the fact he would have tossed you out? Or that he stalks you like prey? Does that so sorely offend you, madam?"

"*Yes!* It does!" she cried angrily. "It is none of your affair, none at all! How dare you challenge him so openly! And to what end? To publicly *belittle* him?" She shoved past the furniture in an effort to be gone from the box, but Alex caught her and forced her to a graceful walk.

He felt a little contrite, but not nearly enough to douse his soaring frustration. "I beg your pardon, but this night is mine, fairly won. It did not include your constant shadow!"

"You did not have to humiliate him!"

"I rather doubt the man is capable of being humiliated," Alex responded evenly.

"And *you*, apparently, are not capable of being civil," she snapped angrily. "What arrogance!"

Alex groaned. "You act as if I have snubbed your lover. Is that what he is? Is that why you allow him to follow you everywhere?" he demanded impatiently, forcing a smile for an acquaintance.

"My *what*?" she gasped behind a frozen smile as they marched, side by side, toward the grand staircase. "Do not even *presume* to answer that! You know nothing about me, nothing at all! You are overbearing, presumptuous, and meddlesome!"

"Your grace, what a pleasure to see you! I hope you are well."

Alex smiled grimly. "Good evening, Lady Fairlane. Indeed, I am quite well."

"Good evening, Lady Fairlane," Lauren said.

"Countess Bergen," the woman responded, a little coolly, Alex thought. They began their rapid descent of the staircase, and with a perfectly placid expression, he muttered, "You were not quite through, were you?"

"Hardly!" she choked on a half-laugh, half-sob. "I thought you many things, but *cruel* was never one of them!" She smiled at an elderly couple approaching them.

"Now you must be quite finished. And let me respond with equally heartfelt emotion, madam . . ." He paused as the couple reached them.

"Good evening, Mr. and Mrs. Bartlett," Lauren said. Odd, but Alex noticed the woman responded with an unmistakable upward tip of her chin to Lauren's greeting.

"Sutherland, caught your speech in the Lords! Very inspired!" the gray-haired gentleman gushed, squinting at Lauren.

"Thank you," Alex said cordially, curious as to Bartlett's overt perusal of Lauren.

"Good evening, Countess Bergen," the old man said.

"Good evening," she replied.

Alex gripped her elbow tightly and pushed her forward. "As I was saying, I may be the most despicable creature you have ever had the misfortune to lay eyes upon, but *you* are the most stubborn, *sanctimonious* little . . ." He stopped as another gentleman approached.

"Sutherland, hoping to catch you at White's this week. I've got a parliamentary bargain for you, old chum, a potential meeting of the minds so to speak."

Lauren snorted at that, and Alex squeezed her elbow in warning. "Shall we say Thursday afternoon, Lord Helmsley?"

"That would be fine. Good evening, your grace." He smiled and bowed low, his gaze sliding surreptitiously to Lauren.

Alex pushed her, none too gently, toward an approaching footman. "The red cloak, please." He jerked around and stared down at her. "Sanctimonious little *coquette*. How many men do you string along, Lauren? How many hearts will you have served on a platter when it is—"

"I am *not* a coquette!" she exclaimed indignantly. The

footman produced the cloak, and Alex reluctantly let her go to help her into it. He watched her warily as he plunged his arms into his greatcoat, and taking his dress hat from the footman, quickly caught her arm again and ushered her out the door.

"In that you are quite mistaken. You string them along like some greatly decorated *kite*. Jesus, I cannot even count them all! Goldthwaite, Westfall, van der Mill, and that brute Madgoose—good God, I wonder what on earth possesses me to want to see you? I must be out of my mind!" he said harshly. He glanced upward; a light rain had begun to fall. With an exasperated sigh, he hurried her down the steps toward his waiting coach. Lauren was oddly silent. He warily looked down; she was staring straight ahead, but he could see the tears glistening in her eyes. "Oh God," he groaned. "Lauren—"

"I am not a *coquette*. I am very honest, I truly am," she said in a trembling voice.

It had the instant effect of a painful slap across his face. He abruptly picked up his pace toward the parade of coaches, dragging her along. "Don't cry!" he pleaded under his breath.

"I know I must seem so to you, but you do not understand, you could *never* understand," she blurted helplessly, stumbling next to him. Alex nodded at one of his coachmen. "I do not want their attentions! I did not *want* to come to London, but I had no choice! I would have been perfectly content to stay at Rosewood, and I am going back as soon as I possibly can, maybe even *tomorrow*!"

The coachman swung the barouche door open, and Alex unthinkingly grabbed Lauren by the waist and lifted her inside. Her hands shot out to catch the sides of the narrow doorway, effectively stopping her entry as she glared at him over her shoulder. "And I did not *ask* you to see me, whatever *that* means!" The coachman nervously bowed his head, obviously wishing he were somewhere else. So did Alex. He gave Lauren a hearty push that sent her tumbling into the lush interior, and followed her by fairly leaping inside and slamming the door shut after barking instructions to the driver.

She had landed on her hands and knees on the velvet squabs, and set about righting herself, murmuring incomprehensibly under her breath, and taking deep breaths against the sobs that lodged in her throat.

"Lauren, dear God, please don't cry. I did not mean to—"

"I do not string them along. Ethan, *he* encourages them, but I have *never*," she mumbled. "He would have me marry the fattest purse, and will not leave me be until I have done so, because there is no other answer for Rosewood. But *I* don't think that! We can trade things, like milk and wool, and honestly, I do not *have* to marry," she said miserably. "And I have explained to Magnus I cannot marry him, but he harbors some fantastic idea that I will change my mind . . ."

He would have kicked himself if he could. He had been angry, irrationally jealous of Bergen, and uncommonly rash with his words. The coach lurched forward and Lauren clutched the squabs, looking so forlorn that Alex instinctively, blindly, came across the coach and gathered her in his arms.

She did not resist him.

"I did not mean to upset you," he muttered against the top of her head. "I would not upset you for the world."

"You cannot upset me." She sniffed, and incongruously wiped a tear from her cheek.

He slipped two fingers beneath her chin and tilted her face upward, forcing her to look at him. "I am sorry," he said. "It was a wretched thing to do, even to Madgoose. But I was mad with—Bloody hell, I do not pretend to understand what it is about you that causes me to act so irrationally, but I cannot help . . . *feeling* the way I do. God,

Lauren, I want you, do you know that? I want you like I have never wanted anyone in my life . . ." His voice trailed off as the enormity of what he had just uttered weighed in around them.

She seemed just as stunned. Her eyes pooled; her bottom lip trembled slightly. It was more than he could bear, and he tenderly kissed her forehead. He heard the soft choke of another sob, and leaned down to kiss her mouth. Her lips were unbelievably inviting—soft and moist, the taste of salt on them. As he shaped them to his own, she sighed softly.

That small sigh awoke a ravenous desire in him. His tongue slid slowly along the crease of her lips, then slipped inside to savor sweet, sweet mouth. Her fingers curled innocently around his wrist, and the seductive allure of that single act pounded away at his considerable defenses. Despite a weak objection from his conscience, he suddenly pulled her to him, crushing her against his body as his mouth plundered hers with a fierce hunger he could not sate.

She softened in his arms, her body molding effortlessly to the rigid contours of his. Desire coursed through him, culminating in rigid attention against her belly. He delved deeper, demanded more of her, and she eagerly responded. With one arm, he firmly anchored her to the arousal that strained against his trousers. His other hand swept over her, caressing her, sweeping the outline of her breast. He began to move against her, a soft undulation that made her press against him. Ripping the gloves from his hands, he held her tightly, almost afraid she would slip away from him and melt into the squabs, on which they were now, somehow, prostrate. Her breast filled his hand as he rubbed his thumb across the satin of her gown. Impatient for more, he slipped his hand into her deep décolletage, stroking the peak of her breast with his palm. She gasped with pleasure against his mouth.

That seductive utterance awakened him from the drugging sensation of her body beneath his. It took every ounce of will he possessed, but Alex forced himself to stop. He raised himself slowly and looked down at her. On her back, her chest was heaving with each deep breath. Her gardenia was crushed. Bloody *hell,* how he wanted her. But he would not ravish her on the squabs of his coach like a harlot, no matter how much he would have liked to. He cupped her face in his hands, gently kissed her eyes, then pulled her up to a sitting position.

Her blue eyes were almost black as she wiped a trembling hand across her swollen lips. An errant strand of hair draped seductively across her face, and Alex had never been more aroused. It was sheer force of will that kept him from instructing the driver to take them to his mother's closed house on Berkley Street, where he could do his desire justice. It would be so bloody *easy.* Alarmed by the direction of his thoughts, he impulsively moved to the bench opposite her.

"I did not know a kiss could be like *that,*" she whispered.

Neither did I, he thought helplessly. "Lauren—" he muttered, raking a hand through his hair. "I should not have . . . you deserve so much more," he ground out. She did not reply, and completely at a loss, he leaned down to retrieve his hat.

She did not reply because she was wondering what on earth he thought could be more than that kiss. She was quite simply stunned, at first by the sweet sensation of it, then by the bright flame it ignited within her. The shivers of the strange lightning she had felt when his lips touched hers had quickly turned molten. Warmth seeped through her, draining all reason. Even though he had ended that extraordinary kiss, she was still caught in a web of physical desire, entrapped by an unimaginable passion stirring within her.

Lauren brushed the loose strand of hair from her eye. She looked down, ruefully noting the gardenia was crushed, and absently tried to fix it. She kept her gaze averted from his, trying desperately to overcome the overwhelming sensations warring in her body, her heart and soul. God, her longing for him had grown greater than she could have possibly imagined, and the fear that she could never have him became even more excruciatingly real.

So real, that at that moment, she thought she would do anything to know what it was to be loved by Alexander Christian. Dear God, she would be twenty-five years old in two months, and had never experienced that which her body ached to know. When the coach turned toward Russell Square, she began to panic. She might never have this chance again, never in her life! *Never* would she love like this, and her one opportunity was slipping away with every *clip-clop* of the horses' hooves on the cobblestone. She would go to her grave desperate for the touch of the man she loved if she did not do something. *Now.*

"Alex?" His head came up abruptly, his deep green eyes searching her eyes. One hand clenched his knee, as if he was afraid he might touch her. *"Alex,"* she repeated, squirming inwardly at the twinge of desperation in her voice.

"What is it, sweetheart?" he asked softly. Her heart skipped erratically at his endearment. She stared at the loosened tails of his neckcloth, afraid to say aloud what she was thinking. But oh, God, he had awakened something inside that could not be satisfied without him, something that she simply had to know. She lifted her eyes, her gaze locking with his, afraid unto death to ask it of him. What she was thinking was decadent. Her thoughts could not be so *very* sinful, could they? She was a widow! Who would ever know? He was *engaged*! But he wasn't yet married. Was it really so terrible? Could the one experience, just one night, sentence her to eternal damnation? Did she bloody well *care* at the moment? She would never have a chance like this again—and she was willing to suffer the consequences. She blushed deeply at her own thoughts and the corner of her mouth lifted in a lopsided, uncertain smile.

Alex lifted a brow.

"Will you . . . ah, sh-show me?" she choked.

Alex raised his other brow to meet the first. "Show you
. . . *what,* love?" he asked cautiously.

She nervously cleared her throat and tried again. "Show
me . . . *how* . . . you know, to ah . . . *love.*" There.
Mortified, she blushed furiously at having actually voiced
her desire aloud, in plain English, so there was no mistaking
it. Incredibly, Alex did not seem offended by her wanton-
ness. Quite the contrary; his eyes darkened immediately
with what she instinctively knew was the same desire she
felt.

"Lauren—"

"Show me," she whispered again, more insistently, suddenly determined not to let propriety stand in the way of her
decision. He looked uncertain; she impulsively leaned
across the coach and covered his hand with hers. "Just one
night, remember?"

Alex was momentarily taken aback, afraid he had misunderstood her, and just as afraid he had not. He was mad,
raving mad, to even *consider* it, but her eyes sparkled with a
light that seemed to come from somewhere deep inside her,
beckoning him. He clenched his jaw against his raging hunger. Lust was surely causing him to imagine things.

"Please?" she whispered, as if assuring him he had not
imagined it, and succeeded in seducing the pants off him
without even a blink of her eye. He abruptly yanked open
the vent in the ceiling.

"Brianson! Fourteen Berkley Street!" he barked. She
smiled, almost gratefully, he thought, and it very nearly
drove him to his knees. He pulled her across the coach and
onto his lap, his thoughts tumbling out of control as he
kissed the curve of her arm and began to slowly peel her
glove away. This was insane! He was a duke! A *gentleman,*
for Chrissakes! Yet there was nothing, no argument his mind
could produce that could stop him now. Every tendril of

conscience that tried to take root was quickly severed. He was only aware of Lauren; every sense, every pore was filled with her, the sweet taste of her, and the fragrant smell of her hair.

He thought they would bloody well never reach Berkeley Street in his lifetime.

It all felt like a dream to Lauren. He slowly removed her gloves, kissing her bare arms, her wrist, then her neck and her lips to the point she was breathless and unable to think clearly. When the coach came to halt, she had no time to think; he quickly lifted her out and instructed Brianson to pull the coach around back. Wrapping her protectively in the folds of his greatcoat, he hurried to the front door. The house he had brought her to was dark; he let her go only to retrieve a key from under the flagstones, then rushed her inside, closing the door quickly behind them.

In the dark foyer, he felt around for a light while her breathing grew more and more constricted. A tremor of panic racked her as the light from a single candle flared. His eyes sought her in the darkness, and when he found her, he smiled reassuringly. Wordlessly, he extended a hand to her. Suddenly frightened, she stared at him, and for a moment, feared she would change her mind. No, she wanted this. Very hesitantly, she slipped her hand into his.

"Lauren . . . if you have changed your mind, it is all right," he said soothingly.

To her utter amazement, she smiled and shook her head. "I *cannot* change it. Believe me, I have tried," she whispered truthfully.

He stood looking at her for a moment, his eyes sweeping her body. And then he began to walk, very slowly, toward a staircase spiraling up to darkness above, her hand firmly in his. Her mind raced far ahead of her feet, struggling with the protests of her conscience that battled with the very strong need to be with him.

He tried to set her at ease by talking about the house, how

it was rarely opened, and the family debate over what to do with it for the long term. They moved down the dark corridor on the first floor, passing two or three doors, she thought, until he came to one and paused. He opened the door and stepped inside, pulling her with him.

She could ask him to take her home. *Now,* before it was too late. He placed the candlestick on a table and turned to face her. Another tremor raced through her; fear was overtaking her desire; fear of the unknown, of her prurient longing and it's consequences.

"You are trembling. Are you certain about this?" he asked softly.

Her heart leapt to her throat. A thousand no's died on her tongue, slain by the longing she had felt since they had first met at Rosewood. "Oh, Alex," she sighed, "I just want to know . . . I mean, I *must* know . . . I realize this must sound very odd to you, very wanton, but it is not something I can explain, really, it's just that it is here," she said, motioning with a shaking hand toward her abdomen and chest, "lodged in here, and I cannot rid myself of it, no matter how hard I try. Every time I look at you, I feel it." He unexpectedly reached inside her cloak, his hand gently caressing the level plane of her abdomen.

Her skin burned where he touched her, igniting the flames in her belly all over again. "I, ah, suppose I could be ill, but I really do not recall ever feeling something quite like this, you know—" She stopped abruptly as his hand slid up her ribcage to the side of her breast. His other hand slipped beneath her cloak, encircling her waist, drawing her into his chest. "I don't think it really an illness, but I suppose it could be indigestion, although that seems unlikely since I hardly ate a bite today," she babbled.

"I do not think," he murmured through a faint smile, "that this is indigestion." His lips grazed her neck, sending another round of shivers through her. "I know what ails you, angel—it is this incredible desire we attempt to deny. If you will allow me, I will fix it." He nibbled her earlobe, taking her earring into his mouth. She inhaled sharply, and he lifted his head. "We will not do anything you do not want, Lauren. We can stop at any time."

That was a monstrous lie, and she knew it. "Alex," she whispered, plunging headlong into the situation she had created, "please, just show me."

He groaned softly, swept her into his arms, and marched to the bed. He paused to sweep the dust cloth from it, then fell with her in his arms onto the elaborate green and gold spread. One arm swept under her and hauled her into his chest as his mouth descended hungrily to hers. Deftly, he discarded her cloak, his hands caressing her back and loosening her hair from its pins. Driven by the urgency to touch him, she swept her hands over his chest and shoulders, feeling the corded muscles beneath his silken shirt.

Her hair tumbled down around them, forming a curtain of dark curl as he unfastened the buttons of her gown with the skill of a lady's maid. Somehow, the gown came off, as did his coat, waistcoat, and shirt. When he pulled the ribbon of her chemise, one breast sprang free. He palmed it, slowly kneading the peak to stretch taut and firm, and dragged his mouth from her throat to lave it. A surge of raw, intoxicating sensation roared through her, and moaning softly, she reached for him.

Suddenly on her back, Lauren grasped his thick hair as he laved the other breast, amazed by the shocking reverberations that rumbled through her body and seemed to settle in her groin. A pressure, sweet and torturous, was building in her belly. She caught a nervous breath when Alex pulled the hem of her chemise upward, then gasped with terrified pleasure when his fingers brushed lightly against her flesh. He thrust his tongue into her mouth as his fingers danced sensuously across her bare skin, skirting the apex of her thighs, then slipping into the wet folds. "My God, you are beautiful," he murmured against her skin.

Terrified by what he was doing to her, Lauren froze. His fingers stroked her skillfully, circling around and over a point of intense pleasure. His lips found hers again, tenderly kissing her while the pressure built to intolerable lightness. "Angel," he whispered, "dear God, I want you." His warm lips fell to her neck as he fumbled with his trousers. When his weight settled on her again, she could feel his velvet tip throbbing against her bare flesh. Each sensation, more startling than the last, was as tormenting as it was exquisite. She impulsively, anxiously, came up on her elbows.

Alex paused and looked into her eyes. Tiny tufts of chestnut curls swirled around her face. Long, silken tresses dropped to the bed behind her and over her shoulder. Propped on her elbows, her magnificent breasts exposed to him, she looked at him with a beguiling softness that made his heart pound. He had never desired a woman so intently. He had never yearned to show a woman what he was feeling, to give her all the pleasure he could, to fulfill her in ways she had never before experienced. Lauren's dark blue eyes fell to his mouth and she tenderly laid two fingers against his lips.

It was more than a man could possibly endure. Alex swiftly positioned himself between her thighs. She was still on her elbows, her breasts rising and falling with each frantic breath as he entered her. He moved carefully and steadily, relishing the feel of her body tightening provocatively around him, pulling him into her depths. Unconsciously, she pulled her bottom lip between her teeth, her gaze drifting to his lips.

"Look at me, sweetheart," he hoarsely urged her. A torrent of emotion flowing through him, Alex slipped a steadying hand behind her back. Gazing into her eyes, he plunged fiercely into her warmth.

With a strangled cry of pain, Lauren buried her face in his shoulder.

Stunned, Alex's body went rigid, his mind reeling with

the realization that she was a virgin. *A virgin!* He lowered her to the bed, murmuring his desperate apology for having hurt her and an equally desperate promise he would never hurt her again. Terribly confused, he tried to make sense of it, tried to understand how a widow was a virgin. It was impossible! But it *was* possible; he had *felt* himself tear through her maidenhead. God, what had he done? *What in the hell had he done?*

Lauren was oblivious to his astonishment; the sudden pain had shocked her. Slowly, it began to ebb, and she shifted against him, instinctively wanting to continue this extraordinary journey, to feel the keen pressure of his body inside her again. He moaned, kissed her softly, and began to lure her into the seductive rhythm of his passion. The pain forgotten, she quickly became entranced with what was happening to her. He buried his face against her neck, his breathing ragged—she intuitively knew he was restraining himself, moving gently for her benefit. His hand found her breast again, and he tenderly rolled the peak between his fingers, sending a jolt of sensation down her spine that landed squarely in the midst of the pressure building in her groin.

Her body screaming for release, she began to move with him. Alex answered her desire by slipping an arm under her hips so he could lengthen his stroke and reach the very core of her. As the pressure began to build toward a frightening climax, Lauren clung to him, afraid that she would virtually explode into pieces. "Let it come, angel," he murmured in her ear. "Let it happen."

Suddenly, the pressure in her spiraled upward and out of control. She convulsed against him as her entire body burst into a thousand pinpricks of light. A cry of pure pleasure stuck in her throat as wave after wave of ecstasy washed over her. Her body felt weightless; she would have sworn she floated above the bed. Alex's strokes took on a new urgency; he answered her soft gasps with a low growl before throwing his head back and pouring his seed deep within her. With a final, powerful thrust, a guttural moan emanated from his throat before he collapsed on top of her, bracing himself on his elbows.

When she could focus at last, she smiled brilliantly, in a state of complete euphoria. *"Alex,"* she whispered. He smiled, stroking her cheek with his knuckles. She could not have dreamed it would be so intimate, so *giving.* Her eyes filled with tears that she tried to blink away.

Alex immediately cupped her face in his hands, muttering an oath under his breath. "I hurt you, didn't I? Darling, I did not know—why did you not tell me?" he moaned as a fat tear slipped down her cheek. She laughed, surprising him, while more tears slipped from her eyes.

"Oh, Alex, I am so glad it was you," she murmured. She reached up and twirled a lock of his hair around her finger. "I . . . I never imagined it could be so wonderful between two people. I was terribly afraid I would never really know you," she said softly, a new flood of warmth filling her from head to toe. "And I so desperately wanted to *know* you."

He looked at her in amazement. She laughed giddily against his neck, never having felt so strong or secure in her life. God, she adored him, and without thinking, she suddenly blurted, "I love you, Alex, do you know that? I have loved you since the day you incited Lucy to almost kill me, and I cannot stop!" She laughed again, a little hysterically. "I have tried and tried, I really have, but I cannot make myself not love you!"

Stunned by her admission of love, Alex held her tightly as she simultaneously sobbed and laughed into his neck. He rolled onto his side, still holding her. Moved by the simple sincerity in her declaration, he marveled at the depth of his understanding. God forgive him, but he was quite certain he loved her just as profoundly.

Which made the extraordinary experience they had just shared all the more difficult, something he forcibly blocked from his mind. "You are," he murmured, "the most beautiful woman in all of England. An angel. A wicked little angel at that, for making me want you so badly."

She giggled. "Do you want me truly, Alex?"

"With all my heart, darling," he responded, somewhat amazed that he would admit as much.

"For . . . for just one night?" she asked hesitantly, tracing the line of his jaw with her finger.

God, if she only knew. "For a lifetime."

Her hand slipped away from his face, and she sank into the pillows. He propped himself on his elbow and gazed down at her, stroking her satin hair. "What are you thinking?"

"How cruel life is."

He said nothing for a long moment. He thought about the possibilities open to them, but the best he could imagine was the occasional visit to Rosewood, or secret trysts in London from time to time. A tear slipped from the corner of her eye as she stared blankly at the canopy above them. He would not allow the magic between them to be marred with the cold reality of their lives. They had one night. He leaned over her and kissed the tip of her nose. "I will think of something, Lauren. I will find a way for us," he said soothingly, and claimed her lips again.

He made love to her again, slowly and gently, reaching another pinnacle of fulfillment he had not thought possible. But when the clock on the mantel struck three, the practical side of him took over.

They rode to Russell Square in silence, his arm wrapped protectively around her, her head resting lightly on his shoulder. She was still smiling, and he could not wrest his gaze away from the beauty he held in his arms. What they had shared had been the most fulfilling physical act of love in which he had ever engaged. He had never been so completely *possessed* in his entire life. Women had writhed be-

neath him before, but none had filled him with her response
or had aroused him to new heights of fulfillment. But what
really moved him was the discovery of something so primal,
so inordinately masculine in the possession of her virginity.
The impact on him was powerful—she was a part of him
now. He had claimed her, had touched her depths before any
other man. She was his angel. *His.*

As the coach slowed on Russell Square, Lauren looked
up, an unreadable expression in her eyes. Strange, but he
suddenly sensed an impending loss that made him oddly
nervous. There were so many things he wanted to say, so
many things he *should* say. And just as many things he
should *not* say, had no *right* to say.

"Lauren, we must talk. I—"

"I love you, Alex. Do not say anything to discourage
me," she whispered, smiling. "I know what the truth is, but
this night belongs to us. Please, let's not spoil it." Her eyes
implored him, and he was struck by the recognition that it
was completely beyond his power to say no to her. With a
heavy sigh of resignation, he climbed out of the coach, then
helped her down. As she glanced furtively toward the town
house, he was gripped again with the unnerving thought she
was slipping away from him. Desperate, he caught her arm.

"I must see you again." Her lips parted, and he quickly
shook his head. "Listen to me. I do not care about anything
else, I just want . . ." The words died in his throat. What
did he want? Goddammit, what did he really *want*? "Look,
just come to me tomorrow," he said anxiously. "Vauxhall
Gardens, nine o'clock, the small fountain near the entrance.
Do you know which one I mean? Tell Hill that you are to see
Lady Darfield. Promise me you will come." He spoke
quickly, frantically, the fingers of irrational fear curling
around his heart. Fear he would lose forever what he had
found tonight.

"Of course I will be there," she whispered, and leaning
up on her tiptoes, kissed the corner of his mouth. She gig-

gled as she pried his fingers from her elbow, then turned and walked briskly toward the door of the town house.

"Don't be late!" he whispered loudly after her.

She tossed an alluring smile over her shoulder and shook her head. He watched as she skipped up the narrow little path and inside, the memory of her smile forever burned in his brain. How extraordinary, he thought, that he would gladly endure the flames of hell for a glimpse of that smile. How ironic that he was well on his way.

Chapter 18

Euphoric and wildly in love, Lauren stepped into the darkened foyer and quietly shut the door behind her. She had never felt so wonderfully complete in all her life. Nothing could have prepared her for the magic of being loved by Alex; her body still tingled with the delicious memory of it. As she slipped out of her cloak, she paused to rub the fabric against her face, recalling the feel of his hands on her skin.

"Enjoy the opera?"

Startled, she whirled around, dropping her cloak. Deep in the shadows, Paul was standing next to the armor. "You startled me!" She smiled, bending to retrieve her cloak.

Paul did not return her smile. "Bergen was here earlier, waiting for you, until it became apparent you were not coming home from the opera. Where did you go?" he asked quietly.

"Ah . . . to a gathering at Harrison Green's," she lied, then asked hastily, "where is Ethan?"

Paul's expression was dubious at best. "In bed. He tired

rather quickly from all the cackling about the five hundred thousand pounds a year the duke apparently earns.''

''Oh,'' she said softly.

''I was under the distinct impression when you left here tonight that you were not interested in his company. In fact, I thought you were most decidedly set against it.''

''I suppose the evening was better than I anticipated,'' she murmured. ''I had a wonderful time, Paul,'' she said, conscious that she smiled too brightly.

''I see,'' he said, and for a moment, Lauren feared that he did. He said nothing, just stood looking at her. Peering right through her. Uncomfortable, she turned and carefully hung her cloak on a wall peg. He sighed wearily. ''Lauren, do you know what you are doing?''

She laughed nervously and turned to face him. ''Doing?''

''Magnus is a good man. He truly cares for you.''

''Goodness, Paul, what are you talking about?''

He moved out of the shadows. ''I want to see you happy. Magnus is a good man. He will honor you above all others.''

Still reeling from her incredible experience, Paul's sudden and uncharacteristic support of Magnus made her thoughts spin like a top. ''Are we speaking of the same Magnus?'' she asked incredulously. ''Count Magnus Bergen of Bavaria? The one you despise?''

''I have a changed opinion.''

''Well, I do not,'' she said sharply and began to walk toward the stairs.

Paul's hand shot out and painfully gripped her wrist as she attempted to pass. ''He will marry Marlaine Reese, Lauren. Nothing is going to change that. *Nothing.* You are only harming yourself with this foolishness!''

Appalled, Lauren jerked free. ''You presume too much, Paul! Have you forgotten that *you* are the one who made that foolish wager? I would not have gone tonight had it not been for that, and now you would fault me for enjoying it?''

Paul shook his head, dismissing her rebuke. "Listen to me! Ethan has exhausted our funds. We will return to Rosewood in a fortnight. If you do not accept Bergen's offer, you may not have another! At least with him, you may expect to live with respect and comfort."

She laughed bitterly. "Dear God, you must be awfully fearful of having a spinster sister!"

"That is ridiculous!" he snapped, then checked himself, glancing uneasily about the cluttered entry. "I only want what is best for you," he continued evenly. "I have invested wisely in stocks and securities, and I am very optimistic I can take care of Rosewood now. Do you not see? There is no longer any reason for you to toil away there, hoping to meet a man who will accept the children. Bergen accepts them. I have thought about it—we could arrange a betrothal agreement whereby you would live at Rosewood half of each year. That's not such a bad solution, and it *is* the best match you can hope for."

Lauren stumbled backward as if he had slapped her, bumping against the wall and rattling two crossed sabers hanging overhead. "I cannot believe what I am hearing! Those children are not a loathsome chore, I *love* them—you know that! Honestly, Paul, coming to London was not *my* idea—I do not *hope* to meet a man, you and Ethan hoped for that! And Magnus may be my best hope for a *match*," she said angrily, "but I do not want to marry him! I do not love him!"

The muscles of Paul's jaw bulged from the clenching of his teeth. He reached for her hand, but she quickly moved away from him. He slowly lowered his arm. "Forget Sutherland, Lauren. He will only hurt you, and I cannot bear to see that."

"For someone who does not want to see me hurt, you are doing a fine job of it," she shot back, and bolted up the stairs before he ruined her glorious night.

* * *

At noon the next day, Lauren awoke and smiled dreamily at the sunlight pouring through her window. Her mind was on Alex, every masculine inch of him. In her dreams, she had relived each and every moment of her incredible experience with him. Even in the privacy of her room, her cheeks flushed pink at the memory of the passion they had shared. She could hardly wait to see him again and eagerly climbed out of bed, but a glance at the mantel clock made her groan. A wait of nine hours was not to be *borne.* With hands on hips, she glared at the clock, wondering how she would occupy her time if she had any hope of enduring the interminable wait.

She began her morning toilette, planning how she might pass the time. She decided to visit the infirmary this afternoon and then call on Abbey, thinking perhaps her friend or her maid could do something unique with her hair. And then, *then* she would meet the love of her life at Vauxhall Gardens.

A delightful little shiver ran through her as she recalled the urgency with which he had demanded to see her again, admonishing her not to be late. Paul was so very wrong! Alex felt the same as she did. He had said as much. *I will find a way for us.*

Oh God. She paused, glancing at her reflection in the mirror as an unexpected surge of guilt came over her. She felt a deep sorrow for Marlaine, but what could she do? " 'My true love hath my heart and I have his, by just exchange one for the other given,' " she whispered aloud. Who could possibly predict where love's arrows would land? She had not sought it, it had just happened! Surely Marlaine would be able to understand there was nothing to be done for it. She shrugged off her guilt and went about her dressing, cheerfully humming the song from *The Two Gentlemen of Verona.*

Still humming when she entered the dining room, she

smiled broadly at Magnus and Ethan. At Magnus's dark look, she pertly tossed her head.

"There she is, just look at her! I knew the lass would fetch me a good annuity!" Ethan crowed before shoving a slab of buttered bread into his mouth. Magnus did not reply, but quietly sipped his tea, his icy blue eyes following Lauren's every move.

"Uncle, what on earth are you talking about?" Lauren smiled, then laughed giddily. Conscious that her glee was a bit inappropriate, she quickly took a seat across from Magnus and focused on the painted pattern of his teacup.

"Just what they were discussing in the clubs this morning! Sutherland at the opera with Countess Bergen!" Ethan blithely continued.

The remark instantly sobered her; her hand stilled on the teapot and she shot a quick, appraising glance at her uncle. "What do you mean?"

"Talk is all over town!" he said, munching a thick slice of ham.

Frowning, Lauren poured her tea and carefully added a bit of cream. "But why?" she asked at last. "I am sure his grace has many female friends. Certainly it is not so unusual—"

"It is the way he looks at you," Magnus abruptly answered her in German, his voice unusually cold.

Lauren cautiously slid her gaze to him. His eyes, locked on hers, looked like two hard nuggets of ice. "I beg your pardon?" she asked nervously.

"His desire for you is quite evident. It is obvious he would have you for his own if he could. After last night, there are many who speculate he will have you soon, if he has not already."

That stung her. Carefully, she placed the spoon on the chipped saucer and leaned back in her chair.

"What did he say?" Ethan demanded.

"He said there is much talk," she murmured.

"A sign of good fortune for the Hill family!" her uncle reasoned spiritedly.

Magnus sliced an impatient gaze across Ethan, who was sopping up the last bit of his eggs with a piece of bread. "I would like a moment alone with your niece, my lord," he said in English.

"Of course, of course," Ethan grinned, still chewing the bread as he heaved himself to his feet. "You two have yourselves a nice little chat," he cackled, and waddled out the door.

Magnus waited for Ethan to depart, staring at Lauren with the most foreboding expression she had ever seen on him. She smiled sheepishly. "Toast?" she offered lamely.

He growled and came to his feet at once, the chair scraping loudly on the pine floor. Grasping his hands tightly behind his back, he began to pace. "I have made a decent offer for your hand," he began in German. "A *very* decent offer. Yet you have put me off time and time again—"

"I have not put you off, I have *refused* you, Magnus," she solemnly interjected.

He paused, piercing her with a furious glare. "Please allow me to finish. I have asked myself why you would put me off," he continued. "Do you think to attract a better offer? Are you so naïve to think your situation is good? But now I understand—you have some fantasy of this duke, do you not? A childish fantasy—"

"How dare you!" she cried indignantly.

He leveled a darkly quelling look at her that effectively unnerved her into silence. "I do not fault you for it, Lauren. Everyone has them at some point. Even as a young man, I had such a fantasy for a woman far above me in social standing. Eventually I saw my infatuation for what it was: a *fantasy*—"

"I am not indulging in a fantasy!"

He suddenly gripped the table and leaned across, his eyes boring into her. "Make no mistake—it is *fantasy*! That man has no use for you other than to warm his bed! And you are not a young maiden with the luxury of time for such daydreams. You are in need of a husband and I offer you a good match, a wealthy existence, and respect.''

''Respect?'' she echoed in disbelief.

Slowly, he straightened. ''And . . . affection,'' he said softly. ''I have much affection for you, Lauren. I have admired you since our paths crossed at Bergenschloss.''

She started to remark that she could hardly believe that, given the way he had acted at Bergenschloss, but he quickly brought up a hand. ''I do not ask you to return my affection. I am not so blind that I do not see your heart lies elsewhere. I ask only that in return for the protection of my name, you respect me as you would your husband. As you respected my uncle. I ask only that, and in exchange for your respect, I will allow your affections to be what they are—for *whomever* they are.''

Her breath caught in her throat. A million thoughts tumbled through her brain, not the least of which was a familiar glimmer of fondness for him. That he would offer himself in such a way—without hope of her returning his affections—touched her very deeply. ''Magnus, I—''

''Do not answer me now,'' he said gruffly. ''Think on what I have said. But I must have your final answer tomorrow, do you understand? I will not stay here any longer, nipping after your skirts like a *dog,*'' he said disgustedly. ''At least consider it. *Honestly* consider it.''

He walked around the table and came to stand beside her. ''Regardless of what you will decide, you must be very careful, do you understand? Do not fool yourself—the talk today is of *you,* not him. These people will cut you dead.''

''You are exaggerating,'' she said weakly.

He sighed impatiently. ''This is England, *liebchen.* They do not tolerate indiscretion in their little circles. They will treat you as if you were as insignificant as the dirt under their feet.''

Lauren glanced at her hands in her lap, refusing to dignify his threats with a response. She had only gone to the opera, for heaven's sake. He was trying to scare her into considering his offer.

"Think on what I have said." In an unusual display of affection, he gently smoothed his palm over the crown of her head before quietly quitting the room.

Lauren sagged as the door shut behind him. She had already considered his offer. She had considered it for *weeks*. She was fond of Magnus, but it was not enough. She did not and could not love him. Not ever. She loved Alex with all her heart, had loved him since the day he had come to Rosewood, and would love him madly for the rest of her life. There was nothing Magnus could offer her that would ever change that.

Oh, Alex! Sighing happily, she buttered a piece of toast.

Alex signed the last of the papers his secretary had left him, the bold strokes falling under words he had not read. It did not matter, nothing mattered anymore. *Christ*, he had done exactly what Paul Hill had feared. Like a rutting stag, he had compromised Lauren beyond reparation, had ruined the only woman he would ever truly love.

And he had betrayed Marlaine.

Marlaine.

A stab of remorse shot down his spine. She did not deserve this, this unconscionable perfidy, just weeks before their so-called wedding of the decade. He dropped the quill and closed his eyes, trying to blot out her delicate features and his guilt.

He did not have to see to know it was Arthur who entered the room unannounced. He opened his eyes to see his brother standing before him, the morning edition of *The Times* stuffed under his arm. Usually much too cheerful, Arthur's dark look surprised Alex. His brother stared at him

for a long moment, then asked bluntly, "What in the hell are
you doing?"

"I am reviewing some documents," Alex said blandly.

"You know perfectly well what I mean, Alex."

"I don't think I do," he responded warily.

"Then I shall be perfectly clear. What in the hell is this
little *on-dit* in the society pages? Why is everyone whispering about a certain duke who attended the opera last evening
in the company of a certain countess?"

Alex snorted impatiently—the last thing he needed at the
moment was Arthur's indignation over some trifling piece of
gossip.

"You apparently left nothing to the imagination, I'll
grant you that," Arthur continued, recklessly tossing *The
Times* onto his desk. "Particularly when the two of you
left—*alone*—and Paddy was escorted home by Mrs. Clark.
Not her favorite nephew, who had escorted her *to* the ball!
The little display you put on was only eclipsed by Bergen's.
Seems *he* spent the entire evening staring wistfully at you
and the countess!" he exclaimed, and fell heavily into a
leather chair.

"What, Arthur, you believe the rubbish you read now?"
Alex asked snappishly.

"It's all over town, Alex. Is it true?" his brother asked
angrily.

Alex sliced a heated gaze across his brother. "Not that it
is any of your affair, but *yes,* I accompanied her to the opera.
Just as I accompanied Lady Fairlane when her husband was
away last week. What of it?"

"This is *different,* Alex. Unlike Lady Fairlane, Countess
Bergen is not married to one of your good friends. You
escorted her while your fiancée was away tending her dying
grandmother. The night you escorted Lady Fairlane, your
fiancée was also in attendance! And Lady Fairlane, for all
her charms, is *not* beautiful. Countess Bergen is breathtak-
ingly so, a fact noted in *The Times,* along with the observa-

tion that you could not have seen a single bloody act last night, as you could not take your eyes from her!'' he shouted, gesturing wildly at the newspaper on the desk.

''What rubbish,'' Alex muttered angrily, shoving the paper aside.

''But damning nonetheless! What of Marlaine?'' Arthur asked, point-blank.

Commanding himself to control his rising fury, Alex said calmly, ''What is wrong with you, Arthur? I thought you enjoyed the titillating pieces of trash they print about me. This is certainly not the first time there has been talk.''

''This is the first time I have heard very unflattering comments about you from acquaintances who saw you with her. I do not *like* hearing indecent speculation about your whereabouts when I am trying to enjoy myself at Harrison Green's. I suppose I just chafe a bit when the Christian name is slandered. But tell me nothing happened, Alex, and I will not say another word,'' Arthur insisted.

Alex looked his brother squarely in the eye and considered lying. But he had never lied to Arthur, and it was one thing he would not do. Apparently, it was the *only* reprehensible thing he would not do. ''I cannot tell you that,'' he said quietly.

Arthur's mouth fell open. ''Are you *insane*?'' he bellowed.

''It would seem.''

Gaping, Arthur leaned forward, bracing his hands on top of his knees. ''That's all you can say? *Jesus,* Alex, have you no more regard for your title than *that*? Has it somehow escaped you that this is the worst possible moment to be flaunting your infatuation all over town? Think of your position in the Lords! For Chrissakes, what about Marlaine? She is about to become your *wife*!''

''Do you think I do not know that?'' Alex shouted angrily. ''By God, do you think I have thought about anything else? What do you want me to do, Arthur? Bloody hell, *would* that I could change it all! But unfortunately, I have not as yet determined a way to turn back the bloody *clock*!''

A tense silence filled the room. Arthur's eyes flashed angrily as he stood abruptly and went to the window. Alex frowned as he regarded his brother's rigid back. He understood his desire to protect the family's good name. That same instinct, coupled with a healthy dose of guilt, had plagued him all night and all morning.

''You must begin to undo the damage. Today. Before Marlaine returns,'' Arthur said quietly.

''I fully intend to,'' Alex responded, and wondered just how, exactly, he could undo it all. He could not stop *thinking* about Lauren, much less navigate a way out of this mess.

''I will help you,'' Arthur said, turning to face him. ''But first, you must promise to *forget* her once and for all! It can never be, do you understand that?''

He understood. The pain in his chest reminded him of it with every breath. ''I think we could both use a drink,'' he mumbled, and went to the sideboard.

Arthur stayed for a while, devising a tale that he convinced himself would make last night look very innocent. Alex nodded at points that seemed appropriate, letting Arthur plot. He was far too distressed by what possible excuse he could make to Lauren tonight to really listen. Did he offer her a sum to forget it had ever happened? The very thought disgusted him. Did he explain that he had responsibilities, and therefore could not consider a continuing liaison with her? Brilliant, Christian, he thought bitterly, a little late for that. Did he suggest she become his mistress? God, how contrived that would seem! And exactly when did he say all this? Before or after he made love to her again, because God knew *that* idea was consuming him.

It consumed him well after Arthur left and up until the moment Finch announced Marlaine and the duchess. Startled, Alex came off the leather couch like a fox caught in the henhouse. The *last* thing he expected or needed today was

Marlaine. God, not now, not *today*, he silently begged, but Marlaine walked in behind Hannah, her face a wreath of smiles. "Alex! I have missed you dreadfully!" she cried as she hurried across the room to him.

He perfunctorily kissed her cheek and wondered madly if she could see the shame burning his face. "I am glad you have returned," he said, mustering as much enthusiasm as he could. "How is Grandmama?"

"Did you not receive my letter? She has made a remarkable recovery! Oh, Alex, the doctor thinks she'll be able to come to the wedding after all! It is simply divine providence, don't you think?" she beamed.

"That's wonderful news."

"Oh my, you do look awfully worn. Have you been eating? I hope you did not work too hard at Parliament."

His excuse for leaving Tarriton knifed through what was left of his conscience. "I have eaten with alarming regularity," he said wearily, and turned to Hannah. "Good afternoon, Mother."

"Alex. I thought you would want to know that Marlaine is staying with me at Arthur's until her mother can return to London." She crossed the room to him, her expression thoughtful as she lifted her palm and pressed it against his cheek. "Did you sleep last night?"

"Of course!" He laughed, and pulled her hand away from his face, fearful that she might feel the heat. "Did the two of you think I would expire?" he joked, and turned away from his mother's probing eyes to Marlaine, motioning her toward the couch. "Come and tell me about Grandmama."

"Of course I shall, but first I must dash off a note to Lady Paddington. I promised my mother I would let her know the moment we returned with the news of Grandmama's condition. Did you not receive my note saying we were arriving today?" Marlaine asked again, frowning prettily.

He had not looked at his correspondence in three days. "I must have missed it," he said, and left it at that. It seemed to satisfy Marlaine; she floated to his desk, chattering eagerly as to what she should put in the note, then lightheartedly ticking off the myriad things she needed to do before the wedding. Alex resumed his seat on the couch, listening to the almost childlike way she spoke. He was fond of Marlaine; there was no question in his mind as to that. She was a sweet, caring person, and if she had a fault, it was that she was *too* caring. Nonetheless, he respected her immensely for it. But she just did not fill his soul.

Lauren filled him, to the very brink.

Marlaine did not seem to have the same enthusiasm for life; she was much too concerned with what others might think. It was inconceivable to him that his fiancée would ever allow herself to venture into a field. She would contribute funds to an orphanage but never shelter the children herself. She would abide his kisses, but she would never *ask* him to make love to her. And he seriously doubted she would respond to him with complete abandon.

She was not Lauren.

Bloody hell, Arthur was right. He had responsibilities that far outweighed these unprecedented feelings of love. He almost laughed out loud at the very idea that he, of all people, might have *feelings* of *love*. What in the hell was love, anyway? Certainly nothing that could justify turning against years of certain beliefs about society, responsibility, and the peerage. Lauren was not of his station. A marriage to her would not consolidate fortunes or create formidable family alliances. Marlaine met these requirements, and she had waited for two years to be married to him. Waited like a good hunting dog, he thought miserably. Remorse washed over him. Whether or not he could have defied convention, it was too damned late. He had made his commitments and had no choice but to honor them. Listening to Marlaine's voice now, he knew he could not forsake her.

"Alex? I would have your opinion on this note," Marlaine said eagerly, and began to read what she had penned to Paddy. Yes, she deserved the wedding she so desperately wanted, the life of a duchess. She deserved far better than the likes of him, but unfortunately, she was unknowingly as mired in this mess as he was.

"That's lovely," he said, smiling thinly as he came to his feet.

"Oh my, look at the time!" Hannah said suddenly. "I promised Hortense to be a fourth at one of her loo tables. Marlaine, dear, I shall send the coach round in time for supper."

"Good afternoon, your grace!" Marlaine called in a singsong voice. Hannah walked to the door, pausing as she grasped the brass handle. Looking over her shoulder at Alex, her eyes flicked the length of him. He thought she might speak, but she abruptly smiled and left.

Marlaine looked up from the desk and smiled prettily at Alex when the door shut behind his mother. He reminded himself again that she would make him a good wife. A comfortable wife. He had never imagined or wanted more, just that she would be a good and comfortable—Goddammit, he did not *want* a good and comfortable wife! He wanted a wife that could stir the deepest passions in him! A lover who would move him to give her the stars! He wanted a wife who would make him thank *God* each day he awoke next to her.

He suddenly strode to the desk and roughly pulled Marlaine to her feet. "I missed you," he muttered, and claimed her mouth, searching hungrily for something, anything to cover the open wound in his heart, any signal that she could fill the void. Startled, Marlaine stiffened, her lips sealing tightly shut. Her hands came between them as he restlessly sought to unleash some response within her. He pressed her against him, insistent. But she was unyielding— she pushed hard against him, forcing him to release her.

Breathless, she took an unsteady step backward. "Goodness, darling!"

"I want to make love to you, Marlaine, right here, right now."

Red infused her face, and she anxiously patted her perfect coif as her eyes darted about the carpet. "Alex, dearest! You would not ask me to do *that* before our wedding, would you?"

"Then marry me now, *today,*" he said impulsively, frantic to lose himself in her, to claim her body and soul, to awaken something in her that would make it all bearable. Anything, *anything* that might wrest Lauren from his heart and replace her with the woman he would marry.

"You cannot be serious!" she exclaimed, her alarm evident.

"I am deadly serious. Marry me now," he said, and reached for her. She reacted convulsively, jerking insensibly out of his reach. Alex drew up, his eyes searching her face. She pressed her lips firmly together, focusing on his shoulder.

Good God, she was frightened by him.

At any other time, he might have found her maidenly angst amusing. But at this moment, he found it bloody irritating. He calmly watched the alarm and dread widen her brown eyes. There was no desire there, no need of him. Only fear. He abruptly turned and walked away from the desk, his hands shoved deep in his pockets. "No, of course I am not serious. I'm just happy to have you back. Go on with your plans, why don't you? There is something I must do, but I shall return shortly." He walked out of the library without looking back.

Vauxhall Gardens was out of the question. Everything, all that he desired was out of the question the moment Marlaine had walked through that door. He had no choice but to send a note.

*   *   *

Marlaine charitably attributed his behavior to a groom's jitters, and was in the process of making a list of things to do when Finch showed Lady Paddington and Mrs. Clark into the library.

"Lady Paddington! I just this moment dispatched a note to your home informing you I had returned!" Marlaine exclaimed happily.

"Oh, I knew you had come. Mrs. Clark and I had heard from Lady Thistlecourt, who heard from—

"The duchess," Mrs. Clark interjected.

"The duchess. What wonderful news that your grandmother has taken a turn for the better! And not a moment too soon, if you ask me!" Lady Paddington declared. She seated herself, her voluminous, stiff satin skirts rustling loudly as she situated herself just so.

"Not a moment too soon?" Marlaine asked politely, coming from behind the desk. Mrs. Clark shot Lady Paddington a frown.

"Did I say that?" Lady Paddington laughed, and looked contritely at Mrs. Clark.

Confused, Marlaine looked at the two women. "Pardon, but did I miss something?"

"Well, of course not! You were only gone a *week,* what on earth could happen in a single *week*?" Lady Paddington fairly shouted.

"Clara!" Mrs. Clark snapped.

"What?" Lady Paddington responded gruffly.

Marlaine's stomach lurched oddly; she slowly lowered herself onto the couch. Mrs. Clark looked askance at Marlaine, then attempted a smile. "Lady Paddington is not quite herself today," she said apologetically.

"I am very much myself, thank you. I just thought the poor girl might have heard some of the ugly rumors flying about, and I thought to tell her straight on that there is not a shred of truth to them!" Lady Paddington insisted.

Marlaine's stomach did another queer flip. "Rumors?" she asked, very certain she did not want to hear them.

"Oh, it's all *rubbish!* A man may escort a woman to an opera. It's done all the time, I tell you!"

"I am quite sure I do not know what you mean. Of course men escort women to operas. Is there some question?" Marlaine asked, swallowing past a growing sense of disaster.

Lady Paddington brushed the lap of her gown very carefully. "No, at least not in *my* mind. Why, just last week, his grace escorted Lady Fairlane to the opera, and no one thought a *thing* of that."

"Well of course not! Lord Fairlane was called away unexpectedly and Lady Fairlane had been so looking forward to the event. Alex was being kind," Marlaine said.

"He is very kind," Mrs. Clark agreed. "They cannot take *that* from him."

"And he kindly escorted Countess Bergen last evening. Honestly, you would think Parliament had passed some sort of law against simple acts of kindness the way the *ton* goes on and on!" Lady Paddington said angrily.

Her announcement dropped Marlaine's stomach to her toes; her heart began to beat erratically. He had said he would be a good husband. He had all but promised in her father's garden to stop this infatuation. She could no longer deceive herself. Instinctively, she knew—had known for weeks—that this infatuation was somehow different. A surge of anger suddenly shot through her as she recalled the way he had kissed her this very afternoon. Although she did not know *how,* she knew his behavior was related in some way to the countess. "The duke accompanied Countess Bergen to the opera last evening?" she heard herself ask.

"My dear, you will not *think* of it. It is silly, idle chatter, nothing more. Sutherland is a good boy, a very good boy," Lady Paddington averred so strongly, that Marlaine could not help wondering whom she was trying to convince.

"No talk about *him,* of course," Mrs. Clark quickly replied.

"Oh no!" Lady Paddington confirmed. "But there are some who think the countess should not have accompanied him. It was really indelicate, particularly when the object of her affections—"

"You mean her *escort*—"

"Particularly when her *escort* was waiting on pins and needles for the return of his fiancée."

"Oh, and he *was,* my dear, you can rest assured of that!" Mrs. Clark interjected. "He has no interest in *her,* none whatsoever!"

"I have always maintained that if a woman can lose eighteen rounds of loo in one setting, there is something not quite right," Lady Paddington sniffed.

Marlaine barely heard Mrs. Clark's opinion of that. She was too engrossed in keeping a sudden swell of nausea at bay.

Chapter 19

At the Haddington Road Infirmary, a distracted Lauren listened to Mr. Peavey for what seemed hours, hardly able to concentrate long enough to form a sentence. All she could think of was Alex. Throughout the afternoon and on the return trip home, she tried to imagine what he was doing, if he was thinking about her. She closed her eyes and saw the way his dark hair curled above his collar, his broad hand resting on hers, his eyes crinkling at the corners when he laughed. She saw the smoldering way he looked at her as he had thrust into her. An involuntary tremble coursed through her, and she rubbed her hands vigorously against her arms.

Once again at Russell Square, she dressed very carefully for the evening. The pale pink brocade gown she chose seemed a little overdone for Vauxhall Gardens, she thought, and burst into gay laughter. She could meet him in the middle of the pumpkin field for all she cared, *anywhere,* as long as she saw him again.

At half past six, she fairly flew outside to wave down a passing hack and cheerfully gave the driver the direction to

Lady Darfield's. Arriving at the Audley Street mansion, she smiled broadly at the Darfield's butler when he showed her to the green sitting room where Abbey was on the floor, playing with Alexa.

Her friend clambered to her feet when Jones announced her. "Lauren! What a wonderful surprise!" she exclaimed, greeting her with a fond hug. "I had not expected you! I am so glad you have come. Michael and I have spent the entire day preparing for our return to Blessing Park, and I could sorely use some company."

"I should have sent a note around, but I was hoping you might do me an enormous favor," Lauren said, clasping her friend's hands.

"Of course! What is it?"

"Would you *please* help me with my hair?"

"Your *hair*?" Abbey laughed. "My, my, Countess Bergen, I have never known you to be overly concerned with your hair!"

"I know, I know, but I want it to look, well, *special*." She dropped Abbey's hands and pivoted around. "What do you think?"

"I think I have been dying to get my hands on those curls for quite some time! What is the occasion?"

Lauren hesitated. Funny, she had not thought of this awkwardness before now. "Uh, it's a . . . nothing," she blurted.

Abbey's eyes narrowed suspiciously. "Nothing, is it?" She suddenly jerked Lauren's cloak open, eyeing her gown. "Oh, my! It's *beautiful*! All right, *don't* tell me, but I can easily guess!" she exclaimed, planting her hands on her hips.

"You can?" Lauren asked fearfully.

"Of course! You are in *love,* Lauren Hill Bergen, and do not think for a moment that you can deny it! Really, it's not as if he hasn't made his affections widely known!" she exclaimed, and stooped to pick up Alexa.

Lauren suddenly could not breathe. Had Abbey heard the talk Ethan had mentioned? Dear God, how did she *know*? "I—I do not know what you mean," she said shakily.

Abbey laughed, hoisting Alexa onto her hip. "Honestly, Lauren, *everyone* knows Count Bergen is wild for you! Oh, I am so happy for you, I truly am! It is going to happen, is it not?"

Astounded and relieved Abbey thought her affections were for Magnus, Lauren laughed uneasily. "Is *what* going to happen?"

"Why, marriage, of course!" Abbey laughed.

"Marriage?"

"You mean he has not *offered* for you?" Abbey asked, incredulous.

"No! I mean, yes— I mean—"

"Lady Marlaine calling, madam," Jones said from the doorway.

"Oh, *wonderful*! We shall have a little party, shall we? A celebration of sorts! Two weddings in one year!" Abbey giggled delightedly. "Please show Lady Marlaine in," she said to Jones, then turned an endearing grin to Lauren. "You must promise you won't say a word until I come back from the nursery, do you promise? Hold onto every single thought!" she exclaimed happily, and fairly skipped out of the room, explaining to Alexa that mummy was going to have a tea party.

There would be no tea party if Lauren could help it. Mortified to the very tips of her toes that Marlaine was here, she searched frantically about the room for an escape, at *least* a place to hide. A wave of bitter shame rumbled through her, and she rushed blindly to the window. At the sound of the door opening, Lauren whirled around, bracing herself against the window sash.

Marlaine looked as surprised as she was, and stood uncertainly at the threshold for a long moment. A little pale, but nonetheless very pleasingly dressed in apple green,

Marlaine moved slowly and elegantly into the middle of the room. Lauren felt like a lump of pearl-pink clay standing at the window as she was, shame and horror seeping through every pore.

"Good afternoon," Marlaine said politely.

"Lady Marlaine," Lauren choked.

"I apologize, I did not mean to interrupt. Jones did not mention—"

"Oh no, please, you are not interrupting—I—I called unexpectedly. Lady Darfield has gone to the nursery, but . . . but she should be back at any moment."

Marlaine nodded and glanced around the room before moving toward a settee covered in gold china silk. Searching for *something* to say, Lauren blurted, "I, uh, I understand you have been away?"

Marlaine's head jerked unnaturally toward her, and Lauren immediately regretted her choice of words. "Yes. My grandmother has been very ill—"

"I am terribly sorry."

"She is much improved, thank you," Marlaine said coolly. She sat gingerly on the edge of the settee, nervously smoothing her hands over her skirt. "I hurried back to London once she started to mend." She paused, looking quite awkward. "You—you cannot imagine how much there is to do before a duke's wedding," she said, looking at her lap.

Lauren's hand slipped from the window sash, falling limply to her side. "It must be daunting," she muttered, swallowing past the guilt lodged in her throat.

"Oh my, yes, indeed it is. The caterer, the florist . . . the trousseau. And it is so very hard to decide what one should take on the wedding trip."

"I am sure." God help her, she was going to expire right where she stood.

"So many details, and then there is the distraction of my very eager fiancé." Marlaine laughed tightly. "He claims to have missed me terribly." She lifted her lashes, looking at

Lauren from the corner of her eye. "I hope you won't think me indelicate, Countess Bergen, but he could hardly keep his hands from me! He actually begged me to run away and marry him. *Today!*" She laughed, a strange, choking laugh.

Lauren's stomach plummeted. Alex could not have asked her that, not today, not after last night. But why would Marlaine lie to her? She focused on the door and swallowed past a wave of nausea, wondering if she could make it there without collapsing.

Marlaine coughed lightly. "He—he *swears* he cannot abide the wait until we are married, but I made it quite plain he must. Do you know I actually considered it? But there are so *many* expectations—he'll just have to be patient a while longer." She laughed again, a little hysterically.

Lauren felt her own hysteria rising. Like a volcano.

"I beg your pardon, Countess. It's just that—" she looked up again, catching Lauren's horrified gaze "—it's just that I care for him desperately. Do you know what it is like to care for someone so desperately?"

Not trusting herself to speak, Lauren weakly shook her head.

Marlaine flashed a smile, one that did not erase the peculiar look in her eyes. "I would do anything for him, you know, but one cannot sprint off to Gretna Green . . . Not in our position, anyway. There are so many others to consider, no matter how anxious the groom! Well, that is quite enough of that," she said, with a dismissive flick of her wrist. "What a lovely gown—are you going somewhere special this evening?"

"No," Lauren choked. "I really must be going—"

"Oh no, I would not hear of it! I did not mean to interrupt your visit with Lady Darfield."

"Really, I cannot stay." On wooden legs, she lurched for the door, desperate to get out of that room and as far away from Marlaine Reese as she could before she burst into a torrent of tears. She rushed from the room so hastily, she did not see Marlaine sink against the settee, press her hands against her stomach, and bend over with grief.

She had no idea where she was going. Walking aimlessly through Hyde Park, blind to everything and everyone around her, she wanted to die. The ache in her chest had started the moment Marlaine had entered Abbey's cozy sitting room, had become intolerable by the time she fled, and was now an unrelenting, throbbing pain in every limb. She was not quite sure which hurt worse. The disgrace and shame she had brought on herself? Or that Alex had wanted to elope with Lady Marlaine today, of all days? God, the rooster could not even *wait* for his wedding! Was she such an incredible *fool*?

She did not see Lord and Lady Fairlane until she was almost upon them. She tried her damndest to smile and murmur a greeting. Lord Fairlane nodded curtly; Lady Fairlane pretended she had not seen her at all as they quickly sailed past. Confused by their behavior, Lauren stopped and glanced over her shoulder at the passing couple. *These people will cut you dead.* Magnus's warning came back to her, and she choked on a bitter sob. A hoyden, that's what she was. A woman of moral depravity, as common as a tavern wench.

But then what was *he*? What about the things he had said, the earnest way in which he spoke? *I will find a way for us,* he had said. *Damn* him! He had meant something altogether different than what she thought! No doubt he meant a tidy little flat somewhere—dear *God,* she had *asked* him to make love to her! An intense wave of shame flooded her, and she brought her hands to her cheeks, forcing herself to walk. All right, all right, she may have asked him, but *he* was the one who had contrived to meet her at the opera! He was the one who said he wanted her as he had never wanted another! He had said so many sweet, *tender* things, but he had not once admitted to loving her. She was so bloody *stupid* to have interpreted his lust as love!

Unable to choke back another sob, Lauren fell heavily onto a bench and buried her face in her hands, sickened by the dawning realization that what had occurred last night had been fantasy. *Her* fantasy. And what in God's name did she do now?

The sun had almost disappeared when she at last lifted her head. There was only one plausible alternative to her bleak situation. She had to get as far away from Alex Christian as she could. As far away from London as was possible. From England, for that matter.

Having made her decision, she stood and slowly began to walk in the direction of Bedford Square where Magnus had taken a house.

Magnus did not like the frumpy man he had hired to be his butler; he seemed to spend most of his time in the kitchens with the scullery maid. The inability to hire good help was the single most annoying curse of being a foreigner, he was quite convinced. If he had not happened to be walking near the entry, no one would have heard the rapid knocking on the door. Grumbling in German, he stalked to the door and flung it open.

He gasped. From the strands of dark hair blowing in all directions, to the hem of her gown stained with the dirt of the street, Lauren looked as if she had been physically beaten. She started to speak, but the words died on her tongue. Alarmed, Magnus caught her before she sank onto the steps and pulled her inside. "*Liebchen,* what is wrong?" he asked desperately, his big hands smoothing the hair from her face. "What is wrong?"

"Magnus, I have to talk to you," she mumbled, shakily wiping a tear from her cheek.

"Do not try and talk now," he said, lapsing unconsciously into German. "Let me get you something to drink." He helped her into the main drawing room and yanked angrily on the bellpull. Seating her on a settee, he nervously took her hand in his. The butler appeared, his eyes rounding with great surprise when he saw Lauren. ''Port,'' Magnus barked. He waited until the butler had gone before asking, ''What has happened?'' Tears pooled in her eyes, and she shook her head. Slowly, she inhaled, obviously trying very hard to regain her composure. ''Tell me! Has someone—''

''No,'' she whispered.

''What is it? What has happened to you?''

''It does not matter,'' she said, flicking a limp hand at the unknown. ''Magnus, I have considered your generous offer. I accept.''

He gaped at her in surprise. The butler entered, carrying a tray with a full decanter of port and crystal glasses. Magnus impatiently motioned for him to place the tray on a table nearby and leave. ''I do not understand,'' he said, reaching for the port.

''I will marry you,'' she said weakly, shaking her head to the port he offered. ''But . . . but I have two conditions.''

Greatly surprised and equally suspicious, he said carefully, ''Go on.''

''The first,'' she said in German, ''is that you allow me to go to Rosewood so that I may settle a few things—and say good-bye.'' A deep sob escaped her throat. He made a move to touch her, but she shook her head, swallowed hard, and continued in a whisper: ''And the second is that you take me to Bavaria.'' She lifted her eyes to gauge his reaction.

He had never seen such misery in his life. ''That is all?'' he asked slowly. She nodded. ''You are certain? Lauren, are you quite certain?''

Her eyes pooled again. A single tear drifted from the corner of her eye, sliding slowly to her mouth. ''I am *very* certain.''

On impulse, Magnus grabbed her, wrapping her into a protective embrace. He kissed her salty lips, grimacing

when she began to cry again. He did not ask her anything—
he had made his promise and he would keep it. There was
nothing he could do but cradle her head against his shoulder
as a river of grief flowed from her body.

She eventually took the port he insisted she drink and
calmly, if not leadenly, talked through the arrangements
with him. They agreed to leave as soon as Lauren could
pack a few things. Magnus was not so certain she would be
able to travel in her current state, but she insisted she would
be quite all right.

When he escorted her home, it was he who broke the
news to a stunned Ethan and Paul. Paul took the news quietly, his eyes traveling frequently to Lauren, who was trying
gamely to put on a smile for them. Ethan, naturally, acted
disappointed. He had set his sights on the duke, but Magnus
knew he would gladly accept his generous settlement. He
even agreed to pay the Russell Square rent through the end
of the Season, as Ethan complained he was just beginning to
enjoy himself. Pleased with that concession, Ethan insisted
upon toasting his latest accomplishment. As the bastard
chortled over his feat of snaring *two* Bergen men, Magnus
stole a glance at Paul. He stared at his untouched brandy, his
mouth set in an implacable line. Lauren looked as if she had
been handed a death sentence.

He left very soon afterward, eager to be away from the
obnoxious Lord Hill.

The gargoyle clock on the mantel chimed eleven times.
From the writing table in her room, Lauren glanced at it and
frowned. Turning back to the empty paper in front of her,
she tapped the quill against her cheek. What she had in mind
was childish, but she could not resist a parting shot for the
scoundrel. She was struggling; she had never been very
good at expressing her innermost feelings, yet she was
deeply compelled to tell him how badly he had hurt her. As

impotent as a few words might seem to him, they gave her a
strength she desperately needed at the moment.

But she was completely inept at describing her utter dev-
astation, and fretted with the end of the quill as she mulled it
over. He had asked another woman to run away with him
after he had sparked a flaming passion in her that was not,
even now, extinguishable. He meant to install her as his
mistress, not find a legitimate way for them to be together as
she had so foolishly hoped. There was nothing that could
soothe her, nothing that could ease the pain he had caused
her. Suddenly reminded of a poem, she dipped the quill in
the inkwell and wrote quickly.

> When lovely woman stoops to folly
> And finds too late that men betray
> What charm can soothe her melancholy
> What art can wash her guilt away?

She anxiously read what she had written. The words, though
clear, did not seem to capture her deep hurt. She thought to
try again, but a glance at the clock decided her against it.
There would be ample opportunity after tonight to perfect
the art of stinging rebukes. She left the note unsigned, sprinkled sand across the ink, and waved the paper impatiently to
dry it before sealing it with candle wax.

Gripping the note, Lauren soundlessly slipped out of her
room and downstairs, pausing on the bottom step to listen.
Voices drifted from the parlor; picking up her skirts, she
dashed down the hall in the opposite direction, almost skid-
ding to a stop in front of Davis's room. She knocked rapidly
and waited, glancing nervously over her shoulder toward the
main hallway, and impatiently knocked again. A faint rustle
could be heard behind the door before Davis pulled it open,
clearly annoyed.

"Caller," she said impertinently, and thrust the note at
him. "Please take this to Twenty-four Audley Street right

away." Davis peered at the note in her hand. "*Please*, Davis, I need you to do this!"

"Sutherland," he said, reading her direction on the note, then lifted his gaze and studied her closely. "Too late," he snapped.

Lauren quickly wedged herself in the door to keep him from shutting it in her face. "All right, I did not want to do this, but I am fully prepared to dispatch a letter to Lord Dowling and tell him how horribly disagreeable you have been during our stay here. I do not know Lord Dowling well, but I am quite certain he will not appreciate that a countess has been treated so ill by a servant in his home. You value your employment, do you not?"

Judging by the sour pucker of his mouth, he did. He glared at her, then the note in her hand. With a low growl, he snatched it from her. "Twenty-four Audley Street," he groused, and would have slammed the door on her shoulder had she not jumped out of the way.

Finch glared at the little man who thrust the note at him and barked, "Sutherland," then turned on his heel and stomped away from the door. The last thing he needed was to bring his grace any more news, of *any* kind. Oh, the duke was in a fine mood. It had begun during the welcome home supper for Lady Marlaine. His grace had ignored all propriety and had actually left the table in the course of the meal to find his butler. Find him, he did, all right, in the servant's dining area, and had dragged him out in full view of the staff.

Finch's second misfortune—the first having been found—was to be the one to tell his grace that the messenger was unable to locate Countess Bergen at Vauxhall Gardens. The duke's face had grown dangerously dark as Finch assured him the messenger had gone to every single fountain in the gardens, big and small alike, but had not located her. He had timidly returned the note that should have been delivered, only to watch his grace rip it into tiny little pieces before marching back to the dining room.

God only knew what news *this* note brought. But there was one thing of which he could be sure, Finch thought as he walked slowly to the duke's private study, the note held before him on a silver tray.

His grace would not like it.

His grace signaled his displeasure by groaning the moment Finch stepped into the room. "What is it?" he barked.

"A note has arrived, your grace."

He growled, slamming the glass of whiskey down on a table. "What time is it?"

"Half past twelve midnight."

The duke rubbed his temples. "Bring it," he snarled, and tossed aside the book in his lap. Finch carefully handed him the note, and then backed out, shutting the pocket doors *very* softly.

Alex could not bring himself to read it.

He paced around the room, clutching the note tightly in his hand. He could not bear to be reminded of the mess he had created or be filled with a new rash of longing. He took a deep breath, ripped past the seal, and looked at the page.

"Bloody hell. *Bloody, bloody hell!*" he shouted at the ceiling. It was unsigned, but he knew *exactly* who had penned it. Good God, who *else* went about quoting from pages of English poetry? He stumbled backward and into a chair. How could she have come to the conclusion that last night was a lie? How in the bloody hell had she judged it a lie? It was not a *lie,* Goddammit!

God, what had he done? he asked himself for the thousandth time as bitter disappointment churned in his gut. Reminded of his strange premonition last evening that she was slipping away from him, he realized he had lost her. He had lost the one thing that had ever mattered to him.

His world was rapidly crumbling.

He glanced at the clock—a quarter to one. There was nothing he could do at this hour, not a bloody thing.

Except drink.

Chapter 20

His head felt like stone. Not only that, he must have eaten mud last evening, so foul was his mouth. God help him, but that woman had caused him to overindulge three nights running now and last night had been his best effort yet. Alex lifted his head from the desk and tried to open his eyes, blinking against the shards of sunlight that knifed his brain.

This madness had to *stop*. He was neglecting his responsibilities and scaring Marlaine half to death. She was trying very hard to be understanding, but she was smothering him with her concern, constantly hovering, asking if there was anything she could do for him, if there was anything he needed. There was something he needed, all right, something she could not give him.

He did not look up when the door to the library opened and closed. "God's blood!" Arthur exclaimed. Alex gestured for him to soften his voice. "You look like hell, man! Judging by the look of you, I suppose there is no need to tell you Countess Bergen has left London—"

"Wh—What did you say?" Alex demanded, pushing himself up in his chair with supreme effort.

"I said you look like hell—"

"Not that!"

Arthur exhaled his aggravation and picked up Alex's discarded neckcloth. "She left. Yesterday."

Sagging, Alex closed his eyes, his head reeling. She was gone. He pinched the bridge of his nose and wished like hell the room would quit moving. "Yesterday?" he croaked.

"In the company of the German."

"Bloody hell," he grumbled.

"God, Alex, when will you end this tiresome brooding of yours? Do you remember you are to be married in a matter of days? You should be treating your fiancée with the adoration she is due on the eve of that fortuitous occasion, and not diving into your cups night after night!"

If Alex had possessed one ounce of strength, he would have cheerfully split his brother's skull open. And Lauren thought *he* was arrogant.

"How long do you intend to let this self-pity continue? How long will you allow the gossip to abound? Do you know that Marlaine attended a concert without you last evening? Told the Delacortes you were ill, but as you managed to make it to White's yesterday afternoon for a *drink,* Delacorte knew it to be a lie. Oh, but do not worry. Your fiancée had a nice time of it with her cousin, Miss Broadmoore. A *smashing* good time by all accounts. Seems the pendulum has swung the other way—now Marlaine is the object of gossip."

Alex rubbed his temples in a vain attempt to dispel the throbbing. "She will be the source of constant gossip once she is a duchess and may as well get accustomed to it. God knows I have."

Arthur's unsympathetic moan reverberated about the room. "Here now, take Marlaine to the Fremont ball tonight. That will end the worst speculation."

"I don't know," Alex drawled as he slowly sat up, grimacing. "I had already promised my attentions to a bottle of whiskey."

"All right, enough," Arthur said impatiently, throwing up his hands. "Look, I can certainly understand your infatuation for the countess—she is beautiful and charming. But that is all it is, Alex, an infatuation. She has *left,* for Chrissakes! And according to Paddy, that rather despicable uncle of hers has announced her betrothal to Count Bergen. So you may stop this adolescent pining for her and resume your life!"

"Tell me, Arthur, is there anything else I might do to please you?" Alex asked bitterly.

Arthur wearily tossed the neckcloth aside. "I think you have lost your mind."

Not my mind. My way, he thought, and forced himself to look at his brother. "I will take Marlaine to the Fremont ball tonight. I will let the entire *ton* see that all is well with Sutherland. We are one very happy family, do not fret."

"Good," Arthur said, and walked to the door. He paused, looking over his shoulder. "Come now, it can hardly be as bad as all that. You will have forgotten her soon enough, just like the others."

Alex snorted as the door closed behind his brother. He would never forget her. There was not enough whiskey in the world for that.

Arthur's indignation, Alex suspected, sent him running to Hannah, as he could think of no other explanation for his mother's sudden appearance. He was sitting in his study, his head lolling against the leather wing-backed chair, staring into the fire. Lauren had left with the Goddammed German, and there was not a bloody thing he could do about it. He himself would be married by the end of the month; he could hardly fault Lauren for doing the same. After all, everyone must make a suitable match, one befitting their station and the *ton*'s expectations. Everyone must eventually settle. He would. She would. Life would go on. And he would learn to endure this agony.

It was that which he was contemplating when Hannah appeared at the door of his sanctuary, her hands on her hips. Hardly in a mood to hear a maternal lecture, he barely glanced at her.

"It would seem my son has a problem," she said imperiously.

That was putting it rather mildly. He sighed impatiently. "What, was there some offense Arthur failed to mention?"

"Sarcasm does not become you, Alexander," she said, gliding into the room. "And Arthur is right. You have behaved abominably these last few days."

"I really must thank Arthur for his complete dossier."

"I spoke with Marlaine earlier," she continued, ignoring his biting sarcasm. "She confided to me that you have been very distant with her. She fears you are suffering from second thoughts. Quite naturally, of course."

"That's rich," he scoffed. "Only Marlaine could make my behavior sound reasonable."

Hannah sat heavily on the edge of a chair next to him. "I have asked myself over and over again why you are behaving this way. You are a fine man, Alex, a decent, *caring* man. You are hardly one to invite gossip or disregard the feelings of others, or intentionally hurt those for whom you care."

"Mother, I apologize, all right?" he said with icy impatience.

But she continued as if he had not spoken. "So I asked myself, Hannah, what on earth would cause him to ignore all civility and act in such a way? What would cause him to cast off the lessons he has learned from the cradle about revering the women in his life?"

"Marvelous. And what did Hannah say?" he said, mockingly.

"That there could be but one reason. That at last, her son had discovered love."

Startled, Alex flicked his gaze to her; she was looking at him pointedly, daring him to disagree. "I have no doubt Hannah had an opinion about that," he said slowly.

She smiled softly. "Only that she prays it is true," she murmured. Alex frowned disapprovingly; it was inconceivable to him that his mother would want what she implied.

But she assured him she did with her smile. "I am a mother, Alexander, and I know my son very well. I know he does not allow his feelings to show, assuming, of course, he actually has any. I know he thinks he has made a very good match, one that will meet with everyone's approval. I also know he does not love his intended, but carries another in his heart. And that he was never expecting anything like this to happen, not in a thousand years."

Stung that she had pegged him so accurately, he snorted disdainfully. "What has love got to do with anything?" he asked contentiously.

"Don't be an idiot, darling. It has *everything* to do with anything," she smiled. With great condescension, Alex shook his head, but Hannah merely chuckled. "Do you recall the day of Lady Darfield's garden party?"

He nodded suspiciously.

"I found that party to be quite extraordinary. I have never seen you look at a woman the way you looked at Countess Bergen, and I knew instantly what it was. The French say, *'true love is like ghosts, which everyone talks about and few have ever seen.'* " Alex rolled his eyes in great exasperation.

Hannah suddenly moved to the ottoman directly in front of him and leaned forward, placing her hand on his knee. "Oh my darling, you cannot possibly know how true that is! I was fortunate enough to know true love with your father, and I cannot begin to convey how very precious it is. In this day and age, when marriages are made for little more than gain, I have despaired that you would ever find true love! I was resigned to the idea that you would marry some silly debutante who wants nothing more than to have people bow and scrape to her—"

"Mother!"

"But I *know* what I saw in your eyes that day, as well as I know what I saw in hers! You *love* her, Alex, and I cannot stand by and allow the opportunity to see you happily married slip away!"

He started to deny it, but he could no more lie to her than he could to Arthur. It would have been useless, anyway. She was ready for him to defy her; he could see it in the set of her mouth. "She has left town," he said slowly, uncertainly. "In the company of the German."

"Ha!" Hannah scoffed with an airy wave of her hand. "I don't really care for him, do you?"

"I don't think she really cares for me," he muttered.

"Rubbish!"

"She believes I used her."

"Well, did you?"

"No," he snapped angrily, then muttered, "I could *never.*"

Hannah took his hand and held it tenderly between both of hers. A silence fell over the room as mother and son contemplated one another. It was extraordinary, he thought, that he actually felt relieved. As if a great, secret weight had been lifted from him. At length, Hannah said quietly, "You should go after her, of course. And do not let that German deter you. She does not love him."

Alex was not about to challenge her wisdom on that front. "What of Marlaine?"

Hannah sighed sadly. "Now *that* will not be easy. She will hate you, utterly despise you. But someday she will thank you for being honest with her."

"Rather hard to imagine," he scoffed.

"Well, I suppose it may take years and years. This may

sound a little contrived, but your uncertainty is hardly fair to Marlaine. She adores you, and you cannot return that affection. Someday, sooner rather than later, I suspect, the bond between you will crack. And who knows? Maybe she would be relieved in some small way? You have hardly been the attentive fiancé.''

Alex cautiously regarded his mother. "You didn't think this way before."

"Yes I did," she said, caressing the back of his hand. "But I suppose I was a bit afraid of the talk. It wasn't until you returned from Tarriton that I realized just how deeply you felt for the countess. And it wasn't until the last few days I realized how devastated you were. Come what may, no mother can see her child suffer so and not want to move heaven and earth to fix it." She lifted his hand to her mouth and kissed it.

His eyes began to sting; embarrassed, he blinked and hastily looked down. "I . . . thank you, Mum. I will think on what you have said."

Hannah grinned at him. "I know you will, darling. Now then, if you will excuse me, I shall be off to improve the life of my youngest son."

"I should hardly think it possible to improve two lives in one day, but let me suggest you work on the nasty little habit he has of tattling on his brother."

Hannah rose, chuckling. She stooped to place a kiss on Alex's cheek. "I love you, Alex. I want only the very best for you."

He grasped her hand and pressed his lips to her knuckles. "I know. And I love you for it."

For the remainder of the afternoon, Alex contemplated his mother's wishes, but eventually dismissed them as sentimental. He could not betray Marlaine. No, he was bound by duty and responsibility to go through with his commitment. She deserved that and the *ton* expected it of him. He was an influential peer, and he had to consider the ramifications of his actions in more than one light.

He arrived at Marlaine's home at nine o'clock, having sent a note asking her to attend the Fremont ball with him. Marlaine's hopeful smile faded when he entered the drawing room. It was little wonder; the expensive cut of his evening clothes did not erase the dark circles under his sullen eyes. He knew he looked awful; he just did not give a damn.

"Shall I fetch you a drink?" she asked carefully, trying hard not to look appalled.

"I think not," he said, his stomach roiling at the mere suggestion. She motioned for him to sit, and sat nervously on the edge of a chair, very carefully avoiding his eyes.

"I offend you," he observed indifferently.

"Never," she gasped.

"God, Marlaine, admit it. I offend myself," he said wearily.

"Well . . . I admit I do not understand," she said softly, her gaze dropping to her lap.

"What, that I drank myself into oblivion or that I am paying soundly for it today?" he asked apathetically.

"I do not understand why you have felt compelled to do it two nights in a row," she murmured.

"Three," he corrected her. "Sometimes men drink. They do not require a reason. They just . . . do." She nodded, her eyes downcast. "Would you prefer I leave you?"

"Oh no! I think we *must* go to the ball, don't you?"

Her eager response struck him as odd. "We must?"

She smiled a little, her delicate hands anxiously working a seam in her gown. "It's just that people have *asked* about you. I—I think it is best we be seen in public. You know, so they will not talk," she said quietly. "Papa says we must all stand united if your reforms are to be favorably viewed."

Ah yes, a subtle reminder from Whitcomb about the almighty importance of appearances. He was not going to argue the point—normally, he would agree. Gossip grew vicious when individual members of the *ton* did not do what was expected of them. The *ton* could go to hell as far as he was concerned, but he had Marlaine to think of. "Then we shall go. Just keep me away from the whiskey, will you?"

She glanced at him, unsmiling. "I will try," she said quietly.

The stifling crowd at the Fremont ball was enough to make a strong man ill; it had Alex downright nauseated. He had danced twice, both times exacerbating his rather enormous headache. For once, he was grateful for David's intervention. Their relationship had been strained since that day at the park, but his cousin seemed to have forgotten it. He paid uncharacteristic attention to Marlaine. He had danced with her twice already, and had even taken her for a garden stroll. But even David, for the sake of propriety, could not prolong her absence. She was back at his side, and his temples were throbbing. There was no air circulating in the ballroom, and he tugged impatiently at his white silk neckcloth.

"Are you all right?" Marlaine asked anxiously for the third time, worry rimming her eyes.

"I am as well as I was when you asked ten minutes ago," he said gruffly, glancing testily about the room.

"We can go if you like," she offered.

"I am fine, Marlaine. Stop . . . *fretting.*"

She smiled demurely. "I cannot do that. I am afraid fiancée's fret."

"Sutherland?"

Alex glanced over his shoulder at Lord van der Mill, a casual acquaintance. He was in no mood to make idle talk. "Good evening, my lord," he said, bowing slightly.

"Surprised to see you. Heard you were indisposed. Good evening, Lady Marlaine. Lovely ball, eh?" the older man chirped.

"Yes, my lord, quite lovely," Marlaine purred. "His

grace is almost completely recovered. It's a horrid little fever going around.'' If there was one thing Marlaine did well, it was play the game of social graces, Alex thought.

"Fever, that so?'' van der Mill muttered, peering closely at Alex. "Not contagious, are you?''

"Hardly,'' Alex intoned.

"Say, your mother still own that house on Berkeley Street?'' van der Mill asked. "Heard you might consider selling it.''

Alex shifted restlessly against the wall he was using to support himself. Van der Mill had all the houses he could possibly want, two in London alone. "Looking for another home?'' he asked.

"Don't know.'' Van der Mill shrugged and glanced askance at Marlaine. "Have a friend who might be interested,'' he said, and winked subtly.

Alex nodded, a little surprised a man of van der Mill's considerable years would still be randy enough to want to keep a mistress. "Why don't we talk? Perhaps you could come around in a day or so?'' he suggested, his curiosity piqued.

I'll do just that,'' van der Mill responded with a queer smile. "Good evening, Lady Marlaine.''

"Good evening, my lord.''

Van der Mill patted Alex's forearm in a friendly gesture. "Hope you are over that fever soon, your grace,'' he said. He turned to walk away, but hesitated, and looked at Alex over his shoulder. "No one living there at Berkley Street, is that right?''

"That's right.''

"Odd. Your driver was not so certain. Said you were there a few evenings ago—with a woman?'' Alex's heart stopped beating; he managed to keep his expression bland as van der Mill shrugged indifferently. "I suppose he was mistaken, then?''

He could have sworn the old man's eyes narrowed

slightly as he waited for a reply. "The house is closed for the Season. He was mistaken," he said evenly. Van der Mill's eyes flicked quickly to Marlaine and back to Alex before he nodded curtly and strolled away.

His pulse pounding harshly in his neck, Alex resisted the urge to look at Marlaine. *Damn* that jealous old rooster! And God save his driver, whose *tongue* he would have for breakfast!

"Perhaps . . . perhaps Arthur was there," Marlaine said softly.

His hands fisted at his side. "He was mistaken. The house is closed."

She nodded slowly, peering up at him. "Is something wrong? You are so pale."

"Would you like to call a physician, Marlaine? Perhaps then you may rest easy I won't expire on you in the middle of the Fremont's dance floor!" he said sharply. Her eyes widened with astonishment, and she quickly looked away. He truly lamented his outburst. "I am sorry, love. I did not mean to snap at you."

"Yes, so you keep saying," she murmured.

He shoved away from the wall. "They are playing a waltz. Would you like to dance with an irritable goat?" She shrugged halfheartedly. Nonetheless, Alex led her to the dance floor and swept her into a waltz. She danced stiffly, holding him at arm's length as was proper, her steps small and precise. It was bloody impossible not to compare her with the way Lauren fit his arms perfectly, the way she flowed with the music. Marlaine gamely attempted small talk, chatting about something to do with the wedding. He hated himself more with every beat of the music. Was he destined to spend his life comparing her with Lauren? It was a wretched way to live; he always comparing, she always trying to measure up to some standard she did not even know existed. *She adores you, and you cannot return that affection.* His mother's words rattled like a loose ball about his brain. He could not return her affection. He could not even muster the patience for one ball for her.

It was a great relief when Marlaine asked to be taken home. He helped her into the coach and sat across from her, closing his eyes and sinking against the plush squabs with numbing fatigue.

"You work so hard, Alex. You need your rest," she said as the coach rolled away from the curb.

Her constant concern pricked at him, and he was an ogre for resenting it. Unfortunately, it seemed there was little he did *not* resent tonight. "What are your plans tomorrow?" he asked, desperate to avoid another discussion about his health.

"I really must finish the invitations. There are so *many*—"

"The invitations have not yet been sent?" he asked, his entire body tightening in response to some internal, primal warning.

She laughed lightly. "Of course not! They are to arrive exactly a fortnight in advance of the wedding, and Friday would be a fortnight."

He stared at her, his mind a sudden whirlwind tossing thoughts haphazardly about his conscience. The invitations had not been sent. The bloody invitations had not been sent. *She adores you, and you cannot return that affection.* It was not too late, he thought madly. "Marlaine—"

"I have completed most of them, mounds and mounds of them. Naturally, *everyone* wants to be in attendance at a duke's wedding," she said suddenly, and unconsciously began to wring the gloves in her lap.

"Marlaine—"

"Your mother is such a dear," she quickly interjected. "She has been an enormous help. So many people have worked very hard for this wedding, you know, so that it is just right. The florist wants to go over the church arrangements one last time, and the caterer, well, he is so *particu-*

lar, when he discovered the number of distinguished guests that were expected at the breakfast, he was quite beside himself. He sent to Paris for special recipes, can you imagine? The entire *ton* is expecting a magnificent event. I—I will make sure the invitations are delivered to the post tomorrow. I won't delay, I promise. They will all be delivered on time, you must trust me,'' she said frantically.

Something preternatural had overtaken him; he felt completely detached from himself and Marlaine. He calmly reached for her hand. *''Marlaine—''*

She shook her head violently. ''No, Alex,'' she whispered.

''We must talk, love.''

''No!'' A tear slipped from the corner of her eye and she bowed her head. Alex moved to sit beside her, wrapping an arm around her shoulders. *''Oh, God, please no,''* she gasped, and began to sob.

''I am so very sorry,'' he said, wincing at how violently the sobs racked her slender frame. ''But I cannot—''

''Don't do this to me, Alex! Don't make a fool of me!'' she sobbed.

''I'm afraid I will make a fool of you if we wed,'' he said miserably. Marlaine stifled a scream and slid off the bench, falling to her knees on the floorboards and burying her face against his leg. Grief stricken, Alex bent over her. Darkness enveloped his mind; he felt despicable, the lowest form of humanity.

''Tell me what I have to do, Alex, and I will *do* it! Just tell me what you want, but don't do this!'' she cried hysterically.

Alex closed his eyes tightly and buried his face in her hair. ''Oh, Marlaine,'' he breathed, ''there is nothing you can do. It is beyond my power to change,'' he muttered sadly.

With her fist, she hit his leg. ''It's *her,* isn't it? You are forsaking me for *her!*" she cried. When Alex did not answer, she hit him again. And again.

By the time the coach reached her father's home on Mount Street, Marlaine had fallen into stunned silence. He tried to help her down, but she pushed away from him and alighted awkwardly on her own. "I will call first thing in the morning and explain to your parents," he said softly, hating the sound of his own traitorous voice.

"Don't bother yourself," she muttered acidly, and pushing past him, walked unsteadily to the door.

After a sleepless night, Alex was shown the next morning to the drawing room of the Whitcomb residence by a butler who regarded him as if he had just crawled up from the bottom of the Thames. As he crossed the threshold, Lord Whitcomb fairly vaulted out of his seat, his face white with anger. Marlaine refused to look at him.

"I don't know what insanity has overcome you, Sutherland, but you had better assure Marlaine that she has misunderstood you!" Whitcomb roared.

"She has not, Edwin," Alex said in a low voice. "I deeply regret what I must do, but I cannot marry your daughter." Whitcomb gaped at him in horror.

"What sort of monster *are* you?" Lady Whitcomb gasped.

"By God, you had better explain yourself!" Lord Whitcomb shouted.

A faint queasiness rumbled through Alex's gut. There was nothing he could say or do, no fabrication he could create that would ever justify or excuse his actions to the Reese family. Not even the diagnosis of complete madness, which he believed was just shy of true. "I have determined we do not suit," he said simply.

Whitcomb exploded. "Do not *suit*? Goddammit, Sutherland, think of what you are *doing*! You are about to erase forty years of association between the Christian and Reese family, do you *realize* that?''

"I do."

Lady Whitcomb sank, dumbfounded, into a chair. "You are *contemptible!* What manner of *gentleman,''* she spat, "would abandon the daughter of Earl Whitcomb for a *wanton—*''

"Do not," Alex said with deadly calm, "cast aspersions on anyone else but me, madam. There is no one to blame for this but me."

Lady Whitcomb snorted in disbelief and glanced at Marlaine, who had yet to look up. "Make no mistake, your grace. We blame you *completely,''* she said haughtily.

"I should have known," Lord Whitcomb growled. "I *defended* you when they called you a Radical! Give the man a chance, I said! *God,* to take it all back now! You must be as mad as they say!"

Alex had, of course, anticipated Whitcomb would abandon his support of reforms. "I would hope your vote would not be unduly influenced by this unfortunate incident. The reform movement is valid and vital to this country—''

"I don't give a *damn,* Sutherland, do you hear me? You can bloody well look for support elsewhere!"

"I will not have Marlaine's name disgraced before all of society!" Lady Whitcomb interjected, oblivious to the exchange between her husband and Alex. "As far as I am concerned, *she* abandoned *you*! And believe me, *everyone* will know why!"

"Say whatever is necessary, Lady Whitcomb," he said blandly.

"Oh, rest assured I will say—''

"Mother!" Marlaine succeeded in gaining everyone's attention. Pale as a ghost, she slowly stood and glared at Alex. "I think enough has been said. I would thank you to leave now, Alex."

He desperately wanted a word alone with her, the chance to apologize one last time. "Marlaine, could I—"

"No! Please go."

"I cannot tell you how very sorry I am—" he attempted.

"You heard her. Get out of my house," Whitcomb growled. Marlaine lifted her chin and stared at him hatefully. There was nothing else that could be said.

Alex turned and walked out of the drawing room.

The next day, Alex made one final call. Pulling his hat lower to shield the blinding rain from his eyes, he marched to the door of the Russell Square town house. When the diminutive butler opened the door to his pounding, he did not pause to shake the rain from his coat, but strode inside and demanded to see Paul Hill. It had been five full days since he had looked into her dark blue eyes or heard the melodic sound of her voice.

Five full days that he had worried unto death he had lost her forever.

He had done what he had to do: wreaked havoc in London. His announcement that Marlaine had ended their engagement had set the *ton* on its ear. This morning, *The Times* had carried nothing else on the society pages except speculation as to what extraordinary indiscretion had forced an end to the Match of the Decade. There were several theories: that he had lost a sizable fortune in East India; that the reforms he pushed had been more than the Reese family could endure; that his sudden drinking, obviously indicating a larger problem, had forced her hand. He was in no mood to explain himself to anyone, and least of all, to Paul Hill. Davis pointed to the parlor, and Alex marched inside.

It was Ethan Hill who greeted him from a chair pulled in front of the fire, his stocking feet propped in front of the flames.

"Where is Paul?" he demanded of the enormous man.

Lord Hill grinned as Paul emerged from the hall, his cane

forcefully striking the floor. "Come calling again, have you?" he asked blandly. Alex angrily yanked off his gloves.

"Not every day a duke with *five hundred thousand* a year comes calling!" Lord Hill noted cheerfully as Alex carelessly tossed his gloves onto a chair. "A brandy! That's what we all need. Shall you have a brandy, your grace?" the rotund gentleman asked, grinning.

"No. I have come to learn the whereabouts of your niece."

"Ah, how marvelous! Had your cousin here a month ago," Lord Hill chortled.

"She has left London with her fiancé," Paul announced, expressionless.

Alex shunted an impatient glare at Paul. "Where is she?"

Paul cocked his head to one side and considered Alex. "You may not put much store in formal betrothal agreements, your grace, but the Hills do."

"Aye, *but,*" Lord Hill loudly and hastily interjected, "until the vows have been said, the Hills will consider *all* offers!"

A muscle in Alex's jaw flinched. "I do not believe a formal agreement prevents her from speaking to me," he said, trying desperately to keep his tone even.

"Unfortunately," Paul remarked, "she does not ever want to speak with you again."

Paul Hill was playing with fire. Alex deliberately turned to his uncle. "It is extremely important I speak with your niece," he said with icy calm. "And I am in no mood to argue that point."

Paul actually smiled at his deadly tone. "Neither am I. You may *think* you can come in here and demand to see her, but I think it only fair to warn you that I will kill you before I allow you to harm her any more than you have. I had your word, Sutherland," he said in a low voice, reminding him of their wager.

"How do you think you will stop me?" he asked incredulously. "I will not let you, or your uncle, or the whole bloody kingdom stand in my way! Tell me where she is!"

"Perhaps you did not hear me. She does not want to speak with you again. *Ever,*" Paul added emphatically.

A rage was building in Alex that he feared he could not contain. "Tell me where he has taken her!" he shouted.

"Haven't you done enough? I will not allow you to trifle with her any longer! God, don't you know that she *loves* you?" Paul shouted, his face turning red.

"And what do you think *I* feel? Why on earth would I come here, demanding to know where she is? Why in God's name would I do that?" Alex roared. Paul folded his arms across his chest, fiercely resolute.

Alex's shoulders sagged. "I have," he said in a ragged voice, "journeyed to the far ends of this earth and seen everything there is to see. I have climbed mountains, forged through jungles, and thirsted in deserts. I have a title that affords me the greatest luxuries, any woman I could ever want, and wealth so great it is obscene. I have experienced it all, or so I thought. Because never—*never*—in all that time have I been so completely and thoroughly *affected* by another human being! Never have I desired to move the sun just to see one *smile*! I have wended my way through the most tumultuous week of my life, have disappointed everyone I love, have neglected my responsibilities, and have thrown all aside for just the *chance* to talk to her! And *you* think to deny me? I swear to God, I shall bring the full force of my name down on your house!" His voice boomed in the small room. "Tell me where in the hell she is!"

"Good *God,*" Lord Hill muttered, for once speechless.

Slowly, a smile crept across Paul's face. "Bloody hell, you *do* love her," he muttered. Enraged, exhausted, and emotionally spent, Alex could do little more than roll his eyes in exasperation and sink into a chair directly across from Ethan Hill.

Paul limped to the sideboard and poured three brandies. "What do you intend to do?" he asked casually, handing the brandies around. "She is formally betrothed to Magnus."

Alex groaned as he accepted the glass. "I do not know," he answered truthfully.

"If you think to end our agreement with the Bavarian, there will be damages to consider," Lord Hill interjected. Alex and Paul ignored him.

"You had best devise a plan, my friend. Magnus Bergen is not an easy man to deal with," Paul warned him bluntly.

"Ha! He pales in comparison to Lauren," Lord Hill snorted. "Now *there* is a stubborn little wench for you."

Paul smiled wryly. "She will not see you, you know that. Unless, of course, your head is on a pike."

"Where is she?" Alex quietly insisted.

Paul exchanged a look with his uncle. "Rosewood. They intend to marry and depart for the continent the first of August."

"Bloody grand," Alex muttered, springing to his feet. He stalked to the door, pausing only to retrieve his hat and gloves.

"Sutherland!" Paul called. Alex's hand stilled on the doorknob as he turned to Paul one last time. "Godspeed." Alex nodded curtly and walked out the door, slamming it resoundingly on Lord Hill's cheerful prediction that there would be a duel before it was all said and done.

Chapter 21

Mrs. Peterman met him at the door of the Rosewood manor wearing the same disapproving scowl she had worn the first time he had come. Folding her arms tightly across her dirty apron, she eyed him suspiciously.

"Is Miss Hill about?" he asked, dispensing with any greeting.

Mrs. Peterman did not answer right away, taking in his clothes, his boots, and even his mount tethered nearby. "Is she expecting you?"

"I rather doubt it," he responded dryly.

"Never know who is going to call anymore," she grumbled. "Bout fell out of my chair, I did, when that giant brought her home. Said he was going to marry her. Poor Mr. Goldthwaite, he—"

"Mrs. Peterman, is she here?" he interrupted.

She frowned. "No, she ain't." Alex's heart lurched against his chest—he had come too late. "Mr. Goldthwaite took her and the children to Blessing Park," she said curtly.

"If you don't mind, I've enough to do to get the children fed today," she said, and closed the door.

Alex pivoted on his heel and marched to his horse.

At Blessing Park, Jones showed him to the gold drawing room, where he anxiously paced until Michael came bursting into the drawing room, a broad grin on his face.

"No doubt you've come to scold me for leaving London unexpectedly," he said, chuckling. "That, or someone has died," he added cheerfully, striding across the room to greet his friend. As he neared, his grin faded. "God forgive me," he exclaimed. "*Has* someone died?"

Alex managed a wry smile and shook his head. "No. I have come . . ." He choked on the words, unable to admit he had come for Lauren.

"Yes?" Michael asked with genuine concern. Alex glanced sheepishly at the Marquis of Darfield. If there was a man in the *ton* who had given in to love, it was Michael Ingram, and he had fought its onset with gusto. But he had succumbed, quite thoroughly, in Alex's estimation. Surely Michael would understand the desperation he himself felt.

"Good God, man, has something happened?" Michael demanded.

Alex took a deep breath. "Is Countess Bergen here?" he asked.

Confusion scudded across Michael's face. "Yes . . . have you brought her bad news?"

"I suppose that depends on one's perspective," Alex said dryly. "My engagement with Marlaine is ended."

Michael blinked, staring at Alex in shock. Then suddenly, he turned and went to the drink cart and poured two whiskeys. "I think," he drawled as he handed a glass to Alex, "I have put two and two together."

"Let me explain—"

He was interrupted by Abbey's cheerful burst into the drawing room, grinning happily. "Darling, have you—"

She drew up short the moment she saw Alex. Neither he, nor Michael, judging by his little chuckle, missed the sudden change in her demeanor. "Oh. Your *grace*. You have come," she said simply.

"I believe, my love," Michael said, sauntering toward her, "you meant to say that mean-spirited, detestable reprobate has come."

Abbey paled visibly and shot an imploring look at her husband. "I have no idea what you are saying, Michael. You must excuse me—I look a fright," she said, taking a step backward. Michael caught her hand and pulled her, against her will, into his side.

"You look wonderful." He wrapped an arm firmly around her shoulders. Abbey's cheeks were suddenly quite red, and she stared intently at the carpet. Michael grinned at a bewildered Alex. "You and I have never minced words, Sutherland," he said laughingly. "I have been hearing about an unforgivable scoundrel for several days now. Apparently you are he."

"I see," Alex muttered.

Michael's grin broadened. "Now I understand why my wife has refused to identify this evil being to me. Undoubtedly she feared I would take your side, as we are cut from the same black cloth," he said, and smiled adoringly at Abbey. "The wedding is off, darling," he said, and quickly put a hand over her mouth before she could shriek a response. "Countess Bergen is in the paddock with my head gardener, Withers," he said cheerfully, and with a playful kiss to Abbey's temple, removed his hand.

"Oh, Alex," Abbey said, and sighing, gave in to their long-term friendship." I am so sorry! But you had best be prepared. Lauren, well, she does not speak . . . very . . . *highly* of you."

Alex nodded and tossed the whiskey down his throat. "I assure you, I have come quite prepared to battle to the death," he said, and strode past them just as Michael gathered Abbey into a loving embrace that he could not help envying.

He could hear the sound of children's laughter as he walked across the west terrace. As he sprang down the stone steps onto a gravel walkway lined with clipped hedges, his heart raced. At the end of the walkway, he paused to straighten his neckcloth, desperately needing to collect his thoughts. As he tried to think, he heard her dulcet laughter.

It literally snatched the breath from his lungs.

He stepped forward and peered around a tall hedge, unnoticed by those in the paddock. His eyes riveted on Lauren.

His angel was standing in her old leather boots, wearing a boy's white lawn shirt and buckskin trousers that fit her curves like a glove. She was absolutely glorious; her hair was bound in a single braid, and she wore a ridiculous-looking hat garnished with a wide variety of fruit. Her cheeks bore a hint of color, her teeth gleaming in a smile. Little Sally clung to her leg, and Withers, a man with fists like hams, was standing next to her, watching a child being led about on the back of an old nag.

Slowly, a smile spread his lips as he watched Theodore, sporting a new pair of spectacles, come eagerly to Lauren's side when she beckoned him to fetch Sally. Lydia leaned against the paddock railing, smiling coyly at the stable boy leading the nag. Young Horace was hanging by his knees from the railing, his head just inches above the ground, shouting for Lauren to look at him.

On top of the nag sat Leonard. He said something that caused Lauren to burst into musical laughter. She moved to help him dismount, tousling his hair affectionately when he refused her offer. But the moment his legs hit the ground, he flung his arms around her waist and hugged her.

Dear God, he had forgotten.

He had forgotten what she meant to this little brood. He had been so engrossed in his own desires, he had forgotten that at Rosewood, Lauren unselfishly bestowed the treasure of human touch on each and every one of those orphans. He had forgotten, and he could not have possibly loved her more than he did at that moment.

His chest swollen with pride, he watched for a long while from the shadows of the hedge, truly touched by her ability to make each child feel special. When Withers at last led the nag away, Lydia stepped in and began to gather the other children. Lauren reminded Lydia that Cook promised oranges before Mr. Goldthwaite came for them. The children, chattering among themselves, filed from the paddock toward the garden, Horace terrorizing them with strategic pokes from his wooden sword. Alex stepped into the cover of the hedge as they passed. Lauren lagged behind to retrieve Sally's discarded doll and Theodore's forgotten book before following them.

She walked through the paddock gate, passing him.

Alex stepped from the shadows of the hedge, his voice failing him for a moment. *"Lauren,"* he choked.

She froze in mid-stride. He did not so much as breathe as she cast her gaze heavenward, her eyes filled with poignant hope. His heart surged with emotion as she turned slowly toward him, her eyes seeking him in the late afternoon shadows. When she found him, her lips parted slightly and her eyes widened, as if she did not believe what she saw. God, she was so beautiful, so earnest, so hopeful, so . . .

"No," she whispered, shaking her head.

Instinctively, he reached for her. "Lauren, I—"

"No!" she said again, staring at him as if at an apparition.

His hand fell, dangling at his side. "I know you were not expecting this," Alex said evenly, despite his racing heart.

She stared at him, obviously unable to fathom his appearance. She said just one word. "No."

Dammit, he had planned what he would say and how he would say it, but at the moment, he could not remember a bloody thing. He glanced uncertainly around him, desperately trying to think.

She moved backward, away from him. "I want you," he suddenly blurted. Her eyes fluttered wide as saucers. And to his utter amazement, she turned and walked away, toward the stables.

Because she could not *breathe*. What did he think, that he could waltz into the paddock and announce *that* after all she had been through? It was bad enough to be caught so off guard by him, to be so instantly disoriented by those incredible green eyes. Her heart was *still* pounding, her throat dry. He was beautiful, so very beautiful, and had just deepened the wound in her heart. It was too much to be *borne,* not after crying herself to sleep night after night, mourning him! Not after agreeing to marry Magnus! Hot tears began to press against the back of her throat as she walked blindly into the stables. She could *kill* him for this!

Her anger melted away to fear the moment she realized he had followed her, his powerful presence immediately filling the stable. She brought a hand to her neck, wondering if she might have to claw her shirt open just so she could breathe. Behind her, he cleared his throat. "Believe me, that most definitely was *not* what I intended to say," he said apologetically.

She was mute, stunned into silence. She could feel him surround her, knew he was closely examining every inch of her. Mortified that he should see her deep hurt, she hugged herself tight, hoping against hope he would not see the tremors that racked her body. She sensed him moving even closer and felt a panic rise in her throat that bordered on delirium.

"Lauren, please look at me." The softness of his voice wafted across her like a breeze, and she clamped her mouth shut, knowing her emotion would betray her if she spoke.

"You are trembling." His light touch on her shoulder scorched her like a flame. She started violently, staggering several steps away from him. "I know you are angry," he said quietly.

She was not angry, she was *devastated*. She could not help herself; she sliced a heated gaze across him. "Angry does not *begin* to describe how I feel," she croaked, immediately despising herself for sounding so wounded.

Alex nodded slowly and looked thoughtfully at the ground, rubbing the back of his neck. "I did not lie to you. London, that night—it meant everything to me," he said quietly. He slowly lifted his gaze. "I have fallen in love with you, Lauren. Hopelessly and completely. I think of you constantly and dream of you at night. I want you to be with me always, and God help me, I do not think I can live without you."

He looked so earnest and sounded so sincere that Lauren gasped softly, touched to her very soul. But it could not be true. Dear God, the man would be *married* in a matter of days—*earlier,* if he could have convinced Marlaine!

"I am astonished, your grace," she murmured coolly, noticing his wince. "Perhaps you think I should *forget* that you begged Lady Marlaine to elope with you after that night!" she stammered angrily. " *'One foot in sea, and one on shore, To one thing constant never!'* "

Alex's complexion darkened. "Who told you that?" he demanded, ignoring the poetic knife in his gut.

"*She* did!" she cried, her voice breaking. "How could you do it? How could you *love* me like that if you loved her? But then, I *begged* you to love me, didn't I?" She laughed hysterically, choking on it.

Alex took a step toward her, his hands clenching and unclenching at his sides. "Lauren, listen very carefully to what I am saying to you. I love *you,* no other, more than I have ever loved anyone in my life. I have come here to ask you . . . no *beg* you—" he paused, glancing wildly about the stable. "I have broken my engagement with Marlaine," he said simply. "There will be no wedding."

She did not think it possible to hurt any more, but those words killed her. The stalls seemed to tilt; she could not, she *would* not believe him! Oh *God,* did he not understand? He had come too *late*! His eyes darted across her face, anxiously gauging her reaction. She could not look at him and squeezed her eyes shut. She hated him for saying the one thing she had prayed to hear, the *one* thing that could break her heart. It was too damned late. "I am sorry for Lady Marlaine," she forced herself to say, and slowly opened her eyes. "But I will marry Magnus."

Raw anger flashed in his green eyes. "Have you heard a bloody word I have said?" he roared.

Lauren stepped backward. "What did you expect me to do? Wait for a stolen moment here or there? Lurk about London hoping to catch a glimpse of you and your wife at some afternoon assembly?" she cried.

"Do not antagonize me, little girl. I have been to the edge of *hell* and back in my desire to find you and set this matter to rights! Ending my engagement was the hardest thing I have ever had to do, but I did it because I *love* you!" he bellowed.

"I am not a *fool*!" she shrieked. Alex's eyes narrowed and he began to stroll toward her, his raw power thinly disguised by his graceful, almost catlike movement. Lauren took several steps backward. "I will marry Magnus," she heard herself say, "and you cannot stop me! Dear God, it is the only thing I can do now!"

"I think you must be quite deaf! I said that I *love* you! I have never said that to another living soul! Do you not *hear* me?"

Oh, she heard him, all right, and if he said it one more time, she was going to have to beg for a truce and lie down in a stall until her heart stopped pounding so erratically. If only he knew how those words wrenched her gut, how she had longed for him to love her! She was already sentenced to a life of hell, knowing she would be haunted by her desire for him, and now he sought to torture her with declarations that were meaningless.

"I *heard* you," she said, fighting a sob. "But it is too *late,* do you not understand that? It is *so* very late; I cannot help but wonder *why* . . . Why now? Dear God, why now? Just go back to London and find another woman to amuse you—"

"I cannot," he breathed. "Unfortunately for us both, apparently, it's *you* I want."

"You want me as your *mistress*! You said you would find a way for us, and I thought . . . but you asked her to elope with you!"

"I wanted you then as I want you now, Lauren—with me always, at my table, in my arms, sleeping next to me," he said earnestly.

"But you *asked* her!"

Impossibly, his face darkened even more. "I bloody well *know* what I asked her!" he snapped. "In a moment of uncertainty, I had to know if she could possibly fill my soul—"

Lauren gasped and turned away, fighting for air, but Alex stubbornly continued. "God in heaven, there was so much at stake, Lauren. Others were depending on me, needing me to lead them, to set an example. But I—I *cannot* be without you. I know that now, but it was *not* a decision I reached lightly!"

She pressed her hands against her abdomen as the full weight of what he had done began to sink in. The reforms. Good God, he had risked his influence over important economic reforms—reforms that Rosewood had desperately needed to survive. Reforms that would benefit the children, others like them . . . No, she could not let that happen. She could not be responsible when so many others . . .

Alex suddenly caught her from behind and jerked her hard to his chest. The impact knocked the breath from her, and she gulped for air as he nuzzled his face against her neck, sending a wave of unwelcome longing crashing through her. "Let me soothe your melancholy, sweetheart. Let me wash your guilt away," he whispered hoarsely.

The poignant use of the poem she had sent him in her darkest hour was her undoing; she swallowed a violent sob and pivoted in his arms. He cradled her face in his hands, peering deeply into her eyes. "I will not lose you again," he breathed, and crushed his mouth to hers, devouring her. She surrendered easily, abandoning everything to him. Love and desire swirled through her, and she responded with the intensity of those powerful emotions, groping for him, until her thoughts began to cloud her passion. Her conscience would not let her abandon herself completely to him; images of Magnus swept across her mind's eye, the recognition of Alex's importance in the Lords. Her passion began to ebb, flowing out like the tide and allowing guilt to seep in. She suddenly broke away, shaking her head.

"Don't stop," he rasped in her ear.

"You shouldn't have come here," she whispered. She felt him stiffen. Wearily, he laid his forehead against hers, breathing deeply. "I can't be with you, Alex. You have to leave."

His head jerked up at that. *"Never,"* he said roughly.

No, never, please God, never, she silently prayed, but pushed softly against his chest. "Maybe it's not too late. If you go back to London—"

"What in the hell are you saying?" he demanded.

"I can't be with you," she said again, her voice quivering.

Alex slowly dropped his hands to his sides. Lauren stepped away, flattening her back against a stall, fighting the urge to fling herself into his arms again. There was simply too much at stake. His expression was disbelieving, incredulous. But he had to believe it.

Pivoting on her heel, she fled the stables, blinded by tears.

* * *

She ended up in Abbey's favorite sitting room. Like a wild animal, she paced around the sewing baskets, books, and magazines scattered about the floor, intermittently crying and suppressing a rifling anguish. Oh, God, why had he come and made such a bloody mess of everything? No, there was no *mess,* she angrily reminded herself, other than her state of mind. Ethan had signed the betrothal agreement, had already posted the banns. What of Magnus? Good *God,* how could she look at him having heard Alex's declaration of love? How could she *lie* with him on their wedding night? That monumental event was just days away—even now, he was in Portsmouth, readying his ship to take her to Bavaria.

To take her away from Alex.

With a sob, Lauren whirled toward the windows overlooking the gardens. *Bavaria.* Where she would wake each morning to the memory of his words: *I love you, no other, more than I have ever loved anyone in my life.* She gasped in abject pain.

When the door quietly opened Lauren spun around, half-afraid it was Alex and she would lose all reason. But it was Abbey who entered, balancing a tray with a flagon and two tankards. Lauren hastily wiped the tears from her face as her friend carefully placed the heavy tray on a stool. Abbey did not look at her as she knelt on her knees next to the stool. "Michael sent Mr. Goldthwaite to Rosewood with the children," she said quietly, "and Alexa is in bed." Lauren did not answer, afraid she would break apart if she did.

Abbey poured a tankard of ale and held it out to Lauren with a sheepish smile. "It's my favorite. Whiskey may seem more appropriate to you at the moment, but it does not go down quite as smoothly." Lauren could not move; she stared at the tankard. "It's none of my affair, but I am guessing things did not go particularly well," Abbey said, and with her head, motioned toward the tankard.

Slowly, Lauren walked across the room, fell to her knees

across from Abbey, and took the tankard. "He has ended his engagement," she said bluntly, and took a long swallow of the foul liquid.

Abbey poured a tankard for herself and settled on the floor, leaning against an overstuffed couch. "Michael told me."

Lauren slid to her hips, perching her shoulder against the couch, and stared into the tankard. "He says he *loves* me." She almost choked on the words.

Abbey took a generous swig as she contemplated that. "I think he must love you dearly to do what he did. It must have been very difficult for him."

"What? To come here *now,* when it is too late?" Lauren asked bitterly.

Abbey smiled softly and shook her head. "No, I think it was very difficult to end his engagement and risk everything he has built." Lauren hid her guilt at that behind another swig of ale. "But," Abbey continued, "I never thought he loved her. I mean, I think he *hoped* he would, but . . . He found you. It's just that the timing is not very good."

"The timing could not be *worse!*" Lauren moaned, and drank more.

"You can hardly fault him for the timing, Lauren. It's not as if you presented yourself any earlier."

"Oh, *fine,*" she snapped, and drank more of the ale. After several minutes, she blurted, "First of all, I did not *present* myself. Secondly, he may say whatever he likes now, because it is just too *late.*"

"Too late? Why is it too late?"

"Have you forgotten? I have to marry Magnus!"

"You do not *have* to do anything. You are not married yet, so how can it be too late?" Abbey demanded.

"Because it *is!*"

"No it is *not,*" Abbey strongly disagreed.

"What are you suggesting?" Lauren asked suspiciously. Abbey snorted loudly and quaffed her ale before speaking. "You do not love Magnus, do you? Do not even think to try and tell me otherwise! It is quite obvious!"

"Is that so? Well, the night in London I came to your house, you thought I was quite mad for him! Seemed obvious to you then!" Lauren countered triumphantly, feeling a bit light-headed.

Abbey gave a curt toss of her head and glanced imperiously at the hearth. "I have had the opportunity to observe you closely since then—"

"You have had the opportunity to listen to me cry about my troubles, you mean."

Abbey abruptly giggled into her tankard. "All right, so I have! But you have told me everything, and my point is that you love him, Lauren, *not* Magnus! And Alex loves you! So much that he ended an important engagement, severed a powerful family alliance, and walked away from everything he has accomplished in the Lords. Therefore, it is not too *late*!" Abbey lifted her tankard into the air, ending with a flourish.

Lauren giggled and impulsively lifted her tankard, tapping it against Abbey's. The two women simultaneously sagged against the couch in a fit of silly laughter. After a moment, Lauren sobered, sighing sadly. "Forgetting, for the moment, that he would always be tainted by my presence if I were to consider your suggestion, I cannot do that to Magnus."

Abbey did not say anything for a long moment. "Do you think," she finally asked, "that Magnus would want to marry you if he knew you loved another?"

Lauren shrugged as she fished a piece of debris from her ale. "He knows. It does not matter to him. It was part of the agreement between us," she said softly. "His affection in exchange for my respect. That is all he wants from me."

Abbey looked skeptical. "Truly? I mean, he may have *said* that, but do you think he could truly mean it?"

Lauren did not immediately respond. She drained her

tankard and helped herself to another. "It does not matter,"
she said resolutely. "I *do* respect Magnus, and I cannot toss
him aside."

"But what of Alex?" Abbey asked as she refilled her
tankard.

"I don't know!" Lauren exclaimed. "I don't want him to
risk it all! He is too important—England *needs* a man like
him. But—but he uses *words* to make me—*want* him," she
said timidly.

Abbey laughed. "Words as opposed to what, his feet?"

Buoyed by the ale, Lauren laughed. "His feet are very
large, have you noticed?"

Abbey nodded. "Almost as big as his head," she whispered gravely. The laughter of both women pealed through
the room, and they spent the early evening detailing all of
Alex's faults. When they had quite exhausted that subject,
they sent for another flagon of ale, then gleefully turned to
Michael's faults. And then those of men in general.

Chapter 22

After depleting the Darfields' ale reserves, Lauren was escorted home by two coachmen and Withers. The next morning, her headache was far too blinding to answer the dozens of questions Mrs. Peterman put to her. She hardly knew what she was doing as she attempted her chores. If she never saw a pint of ale again, it would be too soon.

Unable to endure the housekeeper's disapproving looks, she finally stumbled outside to feed Lucy, but even she seemed to be looking at her questioningly. "*Et tu,* Lucy?" she mumbled. Misery, both physical and emotional, deluged her. In the rare moments she was capable of thinking clearly, she was baffled and drained by Alex's unexpected appearance. She could not think. She did not *want* to think. Dropping the empty feed pail, she began to walk to no particular destination. Just somewhere away from all humanity. Somewhere she would not have to think.

Without realizing how far she had gone, she stumbled onto the pumpkin field and moaned. How apropos that she should end up exactly where her little saga had begun. She dragged herself to a tree and leaned against it, looking out over the fallow field.

There would be no pumpkins this year. Magnus did not like the fact that she had established trade—like Paul, he did not think it terribly befitting a countess. He had bestowed a trust on Rosewood so there would never again be a need to trade. A trust so large that it allowed him a voice at Rosewood. With a heavy sigh, she slid down the trunk of the tree until her legs folded under her. He meant well, but it chafed her that he had come to Rosewood and demanded change, asserting his right to do so simply because she had agreed to marry him. She had not argued with him; she had been too exhausted. Alex had exhausted her of all will.

Alex.

A watery recollection came to her, and she turned her cheek against the smooth bark of the tree. With her eyes closed, she could see every feature of his ruggedly handsome face. As hard as she had tried to push him from her mind since leaving London, he had been constantly with her. It was appalling to her that while Magnus talked of marriage, children, and Bergenschloss, she could sit calmly, pretend to listen, and think of Alex—*long* for Alex. Then yesterday, he had appeared from nowhere and had said the words she had so wanted to hear.

She winced, feeling the pain of his words for the hundredth time. Had it not been for Magnus, she might very well have begged him to take her away from everything. As if she could escape! There was already talk of her in London. The day she had left, she had called on Charlotte to say good-bye, but that horrid Lady Pritchit had not allowed her to see her daughter. Lauren had been so stunned, she had simply turned and walked away. Her glorious night at the opera was the cause, that much she understood. Why had she not insisted he fetch Lady Paddington? Why had she not insisted he take her home? Why, oh *why,* had she . . .

What was done was done, and she was sick of the guilt.

She *had* gone, and now she had no choice but to go to Bavaria. The very thought of leaving wrenched her heart, even if only for half a year at a time. The children needed her so. But more than that, how could she possibly survive without him?

She drifted, the image of Alex vivid in her head. He truly was magnificent, she thought. In her mind's eye she skimmed the broad shoulders, the long line of his muscular legs, the arrogant smile on his face. His poignant words whispered over and over in her head, the feel of his lips on hers so real that she could not be completely certain it was *not* real. She drifted through the waking dream as she lay against the tree, a dream in which the stark reality of her duty to Rosewood and Magnus periodically intruded. Tortured by strong feelings for him, Lauren actually felt ill. It was several hours before she found the strength to return home.

The following day, Lauren absently hung freshly laundered clothes on a line between the new barn and a tree, determined not to think of Alex *or* Magnus. Unfortunately, she could not stop herself, and quickly discovered that she could not think of one without thinking of the other. So perplexed was she by her dilemma that she did not notice the line sagging until it snapped from the weight of the children's wet clothes. She groaned, picked up the clothes, and went in search of Rupert to repair the line. She heard his booming laugh coming from the front lawn as she walked toward the house. Changing direction, she rounded the corner of the house, halting unsteadily when she saw Alex. What was he *doing* here? Surrounded by Rupert, Horace, Leonard, and Theodore, he held a rapier in his hands. A *real* rapier.

"Good afternoon, Miss Hill," Alex called cheerfully, as if nothing was out of the ordinary. As if time had turned back and they had never left Rosewood almost a year ago.

The other four heads instantly swiveled toward her. Speechless, Lauren eyed him suspiciously. "I found this old thing at Dunwoody and thought the lads might enjoy it," he remarked. With a smile, he resumed his detail of the sword for the boys. She edged cautiously toward the lawn, her fingers trailing the brick of the house, disbelieving his casual presence. He had removed his coat and had rolled up his sleeves over sinewy forearms. His hair, a little long now, glistened in the afternoon sun as he demonstrated the basic steps of fencing. She was immediately overcome with a vivid memory of his body above her, his green eyes peering through to her very soul. She unconsciously pressed a palm against her hot cheek.

It was his handing the rapier to Leonard that shook her back to the present. It was Leonard's wild swing toward Horace that made her take several quick, uneasy steps forward. But Alex turned toward her and smiled reassuringly, as if he understood her misgivings. *All* of them. The small but extraordinary unspoken communication startled her. He understood.

"Very good, lad," Alex said as Leonard thrust forward.

"I will try!" Rupert demanded. And so it went; Rupert, then Horace, and then the others. Lauren watched in fascination as each of them turned eagerly to Alex to see if they held the sword just right, if their form was to his satisfaction. They adored him, too, she realized, and a smile slowly curved her lips. As she stood leaning against the house watching the boys thrust their sword into thin air, she realized that the ache was beginning to thaw from her heart. But that, in and of itself, was quite frightening. What was she thinking? In the middle of Theodore's turn, she turned on her heel and walked away, afraid to look at him a moment longer.

Every day thereafter, Alex appeared at Rosewood, usually in the company of one of the children. He explained to a wary Mrs. Peterman that he was overseeing some repairs to

Dunwoody. Lauren did not believe that for a minute, but she kept silent. She did not encourage him in any way, but neither did she ask him to leave as she had at Blessing Park. She knew she should, but the words would not come.

He appeared every day, filling her with his mere presence, assuring her without words. He charmed them all. Even Mrs. Peterman began to soften toward him, even though she still held him fully responsible for Lauren's refusal of Mr. Goldthwaite. On the front lawn, he taught Lydia the latest dance from London, accompanied by his rich baritone hum. The poor girl was so admiring of him that she almost swooned, and did not once mention Mr. Ramsey Baines, the young lad she was determined to marry one day. He brought Theodore two books of fiction, one a pirate story, the other an adventure. He helped Rupert shore up a fence the cattle had crumbled. He took Leonard riding on Jupiter. At the supper table, the children could speak of little else than Mr. Christian and the many adventures he had experienced. Climbing mountains, exploring jungles, and meeting strange people who wore grass for skirts.

She could not help but be drawn to wherever he was, but she kept a respectable distance. At first, she was reluctant to even speak with him for fear of betraying herself and ultimately, Magnus. But it was impossible to resist him. After a few days, she began to respond timidly to his chatter. He asked about her plans for Rosewood. She cautiously explained her idea, rejected by Magnus, of establishing a dairy and trading its products for food and sundry dry goods. She fully expected him to tell her it would not work. He surprised her by proclaiming it a marvelous idea, agreeing that Rosewood could not rely on the land to produce enough grain to sustain them. He offered to help, said he knew a dairyman who could help her get started if she should have the opportunity. Lauren realized she was smiling as he spoke, eagerly discussing her dreams with him, encouraged and enthused by his tacit approval.

She even garnered enough courage to ask him about Sutherland Hall. He grew animated as he spoke of his home, regaling her with tales of three brothers who were constantly into mischief. Every once in a while, if she had allowed herself to be near him, he would reach up and casually smooth a curl from her temple, or let his knuckles graze her cheek. His touch always startled her—she was so sure she would succumb to her desire that she made certain she was never alone with him.

It was very obvious he did not care for her reticence. He tried any number of ways to be alone with her. Part of her desperately wanted to walk with him when he asked, or to ride Jupiter with him, or to accompany him to Pemberheath. But it was too dangerous, too tempting. She forced herself to think of Magnus. She reminded herself that Alex should be in London at the close of the parliamentary session, not Dunwoody, *not* whiling away the time at Rosewood. There was too much at stake—she told herself that so often, that she was beginning to chant it like a mantra.

Though it hardly seemed possible, she grew to love him more each day, and therefore became more confused. She tried to make herself think of Bavaria, of when Magnus would return, of who she was, but she still refused to face her future. She still allowed herself the remnant of a dream. But then a letter from Paul arrived.

He had written to confirm that he and Ethan would arrive at the end of the week. In the course of his note, he wrote that the latest speculation as to the true cause of the sudden breakup between Lady Marlaine and Sutherland was the duke's obsession with a titled woman, unknown to the *ton* before this Season. In so many words, he told her that the gossip about her was malicious.

That might have been enough to confirm her determination to marry Magnus, but Paul had gone on to report that the *ton* was on edge over the potential fate of the reform bill now that it had passed the Commons. Unfortunately, he wrote, most pundits gave it little chance of passing the Lords without the Reese-Christian support, which was now, of course, highly doubtful. Paul's opinion was that for all intents and purposes, the reform bill was dead. From there, he had launched into a discussion about his plans to pick up the mantle of reform, perhaps starting in their home parish. Just as soon as he set Rosewood to rights, he would seek a seat in the Commons, he boasted.

Lauren had burned Paul's letter. The sight of it reminded her of the reality of her situation beyond the bounds of Rosewood. Instead of being in London where he was sorely needed, Alex was here. Instead of swaying the Lords to enact the reforms and change the destiny of the country, he was teaching Lydia to dance. Dear God, even if she *could* end her betrothal to Magnus and follow Alex—which she could not—there was no hope. She was ruined, just as Paul and Magnus had predicted. She would be a source of constant embarrassment to him, a thorn in the side of the Earl of Whitcomb and his family. No one would take him seriously, not after the scandal that was apparently brewing in London. All because of one night.

One extraordinarily beautiful night.

Alex galloped into Pemberheath, reining Jupiter to an abrupt halt at the village stable. He quickly dismounted and irritably tossed the reins to a stable boy along with a few coins. He was at his wit's end, having tried everything he could think of to lure Lauren to him, resenting the hell out of the fact that he could not get close to her, no matter what he did. If there was not a child hanging from her leg, Mrs. Peterman was standing guard. The woman hardly needed to bother; Lauren made quite sure she was never alone with him. He could not even take comfort in the fact that she seemed to be softening a little. Yesterday, she had actually laughed, a rich, full laugh, when Leonard had pelted him with a rubber ball. He became distracted from their game of toss when Lauren had appeared on the lawn in that simple pale blue gown. As a result, he had a nasty little bump on the side of his head.

She had laughed, but she had refused to walk with him. He had almost begged her yesterday, weary of being the gentleman. *Come with me, Lauren. Just a walk about, nothing more,* he had said. Her expression had paled, and she had looked nervously at her feet, telling him she could not. When he demanded to know *why* not, she had scuffed the edge of her old boot into the earth and had murmured, *Magnus would not approve.* That damned German was not even *here,* but his hold on her spanned the bloody little continent!

He had to face the possibility he had lost. Hell, he had hardly *slept* from facing it. What in God's name was he supposed to do? He could not live at Dunwoody indefinitely. There was a dearth of simple human companionship, except the groundskeeper and his wife, whom he rarely saw. With little to keep his mind occupied—save her—he restlessly rambled from room to empty room, absolutely *obsessed* with her.

He hated to admit it, but he supposed it was possible she actually felt some affection for Madgoose. Did that mean she had lost the love for him she had so blissfully proclaimed the night of the opera? He did not know for certain, and it was driving him mad. He would try one last time, he had decided. If she did not come to him now, if she did not give him *some* sign there was hope, he would leave. First to London to wrap up some business, and then, by God, he would leave England, perhaps indulge in an adventure or two. Anything that might cleanse his soul of her.

He stalked toward the end of the main thoroughfare, wondering just where in the hell a person might find a bunch of gardenias in such a godforsaken little village.

"Sutherland!"

Alex pivoted sharply. Scanning the crowded street, he

saw Paul Hill limping toward him, using his cane to force
the carriages and horses to veer around him. "I had thought
I would receive word that the wedding had been postponed," he said breathlessly as he reached Alex.

Alex flicked his eyes to the people around them, then to
Paul. "I did not know you were at Rosewood," he muttered,
and motioned toward a covered breezeway between two
buildings.

"We only just arrived. Ethan has gone to find Rupert.
Damn fool was to have met us . . . never mind that. What
about Lauren?" Paul asked, trying to catch his breath as
they moved into the breezeway.

Alex scowled. "Your sister, sir, is the most intractable
woman I have ever known," he responded irritably, and
leaned over the railing to peer into a babbling stream below
them.

"Well then, what have you done?" Paul demanded.

"Other than be my usual charming self?" he answered
acerbically. "I have done nothing. I cannot get close enough
to her to so much as offer a handkerchief."

"Oh, God," Paul snorted. "That's it? I expected more
from you, Sutherland!"

Alex angrily jerked around to face Paul. "What in God's
name would you have me do? *Abduct* her, for Chrissakes?"
he fairly shouted. "She is, apparently, content to marry that
heathen Bavarian!"

"You are wrong," Paul said evenly. "She has loved you
since the day you stumbled onto Rosewood. She practically
deified you, Mr. Christian. She has wanted no other, not
since the day you almost killed her."

"I did *not*—" With a great sigh of exasperation, Alex
angrily shook his head. "That was before London, before
Madgoose arrived to claim her. She has obviously changed
her mind."

"If you think Bergen stands in your way, you *are* a fool.
Can you not see that Bavaria is a convenient solution for

her?'' Paul blustered angrily. When Alex did not immediately respond, he sighed, glancing impatiently at the stream. ''Look here, she thinks Bavaria is the only place she can go now. And the circumstances being what they are, I have to agree with her. London has branded her—there is no hope for her in England, not the way things are.''

Alex remained silent, his doubts overpowering him.

Paul groaned with exasperation. ''I *know* my sister. I know when she loves, it is completely, without artifice. Would that I had understood that sooner,'' he muttered, more to himself than to Alex. ''She cannot bear to love you without hope—she would prefer Bavaria to that. But you can change that.''

Alex looked again at the stream, slowly shaking his head. ''I have tried—''

Paul gripped the railing. ''What you said in London . . . If you truly love her, if you truly *want* her, you will find a way. But you had best be quick about it. They wed Friday and set sail the following morning.'' He did not wait for a response, but shoved away from the railing. Alex clenched his teeth as he listened to the clip of Paul's cane.

He had four days.

Theodore announced excitedly that Count Bergen was coming down the drive. Lauren's heart sagged with disappointment—she had been waiting for Alex to come. When he had not come around yesterday, she had tried to convince herself that it meant nothing. But as today had passed with excruciating tedium, she had begun to wonder if she had succeeded in chasing him away. If she had been as successful as all that, she was prepared to march right down to the river and throw herself in. Could she do *nothing* right? Without looking at Paul, she slowly put away the socks she was darning and stood, smoothing the lap of her gown.

''Well,'' said Paul cheerfully, ''Bergen's return means you will be leaving soon.'' He smiled and picked up his cane. "You must be very excited. The nuptials, a wedding trip aboard a fancy ship, married bliss in Bavaria."

In her current state, it was beyond her ability to fathom why Paul might try to provoke her, but he was doing a fine job of it. God, she wanted to slap him—this was hard enough without his needling. "Should you not welcome your beloved home?" he grinned, confirming her suspicions. With an icy glower, she walked out of the drawing room.

Magnus was climbing down from his horse when she stepped outside. He smiled at her as he lifted his saddlebags. "You are a welcome sight, *liebchen.*"

"Welcome back," she said, trying to smile. Magnus hoisted the bags onto his shoulder and crossed the drive to her. He slipped a free arm around her waist and kissed her on the lips. "You will be pleased with the ship," he said in German. "I spared no expense to have my cabin made suitable for a bride."

A bridal suite—Lauren felt herself color. She thought of Alex immediately and tried to stuff her traitorous thoughts into some remote corner.

Magnus chuckled. "Come now, *liebchen,* you are not as innocent as all that," he grinned, and winked subtly. Feeling suddenly nauseated, Lauren swallowed a lump in her throat. Magnus frowned. "What is this? Ah, my dove, I will be as gentle as a lamb. You have nothing to fear," he said, and affectionately kissed her temple.

"My *Deutsche* is not terribly good. What were you confessing, Bergen?" Paul asked. Magnus slid his gaze to Paul. His hand slipped from her waist, and he moved away, muttering something that caused Paul to chuckle. She stood, unmoving, staring into a bleak space that resembled her future. She heard Ethan's booming voice, and still she did not move. She might have stood there all day had her eye not caught a movement up the lane.

Her heart leapt to her throat. It was Alex, riding hard toward the manor house. A silly grin spread her lips, which she quickly covered with her hand. As rider and horse neared, her heart pounded against her ribs with every thud of the hooves. He flew onto the drive, reining up hard, his eyes locked on her. Then slowly, the green orbs flicked to the men behind her.

"I see Madgoose has returned after all," he said jovially and gracefully alighted. Lauren did not turn around, but clutched her hands nervously in front of her, clinging to a thin thread of control as Alex tethered his horse and walked briskly to where she stood. Her pounding heart would break free of her breast at any moment, she was certain of it.

"Sutherland," Magnus said very gruffly, coming to stand beside Lauren. "What are you doing here?"

Alex grinned unabashedly. "Wishing the happy couple well, Bergen," he quipped, then turned to Lauren. "Good day."

"Good day, your grace." Oh, *God,* were her cheeks as flaming red as they felt? Judging by Alex's widening grin, apparently they were. Magnus flustered her further by suddenly hauling her to his side in an iron grip.

Alex merely chuckled at his possessive display. "I could hardly let you sail to Bohemia—"

"Bavaria," Magnus growled.

"Whatever," Alex said flippantly, "without saying good-bye. It has been such a . . . *challenge* . . . knowing you, Bergen."

"Sutherland!" Ethan boomed, waddling out onto the front steps. "Unless you've come to up the ante, be gone with you now!"

"Yes, go," Magnus said quietly. He was gripping Lauren's waist tightly, so tightly, she was having trouble catching her breath.

"In due time, my lord," Alex responded, undeterred. "I

brought your angel a gift," he said, and pivoting on his heel, marched toward Jupiter.

"Angel?" Magnus echoed, peering sharply at Lauren.

"Lydia . . . he means Lydia," she hastily responded. Alex reached inside his saddlebag, and returned to the front steps, where Paul, Ethan, and Magnus now surrounded Lauren.

"Miss Hill," he said, and held out a perfect, single gardenia to her. "Would you be so kind? To, ah, give it to Lydia, that is."

Hesitantly, she glanced up at him and saw the warmth in his eyes. Her heart fluttered wildly. Magnus's grip tightened painfully. She coughed uncomfortably and slowly reached for the flower. Alex put it in her hand, his fingertips brazenly brushing her palm.

"I, ah . . . what shall I say?" she asked, mortified that her voice trembled.

He smiled, his eyes fixed on hers, seemingly oblivious to the others. "Tell her, *'the heaven such grace did lend her, that she might admired be.'*"

A tendril of sweet desire coiled around her heart, and Lauren exhaled softly. No one could touch her as deeply as Alex, she thought, and looked at the gardenia in her palm, blurred through a haze of tears. She heard the guttural growl from Magnus and Ethan's angry bluster. Slowly, she lifted her gaze to Alex and returned his warm smile.

"You are not welcome here, Sutherland," Magnus said suddenly, his voice dipping dangerously low. "Get on your horse and go."

Alex reluctantly shifted his gaze to Magnus and actually smirked. "Haven't taken your vows yet, have you, Bergen? I think your presumption of owning the place is a bit premature."

Magnus suddenly let go of Lauren and took a large step forward. A good two inches taller than Alex, he stood only inches from him, arms akimbo, a threatening expression on his face. "I said leave. You are not welcome here any longer."

Alex chuckled and casually shifted his weight onto one hip as he regarded Magnus with a hint of amusement. "I suppose in Bavaria it is impolite to wish a couple well, then. Is that right, Bergen? You Germans prefer the civility of the pagans?"

"Pagan?" Magnus breathed.

"My apologies. What is the word in a language he can understand, Lauren?"

Magnus suddenly lunged for Alex, grabbing for his throat. But Alex was too quick; he whirled around, neatly sidestepping him, and chuckled at Magnus's fluster. "You'll have to be a damn sight quicker than that if you want to harm me, my friend. But in England, we have other ways of settling our differences if you care to explore them."

"Here now!" Ethan called nervously, and Paul hastily limped toward the two men, shoving his cane between them. "There is no cause for that! Bergen, he has come to wish you well, nothing more! And Sutherland, your kind wishes are graciously received. But the count has only just arrived from Portsmouth; perhaps it is best if you call another time. If you don't mind . . ."

"Not," Alex drawled, "any more than usual." He glanced at Lauren, who was paralyzed by what was quickly unfolding in front of her. His eyes quickly flicked the length of her, then landed on her face again. "Good day, Lauren," he said quietly. With a curt nod to Paul, he pivoted and swung onto Jupiter's back, and galloped away in a cloud of dust.

Magnus watched him go, then jerked around to face Lauren, his face mottled with rage. "What in the hell was he doing here?" he demanded angrily in German.

Lauren shrugged weakly. "As he said. To wish us well. If you will excuse me, I should give this flower to Lydia before it wilts." She fairly flew inside, just as Paul clapped Magnus on the shoulder and remarked that it did seem a very kind thing for the duke to do.

Supper was a horrid affair for Magnus. He could not stop staring at her, watching her blue eyes dip to her plate as she pushed her peas about, one by one. Paul was unusually animated, talking incessantly about the blasted duke. And the uncle was orally spending the trust Magnus had given Rosewood as a betrothal gift. He thought the blasted meal would never end, and when it did, he stood abruptly, announcing that he would retire. To the village.

He stalked silently outside, Lauren close behind. Thankful to find that the simpleton Rupert had brought his horse around, he tossed his saddlebags on the mare's back then turned sharply to face Lauren. She stood with her hands clasped behind her back, rocking gently on her feet. The light spilling from the house cast shadows on her face that made her allure even more profound. For the sake of propriety, he had chosen to stay in Pemberheath. But looking at her now, he wished he had decided to stay at Rosewood. Perhaps he might have visited her room. Perhaps he could have removed any thought of the Goddamn duke from her head.

He folded his arms across his chest, growing angrier with each passing moment. He deserved an explanation for the duke's presence, but she said nothing—absolutely *nothing*. Not only did she make no effort to soothe his ruffled feathers, she did not even attempt to send him off with a warm good-bye. And that, he realized, was not a very auspicious beginning for two people about to be married.

"You seemed preoccupied this evening, Lauren. Is there something on your mind?" he asked at last, struck by how harsh his native tongue suddenly sounded.

"Have I? I was not aware. I apologize," she said, and averted her gaze, across the lawn.

"You did not answer me. Is there something on your

mind?'' he asked again, silently willing her to assure him that all was well.

''Why no!'' she said sweetly, still looking across the lawn.

''How long has he been here?'' he asked abruptly.

Lauren stopped rocking and looked at him from the corner of her eye. ''Paul and Ethan arrived yesterday,'' she said softly.

Magnus's hands clenched at his sides. ''I am not referring to your *kin*. How long has *he* been here?'' he asked angrily.

Lauren drew her bottom lip between her teeth for a moment. ''I gather you mean the duke?''

''What in the bloody hell is going on here?'' he breathed, his pulse beginning to beat soundly at his temples.

''Nothing, Magnus,'' she said soothingly, and for a moment, he hoped. ''He came to wish us well,'' she added gently.

He knew he should accept her explanation, but he just could not leave it alone. ''We had an agreement, you and I. You promised to honor me.''

She looked surprised. ''I *do* honor you.''

''You do not honor me when you look at him with eyes as big as moons and blush like a maid when he smiles at you!''

Lauren blinked, then slowly raised her chin. ''I honor you, Magnus. I respect you. I will do so until my dying day. But there can be nothing more,'' she said quietly. ''*That* was our agreement.''

His breathing was suddenly constricted. It was their agreement, all right, *his* Goddammed agreement. Enraged, he suddenly vaulted to the mare's back, yanking the reins hard to keep her from bolting at the sudden impact. He glared down at Lauren, his mind and heart racing. She looked at him so serenely, for a moment he wondered if he had misjudged the situation.

But he knew he had judged it perfectly well, and abruptly spurred the mare into the night. She could sleep soundly tonight, knowing that she lived up to her end of the agreement. But not him. His promise was starting to strangle him.

Chapter 23

Lauren had every intention of apologizing. Magnus was right; she did not honor him by practically fainting over Alex's gift of a gardenia. When he had ridden away last night so furious and wounded, guilt had overcome her with a vengeance. She felt so badly about it that she had not slept well at all, and had awakened Rupert at daybreak to hitch one of the old grays to the wagon. Dressed in one of her best walking dresses, she left a note for Mrs. Peterman and started for Pemberheath to make amends. Beginning with an apology to the man she would marry.

A dense morning fog blanketed the earth and it was impossible to discern the landscape; weather that exactly matched her mood. It seemed of late she had no idea which way was up or down. Every day was a kaleidoscope of confusion, her emotions turning and twisting in her heart and mind. She had had enough, she thought, as the gray trotted briskly along the road. She had selected her fate, had signed all necessary documents, and would honor her commitment. Magnus had been a model of patience, very kind in his own unique way, and had asked for nothing in return but that she respect him. She had promised him that much. She *owed* him that much.

She urged the old gray faster.

Horse and wagon rattled across a small bridge that marked the halfway point between Pemberheath and Rosewood. A screeching noise suddenly rent the air, coming from the wagon, and Lauren frantically drew up on the reins. Sighing impatiently, she climbed down, and hands on hips, surveyed the old conveyance. The working of the thing baffled her, other than that the four wheels were required to turn. She walked to the horse and led her forward. The horrendous sound occurred again, and looking back, she saw the front wheels did not move.

"Oh *honestly*!" she exclaimed, marched back to the heap of old lumber, and impetuously kicked it. She immediately grabbed her foot, wincing in pain. "Damned slippers!" she muttered, and glared hatefully at the dainty emerald footwear that matched her dress. Wonderful. She could hope to walk all of ten feet in the flimsy things! And so exactly what was she to do now? In exasperation, she glanced at the sky. Was it her imagination, or were the clouds thickening?

It was not her imagination, she discovered a few moments later, when the first fat raindrop hit her hand. She moaned, hastening her attempts to free the gray from the contraption. Rupert had fashioned a strange, oddly fixed sort of harness, and she could not see how to unlatch the horse in any conceivable way. The drops turned to a light rain, soaking her bonnet.

It was all suddenly more than she could bear. The rain, the old wagon, *everything*. The last two weeks had been the most turbulent of her life and her nerves were frayed to their very ends. She had no idea what to do about *anything*, let alone a horse hitched to a wagon by some homemade harness! God in heaven, was nothing *simple* anymore? She began to sob uncontrollably. Throwing her arms around the old gray, she sobbed pitifully into her neck, too tired and too confused to think of what else to do.

She shrieked when a pair of strong hands grabbed her shoulders and jerked her away from the horse.

"What are you doing?" Alex asked, pivoting her roughly around to face him.

Relief, exhaustion, and plain frustration with the universe devoured her, and her sobs grew more frantic.

"My God, are you hurt?" he asked, a deep frown lining his eyes as they swept her body, searching for an injury.

"It *broke*!" she wailed, and motioned helplessly toward the wheel.

Alex glanced at the thing, then the horse, and let her go. He tried to move the old gray, but the front wheels locked. He walked to the wagon and squatted, peering beneath. "Ah, there is the culprit," he muttered. He came quickly to his feet, strode to the gray and, to Lauren's amazement, easily unlatched her. Yanking on her bridle, he led her to stand under a copse of trees. Sobbing helplessly, Lauren watched him return to the wagon and pick up the contraption that harnessed the horse. With a mighty shove, he pushed the wagon backward, unlocking the front wheels, and steered it off the road. Then he strode back to her and grabbed her hand. She struggled to keep up as he dragged her with him and fairly tossed her onto Jupiter's back, quickly sweeping up behind her.

"Why did you not seek shelter? There is an abandoned cottage not one hundred yards from here," he said gruffly, pointing toward the stand of trees. Lauren glanced in the direction he indicated. The falling structure had a thatched roof, which she had not noticed through the trees and fog until this very moment. It was a cottage she had played in as a child but had forgotten. It was the final blow to her fragile state of mind, and she sagged against him, sobs racking her body.

She had the sensation of moving, then being lifted. The moment her feet touched the ground, she stumbled toward the crumbling structure, bending low to enter. Just a single room, there was nothing inside except a few bales of hay. The floor was mud; an elaborate cobweb covered one corner, a fireplace held the remnants of some long ago fire, and the place smelled of cattle.

She wept harder.

A moment later, Alex came inside, his hand landing on the small of her back and guiding her to sit on one of the bales. As she cried, he broke apart a couple of other bales and spread the hay around to cover the mud. She watched him shed his greatcoat and shake the rain from it, then spread it across the hay he had scattered. He calmly surveyed his work before turning to Lauren. One corner of his mouth snaked upward in a lopsided grin. "Oh, my darling angel, your morning has not gotten off to a very good start, has it?"

Another surge of tears spilled; she buried her face in her hands. He straddled the bale on which she sat and cradled her head against his shoulder. "There now, it cannot be as bad as all that," he murmured soothingly. "What should make those glorious blue eyes produce such an abundance of tears? I wonder, did old Lucy step on your toe?"

How absurd! Miserable, she shook her head and felt the quiet chuckle deep in his chest. "No? Did your Uncle Ethan, then?"

It was so ridiculous, a smile tugged at the corner of her lip. "No," she muttered, sniffing.

"Hmm. Perhaps Mr. Goldthwaite presented you with a bunch of wilting daisies and proclaimed his undying admiration?"

Lauren sniffed loudly. "Hardly. He is quite impatient with me these days," she moaned.

"Then what, I wonder, should make my angel sob so?" he murmured thoughtfully against the top of her head.

"Everything," she cried, and pitifully clutched his lapel.

Alex slipped a finger under her chin and tilted it upward to carefully examine her face. *"Everything?"* he asked, and slowly bent to kiss the path of tears from one cheek. "That is quite a heavy burden," he murmured, and kissed the other cheek. "Much too heavy a burden for one angel." He gently kissed one eye. "Give me your burden, sweetheart," he whispered, kissing the other eye. "I would gladly bear your troubles as my own." He kissed the bridge of her nose.

His soothing words raced through her like fire. She closed her eyes, savoring each one as every good intention flew from her mind. She very much needed his comfort at the moment, desperately so. Suddenly, nothing else mattered. Not the rain coming down in torrents. Not the horses neighing softly beneath the trees. Not Magnus, not Paul, not any responsibility, nor any claim to dignity. She needed him.

She felt his lips on her forehead, then her temple. "Let me bear it all, love—your fatigue at the end of the day, your hurt when the world looks ill at Leonard. Let me bear your triumphs, your defeats, your uncertainties, your fears, your happiness," he uttered softly.

Mesmerized, she opened her eyes and unconsciously lifted her hand to touch his face. He leaned into it, kissing her palm.

"I will bear your health, your humor, your penchant for notable quotations. I will bear your family, your animals, and your little enterprises. I will bear you in my heart always, and your children. I will bear everything—you will never worry, never hurt, never need anything. Just come with me. Come be with me, Lauren." His voice had grown rough; his green eyes glimmered with the depth of his emotion. Her heart seemed to levitate in her chest, hovering on the brink of a feeling so deep she was vaguely afraid she might fall into it and drown.

He smiled. It wrapped around her heart and squeezed life

into it. She instinctively threw her arms around his neck and kissed him. His lips anxiously crushed hers, his tongue thrusting deep into her mouth, claiming her. She was conscious of her fingers raking through his hair, grasping at any and every fiber of him. The bonnet toppled from her head, the high neck of her jacket flicked open. He deepened the kiss, stroking her tongue, inviting her into his very core.

She was on fire.

They tumbled onto his greatcoat. His hands eagerly swept her frame, across her middle, down her legs, finding the buttons on her blouse. The rain drummed harder against the earth just beyond them, matching the tempo of her beating heart. She sought the warmth of his body, thrusting her hands deep inside his waistcoat, feeling his spine, his ribcage, and the corded muscles in his neck and shoulders. He freed her breast and eagerly brought the rigid peak fully into his mouth. Instinctively, she lifted to him, openly indulging in the sweet, burning sensation against her skin and building in the pit of her stomach.

With his mouth and hands, he exalted in her, and Lauren received his caress with pure elation. He paused, tearing off his coat and waistcoat, ripping the neckcloth away. She frantically clawed at the pearl buttons on his shirt as his hand skimmed below her skirts, drifting up her leg. With his free hand, he easily unfastened her skirt.

"You belong with me," he whispered as he pulled the soiled skirt from her waist and tossed it onto the remaining bale of hay. "You know you do." He slipped a hand beneath her so that he might remove her undergarments. Very slowly, he began to pull the petticoats from her hips. "My God, what an angel," he breathed, his eyes lovingly feasting on her nude body, and reverently, he bent to kiss the flat plane of her belly. "My wicked little angel."

Lauren sighed, adrift on the little bed of unbridled sensation. Everything but Alex was forgotten. She *did* belong with him—every inch of her flared with a burning hunger for his touch. His hardness, straining the fabric of his trousers, pressed against her leg. The soft sensation of his lips against her belly and flick of his tongue in her navel sent spasms of desire spiraling through her. *"Alex,"* she whispered, smiling lazily as he lifted her leg, kissing her calf. His lips traced a warm, wet path up her leg, pausing to kiss the soft crease behind her knee, nibbling the inside of her thigh. One hand fluttered across her breast, kneading gently.

His breath brushed the apex of her thighs, shocking her almost senseless. When his tongue flicked across her mound, it terrified her, almost as much as her own desire. Her breathing grew ragged; she was suddenly gasping for air. He moved between her legs, lifting them over his broad, shoulders, and slowly descended. Spiraling recklessly toward release, she began to writhe beneath him, clutching desperately at his head, moving innately to meet the caress of his tongue. Roughly, his hands clutched her buttocks, holding her to him as he delved deeper, then began to lovingly torment her in the most intimate way imaginable. The pressure building in her was unbearable; she strained to meet him, grabbing the straw around her as she sought to hold on.

His hand slipped into hers, squeezing it tightly as the stroke of his tongue quickened. The experience was staggering. Soaring higher and higher, she suddenly plummeted into a pool of sweet oblivion. Her own, guttural moan rang in her ears as the extraordinary sensation washed over her in wave after wave of stunning delight.

Alex left her for a moment to kick the trousers from his legs. His heart raced madly as he gazed at the beautiful creature stretched before him. It was so different this time, he thought, as his swollen manhood skimmed her leg. So very right. A tender smile creased his lips as he beheld the woman he loved with all his heart. "God, I do love you," he whispered.

Her dark blue eyes widened, then her lashes fluttered as she cupped his chin. *"Alex,"* she murmured huskily.

He bent to kiss her, the taste of her still on his lips. He found her hand, guided it to the velvet head of his manhood, and wrapped her fingers around the pulsing member. Her touch was exquisite; his tongue thrust into the corners of her mouth in rhythm with her hand, gliding over her teeth and gums. Desperate to prolong this incredible experience, he suddenly grabbed her hand, pulling it away from him as he quickly found the opening to her sheath. He lifted his head to look into her eyes and plumb their depths, to bear witness to the emotions of an angel he had fallen in love with so many months ago.

"God forgive me, but I want you," she whispered.

It was the most erotic thing she might have said. With a powerful thrust of his hips, he buried himself deep within her. Crying out in ecstasy, she wrapped herself around him, and Alex had the sensation of being deeply drawn into her warm depths. He moved slowly, pulling almost completely free, then plunging again, marveling at the passion sparkling in her eyes each time he did. She rose to meet each powerful thrust—her body tightened around him, coaxing him to the brink of fulfillment. But he kept his long strokes deliberately slow, antagonizing himself to the point of insanity.

In a swift, graceful movement, he abruptly rolled to his back without missing his stride, taking her with him. She was on top of him, bracing herself against his chest, kneading his muscles, fingering the hardened nipples. His strokes took on a new urgency, one she seemed to understand completely as she gazed down at him. Her body seemed to flow into his, meeting him in perfect harmony as he bucked beneath her. As the pressure in him began to give way to an eruption of rapture, Lauren suddenly threw back her head in sensual triumph, her hair tumbling to his legs.

He cried her name with his last powerful surge inside her and convulsed into her, giving his life's blood to her womb.

Panting, Lauren fell on top of him, her hair spilling over his chest and face. He turned slightly; their bodies still joined, he lightly stroked her back as he tried to regain his breath.

"Oh, God, how I *love* you," she moaned as he brushed her hair from his face, then hers, and tenderly kissed her.

"I love you, sweetheart," he whispered. She twisted in his arms, propping her chin on his shoulder, gazing up at him with the same adoration he felt through to the very center of his soul. They remained that way, silently gazing at one another, taking in every feature, quietly marveling at the joy they had created. As he memorized her body with his fingertips, Alex could not remember ever feeling so remarkably at peace.

At last, he smiled and kissed her softly. With the back of his hand, he carefully smoothed the curly tendrils of hair from her temple, his gaze languidly roaming her face. "I am a most fortunate man," he mused, and cupped her full breast. "I must have done something right along the way. I would that I could loll about all day with you naked in my arms and make love to you over and over again." He kissed the curve of her neck and shoulder, unable to sate his desire to touch her. It was amazing to him that a man of his years and experience could be, quite simply, rocked off his feet. But Lauren was so . . . *different.* What she lacked in experience she made up for with passion so intense and heartfelt that he was left reeling. *God,* he loved her. He had never known it possible to love so deeply.

"When I think of the moments we have already lost," he sighed, stroking her hair. "I suppose I shall just have to work doubly hard to make up for them." Lauren responded by burying her face in the curve of his neck, her fingers gripping his shoulder tightly. He smiled at her modesty, and glanced down at the long line of her body, her legs tangled with his. This, the two of them, was so *right.* "There will be no more lost moments, Lauren," he said, kissing her shoulder. "There is nothing that can keep us from one another ever again."

It was then that he felt the wetness of her tears on his shoulder. His gut twisted, warning him. "Lauren?"

She slowly lifted her head, her eyes glistening. "There can be no us," she whispered hoarsely.

His stomach moved again. Violently. "What ever do you mean by that?" he asked roughly. "Of course there can be an *us!*" Struck by the absurdity of it, he attempted to laugh. They had just shared an extraordinary demonstration of their love for one another. He was being ridiculously apprehensive.

But Lauren just lay there in his arms, an expression on her face that looked as if she would be sick at any moment. He stared at her, waiting for her to allay his fear, *needing* her to comfort him, to tell him he misunderstood. A tear slipped from her eye and ran down her cheek. "What is the matter with you?" he demanded, quite certain he did not want to know.

"I—I know what you must think, b-but I am engaged to be married," she stammered in a whisper.

"What?!" His mind began to reel. She could not—she could *not* mean what she was saying. What the hell did she think had just occurred between them?

"Friday. I marry Magnus on Friday."

He suddenly shifted, dumping her out of his arms as if she had burned him. It was inconceivable, totally unfathomable. Had he just imagined what had occurred between them? Could she respond to him so . . . so *completely* then turn around and marry another? Was she *mad*? Was she playing him for a goddam fool?

Unthinking, he sat up and grabbed her arms, jerking her into his chest. "What in the hell is wrong with you?" he shouted. Lauren cringed, closing her eyes. "*Look* at me! You cannot mean it, Lauren! You cannot mean you will *marry* him!" She tried to turn away, but he held her fast, angrily shaking her. "I don't know what nonsense is in that head of yours, but what in the hell do you think just happened here?" he bellowed.

"I—" Her eyes flew open and frantically searched his chest. "God help me, but it does not *change* anything. I made a commitment!"

Stunned, he pushed her away. She caught herself on her elbow, one hand slowly rubbing the spot on her arm he had gripped. He gaped at her, racking his brain for even a modicum of understanding. He could find none—damn it all to hell, he could *not* understand.

Bracing his elbows on his knees, he slowly ran his hands over his hair, fighting for control. "What just happened between us was *honest* and *real.* Doesn't that mean *anything* to you?"

Her head dropped to her chest and her hair fell around her, shielding her face from him. Desperate, he reached for her, but she quickly brought her arms up and covered her breasts. "D-don't," she said unsteadily.

"Lauren—"

"*Don't!* I cannot . . . *think* . . . when you touch me," she rasped helplessly.

Dismay engulfed him and he frantically thought how to convince her. "The . . . the evening you sent me that poem, that poem which *still* plays on in my head," he sputtered angrily, "I realized how much you meant to me, even though I was committed to another. Just like you, Lauren, at the most critical juncture in my life, I was committed to another. It was insane! Yet I didn't understand completely just *how* insane until you were gone! I did the hardest thing I have ever had to do and followed you here, with but one thought in mind!" he said angrily.

Lauren buried her face in her hands.

"That one thought was to *find* you and *marry* you. I have this . . . this *overwhelming* need to give you everything I can!'' he said hoarsely. ''I want to give you the whole God-dammed world to make you happy!''

Lauren caught a sob in her throat as he leaned forward, his face just inches from hers. ''I *love* you, Lauren! How many ways can I say it? I love you more than I thought humanly possible. I love your wit and the fact that you quote old proverbs and English poets. I love your undying loyalty to your family. I *love,*'' he choked, ''that you would give yourself so completely to those children and treat each and every one of them as if they were your own.''

Her body shook from the force of another wrenching sob. ''Today, more than ever, I love you,'' he hastily continued. ''I want to marry you, and I don't give a damn what anyone thinks. What matters to me is that you are who you are— guileless, beautiful, and so giving of yourself. *That* is what this is all about!'' he shouted, gesturing wildly around them. ''Do you understand me? We made *love* and Goddammit, I heard *your* admission of love! I bloody well *felt* it!''

She fell to her side, crying uncontrollably.

Disbelieving, Alex gaped at her. ''Lauren, *please* do not do this,'' he begged her.

After what seemed to him like a hundred years, she slowly raised herself. ''You don't understand. I have ruined your life,'' she muttered hopelessly, and shook her head when he attempted to debate that. ''Whatever you do, my presence will always poison it! I cannot allow that to happen, don't you see? The people of this country *need* someone like you, Alex! Rosewood cannot possibly survive without the reforms you can make happen!''

''I don't care!'' he shouted.

She gasped through another uncontrollable sob. ''And . . . and I have made a commitment I *must* honor. I cannot do this to him.''

''Cannot do this to *him?*'' Alex echoed incredulously as the pounding of his heart rapidly intensified. Teetering on a precipice of complete dejection, his eyes suddenly swept her naked body, the flush of their lovemaking still glowing on her fair skin. It sickened him—she had ripped his heart in half. He glared at the streaks of tears on her face, the pathetic way she hugged herself. Damn her, but she was beautiful, and he suddenly hated her for it. The woman had sorely abused his love, and a rage like he had never known blinded him.

He lunged for her, shoving her onto her back.

"Alex!" she shrieked.

Determined, he angrily grabbed her flailing arms and pinned her to the ground beneath him. "Perhaps I was not persuasive enough," he muttered bitterly, and crushed his lips to hers, kissing her fiercely. It caught him as much by surprise as it did her, and it unnerved him badly. He recoiled; even now, the wicked little angel was capable of evoking a response, and that only heightened his rage.

His loathing was suddenly like a river, running deep. Loathing of himself. For loving her. For being a damned slave to it. It frightened him; he would not have thought it possible to be brought to his knees, begging violently for the return of his affections.

Wild with fury, he kissed her again, battering her lips with his tongue. At first she refused him, her lips pressed tightly together. But he would not relent, madly convinced she did not yet understand, that he could *make* her understand. Gradually, the stiffness began to ebb from her body and she began to respond to his fury. He gentled the kiss, touching her tenderly, his hands caressing her satin skin. Lauren's teary eyes did not waver from his face as he positioned himself between her legs and slowly entered her. "Do you feel it?" he whispered hoarsely. "Do you *feel* how much I love you?"

She nodded. "I feel it," she whispered. "And I love you Alex. You must know that I love you with all my heart." More tears slipped from her eyes. He groaned and lowered himself to her, longing to release himself deep inside her, to bury himself to the hilt. He crushed his mouth to hers in another gentle assault to block out her tear-filled eyes. His heart simply could not accept what he knew would come.

Almost unconsciously he moved inside her, aware that when she reached her climax, the words of love she whispered would be the last. He found his own release more violently than before, and lay against her, unwilling to accept that he had lost her.

"Oh, Alex, my love," she whispered sadly.

He dislodged himself from her and rolled away, his breath harsh in his lungs. He dragged his gaze to the object of his pain. Emotionally and physically spent, she lay on her side, her face covered in the crook of her arm, her shoulders trembling with silent tears. His heart lurched painfully—he stumbled to his feet, yanked on his trousers, then his boots.

"Alex, *please* try to understand . . ."

He would never understand, not in a thousand years would he understand. And for that, she could rot in her little Bavarian hell for all he cared. He plunged his arms into his shirt, and gathering the rest of his clothes, he stalked out of the little cottage without looking back. Once on Jupiter's back, he gave the cottage a final glance, then spurred Jupiter with all his might, galloping away from her and the indescribable pain that engulfed him like a raging fire.

Chapter 24

A steady rain had begun two days ago, when Paul told her Alex had returned to London. For two days she had sat in the same chair, staring out the same window. Staring into the same blank landscape.

Seated in a chair pulled up to the drawing room window, Lauren watched the path of rain rivulets on the glass panes. She had never known such misery. Nothing could ease her heartache; every time she closed her eyes she saw Alex striding away from her, half-dressed. Half-mad. She had no one to blame but herself. He had professed a depth of love that still made her tremble. And she, in all her infinite wisdom, had ignored the utterance of his heart, as if their lovemaking had meant nothing. No wonder he had looked at her with such loathing.

She loathed herself.

Not only had she turned away—*rejected*—the only man she would ever love, she had betrayed Magnus. Deeply ashamed, she could hardly bear to look at him any longer. That she could betray him so completely just four days before they would marry sickened her. The whole, sordid mess sickened her. She hardly knew herself any longer—she was a woman who had betrayed two men and had destroyed another woman's future as well as herself in the process.

One of those men was seated on the couch, quietly reading. For two days, while she had stared out the window, he had sat on that couch, reading. She forced herself to look at Magnus. As if sensing her thoughts, he glanced up and smiled thinly before lowering his gaze to his book again. It was obvious that she was making him miserable, sucking him into her nightmare. Magnus did not deserve this. He was a good, decent man. How sad that she would never love him, not like—

"Do you like it?"

Lauren started and looked toward the door as Lydia bounced into the room, wearing one of her London gowns Mrs. Peterman had altered. Lauren smiled weakly as Lydia twirled around. "You are beautiful, Lydia," she murmured. Magnus glanced up briefly, but quickly resumed reading.

"It is *divine*." Lydia sighed with all the angst of a thirteen year-old, and fell onto a settee. "Why don't you want it any longer?"

"I have no need for it. Mrs. Peterman did a fine job, did she not? You will be the prettiest girl at the harvest assembly."

"I hope Ramsey Baines thinks so! He has hardly even *looked* at me since the church picnic!" she moaned, and sat up, meticulously arranging the full skirts to their best advantage. "He dotes on Eugenia Prenshaw, but when he sees me in *this,* he'll change his mind!"

Lauren frowned. The girl was obsessed with Ramsey Baines, constantly incensed that the young man held some sort of unshakable esteem for the plain daughter of a solicitor. Master Baines seemed to be Lydia's single goal in life, but from everything Lauren had seen, the young man's single goal was Eugenia Prenshaw. "I am quite certain he will notice how lovely you are, Lydia, but you mustn't set your hopes too high. One cannot hope to contrive the affections of another; it must come naturally."

Magnus looked up from his book at that and thoughtfully considered her as Lydia sprang to her feet and wandered impatiently to the hearth. "But if he thinks *me* lovely, then he will no longer love Eugenia!" she protested. "She is not so very pretty, you know."

"Too much pride is unbecoming, darling," Lauren softly rebuked her.

Lydia sighed heavily and wandered to the window, tracing her finger down the edge of one pane. "I don't *mean* to be prideful, but everyone says I am much prettier than Eugenia Prenshaw, so Ramsey Baines must think so, too. And when he sees me in a gown as fine as this, he shall love me, I know he shall.

When had such monstrous conceit overtaken Lydia? " *'Beauty lives within the eye of the beholder.'* Do you know what that means? Sometimes, the most beautiful people are not the most handsome. Ramsey Baines sees a beauty in Miss Prenshaw that attracts him, and you cannot force him to have that same affection for you. It must come naturally."

Lydia came to her side and leaned against the chair, swaying softly as she absently fingered a curl on Lauren's head. "But it did not come naturally for you, and now you love Count Bergen! When you came home from Bavaria, you said he was a goat, but he made you love him. Why can't I make Ramsey Baines love me just the same?"

"I respect the count." The words rolled off her tongue without thought or feeling, as if she had rehearsed it a thousand times. Unwillingly, she glanced at Magnus from the corner of her eye; he was watching her closely.

"There, you see? He made you change your mind," Lydia observed, stroking her hair. "I should think it only a matter of determination," she said with supreme authority.

For the first time in her life, Lauren felt angry with Lydia for being so incredibly foolish and unwilling to see that she would only harm herself with such coquettish ideas. She responded sharply, "He may fall prey to your good looks for a time, my dear, but soon enough he will not be able to hide what simply is not there." Holy Mother, what was she *saying*?

Clearly startled, Lydia stepped away from the chair and shrugged defiantly. "So?"

"*So?* You will always wonder if he is thinking of Eugenia when he looks at you!" she cried angrily.

"Lauren . . ." The count's deep voice carried a warning that she ignored.

"Day after day, you will find yourself wondering if his smile is for *you* or if he is daydreaming of *her*! Every word he speaks will be held up to your scrutiny to see if it is sincerely spoken! When he goes to London for a day, you will wonder if he goes to Eugenia!"

"*Lauren!*" Magnus said more forcefully.

Lydia's face fell. Her bottom lip trembled slightly as she looked down at her new gown. "But . . . but he *might* learn to love me!" she said softly.

"No! He will *not!* You cannot *force* him!" she cried, her voice breaking. She gripped the arms of her chair. What was she doing? Taking her frustration out on Lydia, that was what. She came swiftly to her feet and hugged Lydia tightly to her. "I am sorry, I did not mean to speak so harshly. Oh, darling, I so want you to be happy, but I don't think you will be if you try to force the lad to return your affections. Perhaps he will come to esteem you, but if he does not, if he loves Eugenia, then there are plenty of boys in England who would die for just a smile from you."

Lydia sniffed against her shoulder. "But I love Ramsey Baines," she muttered stubbornly.

Distressed, Lauren sighed. "Do you know what I think? I think lilac would look very well with your new gown."

"Really?" Lydia asked, pulling away from her. "There is some in the garden."

"I think the rain has broken for a time. Why don't you fetch some and try it?" Lauren urged.

"Oh yes, that's a wonderful idea!" Lydia proclaimed, and hurried to the door, seemingly oblivious to Magnus, who had come to his feet.

"Be careful not to soil your dress!" Lauren called.

"I won't!" her youthful voice echoed as she rushed from the room. Lauren stared after her, completely spent. Her own words had done a rather fine job of pointing out the tremendous mistake she was about to make. She could hardly ignore her own advice, could she? A sense of bitter relief suddenly washed over her as she carefully resumed her seat. Days of frustration were gone, replaced by a new anguish—the anguish of facing a horrid task, of hurting someone for whom she cared. A painful pounding started at her temples the moment Magnus spoke.

"Are you angry?" he asked, frowning.

"No!" she exclaimed, a little too emphatically, and shifted uncomfortably.

"What is on your mind, *liebchen*? You look as if you have something you would say." Yes, but her tongue suddenly felt the size of a watermelon. "What is it, Lauren?" Magnus asked quietly.

The pounding in her head was deafening. She glanced uncertainly at him. How could she, practically on the eve of their wedding, tell him she could not marry him? How could she *not*? Heaven help her, she could not be with him day after day and long for Alex. She thought too much of him to . . . to *try and hide what simply was not there.* Oh *God,* she regretted not coming to this conclusion sooner! She slowly sank into her chair.

"If you cannot speak, then allow me," he said, his German quiet and calm. "You have been sitting in that chair staring out that window for two days. Two days almost to the hour since the duke returned to London.'' Lauren tensed and quietly sucked in her breath. ''I am not a physician, but I know what ails you. You mourn this . . . man you love.''

She could not breathe, the pounding in her head having spread to her neck and chest. *''Magnus—''* It was all she could bring herself to say.

''Say it, Lauren,'' he said evenly.

She started to speak, choking on her own words. Magnus did not move an inch, waiting patiently for what he obviously knew she would say. ''It—It is with great . . . *regret* . . . that I must tell you I—I—'' She could not say it. God help her, she could not *hurt* him so! Tears filled her eyes, and she picked helplessly at the arm of her chair, trying desperately to think of words that would make what she would do seem less . . . *egregious*.

''You must tell me what?'' he asked, his voice oddly soft.

''I . . . I must tell you that I am very sorry for chiding Lydia so harshly!'' she blurted. ''God knows I did not want to, but the girl is so *foolish* . . . I mean, I would rather *die* than hurt her, but I could not . . . *pretend* that everything would be all right!'' she exclaimed, aware of how ridiculous she must seem and despising her lack of courage.

His jaw clenched shut for a long moment. When at last he spoke, his voice filled the room. ''Lydia loves Ramsey Baines, it would seem.''

Lauren nodded frantically. ''Yes, yes, she loves him truly, and although he is quite *fond* of Lydia, and I think truly *respects* her, he cannot quite . . . *love* her. But he has tried! He has *really* tried! It's just that . . . it's just that . . .''

''There is someone else?'' he offered helpfully. Lauren cautiously nodded, gauging his reaction from beneath the cover of her lashes. With a rueful smile, he dropped his gaze to his hands.

Tears suddenly spilled from her eyes. ''Oh, *God!*'' she gasped, and looked helplessly to the ceiling. There was no use in pretending, no point in putting off the inevitable. "I was so very wrong to have accepted your offer, Magnus, but I honestly thought—" She nervously gasped for air. "You would come to despise me, don't you see?"

"Yes," he said simply, and reached for her hand.

It was such a kind gesture, too kind considering what she was doing. Her eyes riveted on the large hand covering hers. "We . . . had an agreement, but . . . but it was a foolish agreement, I think."

"It was foolish," he agreed.

"Do . . . do you really think so? I thought . . . I thought you would be so angry with me. But I could not bear it if you wondered every day if . . . if . . ."

Magnus smiled thinly. "I would see the evidence of it every time I looked into your eyes, I can assure you," he said softly. Distraught by that, Lauren bowed her head in shame. Magnus sighed and stroked her hand with his thumb. "I thought—I *hoped*—that you would one day return my affection, but I no longer believe that is possible. You love him too deeply, I think." She glanced up; his clear blue eyes locking with hers. "And I thought I knew what I wanted—a wife to give me an heir, nothing more. But now I realize I want the woman I marry to return my affection. I want to see the tenderness in her eyes when she looks at me. I do not want her to dread the touch of my hand."

"Oh *Magnus*," she whispered, a fat tear falling on his cuff. "I am so *sorry!* I should not have . . . I did not plan for this—"

"Lauren," he said hoarsely, "if I thought you had a choice . . . We never plan the great events of our lives, they just happen. I think you are as helpless as I am to alter your heart. I am—" He swallowed convulsively and looked about the room. "I am disappointed, I will not deny it. But I cannot fault you for following what is in your heart." Slowly, he brought her hand to his mouth, his lips lingering on her palm as he quietly regarded her, then he put her hand

in her lap and rose. "I will speak with your uncle." He
paused, his blue eyes skimming her face one last time as his
fingers lightly brushed her cheek. "Have a care, *liebchen*. If
you ever have the opportunity to be in Bavaria, promise me
you will visit. The Potato Man misses you."

Lauren smiled tremulously. "I promise," she whispered.

There was nothing left to say; he turned and walked out
of the room. And she finally gave into the relief and anguish,
letting a river of grief and remorse flow from her until she
had exhausted herself.

She drifted for days in a state of numbness. Guilt, remorse, and a keening sense of loss invaded her and would
not release its grip. The children cast wide-eyed looks at
her, intuitively whispering in her presence. In her own direct
way, Mrs. Peterman attempted to make her smile, but inevi-
tably shook her head in dismay and left Lauren alone. Obviously having heard the news, Mr. Goldthwaite appeared
very quickly on the scene, brandishing an armful of overgrown daisies. He did not stay long. Even Ethan, forever
counting the next pence, did not once chastise her for the
loss of the annuity promised in her betrothal agreement,
apparently taking solace in the generous trust Magnus had
endowed and left intact for Rosewood.

Paul watched her closely, apparently afraid she might
crumble at the slightest thing—and that was not far from
true. Only Rupert said much of anything to her, but then
again, he was completely oblivious to everything that had
happened, and equally oblivious to her somber mien. Melancholy threatened to drown her. After several days, she desperately needed something to keep her mind and hands
occupied. Something that would give her refuge.

So she made jam.

She made jars and jars of it, sending the children out
each morning in search of fruit until the apple trees, berry
vines, and fruit bushes were depleted. Rupert was sent to

Pemberheath in search of jars twice, his pockets jangling with the coins Paul supplied.

One morning, as she stirred a boiling cauldron of strawberries, Ethan came into the kitchen and landed heavily on a wooden bench, causing the jars lined neatly on the table to knock against one another. His expression was stern as he propped his hands on top of his huge belly. Lauren stood, a wooden spoon in her hand, waiting for him to speak. When he did not, she numbly turned back to her task.

"Paul is returning to London," he said abruptly. Mildly surprised, Lauren looked over her shoulder. "Lord Dowling has sent word he will not return from America until Yuletide and has accepted payment for the lease of his home until then."

"Why?" she asked indifferently as she placed two more filled jars on the narrow windowsill to cool.

Ethan waved an impatient hand at her question. " 'Investments,' he says. I rather suspect it is the gaming hells of which he is so enamored. Fancies himself quite the man about town." Lauren nodded apathetically and rummaged in the big tub she used to sterilize the jars, pulling two free and balancing them on the edge of a workbench already overflowing. "Parliament will adjourn in two weeks," Ethan continued, "and if I had to guess, I would say this could be your last opportunity."

Lauren frowned up at him as she wiped a jar clean with a linen cloth. "Magnus bestowed a very generous trust on Rosewood. Surely you are satisfied with that," she said dispassionately.

A faint smile lifted her uncle's lips. "No, I do not seek another offer for your hand."

"That's grand, because in case you have not heard, I am *persona non grata* in London," she said, a little petulantly.

He nodded, the light smile developing into a decided smirk. "Perhaps. As I was saying, it would appear to me that this is your last opportunity. Sutherland is bound to leave

London soon. He got the Catholic emancipation bill through the Lords, you know. Quite a fiery speech, I hear. I reckon there is nothing left for him to do this Season, so you had best go to him now.''

She was astonished by what he was saying. The mere mention of Alex's name made her queasy. She carefully placed the jar on a narrow workbench. ''I beg of you, do not mention his name—''

''Nonsense!'' he interrupted. ''Enough of this brooding! You've come too far to go on hiding at Rosewood and making *jam* for the rest of your life!''

His suggestion was outrageous—not even worthy of a response. She picked up the spoon and began stir the boiling contents of the cauldron with a vengeance. ''You do not understand, Uncle! He does not *want* to see me—''

''Doesn't he?'' Ethan asked quietly, startling her.

''No! He despises me!''

''Funny thing to say about a man who broke off an important engagement at the last possible moment and chased you to Rosewood like a madman. From what I saw, he would have done anything to make you change your mind. He does not *despise* you, lass, he *loves* you. And you love him, don't you? Love does not fade overnight.''

Shocked that such sentimental words came from Ethan's mouth, Lauren gaped at him. ''Yes it does—it does when—'' she broke off, dropped the wooden spoon, and gripped the edge of the workbench. A moment passed before she could look at Ethan again. ''I *hurt* him, Uncle,'' she said hoarsely.

Ethan shrugged and picked up a jar of cooling jam and stuck his finger in it, smacking his lips as he tasted it. ''I did not say it would be easy,'' he remarked, and tasted another dollop. ''But I had thought you the bravest woman I have ever known—at least until now.''

She jerked her head up. ''You thought *what*?''

''You walk about like the dead,'' he blithely continued,

"making mountains of *jam* for Chrissakes!" He put the jar down and propped his pudgy hands on his knees as he looked her squarely in the eye. "This is the most important moment of your life, Lauren. Don't let it slip through your fingers without a fight. God in heaven, do not lose heart now, lass!"

Stunned that this conversation was even *happening,* Lauren whirled around and stared blindly out the window. God knew she longed to see him, to feel his green eyes pierce through to her heart. But what if he looked at her the way he had when he had left her in the cottage? The pain, the disgust . . . she would not be able to bear it. But neither could she remain at Rosewood forever, never knowing. All she had been through paled in comparison to the prospect of always wondering, of always needing closure.

"Well then, don't dally about it! You know I am right," Ethan said, as if reading her thoughts.

Touched by Ethan's uncharacteristic concern for her, and still reeling from the notion that he was even *capable* of it, Lauren pivoted suddenly and went to him, throwing her arms around his enormous shoulders and kissing him on the cheek. Ethan scowled, red-faced. "Enough of that," he groused as a shy smile toyed with the corners of his mouth.

"Why, Ethan?" she asked, ignoring his gruff response.

He shrugged and looked at the jars of jam lined neatly on the table. "Believe it or not, silly girl, I was in love once."

With that admission, he could have knocked her over with no more than a sneeze. "You *were?*" she gasped, incredulous. "With who?"

"Well, who do you think? Your Aunt Wilma, of course!" he blustered, then sighed longingly, "God rest her weary soul." Embarrassed, he began to wave an impatient hand at her. "Go on with you now!"

Lauren smiled, for the first time in days.

* * *

"What shall we do? We cannot allow him to continue like this!" Wringing her hands, Hannah anxiously paced the floor of Arthur's spacious drawing room on Mount Street. "Did you *see* him last night? Lord Barstone came dangerously close to calling him out!"

"*We* are not going to do anything. I would strongly advise against meddling in Alex's affairs," Arthur answered. "I also would strongly advise you stop pacing before you wear a hole in my very expensive carpet." Seated in a floral damask chair, one leg dangling negligibly over the other, Arthur thought Hannah looked as if she wanted to slap him.

"I will not sit by and watch my son's heartache turn him into a bitter man," she said sharply. "Assuming he does not *drink* himself to death first!" She bestowed an imploring look on her youngest son. "Will you not at least *speak* with him, Arthur? God knows I have tried, but if I so much as *mention* Countess Bergen, he flies into a black rage!"

"Mother, I *have* spoken with him. He will not talk about it. Whatever happened is locked away forever, I fear."

"But there must be something we can do! Dear God, he loved her so! *Loves* her! Can you not see how he is hurting?"

"I can see how he is enjoying the company of a variety of females," Arthur muttered. Since returning from Dunwoody, Alex had thrown himself into the final festivities of the Season with abandon. It was so out of character, so unlike Alex, that Arthur secretly shared his mother's grave concern. Alex attended one mindless rout after another in the company of different women, and usually married ones at that. It was the appearance of Lady Barstone on Alex's arm last night that had Lord Barstone strutting about like a rooster, making loud, threatening comments concerning Duke Sutherland's person.

And Hannah was right; Alex had, of late, developed quite a liking for Scotch whiskey. His disdain for everything and everyone had grown so blatant that rumors were flying wildly. In salons across Mayfair, the Quality whispered about the immoral affair that purportedly led to the end of his engagement. Thanks to Lady Whitcomb, everyone knew that a disreputable *foreign* countess was the cause. Lady Pritchit made sure that no stone was left unturned by spreading rumors of some terribly compromising event that had forced Lady Marlaine's hand, finishing off her little tale with a whisper that Alex still held a strong *tendre* for Lady Marlaine. Naturally, a well-heeled young woman such as Earl Whitcomb's daughter would have nothing to do with such a scoundrel. Nothing could actually have been further from the truth—Alex hardly seemed to notice Marlaine. Whatever had transpired at Dunwoody between him and the countess had wounded him deeply.

Arthur looked at his mother, not liking the lines of worry he saw in her face. He placed his brandy snifter on a cherrywood table, rose, and walked to her side, taking her hand in his. "I will speak with him again. Actually, I happen to know of something that may spark his interest. Paul Hill has returned to London."

Hannah's eyes glistened with gratitude. "Oh, Arthur, please! *Anything* you can do before he is completely ruined!"

Alex helped himself to his fifth glass of champagne, noting bitterly that it was doing nothing to dull the ache that dogged him every day. It was a numbing, nauseating ache that stabbed at his gut every time he thought of Lauren—which was too Goddammed often to suit him. Even though she was married and gone now, he could not stop thinking about her, and he hated her for it, but he hated himself worse. He could hardly bear to think how easily he had given in to such an adolescent notion as love. *Good God!*

"Your grace?" Beside him, Lady Fairlane gave him a playful, familiar nudge. "I asked if you have had seen Lord Fairlane's prized hound."

Alex swung his gaze to the redhead with the inviting mouth. "I have not seen his hound, madam," he said curtly. "I have not been to Fairlane Manor in over a year."

Her mouth curved enticingly. "We shall have to remedy that, shan't we?" she purred. "We are planning a weekend affair two weeks hence. Perhaps you could come?"

He saw the lascivious look in her eye, and gave her a sensuous, lopsided smile. Lady Fairlane's eyes twinkled with delight. "Perhaps I could do just that," he said smoothly, "if I have no other engagements."

Her gaze slid slowly down his chest, lingering covertly on his groin. Her sensual lips curled into a deeper, more suggestive smile. "A popular man," she mused unabashedly. "How shall you judge the merits of all the invitations, I wonder?"

How would he judge them, indeed, he thought and openly beheld her breasts, threatening to spill out of the deep décolletage of her gown.

"I beg your pardon, my lady, but Lord Fairlane appears to be trying to gain your attention." Alex winced at the sound of his brother's voice; God, but he was a determined shadow.

Lady Fairlane glanced at Arthur as he strolled toward them, chuckling low in her throat. "Yes, I rather suppose he is." She sighed silkily, and with an explicit look at Alex, curtsied deeply. "I hope to see you at Fairlane Manor, your grace." As she walked away, she made sure her satin skirts swung suggestively. Alex, quaffing his champagne, brazenly admired the view.

"Quite obvious in her admiration, is she not?" Arthur drawled.

Alex handed his empty glass to his brother. "And what if she is? She is married to an old goat," he said coldly, and shoved away from the column on which he was leaning.

"She and others like her are making you a very unpopular fellow, Alex."

"I suppose that should alarm me? I don't give a damn what anyone thinks." *Not even Lauren.* Disgusted, he frowned to himself as he picked up a sixth glass of champagne from a passing footman.

"The point is that you are making a spectacle of yourself," Arthur said gruffly.

"Save your opinions for your tea with Mother, Arthur," Alex sneered. "You and the duchess can amuse yourselves ad nauseum about me then."

"Your grace, may I be so bold as to request an introduction for my daughter, Eliza?" Alex turned sharply and eyed the portly Lord Stepplewhite and his equally portly young daughter. She turned bright red under the duke's marked glare, making her look something like an overripe tomato as she bobbed a clumsy curtsy.

"Miss Stepplewhite," he mumbled, skipping the formality of a bow.

"Good evening, your grace. Are you enjoying the ball?" she chirped.

Ah, polite little banter undoubtedly learned in her drawing room. The only thing that could possibly be worse would be for the little tomato to quote some ancient proverb or rattle off a pithy little poem. She probably expected him to add his name to her dance card because it was a *nice thing to do*. The memory of that long-forgotten Harris ball jabbed at him. "Yes," he answered curtly, then slid a heated look to Lord Stepplewhite before stalking away, leaving the pudgy young woman to stare after him in hurtful shock. It served her and her overreaching father right.

"That was not very well done," Arthur said disapprovingly, as he followed closely behind.

Alex whipped around and glared at his brother. "If you are worried, you are welcome to soothe her tender feelings," he responded nastily.

"All right, Alex, that's enough. I know you are hurting—"

"And you are beginning to sound like an old woman!"

"But there is no need to take it out on an innocent girl," Arthur continued evenly.

"And since when did you become my conscience?" Alex snarled.

"Since you seem to have misplaced yours!" Arthur shot back irritably.

Alex downed his champagne. "Is there a *reason* you have appeared at my side?" he asked, leaning against the wall and surveying the crowd with disgust. "Other than to point out my numerous faults?"

"As a matter of fact, there is. There is someone with whom I thought you might want to speak."

Alex's heart slammed into his ribs. It was Lauren. For one insane moment, he *wanted* to see her and those sparkling blue eyes. But his determination to cut her from his heart quickly regained control. "I am not interested in anything she has to say," he muttered, not realizing what he had revealed until he saw Arthur's smirk. His scowl deepened dangerously.

"I was referring to Paul Hill," Arthur replied. "I saw him in Southwark just last evening."

Alex had not wanted to hit his brother since they were in short pants, but he was perilously close to putting a fist in Arthur's nose. "You are mad," he muttered angrily.

"No, but I have certainly considered the possibility that *you* are," Arthur said with deadly calm.

"By all that is holy, Arthur, I am just a hairbreadth away from breaking your face," Alex warned sincerely. "Do us both a favor and get out of my sight."

Arthur merely shrugged. "What harm is there in talking to him?"

"What the hell for?" Alex growled, and snared another glass of champagne from a passing servant, trading his empty glass for it.

Arthur frowned at the crystal flute. "You are pitching

headlong for ruination, Alex. There are men in this room who are itching to call you out because of your open regard for their wives. You drink yourself mindless at every opportunity, your mother is frantic with worry, and you haven't looked at our books in weeks! All because of some obscure lover's spat—''

"*Jesus,* you must want a broken nose!" Alex growled. Arthur snorted angrily as he lifted the champagne to his lips. But he could not tell Arthur what had happened, not without breaking. No, it was better this way. Mind-numbing indifference was infinitely more desirable than the hell she had put him through. Was *still* putting him through.

Arthur sighed and turned away. "Your self-pity is—" he suddenly stopped, his eyes focusing on something across the room. Suddenly conscious of the murmuring in the crowd, Alex glanced in the same direction.

His heart stopped. He had to remind himself to breathe as Lauren floated into the crowded room on the arm of his own cousin, David Westfall. Goddammit, she was *beautiful.* Wearing a creation of gold and creme chiffon, her skin positively glowed. A mass of chestnut curls was piled on the crown of her head, adorned with gold filigree.

The crowd's murmuring seemed to intensify, and slowly, he realized they were whispering about her. From Paddy, he knew some of the things that were said about her, owing chiefly to Lady Whitcomb, who had struck like a mother cat when he had ended his betrothal to Marlaine. But he had not realized until this moment how intense the talk apparently was.

"My God," said Arthur, glancing about them.

Every eye in the house was on her. Across the room, Lauren searched the crowd until her cobalt eyes found him. His heart slammed against his ribs, warning him, but Alex could not tear his gaze away. She looked at him very poignantly, and he stared hard at her, inwardly fighting the overwhelming desire to go to her.

The hurt that plagued him won. He had no idea what she was doing here, and at the moment, he bloody well did not give a damn. In the space of a single morning, she had utterly destroyed him. Without a word, he put the flute down and walked in the opposite direction of her, through a throng of people and out the door, in search of his driver.

Chapter 25

After days of moping about, Lauren had cried her last tear, determined to occupy her thoughts with more pleasant matters. Exactly how to do that had required some creative thinking, and she had finally decided that taking a box of jam to the infirmary would do as well as anything to cheer her.

The last few days had been sheer hell. She had no one with whom to even talk, unless one counted Davis, but she was not quite that desperate. As usual of late, Paul was away from the house, enjoying the last few days of the parliamentary session. He was absolutely besotted with Home Secretary Robert Peel, the man who had led the Catholic Emancipation through the Commons. At breakfast, he had talked excitedly about one day following in Peel's footsteps.

Paul had found purpose in his return to London, but her return had been a complete disaster. For days now, she had sought ways to speak with Alex but had been thwarted at every turn, beginning with the Harris's closing ball. She would never forget the look of revulsion on his face when he had seen her across that crowded room. It was matched only by the ghastly disgust he had shown when he had turned on his heel and marched from the room. It had wounded her deeply and she had been forced to endure her public humiliation for the rest of the evening—an evening in which she also had discovered she was a pariah among the *ton.*

Everyone avoided her.

With the sole exception of Lady Pritchit, whose disdain for her had swollen to terrifying proportions. At one point, she had sidled close to where Lauren was standing, and very loudly explained to a friend that Lady Whitcomb laid the blame for ruining Lady Marlaine's future as a duchess at Lauren's feet. A foreign wanton, she had called her. Lady Pritchit's friend had turned bright red as the old bag had added that what *might* be acceptable behavior in the nether regions of the continent was most certainly *not* acceptable in London.

Mrs. Clark's afternoon tea had been another nightmare, she thought, as she methodically stuffed a box with jars of jam. The jovial widow had called on her personally to insist that she come, obviously and very nobly trying to deflect some of the talk surrounding her. She had not wanted to go, but Paul had thought that perhaps Mrs. Clark could help.

Despite her deep misgivings, Lauren had gone. She had been standing in the foyer, nervously fidgeting with her reticule and trying to muster the courage to enter a drawing room stuffed to the rafters with ladies. Much to her great surprise, *he* had come, escorting Lady Paddington. He had looked right through her, as if she did not even exist. As she tried desperately to find her tongue, he had bid his aunt farewell, then had turned and walked out of the foyer. She was still gaping at his broad back when Lady Paddington had greeted her with great uncertainty. At least it was not the complete disdain she was to see on the face of every other guest.

She continued stuffing the box with jam, her thoughts

flitting to the Harrison Green rout to which Paul had insisted she accompany him. Dear God, what a *catastrophe* that had been! Except for rather sharply correcting Lord Brackenridge, who had clumsily grabbed her hand and drunkenly suggested she was now considered "for the taking," she had hardly said a word all night. Everyone avoided her as if she carried the plague, but she was acutely aware of the little tête-à-têtes that occurred behind gloved hands. Simply put, her presence was not tolerated.

Especially by Alex. Her ill-timed attempt to speak with him had gotten her a cruel, public dismissal. Unfortunately, she had caught him by surprise, coming up behind him and touching his arm. He seemed to jump a good two feet before whirling around, his face going white when he saw her. Everyone within a ten-foot radius saw it, too, and closed in on them, straining to hear the exchange between the Duke of Sutherland and the woman who was rumored to have ended his betrothal.

"Your grace, good evening," she had murmured, suddenly devoid of any coherent thought. His green eyes had flashed with fury; his jaw had clenched shut as his eyes flicked to those around them. The situation notwithstanding, she had frantically grabbed at the opportunity. "I had hoped . . . I need to talk to you, Alex," she had whispered, her heart roaring in her ears.

"I am engaged at present," he had said coldly, and had presented his back to her as he smiled charmingly at his blond companion. It was an appalling cut. Up until that very moment, Lauren thought the hardest thing she ever had to do was to end her engagement to Magnus. Oh, how *wrong* she was! The hardest thing in her life was to hold her head high as she had walked away through a throng of gaping onlookers.

After that, she had begged Paul to return her to Rosewood, but he had refused, and they had argued heatedly before striking a bargain. Some bargain! Paul had *coerced* her into trying one last time, but not in a crowded salon or ballroom, where he effectively argued that Alex's pride was at stake. The only reasonable place, he insisted further, was at the duke's residence on Audley Street, since it was apparent he would not be calling on *her* anytime soon.

Reluctantly, she had finally agreed. The truth was that in spite of her very strong misgivings about Paul's idea, she desperately needed to end this insanity once and for all. So she had gone to Audley Street, only to have her courage fail her miserably when she had seen him through a window. The next attempt was equally as daunting, as was the next and the next. Every day at promptly three o'clock, she had walked past his house. And every day she was quite unnerved by the sight of his dark head through a corner window.

This whole messy affair had become impossible to cope with. Last evening, she had cried for what seemed the hundredth time since returning to London. This surveillance of him was ludicrous! As if the *ton* did not have enough to talk about without her walking up and down Audley Street each day seeking the nerve to knock on the blasted door! Her lack of courage angered her, and she was weary of tears. She simply had to *make* herself see him so that she could return to Rosewood without delay, because she had absolutely no hope he would receive her apology with anything less than hatred.

She was as prepared as she would ever be, but it was hours yet before she could go. In the meantime, she would take her jam to the infirmary. They would welcome her—they welcomed *anyone* who took the time to call. Yes, it would be the perfect diversion from her misery.

A generous patron of the Haddington Road Infirmary, Hannah Christian made a point of visiting every third Friday of the month. Her pattern was the same: she listened to Mrs. Peabody's catalog of complaints, read a weekly paper to Mr.

Croyhill, and visited the newcomers. Having completed her rounds this month, Hannah walked to the infirmary door, listening to Dr. Metcalf expound eloquently on his plans to operate a wing for those suffering from consumption. As she pulled on her gloves, a commotion outside caught her attention, and distracted, Hannah glanced through the front door's thick panes of etched glass. Though her view was distorted, she could swear it was Countess Bergen. She took a step closer to the door, and lifted her quizzing glass.

It *was* Countess Bergen! Her arms extended, she was nervously urging a hack driver not to drop the box he edged from the top of the hack and held high above his head. The man stumbled backward, but quickly regained his balance, squatted, and slowly brought the box down to rest carefully on the sidewalk. Curious, Hannah watched as Countess Bergen extracted what looked like a small jar and handed it to the driver. They exchanged a few words, and she produced another jar. His face beaming with delight, the driver dipped his hat no less than three times as he returned to his hack, gripping the two jars against his chest.

Hannah smiled as Dr. Metcalf came to stand beside her and peer outside. "Who is that? Oh my, Countess Bergen!" he exclaimed with some dismay.

"Has she been here before?" Hannah asked, watching as the countess knelt to rearrange the contents of the box. She smiled up at a passerby, responding with a cheerful nod to his greeting.

"She has visited from time to time," he muttered. "But that was before we *knew*," he said, and reached for the brass handle.

Hannah glanced at him. "Knew what?"

The doctor colored. "Before we knew of her . . . *reputation*," he said, almost strangling on the word. "I shall take care of this." He slipped out the door before Hannah could stop him and marched down the steps to where Lauren stood. Hannah could see her beatific smile; it was no wonder Alex was so in love with her.

That glorious smile faded rapidly, however. Motioning to the box, Countess Bergen exchanged words with the doctor. His back to the door, he brought his hands to his hips and looked down at the box, adamantly shaking his head. The countess paused, her hand delicately brushing a loose curl from her cheek. Clutching her reticule, she glanced uneasily up the street. Dr. Metcalf said something else, his head bobbing intently like a little bird. Countess Bergen nodded slowly and turned toward the street, leaving the box at the edge of the infirmary steps. The doctor called a man working nearby to fetch the box, and turned toward the door, his step light as he bounded up the steps. As he entered the foyer, he grinned at Hannah. "Nothing to fear, your grace," he announced grandly. "I have sent that woman on her way."

"Have you indeed?" Hannah seethed. "Pray tell, sir, why in God's name would you turn a benefactress away from this institution?" she bristled.

The young doctor reddened. "But . . . she is without care for her *virtue,* my lady! I should think we do not *want* her benefaction!" he blustered uncertainly.

Hannah's eyes narrowed as she angrily adjusted her bonnet. "Her *virtue,* my good man, is a generous spirit with which she donates to your very worthy cause! How dare you be so presumptuous as to deny her gift!" she said coldly, yanked the door open, and marched toward her coach.

"Your grace!" the doctor called as he raced after her. "Please, your grace! I shall accept the jam!"

It was the last thing she heard as she was helped into her coach. "Turn this buggy around, Geoff, and find a young woman clad in dark blue!" she snapped.

Dejected, Lauren numbly walked away from the infirmary. The whole of London had turned against her; she herself had not realized how terribly bad her reputation was until Dr. Metcalf had asked her to kindly remove herself from his respectable institution. Good heavens, he had refused her *jam*! It was hopeless, utterly hopeless! She was the consummate *fool* for having come to London. She should have stayed at Rosewood where she belonged. She should have—

"Countess Bergen, good afternoon!"

She whirled around and saw a black coach sporting the Sutherland ducal crest coast to a stop. From its window leaned the duchess, smiling cheerfully and waving a handkerchief. Good God, what on earth was she doing? Surely his *mother* knew of her reputation? Did she not understand how this would *look* to everyone?

"Might I offer you a ride to your destination?" she called cheerfully, and motioned for a coachman on the back runner to open the door.

Lauren glanced surreptitiously around her. Several people on the street had paused to look at the duchess, some openly gaping at the ornate coach. "Thank you, your grace, but no."

The duchess's face clouded; she muttered something under her breath. Her head disappeared from the window, but appeared a scant moment later in the door. Grasping the coachman's shoulder, Lady Sutherland hauled herself to the ground and marched to stand directly in front of Lauren, a smile plastered on her face. "Please, my dear, get *in* the *coach*. I should very much *like* to drive you to your destination," she snapped through her smile.

Taken aback by her forcefulness, Lauren gulped. Acutely aware of the eyes upon them, she nodded faintly, and followed a smiling duchess to her coach. Once inside, Lady Sutherland frowned mightily. "Why in God's name would you refuse me?"

"I . . . ah, I have a very good reason," Lauren stammered, mortified. "I am concerned about my . . . *reputation,* your grace."

The duchess rolled her eyes. "And you think that signifies? I don't give a hoot what they say about you *or* me! Now, where did you think to go on such a lovely afternoon?" she demanded.

Lauren swallowed her surprise. Where did she think to go? To beg her son to forgive her, that was where! But that was absolutely out of the question—she could not expect him to see her; dear God, the good *doctor* would not see her! "I, uh, was on my way home . . ."

The duchess's face lit with her smile. "Splendid! No particular destination and I know of just the place!"

Lauren did not like the sound of that at all. She liked it even less when the coach pulled into the courtyard at the Audley Street mansion. When Lady Sutherland reached for her hand, Lauren gripped the squabs in stubborn refusal. The duchess frowned. "Countess Bergen, do you not think this has gone on quite long enough? It is time you and my very obstinate son spoke to one another."

"Lady Sutherland, I understand what you are trying to do, but I do not think you understand! It is impossible!"

"All right then," the duchess said, and folded her arms across her middle. "Make me understand! Expound if you will, Countess Bergen, on why it is so *impossible*!"

"It's rather a long story—"

"I have all day."

Lord, why had she gotten in this coach? "He does not want to talk to me. I . . . I accompanied him to the opera one night when his . . . Lady Marlaine . . . was away. Shortly after that, he ended the engagement—"

"*She* ended it," Lady Sutherland interjected, "or at least that is what we say."

Lauren blinked and looked down. "There are those who think *I* had something to do with it—"

"You certainly did, thank God, but that is none of their concern."

Lauren's head snapped up. "All right, well, *then* he came to Rosewood—my home—but I had . . . I had . . . signed a betrothal agreement, and I did not think I could break my commitment—"

"But obviously you did," the duchess said, clearly enjoying herself.

Lauren swallowed and clasped her hands tightly in her lap. "Well, yes, I did, but that was *after* he left. You see . . . I . . . I *hurt* him rather badly, I think, and he does not care to see me. And now, everyone thinks I am a . . ." She glanced at her lap, chewing on her lip. "A woman of ill repute," she muttered.

Lady Sutherland snorted.

Frantic, Lauren looked at the duchess. "I did something quite horrid, and even if he *were* to forgive me—and believe me, he is *not* so inclined—there is little one can do when an *infirmary* will not even take a donation of *jam*. . . ."

Smiling broadly, the duchess waved a hand to stop her. "If there is a man who can change the collective opinion of the *ton* about anything, it is my son. He is the nonpareil of influence in this town, and can be quite convincing when he is not being a stubborn, boorish *oaf.* Haven't you heard of the extraordinary vote in the Lords allowing Catholic representation? I know Alex has been hurt, but that is bound to happen when one opens one's heart. Of course, *he* does not understand that, because he is so—" She paused, catching herself before launching into a discussion of her son's faults, and smiled charmingly. "He obviously loves you very much."

Lauren winced and dropped her gaze. "I think he might have once, but not any longer. I do not think he will ever forgive me."

"We will never know sitting in this coach, will we? Come along," she said, and grabbed Lauren's hand. "I do not intend to let his true love slip away, my dear," she avowed, and fairly yanked Lauren from the coach.

"Enter," Alex called at the light rap on the door of his study. He glanced up as Hannah sailed into the room, her hazel eyes blazing. "Good afternoon, Mother. Something on your mind?" he drawled.

"As a matter of fact, there is," she said, and marched to his desk. "Do you know what I saw today? I saw an otherwise compassionate doctor turn away a donation of jam to his little infirmary. Not just any jam, mind you, but a box *full* of it! And what do you think made him do that?" she demanded, her fists punching her hips.

Alex leaned back in his chair. "I am quite sure you are about to tell me."

Her flashing eyes narrowed. "He refused the donation because the woman who brought it had a rather unpleasant reputation. Can you *imagine*? Refusing a donation because of *hearsay*?"

He could not, and he shook his head. "It would seem rather narrow-minded."

"Narrow-minded? It was the most *contemptible* act I have ever witnessed!" she blustered angrily.

Amused by her outrage, Alex smiled. "Would you like me to force the jam down his throat?"

"The woman was Countess Bergen! And before you insist her name not be mentioned in your presence, I will *remind* you that a memorable waltz requires the participation of at least *two*!"

Alex's good humor rushed out of him. He sliced an angry glance across his mother, and quickly turned his attention to his work, effectively dismissing her. "Thank you for that reminder, Mother. If there is nothing else—"

"Oh, but there is," she breathed. "She is suffering the disdain of this entire town, but she was not alone in her violation, and *you* are a *beast* if you allow this to continue!

Dear God, you loved her enough to end your engagement, but apparently not enough to keep her from ruin!''

Alex slapped a hand hard down on the desk, scattering several papers. ''That is *enough*!'' he bellowed.

Hannah smiled wickedly. ''Yes, I think it is,'' she said, and pivoting on her heel, marched out of the room, slamming the door behind her.

Alex glared at the door. She was a foolish, meddling woman who had no business intruding in his affairs. Did she honestly think he did not know Lauren's reputation was the direct result of his overwhelming desire for her? And just what was he supposed to do about it? *She* had turned her back on *him*, not the other way around! She had made a fool of him, and now he was supposed to come rushing to her rescue?

He started at the soft rap on the door and briefly considered locking it against another of his mother's invasions. ''Enter!'' he barked, and busied himself with the invoices he was reviewing. Let her rail at him if she wanted; he had work to do. He heard the rustle of her skirts as she entered and wished to high heaven she would just say whatever it was and get out. The faint scent of gardenia irritated him; she would have to wear *that* scent, of all the scents bottled on her dressing table! He dipped the quill in the inkwell.

''I am so *very* sorry.''

Lauren. His head jerked up just as his hand inadvertently sent papers flying from his desk. Dropping the quill, he clumsily stumbled to his feet, gripping the edge of his desk, speechless. God help her, but his mother would sorely regret this!

''I am so sorry, Alex. I never meant to hurt you, I swear to God I did not.''

She was *sorry*? Such empty words for having drawn a depth of love he had not thought himself capable of feeling and tossing it back in his face. She walked unsteadily toward him, her dark blue eyes glistening. "Magnus has gone back to Bavaria," she said.

He clenched his jaw against a soaring indignation at the mere mention of that man's name.

"I cannot stop thinking about you, you know. I have . . . oh God, I have relived your words over and over again until I think I will go mad!"

He *had* gone mad. He had relived every moment of that morning, over and over, a thousand times over. Their union. Her refusal. A shot of pain ripped down his spine as he remembered her lying naked in that cottage, prepared to marry that German. "I have nothing to say to you," he said hoarsely. "Get out and don't come here again." He pivoted away from her to stare blindly out the window, his body rigid.

Lauren's knees buckled; she caught the edge of the desk and stared at his broad back. It was over! God help her, it was over. She had lost him. Humiliated, she retreated, un-seeing, to the door. It was foolish to have come here. It was wrong to have ever *loved* him! God, what had she been thinking when she had come to London? Why hadn't she just let it die?

Her hand closed around the brass door handle, and she slowly pulled it open.

You belong with me.

He had whispered those words to her in the cottage, and she knew in her heart that he had believed them. He had come for her. He had forsaken his duty—everything—and had come for her. The memory suddenly made her angry. This had been impossible for them both, yet he seemed to think his pain was greater, that he was the only one who had suffered.

She glanced over her shoulder. He was still standing at the window, his hands clasped tightly behind his back, his legs braced apart. How *dare* he? Her hurt, her anger, her frustration, all bubbled to the surface, and she suddenly shoved the door shut and whirled around to face him. The sound startled him; he jerked around, his eyes blazing. "You are a hypocrite, Alex! You said I belonged with you and I *believed* you!" she cried out in anger.

"God's blood," he cursed furiously, and quickly turned away again. "You don't belong with *anyone* Lauren! You are a selfish—"

"Selfish?" she gasped in disbelief, then laughed hysterically. "Of course! I am so bloody selfish, aren't I? That is why I have *humiliated* myself in front of the whole damned *ton* just for the one chance to tell you that I love you desperately, Alex! I have loved you from the moment you appeared at Rosewood, and God help me, I shall go to my *grave* loving you!"

He half-turned, his expression livid. "Please God, spare me this little scene, madam. It is too . . . *pathetic,*" he said acidly, and folded his arms defensively across his chest.

Damn him! *Damn him!* She marched into the middle of the room and furiously swiped at the tears on her face. "Do you hurt so much that you want only to destroy me, Alex?"

He snorted contemptuously. "Don't flatter yourself. I feel nothing for you!"

"You are a *liar!* I *know* how badly you are hurting— because I hurt *just* as badly, whether you want to believe it or not! But at least *I* am not lying to myself!"

His nostrils flared, and he unconsciously tightened his arms across his chest. "I do not lie to you *or* myself, madam. Whatever I foolishly thought I felt for you is blessedly gone! Dashed! It has been pummeled and beaten out of me until it cannot be resurrected, do you understand? Do not be a fool and delude yourself into thinking otherwise!" he shouted.

He could have knifed her in the heart and it would not have hurt so much, but she knew he was lying. She raised her chin. "Don't delude yourself! Or are you so very arro-

gant to believe you are the *only* one to have felt the shackles
of your duty and your word?''

His eyes narrowed dangerously, but he did not respond.

''Rest assured, I *know* what it is like to love without
hope,'' she stubbornly continued. ''To . . . to dread the
night because dreams of you torture my very soul.''

He blinked rapidly; she noticed for the first time the
bright sheen in his green eyes. He knew, too, and her traitorous heart went out to him. ''I *know,* Alex! I know what it is
like to love so *completely* that I would forsake everything for
one *touch*! I would sell my soul for your kiss. You have my
heart in your very hands, don't you know that?''

Her wrenching words echoed in the silence, snaking into
the empty pit of his soul. ''I don't have your bloody heart,
goddammit!'' he snapped furiously, refusing to acknowl-
edge the painful tightening of his chest at the lie. ''If that
was true, you would have never let me walk away that morning! How could you have let me walk out that door,
Lauren?'' he roared. A tremble overtook his body at the
force of his emotions. He felt the sting of tears in his eyes,
and hastily turned his back to her. But he heard her strangled sob.

''Because of your *work,* Alex! Everyone said you were
the only one who could do it. You were the only one who
could change things for so many people! For *Rosewood*!
The whole *country* needed you, not just me! I didn't want to
ruin your career. I had already caused enough damage,
enough scandal. And . . . and I had given my word to another. My sacred word!'' She made a sound of grief. He
grimaced; the pain of her rejection, so vivid and strong just
moments before, was slipping away like the tears he suddenly could not control.

''God, I am so *sorry*! I could give you the heavens and it
would not convey how sorry I am!'' she sobbed. He turned
slowly and looked at her, his face ravaged. ''But I belong
with you, and you *know* in your heart it is true! If you can't

believe that, if you can't forgive me that which you yourself are guilty of, then give me back my heart! Give it *back,* Alex! I want it *back*!'' she demanded wildly.

A moment of stunned silence passed. A moment of clarity when his love for her strangled the remnants of his anger. ''No,'' he said hoarsely, and winced as she covered her face with her hands in abject defeat. ''You gave it to me. God knows maybe I don't deserve it, but I won't relinquish it, not now, not ever. It belongs to me.''

Lauren stopped breathing, and slowly lifted her face to look at him in astonishment.

''I'm sorry, angel,'' he uttered softly, and shakily brushed the tears from one eye. ''Please forgive me for hurting you,'' he choked. Doubt flicked across her face, and his heart lurched in his chest. ''If you can't forgive me, then at least promise me you will continue to walk past my house every day at three o'clock.'' He glanced at the window. ''Promise me you will walk by that window so I may be suitably reminded—every damned day—that had I not been blinded by my foolish, *foolish* pride, you would have been mine.''

She gasped softly, and he turned to her, smiling tremulously. ''Then . . . then, I belong with you?'' she whispered in wonder.

''You must belong with me, angel, because I have your heart just here,'' he said hoarsely, and tapped his chest. ''And God knows I have been without mine all these tortuous weeks.'' With a cry, she flung herself into his arms, tears spilling from her glorious eyes. Silently he promised himself that he would never pass another day without gazing into them, and smothered her in a fierce, soul-claiming kiss. ''Forgive me, Lauren,'' he murmured. *''Forgive me.''*

Hannah had waited at least a half hour outside his study, pacing nervously. She could not hear a blasted *thing*! She had expected the shouting, but that had ended some time ago. And now there was nothing—just silence.

The turning of the door handle startled her out of her wits, and she quickly jumped to one side, behind a console. Alex emerged first, dragging the countess with a hand wrapped tightly around her wrist; she was running to keep up. He was throwing her out! Defeated, Hannah sagged against the wall as they hurried down the corridor. Oh, that wretched son of hers! Could he not *see* how much they loved each other? Stupid man!

She pushed away from the wall, prepared to intervene, when the countess caught his arm and stopped him. To Hannah's amazement, she reached up on her tiptoes and whispered something into Alex's ear. He threw back his head with a hearty laugh. "By God, you *are* a wicked little angel!" He kissed her hard on the lips, then swept her into his arms. Hannah pressed a hand over her mouth as Alex took the stairs two at a time as the countess smothered him with kisses.

As they disappeared into the floors above, she strolled out from behind the console, her hands on her hips. "My, my, the *impropriety*!" With a gay laugh, she turned on her heel and walked in the opposite direction, smiling broadly.

Epilogue

Paul Anthony Christian was born at Sutherland Hall in the late fall of 1830, with his mother's dark blue eyes and a shock of his father's brown hair. He was a lusty child, and when Alex held his son in his arms for the first time, he felt the draw of unending love starting at the tips of his toes and spilling out of every pore. With Hannah at his shoulder, he stuck his little finger in the boy's tiny mouth. Tiny fingers curled around his, making his finger look like a sausage. Delighted, he turned to Lauren. "He is beautiful, angel. Beautiful and perfect," Alex said proudly.

"You did not think he was perfect a half hour ago," she said with a weary smile of great pride.

Alex walked to the side of the bed, holding his newborn in one arm, and sat gingerly beside her. "It did seem a rather frightening prospect at the time."

Lauren laughed and held out her arms. Alex carefully handed her the baby, then observed with frank fascination as she held the baby to her breast to suckle. The vision created of a mother and her child was beautifully moving, and Alex was barely able to contain his emotion.

"He was a loud one, wasn't he?" Lauren smiled as she caressed his little cheek. *"My mother groaned, my father wept, into the dangerous world I leapt. Helpless, naked, piping loud, like a fiend hid in the cloud."* She yawned, missing Alex's playful role of his eyes. Hannah chuckled; they were all quite accustomed to Lauren's little quotations for every occasion.

It was not long before Lauren's lids began to grow heavy, but little Paul did not seem remotely sated. At Alex's worried look, the baby's new nurse came and took him. "He shall be a healthy little tike, your grace," she said as she took the child from his mother.

"Of course he will. He shall be a leader of men," Lauren sighed softly, her lids fluttering closed. Alex leaned forward and brushed his lips across her forehead. "Thank you, darling. The greatest gift you have ever given me is my son," he whispered. With her eyes closed, she smiled. Alex lifted her hand to his mouth and kissed her fingers, then with his mother, left the room to allow his wife to sleep.

In the summer of the following year, when Alex was convinced his strapping young son was strong enough for travel, he took Lauren and little Paul to the extensively renovated Dunwoody. They arrived with a coterie of nurses and maids, and infused a life into the old manor house it had not seen in decades. The shout of children's laughter and the gurgling of a happy infant could be heard in all corners of the house.

When Arthur arrived for a visit several weeks later, he found the duke and duchess sitting on the back terrace, watching a handful of frolicking children on the bowling lawn below them. Nearby, a plump nurse kept an eagle eye on the heir to the Sutherland fortune. "My God, is this the same Dunwoody?'' he asked appreciatively after exchanging warm greetings and settling into a wrought iron chair.

''Amazing, is it not?'' Alex chuckled. He pointed to a young man of about fourteen who was standing in the middle of the children with his arms folded across his chest. His face was marred by a large splash of purple, but none of the other children seemed to notice. A little girl leaned against one leg as the young man peered down at Master Christian.

''That is Leonard,'' Alex explained. ''Hanging onto his leg is my son's most ardent admirer, Sally. She is wont to smother Paul with kisses, which Leonard fiercely resists. He is quite afraid she might succeed, and, I rather think, so am I.''

Lauren laughed. ''There,'' she smiled, pointing, ''is Theodore, who has his nose in a new science book. The boy with the rapier—'' she paused, frowning disapprovingly at Alex, ''—is Horace. He shall be the captain of all Alex's ships one day. Simultaneously, I understand.''

''Who is the young lady?'' Arthur asked.

Lauren sighed. ''*That* is Lydia. Honestly, she'll be the death of me yet. I had no idea so many eligible young gentleman lived in and around Pemberheath!'' she exclaimed. ''Uncle Ethan is forever grousing about the constant stream of young gentleman callers.''

''When he is not counting their fortunes, you mean,'' Alex playfully reminded her, to which Lauren laughed.

Arthur dragged his gaze from the pretty fifteen year-old and glanced at his sister-in-law with admiration. Since the birth of her child, she had an air of sophisticated maturity about her. Lauren was, he thought a little enviously, stunningly beautiful. How fortunate it was that the scandal of their marriage had faded with the birth of the heir. His mother was right; no one would turn against the Duke of Sutherland for long, no matter what crime he was perceived to have committed. And it had only been a matter of time before Lauren had charmed her way into the *ton*'s heart once again. Now everyone proclaimed the Sutherland marriage the love match of the decade.

"I have news from London," Arthur announced. "Paddy and Mrs. Clark have at long last overtaken the championship of the loo tables. This feat, I am given to understand, is eclipsed only by the number of games my sister-in-law lost one particular Season. Twenty-six hands in one outing?" he asked laughingly.

Lauren squealed gaily. "It was only *six,* I swear it!"

Alex caught her hand and squeezed it affectionately. "Paddy would not exaggerate, angel. It is rather well known that you are horrid at loo."

"I have more news. As you know, since Paul and I have become partners in the investment venture I started some months ago, I have occasion to see him. He has sent a letter along, no doubt full of his excitement at having been elected to the Commons. Swears he has the votes for the economic reforms," Arthur said, smiling, and handed a note to Lauren.

Beaming, Lauren eagerly opened the missive and scanned it quickly, then lifted a glorious smile to her husband and brother-in-law. "Everyone in the *whole* parish knows of Paul Hill, you know. We are all quite proud of him! And he is so very happy, because *'the entire sum of existence is the magic of being needed by just one person,'* " she said, beaming proudly.

Alex exchanged a look with Arthur. "A new book," he offered blandly.

"I have news for you, brother. Thought you might be interested to know that your very own randy cousin, David Westfall, is quite smitten," Arthur continued.

"My God," Alex exclaimed. "Do tell!"

"Rumor has it he will offer for Lady Marlaine by the end of the Season." Much to Arthur's delight, Alex and Lauren exchanged looks of amazement, then grinned happily at one another.

"How very wonderful!" Lauren exclaimed, genuinely happy.

"And how very extraordinary," Alex chuckled. "It rather explains—" He paused, shook his head lightly, and smiled at Arthur. "I couldn't be happier for them."

A cry rose from the lawn and Lauren quickly came to her feet. Little Paul was holding on to his rattler and crying loudly. "If you will excuse me," she said, and skipped down the terrace steps to the children below. Alex and Arthur both admired her graceful movement as she walked out to the blanket spread on the lawn. Several of the children ran forward to assure her they had done nothing to the baby. The men could hear her melodious laughter as she assured them that babies often cried for no apparent reason.

"She's a breath of fresh air, Alex. You were an idiot for almost letting her slip away."

"Thank you for that gentle reminder," Alex snorted.

Arthur chuckled as Lauren fell to her knees beside the wailing Paul and scooped him onto her lap. "It's a wonder she doesn't remind you each day."

"Rest assured, she does—unwittingly. Not two days ago, we received word that Madgoose, on some *insane* excursion, heroically rescued a young Englishwoman kidnapped and held for ransom by a Russian prince. Rather exciting story, really, but when I saw the look in Lauren's eyes, I realized how close I had come to losing her. She is, remarkably, rather fond of that damned Bavarian."

Arthur glanced at his brother from the corner of his eye and felt a small tug around his heart. He was constantly amazed by how much Alex loved her. What was it he had said of her? She was all that was grace to him.

Below them, the baby Lauren was holding put up a valiant struggle to be freed. Once she realized the boy would not be calmed, Lauren relented and handed him over to his nanny, who began a prompt march for the young boy's cradle. Lauren stayed a little longer on the lawn, talking with the children who obviously adored her. Eventually, she started back to the terrace. As she walked slowly toward them, Arthur chuckled.

"What?" Alex asked.

"It's an irreverent thought," Arthur mused, and slanted a devilish look at Alex. "I had an idea for a small wager on what she might say."

"Say? About what?"

"That's irrelevant," Arthur chuckled. "My wager is that it is a quotation." Alex looked at him as if he had lost all semblance of reason. "Come now, Alex, surely you have noticed she has a penchant for quoting old proverbs and poems, particularly when she has just received a new book?" Arthur laughed.

"It is part of her rather enormous and immeasurable charm," Alex responded playfully.

"Nonetheless—come on, quick with your answer, she is drawing near. A gold sovereign for my very fine nephew if she utters a quote?"

"And one if she does not?" Alex shot back.

"Naturally," Arthur said, now trying to hide his mirth from Lauren.

Alex jumped to his feet and met her at the top of the terrace steps. "I see my hellion of a son is quite out of sorts," he said, taking her hand in his.

Sighing, Lauren nodded. "Afraid so. *'Of all the animals, the boy is the most unmanageable,'* you know."

"Ha! Plato!" Arthur cried, and triumphantly slapped the wrought iron arm of his chair with such force as to startle Lauren.

"What?" she asked, turning to Alex.

Grinning, he cupped her face in his hands. "Lauren, my angel"—he smiled as his mouth descended to hers—*"shut up."* Ignoring Arthur's very tasteless cheering, he devoured the lips of his cherished, proverb-quoting wife.